ANYTHING FOR LOVE

ANYTHING FOR LOVE SERIES BOOK ONE

GRACIE BOND

WATER
BEARS
Publishing

James L Nunn illustrated the cover.

Book Cover Update and Publishing Assistance Provided by: Michelle Morrow www.chellreads.com

To my partner John, for supporting my dreams in writing this book, which is based on my award-winning screenplay. I would also like to thank Joan, who helped that dream to materialise and Christine, for listening.

I dedicate this book to two great Yorkshire guys:
John and beautiful Tom.

1

LEAH'S DILEMMA

W *hitby, North Yorkshire coast*
Leah Jensen ran down Abbot's Bridge Road, the sea winds buffeting her long fair hair around her face and sending the spring blossoms dancing on the trees. It was coming on for summer and the small coastal town, with its Dracula connection and history of whaling and jet mining, was welcoming its fair share of visitors.

Leah let herself into her grandfather's Victorian terraced house and dumped her handbag and jacket on the old-fashioned hall-stand. She yawned. Her shift at the Gingerbread Café had been very busy; she'd been serving customers, cooking the light meals on the menu and helping the owners to clear up after closing time at 5 p.m. Whitby had lots of excellent cafés of all kinds and competition was fierce; the Gingerbread's main attraction was the generously-sized gingerbread men and women which Leah herself baked and decorated with humour and originality.

The house where she had lived for the past sixteen years was very quiet, Leah noted. There was no sign of her Grandad Thomas, nor of her Cousin Joey. The young woman frowned, *her underlying worry resurfacing as it so often did. Thomas suffered from osteo-arthritis in his knees and had been refused treatment on the NHS. To have the arthroscopic surgery he needed would cost thousands. Come on, think, she ordered herself. How can I get hold of that kind of money?*

'Ey up, lass – is that you?' She poked her head around the sitting-room door and saw Thomas lying propped up on the sofa, a blanket over his knees. She hated seeing him in so much pain.

'Hello yourself, Grandad. Do you fancy a hot chocolate? I'll put the kettle on,' Leah offered, hiding the anguish she felt inside.

Thomas looked at her fondly, his voice pure Yorkshire as he replied, 'Yes, kiddo, Ah'd like that. Ta.'

'Will you need your morphine? And is there something else I can get you with your drink – a snack of some kind?' Leah would have done anything for her grandad. He'd been there for her when her parents had died, now it was her turn to help him.

Thomas Jensen blinked back the tears so his granddaughter didn't see. 'Well, I dote like givin' into drugs, but how about one o' your gingerbread men - unless o' course Joey's eaten 'em all.'

'You're in luck, he's left you one. He's in the basement kitchen creating your favourite pudding for tomorrow's Sunday lunch. We're having roast beef and Yorkshires too.' Leah then cajoled: 'Will you have just a teaspoon of morphine?'

'Ah dote need mollycoddling, you know,' Grandad Thomas said mock sternly. 'Tell our Joey Ah'll look forward to me pud an' that Ah'll want custard wi' it - none o' that fancy fromage fraisy. Tell him he's not buggering off neither. I want a proper family Sunday lunch.'

'And the morphine?'

'Fiddlesticks. Ah'll take one half-teaspoon. By 'eck you're

worse than your father was for nagging.' 'Your father' was Thomas's late son Darley, whose wedding photo with Leah's mother Rosie was propped on the piano in a silver frame.

Leah nodded. The morphine sent Thomas to sleep and that was his only relief. She turned on the TV so he could watch *Antiques Roadshow* whilst she was out of the room, and thought again how her Cousin Joey's very recent return to Abbot's Bridge Road had helped; at least now she had Joey to talk things over with, and his presence back in the house had brought a smile to Grandad's face.

Leah herself had secretly insisted that Joey come home for a while; *obviously he didn't yet know why he was here and Leah knew she couldn't talk about it in front of Grandad because he would say that he didn't need an operation. Leah was hoping that Joey might be able to help her come up with a plan. Short of winning the lottery, she herself had run out of ideas.*

AFTER MAKING HOT CHOCOLATE AND TAKING THE LAST gingerbread man in to Thomas, along with his medication, Leah came back into the kitchen and made a cup of coffee.

'Joey, your coffee is ready. Don't let it go cold,' she shouted down the basement stairs.

'I will be up in a mo', Lee-Lee,' he called back.

'OK.' It was so nice to have him home, even if she did have to clear up after him. Her cousin always left a mess, but it was worth it as he was a gifted cook. She wished he wouldn't insist on drinking coffee so close to bedtime though as it made him even more like a child high on E numbers. Joey was well over the top already, without the added boost of caffeine.

'Those servants' stairs will do me a mischief one day,' he complained breathlessly as he ran up into the small kitchenette, his prize pudding balanced between his hands. In a china bowl, wrapped in a covering that ended in a bow, lay the mystery pudding. At twenty-six, two years older than Leah, Joey was drop dead handsome, charming, and as camp as a row of tents.

'Why do you use the Butler's kitchen when there's a perfectly good kitchen up here?' Leah asked, pushing his coffee towards him.

'What - and get in *your* face? Ooh, I hardly dare.' Joey pursed his lips. 'I know my place – it's in the servants' kitchen, downstairs and out of the way of prying eyes, and before you ask, yes, I have washed up. I've just left the dishes to drain. I'll cook this pud tomorrow and by gum, it'll make Grandad's ribs stick together.' He grinned, then became serious. 'Now what was so urgent that you summoned me back up here?'

Leah put a finger to her lips and whispered, 'Grandad will go up to bed soon. We'll talk then.'

Joey put the pudding down on a wooden board. 'I love a nice secret.'

'Not this one, you won't. I just wish . . . oh well, never mind. We can discuss it soon.'

Joey picked up his china cup and with his little finger sticking out in a genteel way he slurped his coffee, then broke wind. He looked across at Leah and they both burst out laughing like the kids they'd once been.

'Joey,' said Grandad Thomas from the doorway. 'Your parents didn't drag you up, did they?'

'No, Grandad, excuse me.'

'Nor did I teach you 'ow to do that. We fart in t'water closet, dote we?'

'We do, Grandad. Oh yes, we do.'

'Cum 'ere an' gi' me a hug and tell me why you stayed away for the past six months. I thought we'd done sommat wrong. Poor Leah was working like crazy, as well as looking after me. Why, if I hadn't of insisted she go and blow her cobwebs away on the beach at a full-out gallop, I think she would've wasted away wi' the worry of it all. I'm just so glad Cyril gave her a horse every time I asked, but mind, that's what friends are for.'

'Oh, Grandad, I'm so sorry.' Joey rushed over to the old man and hugged him gently. 'I was so afraid you wouldn't understand.'

'Joey, you daft young thing, I knew when you were eight that you were goin' to bat for t'other side.'

'You did?' Joey pulled back. 'So I could have come home sooner?'

'Ah did, an' if you'd just had the sense to say sommat instead o' bein' scared, I wouldn't have had to miss you so much. Besides, why didn't your dad talk to me? It seems everyone, includin' you, Leah,' he looked sternly at her, 'were tryin' to keep sommat under covers that I already knew about.' The old fellow sighed. 'I'm going to me bed. You have an early start tomorrow, don't you, lass.'

'I'm sorry, Grandad.' Leah kissed his wrinkly cheek. 'Love you. You do know that I didn't think it was my place to tell you.'

'Ah know, an' I love the both of you. An' I'm looking forward to me Yorkshire puds and me surprise sweet pudding – wi' custard, remember,' Thomas emphasised and then he walked out, bracing himself for the slow and painful journey up the stairs. Joey went after him, to check that Grandad Thomas was safely undressed, washed, and had gone to his bed in his pyjamas with the crossword to help him get to sleep.

Once back down again, Joey set about making another cup of coffee, saying: 'OK, what gives? It must be something bad if you're not telling me in front of Grandad.'

Leah went over to the kitchen drawer and took out a letter from the big hospital in York.

Her cousin read it, then said: 'What the hell do we do now?'

'We brainstorm ways to raise money for this new type of surgery.' Leah filled a glass with cold water from the fridge and took a gulp. 'It's obvious to anyone that Grandad is in agony. He can't carry on like this.'

'But the NHS won't pay.' Joey was appalled; as the news sank in, tears began streaming down his cheeks. The young man was very fond of his grandfather. 'I can't believe they won't help him.'

'There's a panel we can see, but they don't meet for another three months and meanwhile, Grandad is going downhill. We need action now.' Leah pushed her hand through her long hair, fair like Joey's. 'I know – I shall start a collection.'

Joey looked sceptical. 'It'll have to be one hell of a collection if it's going to pay for an operation.'

'With travel and accommodation, I reckon around five thousand pounds.'

'Holy shit! That's a colossal amount.' Joey took a deep breath. 'What savings do you have? Does Grandad have any savings?'

'There are four hundred pounds in my account. Grandad used most of his savings on the new central heating system last winter. And you?'

Joey squirmed. 'I'm overdrawn. No savings. I suppose I could take back the fifty-pound chinos I bought the other day and have never worn. I still have the receipt.'

Leah sat at the kitchen table. 'What about friends? Could they lend us the money?'

Her cousin was shaking his head. 'No, they're all tight-arses,' he said cheekily, adding, 'In more ways than one!'

'Joey! Then we have no choice but to fundraise,' Leah said, reaching for a pad and pen. 'So give me your ideas.'

'How long do we have? Have you been in touch with my dad?'

'Yes, and he made his feelings very clear. He's not interested. You know he's never got on with Grandad.' Leah bit the end of her pen. 'We've got a deadline. The only man in the country who can do the operation has a window in four weeks. So - let's brainstorm.'

'You brainstorm, I will pray for a miracle. I don't know why I mentioned my dad; he's so bloody selfish.' Joey looked depressed.

'You think it's impossible, don't you?' Leah said.

'Not exactly . . .' Joey looked thoughtful. 'You see, I can offer a last-resort strategy, but it's purely for emergencies only. So I'll hold off on telling you more about that for the time being.'

Leah gave a huge sigh, at which her cousin came up to her and put his arm around her. 'We'll figure something out,' he said kindly. 'You watch. We won't let our grandad down.'

Leah looked at the clock. It was 1.39 a.m. and she was still fretting about how they could get several thousand pounds together. She thumped her pillow and closed her eyes – only to jump up ten minutes later and go downstairs for a cup of milky cocoa. She opened the back door to the mild night air and that was when she saw her first hedgehog of the year.

'Hello, Harry hedgehog, can you help me sleep?' Leah whispered as the prickly creature trotted over to the plate of meaty cat food she'd put out.

'First signs of madness, talking to a baby hedgehog,' called a low voice from the upstairs window.

Leah did a double-take. 'What on earth have you got on! Is that my new négligée, Joey? Take it off! I've only just bought it.'

Joey laughed. 'It looks better on me than it does on you.'

It was true, Leah thought. He did look good in the pink chiffon and lace.

'Oh, bloody-well keep it,' she said good-naturedly. 'Along with your posh chinos. Night, night, Harry hedgehog. Enjoy your dinner.' Then Leah went inside, locked up and went to bed. This time she fell fast asleep.

AFTER AN EARLY START TO HER SHIFT AT THE GINGERBREAD Café, Leah worked steadily, serving breakfasts to locals who sat reading their Sunday papers, followed by visitors who asked for hot drinks and one of the quaint gingerbread people. She smiled - she mustn't forget the errand before going home; she made a mental note.

At noon, she handed over to Johnny, a lanky lad with a Geordie accent. She felt as free as a bird as she walked across the East Cliff, shouting her cheery greetings to the fishermen, at one point stopping to peer over at the famous whale jawbones on the West Cliff, which had always fascinated her since childhood. Along with the spooky St Mary's Church and the now-ruined Whitby Abbey, these well-known landmarks loomed protectively over the harbour town below.

It was time to join her menfolk for their Sunday lunch. Leah just loved family gatherings. Thankfully, modern cookers with automatic ovens made the job an easy one. She couldn't imagine how her great-grandma had coped, conjuring up a robust Sunday lunch for twelve on an old-fashioned range.

When Leah entered the house, the aroma was sensational. Joey had been busy cooking for them, like he always used to. A roast rib of beef surrounded with whole onions and potatoes was a rare luxury these days, ever since his departure from Whitby.

Leah washed her hands then did the last job – to whip up the batter and put the Yorkshire puddings into hot fat. As she closed the oven door on them, she heard the batter sizzle. Joey had prepared the vegetables this morning, or so Grandad Thomas had said, so it was obvious he'd gone to bed (removing her négligée first, Leah hoped) reasonably early last night.

Speak of the devil and he shall return, she thought as Joey walked into the kitchen shortly afterwards. He gave her a hug, saying, 'I hope the morning shift went quickly.'

'Yeah, a writers' group came in for their breakfast. They're studying . . .'

'Dracula!' Joey interrupted. 'Of course, they all study Bram Stoker. I reckon they think Dracula was real – I know some of them look for his grave in St Mary's Church.'

Leah laughed. 'Now how did you know that?'

Joey said airily, 'I know more about Dracula than I know about the Wombles - and I'm an expert on them.'

'Of course you do, you took the guided tour on Dracula a few years ago.'

'And it's branded in my memory.' Joey inhaled. 'Oh Leah, I've missed our Sunday lunches.'

'So why didn't you come home?' Leah asked. 'Are we that scary?'

'No, but you see I met this guy.' Joey sat down, only to remember to say, 'Oh, by the way I've set the dining table.'

'"This guy" - is that all I get? Come on, tell me more,

please,' Leah prompted. 'I tell you about my non-existent love-life.'

'Huh, precisely - non-existent. What kind of love-life is that? You love animals before men.' Joey snorted.

'It's not my fault I have a particular taste in men. I've just not met Mr Right yet.' Leah stared threateningly at Joey. 'I won't ask again - I will just come over and tickle you.'

'OK, OK, his name is Olly, all right? We had a fling and I broke his heart,' Joey mumbled without looking at Leah.

Leah opened the top oven door and took out the puddings.

'You broke *his* heart? Why do I doubt you?' she asked as she then carefully lifted the beef out of the bottom oven. 'I will let the meat rest a while.'

'OK, I told him I had a family emergency. I didn't invite him as I didn't think he would be interested in coming here.'

'Why not? Whitby's a great place. Lots of important people come here and love it, like James Martin the chef and TV presenter - but then he's a Yorkshire man. Besides, it's your home. The place you were born. You should be proud.' Leah picked up the sharp carving knife. 'Can you tell Grandad lunch is ready.'

ALTHOUGH THOMAS WAS UNCOMFORTABLE AND CLEARLY IN pain, he insisted on sitting at the table and joining in the conversation. He asked for a small portion of the main course and thoroughly enjoyed every mouthful. When the others had finished, he addressed Joey, saying, 'So then, lad, exactly what have you been up to in London?'

'Well, I was working for a coffee house. A very posh place, but I was drinking all their profits. You know what I'm like for my coffee.' Joey jumped up.

'No wonder you're skittish,' the older man cackled. 'All that caffeine isn't good for you.'

'Hark at kettle calling pot.' Joey smiled at Thomas as he saw the teasing in his eyes. 'If everyone's ready for their afters, I'll fetch the pudding, shall I? Won't be a tick.'

Thomas rubbed his hands together. 'What delights do we have in store?' he wondered aloud. 'Oh, and Joey lad, if that pud is as good as the roast beef, it'll be fine and dandy.'

Joey was back a few minutes later, announcing, 'It's steamed Spotted Dick. I know it's your favourite and I've made proper custard with vanilla.' He had popped off into the kitchen to remove the bubbling saucepan from the stove and lift out the pudding from its basin before making the custard. It gave the others time to digest their first course, was the way he looked at it.

'So, has he told you why he's here?' Thomas asked Leah in an undertone. 'I reckon yon lad is up to sommat, dote you?'

Leah was saved from answering by a high-pitched scream coming from the kitchen.

'Oh no, I forgot to put the currants in! The Spotted Dick's got no spots.' Joey had unwrapped the cloth and instead of a Dalmatian-dog-style vision had uncovered a pale imitation of a suet pudding.

Both Leah and Grandad Thomas looked at each other and laughing, said in unison, 'Dick pudding!'

2

WHO PRICKED THE CONDOMS?

C ity of London, skyscraper

Surreptitious hands closed the office door and the intruder walked across the luxuriously carpeted floor and sat in Dan Ryan's leather chair as if they belonged there. Pulling the bottom desk drawer open, they knew exactly where to find his private stash of condoms. Taking each packet out of the box, the intruder pricked them with a very fine needle then placed them tidily back, returning the box to the drawer.

Satisfied, they stepped back to the door, quietly opened it and looked each way down the empty corridor before leaving as stealthily as they had arrived.

SOPHIE RYAN SCREAMED CLASS. WITH HER SLIGHTLY FULLER figure tucked into a navy pinstriped skirt-suit, white silk blouse and navy patent leather court shoes, she was a woman of distinction. Standing up away from her desk, she pulled the cord of the cream blinds in order to peer out of the window overlooking the busy street at the heart of the City. She smiled as she caught sight of her handsome son, Dan, who glanced up, raised a hand in silent acknowledgement and disappeared into the building below.

Just then, her office door opened and someone barged in. It was Ruby, Sophie's personal assistant. A well-built Caribbean lady in her fifties, the same age as Sophie herself, Ruby sauntered in, kicked off her heels and flung herself into an easy chair, which creaked.

'I'm knackered,' she announced. 'I followed her in a cab all the way to Knightsbridge where she got out and went into Harvey Nicks. I just had time to jump out myself and find her in the crowds. I followed her to the lingerie department, where I'm sure I looked like a shoplifter as I was hiding behind racks of nightdresses most of the time so she didn't spot me.' Ruby stopped to fan herself before continuing, 'She bought lots of expensive crap on *our* company credit card. The cheek of it, I ask you.' She reached across and stole the half-cup of cool coffee from the coffee table.

'Do you mind? That was my coffee. I hope you'd pinch my grave as quickly, you rotten tea leaf.'

'No, I wouldn't – and by the way, I'm a coffee leaf, not a tea leaf.'

They both chuckled.

'So what exactly did she buy?' Sophie asked as she poured herself a fresh coffee and re-filled Ruby's cup. The 'she' in question was Dan's twenty-eight-year-old PA, Chelsea Saffer, a glamorous brunette who had her eye on becoming more than his assistant.

Ruby snorted. 'Black stockings, suspenders, a very fancy bra and matching French knickers. Who's the lucky guy?'

Sophie pulled a face. 'I think we both know that. Ugh! She's definitely not daughter-in-law material. You do know I will have a proverbial dickie-fit if she gets to my son.'

'And I will run her over with the cleaning trolley. Twice!'

Sophie said grimly, 'This is no time to joke, Ruby.'

'I can assure you I'm not joking.' The big woman was indignant. 'Tina the cleaner ran into me with her trolley, and it shaved an inch from my beautiful ankle. Of course, I asked her to make the other ankle the same. Fear not, old woman, if that Chelsea gets up to her tricks with Dan, I shall be like Colonel Rosa Klebb in a Bond movie.' Ruby kicked her foot out in a dramatic move. 'I will stop her little game, all right.'

Sophie sighed. 'Does everything have to be like a Bond film?'

'Not everything, M, but I love danger.'

'We need to think seriously about what will happen if that bitch Chelsea does somehow get her claws into my son. I know she's been trying for a long time. They did have a little fling several years ago, when she first started working for Ryan's, but it didn't last. I think she's never let go and still hopes that Dan will go back to her.' Sophie shuddered. 'I really couldn't bear that.'

'Something will come up; it usually does when we're in a pickle,' replied Ruby calmly.

'It had better. I have decided to get Scotty and Sisco involved,' Sophie informed her, reaching for the telephone.

LEAH HAD HER BLONDE HAIR PINNED UP AS SHE SERVED customers in the queue at the Gingerbread Café. Surreptitiously, she pushed a box forward. The label read *Please donate for surgery for my grandfather who is in pain. The NHS will not pay.*

Leah sighed as a few people put pennies in the box. What on earth was the matter with them, she wondered. She always put into collection boxes for a good cause, so why couldn't they do the same? Her heart was literally in her boots.

Joey walked in from the back kitchen, picked up the box and shook it. 'This is going to take years,' he pouted, pushing the box under a customer's nose. 'It's for a great cause.'

The little man looked over his glasses and read the thick, bold writing. 'They're all good causes.' He dropped a five-pence piece in the box and went and sat at a table.

'Years and years and years,' muttered Joey from behind Leah.

'So, we leave the box in here, and we tackle item two on our list,' said Leah. Then: 'What *is* item number two?'

'You are washing windows, I believe,' replied Joey.

'What about you?'

'I don't do heights. I will wash the bottom windows,' he said magnanimously.

'That's big of you.' Leah frowned.

'Huge - massive even.' Her cousin smirked. 'I'd do most things but never heights.'

'OK, OK, I will do the top windows.'

As Joey walked back into the kitchen, Leah saw several dog-walkers looking through the café window. She went to the door and told them regretfully, 'I'm so sorry. The owner doesn't allow dogs in the café.'

'It's the story of our life. The penalties of loving your dog, I guess,' said one gentleman with a Westie by his side.

'If you'd like a coffee to take out, I'd be happy to make you one, and I will fetch some water for the dogs,' said Leah, feeling sad that they couldn't welcome the dog-walkers of Whitby.

As she made her way inside, she thought of all the local customers and dog-owning tourists and day trippers who would call in for refreshment and a sit-down if only their canine friends were welcome.

THAT EVENING SAW LEAH UP THE RICKETY WOODEN LADDER cleaning her next-door neighbours' windows, whilst Joey buffed the ground-floor sash panes.

Although Joey liked peering into other people's windows and sneaking a peek at their bits and pieces, he was already developing an ache in his arms. 'You know, I hardly think we're going to make thousands doing this,' he moaned.

Leah carefully climbed down. 'Actually, I think they only said yes because we are neighbours,' she confided. 'It was out of the goodness of their hearts. So, what's next on the list?'

'Dog-walking. I mean, what can go wrong with dog-walking?'

'OK, we'll give it a go. I've lined up a few dogs to take on the beach so I'll ring round and let them know we can do it tomorrow.' Leah swilled the murky water down the drain and jumped away when the drain spluttered back and covered her in grimy window water.

'Only £4990 to go. Oh, but we have your four hundred to knock off. Yippee,' said Joey, deadpan.

They couldn't help laughing slightly hysterically.

'Yes, and I may have an extra tenner in tips,' said Leah with a wry smile. 'Ooh, I've just remembered, Cyril said we could muck out his horses in the morning. That will bring another twenty pounds in, but we will have to be up extra early for that. You know he likes the stables cleaned well.'

THE FOLLOWING DAY SAW LEAH AND JOEY MUCKING OUT.

'I forgot what a delicious aroma horse poo has,' said Joey as they worked on a stable each.

'Yes, it's wonderful, isn't it?' Leah replied.

'I meant it was stinky!'

'Not like pig or cow muck. That's stinkier. Anyway, we're almost finished.' Leah brushed the last cobble as clean as she could get it.

'It doesn't have to be spotless, you know,' yawned Joey.

'I do know, but he's paying us well and besides, we can ride on the beach later in the week. Now, it's time to go dog-walking.' Leah put the broom down and walked out into the sunshine.

Joey followed her, grumbling, 'And I've broken one of me nails.' He looked at his shoes, where he'd trodden in some horse manure and gave a tiny scream. If Leah thought he'd wear wellies, she had another thought coming.

AN HOUR LATER, LEAH AND JOEY WERE WALKING EIGHT DOGS on a blustery beach. The waves rolled in in earnest as the gusts of a cool wind whipped the bare legs of Joey wearing his Bermuda shorts.

'I'm blummin' freezing. I should have known. This east coast can be so unforgiving. I'll never get my legs tanned. How do you manage not ending up in knots with these dogs?' he fretted, getting caught up in the leads.

'Easy, put two in each hand.' Leah demonstrated. She frowned. 'We need a solution that pays well.'

'And I gave you the ideal solution.'

Leah gasped. 'That's not a solution. It's out of the question and I don't want to discuss it ever again.'

But Joey was distracted. 'Do you reckon that Dog Warden is waving angrily at us for a reason?' he asked, looking towards the harbour.

'I've picked up any poo so we haven't done anything wrong. What time of year can't you walk dogs on the beach?'

'Looks like it's now.'

'I think we ought to make a run for it because he looks very hot under the collar and he knows where I work. Come on, dogs.' Leah encouraged their charges into a gallop towards the steps.

Joey panicked as the dogs dragged him behind Leah, who was going hell for leather.

'Leah, stop, stop! They're going to pull me over,' he shouted.

'I'd rather that than meet up with him. He's one tough cookie,' Leah panted, looking back at the puce face of the Dog Warden.

'Yes, but Leah, you can soft-talk him,' Joey said equally breathlessly. 'I've seen you in action before. Remember those coppers on the beach - how you told them you had to gallop because Champion the Wonder Horse was looking forward to his breakfast.'

'I do.' Leah chuckled at the memory.

'The irony of it was that you were riding a mare called Frosty and she would have bitten them had they got any nearer,' Joey said, barely able to keep up with Leah.

'She was only like that because some cruel men had ill-treated her. She was always OK with women, which is why Rachel and Yvonne have her now.' Leah got to the top of the path with her four dogs but kept on until she reached the streets.

Back on the clifftop, Joey managed to stop the dogs. 'Holy shit, that was exciting. I'm in the swing of it now. What's next on the list?'

Leah grimaced. 'Isn't that wing-walking?'

'Yes. Hmm. Harry said he'd arrange it. You could have a flag asking for money streaming out at the end of the plane,' suggested Joey.

'He's your friend - you should be doing it, not me. Again, it's down to good old Leah.' She glowered at Joey.

'Face it – I'm not as brave as you. And anyway, you know what I'm like with heights. Anything higher than a step-stool and I'm crapping myself - and I don't think Harry would like that.' Joey was pouting.

'Enough already, I get the picture.'

'You've got a head for heights, whereas I am the brainy one,' Joey said, preening himself while looking down the path from the beach. He then suddenly yelped, 'Dog Warden alert!'

Leah ran over the road with her canines and they disappeared in the network of streets. 'We'll debate that later,' she called behind her. 'Get your skates on, Joey.'

By the time the breathless Dog Warden had reached the top of the cliff, there was no sign of his quarry. He shrugged and began his way back down to the beach, a naughty smile spread across his face. He'd only wanted to tell them the beach was still officially open to dogs.

AS LEAH AND JOEY STROLLED BACK WITH THE DOGS, WHO HAD had a wonderful run, Joey pondered, 'Wasn't it the water-skiing stunts that were the next on the list?'

'You mean I'm being spared the wing-walking for another day or two? So, what tricks do *you* do on skis?' asked Leah nonchalantly, but still knowing his answer.

Joey growled, 'The water is far too cold for me, Lee-Lee, especially at this time of year.'

'How did I know you'd have an excuse?'

'Because you know me better than anyone.'

'So what about Olly? Tell me more. He broke *your* heart, did he?'

Joey quietly said, 'I've never been in love before. He even invited me to meet his mamma and his papa. Of course, you and I can both speak nicely when we want to - Mrs Winters the elocution teacher made sure of that. But Olly's mother was so upper-crust I think she might have swallowed the family silver in one gulp. I mean, I thought the house had come out of a 1950s novel and I had to teach Olly how to dress modern, because trust me his jackets were three sizes too big!'

Leah smiled. 'But you fell for him anyway. What's it like, being in love?'

'You mean apart from the amazing sex? It's like having someone who shares every breath you take. A person who loves the space you occupy and a man who can read your thoughts so accurately it's scary,' said Joey thoughtfully.

'So what happened then?'

'His mother happened, that's what. Joey Jensen simply wasn't good enough for her boy. Anyway, enough wallowing, we have activities to discuss.' He paused. 'We can always go to Plan B.'

Leah stared at him aghast. 'No way, never. I told you - over my dead body!'

IT SEEMED LIKE FAR TOO SHORT A TIME BEFORE LEAH WAS skiing behind a motor boat in the harbour, getting herself into a comfortable rhythm. Joey was sat in the boat looking very queasy.

'If you were to sway the boat, Clem, she'd fall in,' he said to the man at the wheel.

Clem shook his head, saying, 'She'll get wet anyway, you daft bugger.'

Joey pulled a face at Clem then signalled for Leah to start performing stunts as several people were watching from the harbour and the beach. Secretly he'd always wished he was as good as Leah at water-skiing and horse-riding, but that was never going to happen. A natural athlete, his cousin was so easy-going sometimes she was almost horizontal. She'd never been afraid as their grandfather had encouraged her to do many sports, whereas his parents had been more interested in his older sister, Carrie, and her dancing career. True, Joey was a great dancer too.

As Leah began her routine, jumping high off floating blocks, Joey held a sign whilst trying to balance in the motor boat. *Money for our grandad's operation. Give generously in the saddlebag of the black donkey ON THE BEACH!*

The boat suddenly lurched, and with a scream that could be heard on the quayside, Joey lost his balance and fell overboard, making a big splash. On surfacing thanks to his life-jacket, he saw three kids nicking the money from the black donkey's saddlebag then running towards the amusement arcade.

'You thieving little twerps. Put that cash back! Any winnings from the arcade you *will* put back in the saddlebag of the black donkey,' Joey spluttered, but his heart wasn't in it.

THE MOST TERRIFYING ITEM ON THE LIST STILL REMAINED TO BE carried out. So the next morning, trembling with a mixture of terror and sheer cold, Leah flew over the harbour, clamped to the upper wing of a Boeing Stearman bi-plane and screaming constantly. A flyer streamed behind the plane, reading *PLEASE GIVE GENEROUSLY FOR MY GRANDFATHER'S SURGERY. I'M DESPERATE, TIRED AND FED UP WITH YOU STINGY YORKSHIRE FOLK! DIG DEEP AND THANK YOU. WE LOVE YOU ALL.*

Joey was looking up at the plane as it flew in low over the harbour.

'You go, girl. You go!' Joey felt guilty as he saw Leah yelling. It had been his idea and he didn't want Leah to be afraid. He shook the box as people were giving quite generously.

A man walked up and popped a pound coin in the box. 'That young lady is really enjoying herself, isn't she?'

'Is she?' Joey looked again as the bi-plane came past for a second time. He saw Leah screaming and thumping the air. 'Yes,' he lied. 'She's quite an adrenaline junkie!'

SEATED AT THE KITCHEN TABLE IN ABBOT'S BRIDGE ROAD while Thomas rested on the sofa watching *Judge Judy* on the TV, Leah and Joey counted the money.

'Four hundred pounds and the odd few pence,' Leah concluded, 'plus a foreign coin I can't really distinguish.'

'It's better than nothing. We've got almost two thousand pounds now, including your contribution,' stated Joey. 'But you know what? I really do think we should discuss working for Madam Butterfly, even though I know you hate the idea.'

Leah got up from the table and walked over to the bottom cupboard; from it, she took out a bottle of brandy and two tumblers. Half-filling one, she handed it to Joey then poured herself a measure. Leaning against the cupboard, she said wearily, 'How many times would we have to do it?'

'Madam Butterfly has some fairly exclusive clients. They pay well, of course, and I won't let you do this by yourself.'

'Too damn right you won't!' Leah paused for a while. 'Just exactly how did you come to know of this Madam Butterfly?'

'Well, someone I met in a gay bar had told me about this woman and her set-up. I never thought I'd be using it, but at the time it was a godsend. It was before I met Olly and I needed to earn some pennies.' Joey's voice had gone quiet: he wasn't exactly proud of this part of his life. In fact, he could never bring himself to tell Leah about the time when he'd briefly gone off the rails - bigtime.

'I'm not doing anything like that for pennies,' shuddered Leah. 'That is our last resort. I mean it, Joey.'

'It probably won't even come to that, so don't worry your pretty little head,' Joey reassured her with a woeful look. Sheer common sense told him it probably *would* come to that, but he would break the news to her then; all in good time.

3

A LIFE-CHANGING EVENT

hree days later

Leah stood in Kings Cross station in London by one of the cash machines, staring at the balance in her current account. £2003. Not enough. During the journey down from Whitby, she and Joey had looked at their copy of the London A-Z and estimated it was about a 45-minute walk to Soho or a five-minute journey in a black London taxi. It was a fine May day, ideal for a stroll, but with her high heels and after a long journey from home and having to change at Darlington, it was always going to be a taxi. Leah didn't feel remotely in the mood for what they had planned, but she and her cousin had made a pact that they would carry it through. However, she would only do it once: that was her one rule.

Am I doing the right thing? Leah agonised. But Grandad needed that operation and time was pressing. They had provisionally booked the free slot available with the specialist surgeon – but a deposit would soon be needed, let alone the full cost. What with Joey's parents still away in the Australian Outback, what choice did she and Joey have? Someone had to take action! *If Joey and I can get through this and earn enough money together without giving our souls away, then it will all have been worth it,* thought Leah as they arrived at the address in Soho's Dean Street. Before knocking at the discreet black door, she checked her mirror and added more lip-gloss. She was wearing her best outfit, from sexy underwear to pretty jewellery. But she was shaking all over.

A smart-looking woman let them in and guided the pair through to a classy drawing room where an older woman – Madam Butterfly herself – awaited. Leah secretly crossed her fingers behind her back. Part of her wanted to laugh as she recalled the scene in *Shirley Valentine* when Shirley is in a hotel and bumps into her ultra-respectable and posh former school-friend, played by Joanna Lumley, only to find out that the latter now works as a hooker and is waiting for a client. Then she wiped the smile off her face. Here she was, ready to face her fate. All she knew was that she could never do this for anyone else, ever. To Leah, her grandad meant the world. He was her mum, dad, grandad and her best friend and confidant all rolled into one.

SAT IN HIS CHAUFFEUR-DRIVEN CAR, DAN RYAN STRETCHED OUT his long legs. At only twenty-seven years old, single, rich and nearly six feet tall, he was most girls' idea of a perfect date. As he looked out at the passing countryside on the drive back into London, he became more and more agitated. He didn't usually argue with anyone, except his mother Sophie - and that was generally about business - but after the company meeting in Basingstoke, his PA, Chelsea, had driven him crazy. How dare she demand that he take her out to dinner and a show! No way did he need this aggravation after his back-to-back talks around a boardroom table. Fed up, he had sent her back to London on a first-class train ticket.

He pressed the intercom button.

His Chief Security Officer in the front passenger seat looked back over his shoulder. At two inches under five feet and a mature fifty-eight years old, Scotty – nicknamed thus because his home town was Inverness - was the most bizarre choice for a security man. However, he was a good friend of Dan's mother and had proved to be quite a useful asset. His face was unique as was his personality, but there was something about him that Dan liked, maybe because he missed his father and Scotty had been there forever. Scotty and the driver, Sisco, made a great double act, Dan thought. He trusted both men implicitly.

Scotty answered immediately, 'Yes, Mr Dan?'

Dan babbled, not quite believing his own words: 'I want a hooker and a hotel room. Fix it for me, please, Scotty.'

Scotty almost choked. He was shocked to the core. 'Do what, Mr Dan? Did you say "hooker" – as in . . . er . . . working girl, sir?'

'Yes, that's what is generally known as a hooker,' came the terse reply.

'Any particular kind of hooker, sir?' The small man could feel his ears going red.

'One that falls out of the bloody sky,' Dan said irritably. 'I don't care what kind.'

'But sir, this is not like . . .'

'Just do as you're told for once, man!' Dan grunted rudely. Scotty was right – this behaviour was quite unlike him.

Scotty phoned Sophie immediately. 'It's me,' he murmured, although Dan couldn't hear him. 'I think your son has gone quite mad. He's asked me to get him a hooker and a hotel room.'

'Hmm. Interesting. What on earth's got into him?'

'He's had a right old ding-dong with that Chelsea. She was nagging him to take her to Heston Blumenthal's restaurant at the Mandarin Oriental Hotel in Hyde Park and then on to a show.'

'So that's her game. As I said, it's obvious what her plan is. Seduce my son, trap him and live on Easy Street for the rest of her life.'

'Young Mr Dan said he wants a hooker to fall out of the sky and he doesn't care what kind,' confided Scotty. 'He insisted. How are we going to manage that, madam?'

'As long as it's not Chelsea, that seems perfectly possible. I'll call you back.' Sophie spent a couple of minutes thinking, then took her phone out of her bag and made a call. 'I've got this, Scotty,' she told him when she hung up and got back to him. 'Just get Mr Dan to the Byzantine Hotel in Belgravia by nine p.m. He's booked into the King Room. The balcony there is gorgeous and very private, as I recall from a very pleasant afternoon spent there a few months ago, ahem,' she cleared her throat, 'and it certainly has room for happy landings.' The woman was in high spirits, admiring her son for his outlandish request.

'I will now ring Madam Butterfly's establishment,' Sophie went on. 'Goodness knows we've passed enough business her way with our overseas clients in the past. I have absolute confidence that she and her staff will be able to find a beautiful girl for Dan who is also gutsy enough to accept this daredevil date. Money no object, of course. She will deserve a good fee for this extra. I will get an assurance of secrecy from her, of course, and from the hotel. They are very discreet.' And she hung up.

Sisco, the Cuban chauffeur, had heard the entire dialogue. Slapping Scotty, who was half his size, on the back, he said, 'The Byzantine Hotel it is then. But first I need to drop him back at the office to pick up some overnight things and the documents for tomorrow morning's meeting.' For once, he thought, pressing on the accelerator, the M25 motorway was clear. They should make both places with time to spare.

JOEY'S FACE CONTORTED EFFEMINATELY AS HE WHISPERED TO Leah, 'Sad that it's come to this. Never thought I'd see the inside of this place again. Grandad would be livid if he ever found out.'

'I know. Look, I love him, but I can't and won't do this stunt they've got lined up for me,' Leah stated. What on earth were they asking of her? It was downright dangerous.

'The client was very specific,' Joey said doubtfully. 'He will pay you very well indeed and he also pays Madam Butterfly.' The woman had left the room to give them time to talk for a few minutes. Shelley Collins, the real name of Madam Butter-fly, had taken a shine to the natural-seeming young woman with a faint Yorkshire accent. With her knowledge of human nature, the woman could tell that Leah would not be coming back to her to work on a regular basis, so the girl might as well get the most out of the experience. And Dan Ryan was a gorgeous man. If Shelley wasn't gay, she'd fancy him herself.

'I'm scared.' Leah sank onto a gold-embroidered chaise longue.

'Of sex?'

'Er . . . no. Sex is the easy part. But take a look at this.' Leah passed Joey her instructions.

'Holy shit! I'd be crapping myself!' he exclaimed, genuinely shocked. 'But you know what, if anyone can do this, you can. It's right up your street.' He burst out laughing suddenly. 'You, Lee-Lee, are the ideal candidate.'

Leah grabbed the instructions. 'Oh, all right then. Let's see - I have to be in Belgravia, wherever that is, for nine o'clock. Madam Butterfly is sending me in a car and I'm to be taken up onto the hotel roof next to the swimming pool where I'll be doing a bungee jump down to the fourth floor.' She shivered with nerves. 'Oh Joey, please come with me and hold my hand. I'll phone you tomorrow morning and we'll meet at King's Cross for our lunchtime train. Will you be OK, staying with your friend?'

'Yes, don't worry about me. We're meeting at Heaven, a club near Charing Cross, and we'll dance all night. But phone me at any time if you need me, Lee-Lee. I will be by your side as soon as I can.'

DAN STRODE DOWN THE CORRIDOR OF THE BYZANTINE HOTEL with Scotty running after him carrying his overnight case. The little man would not allow the bell boy to take it from him.

'You're in the King Room,' said Scotty, biting his lip to smother a laugh.

'Really?'

'You need to keep a low profile,' the little man joked, 'so you should ideally have checked into the Bridal Suite. No one would look for you there. You signed in as Mr Harrison; you should be well under the covers with that name.'

As they arrived at the pale grey and gold entrance, the bell boy slid the card key in and opened the door. He opened his mouth to explain the amenities to them but Scotty tipped him and he gave up and went away, whistling.

'Where is she, then?' asked Dan, pacing nervously.

Scotty handed the card to him. 'Can't you wait?'

'I will need the car here at six-thirty tomorrow morning,'

Dan said tersely, ignoring his jibe and indicated where he wanted his bag putting down.

Scotty gave a wry smile as he left the room. 'Goodnight, Mr Dan, sir. Have a pleasant evening.' Then he whispered, 'She'll be arriving from the skies any minute now, Mr Dan. Tart or Princess. Tart or Princess. Let's hope it's a Princess, eh?' He closed the door and sailed down the corridor, looking forward to a night with some old friends, a game of cards and a tot or two of his favourite malt. He'd have to be up early to get back here.

DAN RIPPED OFF HIS JACKET, POURED A DRINK FROM THE MINI-bar and slugged it down in one. Needing air, he walked out onto the terrace and gazed out from the fifth floor at the illuminated city beyond. Taking the packets of condoms out of his pocket to check which ones he had selected, he wondered when his companion for the night would arrive.

Just then, before he had time to react, there was a muffled sound as something akin to a dark angel hurtled down past his balcony - attached to a bungee rope. The apparition disappeared, followed by a scream as it bounced back up towards him, returned to the roof and then *boinged* back down. Dan ducked just in time as on its return journey the figure made a desperate attempt to clutch at his balcony railings. It missed, and went whizzing upwards again. Just as Dan was thinking should he call Security - *Smack!* - he was knocked clean off his feet as the flying intruder landed heavily on top of him, sending his condom packets flying in all directions.

Leah clutched at a nearby bush, panting. Her eyes had nearly popped out of their sockets and all the breath had gone from her body; in fact, she didn't know if she was coming or going. This experience had been far worse than wing-walking or water-skiing, she thought dizzily.

Dan too lay winded, the pair of them sprawled in a pile-up on the terrace floor, moaning.

'What in God's name?' Dan held his bruised face. 'I could have broken my neck.'

'*You?* I could've broken *mine*! What are you - some psychopervert - to get me to bungee-jump in? Does it turn you on?' Leah clutched the knee she'd bashed. Always a gentleman, Dan unharnessed her, picked her up and carried her inside the room. So this was his hooker: but not quite what he'd visualised earlier today.

Leah's mouth dropped open. 'Flippen 'eck,' she gasped. 'Is this a room for a royal couple?'

Dan couldn't resist a smile. 'Maybe.' He placed Leah onto the huge, soft bed. 'So, crazy woman, care to explain?'

Leah looked up and babbled, 'I . . . er . . .'

Dan studied Leah's face. She was beautiful, blonde and there was something rather vulnerable about her too.

'*Me* explain? I was asked to drop out of the sky - on your instructions, I might add,' Leah said crossly.

'For the love of God, he can't even get this right,' Dan muttered to himself. 'Stupid man.'

'That's right, blame someone else.' Leah gazed at Dan's Adonis-type face and her heart skipped several beats, but there was something in his eyes that touched her. Then she took a deep, calming breath and pulled the zip down on her all-in-one suit, revealing an ivory lace camisole. She was here to work, after all, and had better start earning her fee.

'I thought you must be kinky,' she said.

Watching her, Dan said, 'Oh, but I am. Very kinky. Allow me.' And he took over unzipping her – but very, very slowly.

LEAH WAS WRAPPED IN A TOWEL IN THE BATHROOM WITH THE door ajar when her iPhone started ringing; her landline number appeared on the badly cracked screen. 'Oh. I can't answer the phone right now, Grandad,' she said aloud. 'Not now. Remember, I'm doing this for you. I love you.'

Dan appeared in the doorway in his boxers. 'Who is that?'

'Wrong number. I get crank calls all the time. Don't you get them?' Leah lied hurriedly. 'PPI, boiler changing and erm . . . double glazing.'

'Not at 2 a.m. Nor do I tell them that I love them, whoever they may be. Come here; I want to show you something.' Dan took Leah's hand and led her back to the bedroom.

Leah sat on the bed, while Dan reached into his bag and removed the object d'art he'd purchased at Sotheby's auction house in Bond Street before setting off for Basingstoke the day before. He'd always wanted to own one of these precious items. 'Close your eyes and hold your hands out,' he instructed.

Dan gently held her hands and put into them the *Fabergé* egg which was encrusted with diamonds and aquamarines. 'Now you can peek.'

Leah opened her eyes. 'Oh wow.' She ran her fingers over the gems. 'This is the most beautiful thing I've ever held. Are these real diamonds?'

'They are.' He was watching her, with her tousled hair in her eyes and he felt a stir inside him. This woman was something else.

'Exquisite.' Leah looked across at him as he sat on the bed next to her.

'*Not* quite as exquisite as you.'

Leah looked into his eyes; he was laughing.

'Too cheesy?' he asked.

Leah nodded. She handed the gem-studded egg back to him and Dan put it in his bag.

'So, what's your name?' asked Leah.

'That's for me to know and you to find out.' Those eyes were smiling at her again.

Leah awkwardly reached up and kissed him. She dropped her towel, whispering, 'I don't care. I want more.'

Dan gazed into Leah's face for an age before he kissed her. In a frenzy, they made love until they were left exhausted and wrapped in each other's arms and legs.

AS THE SUN FILTERED INTO THE ROOM, DAN GENTLY UNTANGLED himself, showered and dressed, all the while watching the woman he was loath to leave. He touched his bruised face and smiled. Dan then picked up her phone, which lay on the night table. A photo was stuck crudely with Sellotape to the back. It showed someone who looked like Leah standing on the wings of a plane with a message trailing behind the aircraft. He peered at the message as it was quite small, but disappointingly, part of it was obscured.

Looking across at her fast asleep in bed, he wanted so much to stay and get to know her more. He noticed the missed call was from her grandad and that endeared her to him. On the floor, her debit card lay face up. Picking it up, he felt the raised name with his thumb. He'd never really thought about her name, but yes, Leah Jensen suited her. He knew there were not many Jensens left in the world, so if nothing else, she was a rare and beautiful find, as were the Jensen cars.

Dan put a kiss on his finger, then placed it on Leah's lips.

She turned in half-sleep, mumbling, 'You owe me nothing. You were amazing.'

Dan reached down, and as she wrapped her arms around his neck, she dreamily breathed in his aftershave.

'You are the amazing one.' He delved into his top pocket, retrieved a business card and wrote on the back. He left the money Scotty had given him, glanced back as he reached the door and had to force himself out of the room, closing the door softly behind him.

LEAH'S TELEPHONE RANG AND RANG. SIGHING, SHE ROLLED over and reached for it. Joey's number appeared on the cracked screen.

'Wakey, wakey, Lee-Lee.' Her cousin sounded bright and breezy.

'We could have been doing It!' Leah complained. 'What if we'd been doing It and you interrupted?'

'True, but you weren't. So, was he a hero or zero? And I'm guessing you survived the jump.' Joey laughed at his joke.

'The jump was horrendous, but he was amazing - and now he's gone,' Leah said sadly.

'Obviously married,' Joey said. 'More importantly, did he pay up?'

Leah looked at the bedside table and saw a scribbled note on the back of a business card and a wad of money. 'Gosh, he's left me a note.'

'Quickly, dish the dirt,' urged Joey.

Leah pulled the sheet up against her and read the note. 'Firstly, it wasn't dirt! It was wonderful,' she objected. 'And yes, he's paid. It says, *You are an extraordinary, gorgeous girl and far too good for this game.*'

Leah touched the business card as if she longed for his

touch again. 'It ends, *What an entrance. Dan xx P.S. Do something amazing with your bonus.*'

'What entrance?' Joey asked cheekily. 'Yours, do you mean? And what's that about a bonus?'

'We agreed on a thousand pounds for the night. He called me gorgeous, Joey . . .'

'A grand! That's far too much for your first dabble.' Joey was rather outraged. 'When I did it, I charged men £500.'

'Men? As in plural?' Leah gasped. Just then, she spotted her bank card poking out of the wad of £50 notes. 'I think he's taken my bank details.'

Joey screamed down the phone, 'Forget Kings Cross - meet me outside the hotel in half an hour. I'm just around the corner having a few coffees. You can pay for them as you're so loaded.'

'Give me time for a scrub, Joey. I want to soak in the copper bath and eat the tray of goodies 'cos I'm flipping starving. Let's meet downstairs in an hour and a half,' insisted Leah.

LEAH GRABBED HER SNAKE RING FROM THE BEDSIDE TABLE AND remembered how, only a few short hours ago, she had run her fingers through his dark hair; several strands were still caught in the snake's tail. Before leaving, she looked out across a panorama of London roofs – a sight she would never forget. Slipping the ring in her pocket, she found her way out of the King Room and took the lift down to the foyer.

As she stepped out of the elevator, she felt conspicuous in her all-in-one bungee suit as she went to the desk to hand over the card key.

'Ah, madam, a parcel came for you a few minutes ago.' The receptionist handed over a gift bag in gold, bearing an elegant card which read: *This is for you, for falling from the sky for me. D x.*

'Thank you.' Leah smiled a little awkwardly. She turned and went thankfully outside into the sunshine.

'At last!' Joey said rather loudly. 'You look like Amy Johnson in that get-up, Lee-Lee. Where's your Gipsy Moth called *Jason*? Never mind, I've got all your clothes in this here bag. Come on, I can see a taxi over there,' and he began gesticulating at a black cab which had its light on, showing it was free for hire – only to see another couple step inside it and be driven away.

Leah cringed as Joey tossed his blond head and began to shriek in a most unladylike voice all the swear words he could think of, expressed in a fruity Yorkshire twang.

Even though Londoners were used to all sorts of goings-on, some passers-by did stop to watch while Leah closed her eyes hoping a sinkhole would engulf her.

Hearing the commotion, the concierge emerged from the hotel and hailed another taxi with one imperious gesture.

'I think you'll find this taxi quite convenient for purpose, sir,' he said smoothly to the fuming Joey. 'There are several thousand taxis in London, and *this one* is *most assuredly yours*!'

4

GOING HOME

'Leah, stop gawping at everything and put your card in this flaming ATM,' demanded Joey, who was getting hot under the collar. The taxi had dropped them at the side entrance to Kings Cross and there was time before their train departed to check Leah's bank balance.

'Pin number, quick,' he nagged, running a distracted hand through his mop of fair hair.

Leah entered the PIN number then glanced at the screen. 'See? Same amount as this morning.'

Joey squinted at the figures. 'How much did you have in? I can't read it properly but there's a few noughts.'

'What?' Leah stared more closely. 'That's impossible.'

Joey grabbed her by the shoulder. 'Do you see what I see?' he asked, his voice faint.

'I had two thousand and three pounds in it earlier. Holy smoke . . . Let me check again. Joey, Joey, we've done it! We've done it!' Leah jumped about like a small kid.

Joey printed the balance off, muttering to himself, 'Whatever happened last night surely wasn't worth ten flipping grand.'

'Eleven - *if* you don't mind. I have a thousand pounds in cash.' Leah lowered her voice at this point in case any pick-pockets were listening. 'And you know what? It must have been special to him. Maybe he loved me. It was certainly special for me.' Her voice was wistful.

'Don't be getting any ideas,' Joey cautioned. 'I know men, honey, and they're all bastards. Did he say he loved you?'

'Well, no.'

'Huh. Anyway, what's in the gift bag?'

Leah sat on an empty seat near the row of ATMs while Joey stood by her as passengers streamed past, often knocking into him or even running over his feet with their luggage. He checked the clock and the Departures board and was satisfied that their train was on time. Because he'd already had enough of London.

Inside the gold bag was a smallish box. Opening the wrapping with shaking fingers, Leah then fiddled with the box lid, eventually getting to her prize, and what a prize it was! A beautiful white iPhone nestled in its satin pouch.

Joey rifled in the gift bag and found some paperwork. 'Witch, you must have had this man under a spell. It says it's on monthly contract for two years. Two years - I ask you! Just for a shag.'

Leah blushed as a passing man looked round on overhearing the word 'shag'. She protested in a whisper, 'It wasn't like that, Joey. It was making glorious love. We made love and I told him I didn't want any money.'

'You told him *what*?' Joey was horrified.

'I might have mentioned he didn't owe me anything, but instead he gave me a phone and . . .'

Joey shook his head, 'And ten thousand pounds. Plus the one grand cash. He's either crazy or minted - or both.'

FIVE MONTHS HAD PASSED SINCE THE TRIP TO LONDON AND Leah was blooming. The October sun shone over Whitby in a glorious Indian summer as she and Joey arrived at the café that morning. She looked up at the new nameplate above the café door: she got a lump in her throat every time. The sign read *The Amazing Dog Friendly Café*. The designer had dogs frolicking around the letters: it was perfect. This was her future now - then she rubbed her small bump and amended mentally, *Our future, kiddo.*

Joey, as ever her loyal companion, grabbed Leah gently by the shoulders. 'Come on, cousin, we need to get our skates on if we are going to do the grand opening on time.'

'We do, we need to get ready to build our empire.' Leah grinned. 'It was a great idea of yours to make gingerbread-style bones for our four-legged customers containing doggie ingredients. With luck they should run off the shelves.' She got the keys to the door from her bag.

'Do you ever wonder why Frank did a U-turn on the price for the lease?' Joey enquired.

Leah placed the key in the lock and turned it. 'I do, but in the end I think, who cares? I signed the lease so let's get baking.' She gave Joey a hug. 'You do realise that I've always dreamed of this day, of turning this café into a dog friendly place.'

Joey hugged her back, with real tears in his eyes, then he screeched: 'Once I've got the coffee machine on the go and your first batch of goodies is set out and ready, I'll turn the sign to Open. So I'd better get started.' After washing his hands in the little sink, he began to display the cakes that had been made at home. 'I'm so excited!' he sang out, dressed in his pink apron with its design of assorted dogs. In the glass-fronted slab he stacked the crusty bread sandwiches, sourdough butties and granary subs, and on the cake towers he arranged – artistically, of course - the Red Velvet cake, walnut and lemon sponge, and the scones, still warm from the ovens at Abbot's Bridge Road. Leah had filled the cash register with change and taken the butter pats out of the fridge and the tiny pots of jam for the scones. She checked the paper napkin dispenser and watered the plants on the windowsills. As Joey turned his attention to the big coffee machine, she knew they were nearly ready.

Leah almost skipped into the kitchen, picked up her own new apron with a smiling puppy on it, then she switched on the oven. She and Joey had been working flat out to update, decorate and stock the café. They both had their hygiene certificates already and Leah had chosen to use the same suppliers as before. However, the bulk of their food was to be homemade, fresh and delicious.

Joey slumped against the door as he switched the sign to Closed. Like Leah, he had been cooking, serving and waiting on tables all day. 'I'm fagged out, but I had a great first day.'

Leah smiled at him tiredly. 'You've worked so hard, Joey – I couldn't have done any of it without you. I'm shattered too, but seriously, if this place is going to be this busy, I think we need another front-of-house person to help. I mean, we still have the cleaning to do and then more baking tonight.' She sat down with a sigh. 'Now Grandad's on the mend after his op went so successfully,' at which she and Joey stopped to perform a quick high five, 'we have more time on our hands, but it's still not enough.'

Joey plonked himself down beside her. 'Oo-er. Get you, with your front-of-house. We are hardly one Michelin Star yet.

On a different tack, are you going to get in touch with Papa?'
Joey pointed to her tummy.

'I tried, I told you. I wanted to leave a message with his PA
but she said he's moved to America and he's not coming back.
And you know what, Joey? I'm thinking like you, I reckon he's
married and he doesn't want to know.' She yawned. 'Come on,
let's go home to Grandad. Apart from you, he's the main man in
my life – he's my rock.' Leah stood up and went to get her light
jacket as the sea breezes could be chilly by teatime. 'If I have to
start a new life without Dan, I start it now with my Amazing
Dog Friendly Café. In one way, Dan has given me a future for
me and my baby - and you, mustn't forget you, Joey. We are
family.'

THE WEEKS FLEW PAST IN A BLUR OF COOKING, WITH ANY
leftovers going to the homeless - in many ways that was Leah's
favourite part of the day. Christmas at the café was a marvellous
time, with special treats for all their regular customers, both
two- and four-footed. Leah was working so hard she barely had
time to fit in the necessary hospital pre-natal appointments. If it
hadn't been for Joey's incessant badgering and Thomas insisting
on escorting her to each and every appointment, she probably
wouldn't have gone. And Joey and Thomas together had taken
charge of ordering baby clothes, nappies, the crib, cot - and all
the other items a new mum needed. Truth to tell, both men had
thoroughly enjoyed themselves, and Grandad Thomas was
chuffed to pieces at the thought of greeting his first great-
grandchild.

That particular day, towards the middle of February, Leah
was up to her elbows in baking 'Rocky Roads with a Twist'.
The orange twist was by far her customers' favourite, but her

own was the lime and lemon twist. The café had closed and it was nearly dusk outside as she was grating a little chocolate over the last tray. Suddenly, she doubled over in pain.

'Ow,' she whispered, but not quietly enough as Joey flew into the kitchen.

'OK, where's the pee?' he said officiously, flouncing around to look for some kitchen roll. 'I must clean up or Environmental Health will close us down.'

'My waters have not broken,' Leah said feebly. 'It's just a twinge. *Ow.*'

'Twinge or not, I'm calling for an ambulance. It's a long way to Scarborough.' Joey ushered Leah into the café and to a table near the door.

Marisa, an older lady who had been working for them for several months now, put down her broom and hastened over to Leah. Gazing at her very small bump, she said, 'Are you premature, dear?'

'No, Marisa, I'm smack on time if he comes today.' Leah had been trying to ignore the fact that the birth was very close now. She just had so much still to do.

'Don't take it as read that he's a boy from the scan, they've been known to be wrong. My great-niece should have been a boy - or so the stupid scan would have had us believe,' Marisa related to Leah for about the fifth time.

'Are you phoning the ambulance or what?' Leah asked Joey, then had to stop for a few seconds, and just breathe. '*Aaah . . .* That was a real contraction, I think,' she gasped when she could speak again.

'I was going to phone Grandad first.'

'No! Just ring the flaming ambulance, Joey, like you said you were going to. What can Grandad do?' Leah protested, then bent double again for a minute or two as another contraction seized her.

Marisa pushed the sugar cubes in front of her. 'Here, suck on one of those, take your mind off the pain. Joey, get on that phone.' Marisa could tell the contractions were only minutes apart. It was time to get going.

'Huh, if only she'd sucked . . .'

'Joey, shut *up*. I don't need a lecture. *Ow!*' Leah screamed and stood up. 'Marisa, can you open the door for me, please.'

'Oh no, dear.' Marisa stood in front of the door. 'You are not breaking your waters on the pavement for anyone!'

Joey stuck his nose in the air and punched out the numbers 999. 'Hello, yes, we are having a baby and I don't want any mess in my café!'

'Sir, this is for emergencies only. Is it an emergency?' asked the operator.

'Whose café?' screamed Leah.

'Sorry, she's rather irritable. I think I'll put a bucket under her legs just in case she drops the sprog before you arrive.' Joey knew he was gabbling but somehow, he couldn't stop. 'Actually,' he rabbited on, 'can you advise if she should look like Medusa. Head swelling, eyes bulging kind of look.' Flustered, he blurted out, 'Well, we need an ambulance so just make it quick, will you. Please. We're at The Amazing Dog Friendly Café on the West Cliff in Whitby, and yes - it's an emergency all right.' He placed the phone on the counter top with trembling hands. 'Now for the bucket.'

Both Marisa and Leah shrieked at him in unison, 'No bucket!'

'All right, ladies, keep your clouts on. Towels then, we practised towels, Leah.'

'Yes – *ow* . . . yes, towels.'

'Oops, shouldn't you be breathing, Lee-Lee? Panting, I mean, like the bitches when they're hot.' Joey brought a handful of bath towels.

'They're the dog towels,' Leah managed to say.

'Oh. You want the *new* towels?'

'Yes, Joey, I do. Ow, and I want them now!' she screamed.

'Keep your helmet on, I'm getting them,' Joey said tartly.

He'd never known his cousin Leah to be quite this objectionable. As he appeared in the doorway, fetching the towels through, they all saw the ambulance pull up outside the café.

'Thank God,' whispered Leah.

When the ambulance staff had come in and were helping Leah to stand, Joey was straight in with the question: 'Why haven't her waters broken when she's having contractions?'

'This is absolutely normal. There's nothing to fret about, but I know as an expectant father it must be worrying,' said the male paramedic.

'Huh, I didn't screw her,' Joey murmured to himself. 'Please, I'd rather do him getting out of the driver's door. *He's* seriously hunky.'

'Now,' said the female paramedic to Leah, 'how often are your contractions?'

'Well, she's only just started having them, but I have to say she's becoming obstrocolous.' Joey motioned to the coffee machine. 'Would you like a latte?'

'Joey! I'm having a baby, not waiting for the buns to come out of the oven.' Leah turned to the paramedic. 'About every few minutes. *Aaarrrgggghhh . . .*'

'We've got time then. Gently does it.' Together, the little group made it to the ambulance, leaving Marisa behind to look after things.

LEAH LOOKED AT THE BUNDLE IN HER ARMS AND SAW THE MOST amazing eyes peering back at her. She kissed her baby son's forehead and inhaled his smell.

Joey pranced in. 'At last I get a proper view. Well done, Lee-Lee. Oh, isn't he gorgeous . . .' Joey's eyes filled with tears of wonderment and joy, for his tender heart was easily moved. 'So,' he said, clearing his throat, 'are you calling him Joey after me?'

Leah smiled. 'Silly boy. I'm calling him Tom after Grandad, as we agreed.'

'I thought you might have forgotten, what with baby brain and everything going on. On a plus point at least you didn't wee on the café floor and that Medusa look has gone completely.' Joey hesitated. 'Can I hold him? My hands are clean. I've always wanted a baby.'

'You have?'

'Oh yes, of course I'd have to adopt, but one day when I meet Mr Right . . .'

As he took little Tom into his arms, Joey couldn't hold back more tears. 'Oh Leah, he's perfect. Look at his little fingers and those cute little toes and just wait until he can make gingerbread people. It's so sad that his father doesn't want anything to do with him.'

'Yes, it is,' Leah said sadly. 'His PA made it clear he isn't interested.'

'Did you tell her that you were up the duff?'

'Of course not. That's our business, not hers.'

'Then it's just us Jensens, kiddo, and we'll do our best to raise you good and proper. I will show you how to decorate pink gingerbread men,' he whispered as he noted Leah was asleep, and carefully placed the tiny newcomer in his cot. 'Better ring your great-grandad now, Tom junior, tell him you've arrived with your jet-black hair and beautiful blue eyes. Looking at you now, you'll have all the girls - *or the boys* - chasing you.'

5

THE PAST COMES BACK TO BITE

Nine years later

Leah carried in the gingerbread people and dogs from the kitchen and placed them onto the rear work surface. She waited for Joey to finish serving.

'Will you decorate these, please?' she requested, then warned him: 'And don't go over the top, if you don't mind.'

'I fancy putting the men in fairy blue suits today, with purple trimmings. All very butch.' Joey felt a delicious shiver run through him as he thought of his latest, very butch Grindr 'brief encounter'. Such a pity that these short liaisons led nowhere. Joey was getting to the age where he'd like to settle down, but so far, the right man hadn't come along. Sex there was a-plenty if he wanted it, but long-term commitment was out of the question. For the moment, however, Leah, Tom and Thomas senior still needed him at Abbey Bridge Road.

'Suit yourself. But don't forget the next batch of dog treats are in the oven,' Leah reminded him, just in case he forgot. 'I've put the timer on. I'll have to be off soon to pick Tom up from school.'

Joey started making a salmon and cucumber sandwich for

Eddie, a regular customer who, because he could bring his best friend Bertie the Basset Hound here with him, arrived every single afternoon around the same time, and always ordered the same sandwich, along with a doggie 'gingerbread' man. Now, taking the generously-sized sandwich from Joey and sitting down, Eddie took a huge bite, watched carefully by Bertie.

'You know, Lee-Lee,' Joey began cautiously, 'when I picked Tom up from his piano lesson yesterday, he was asking about his father again for the school gig thingy tonight. You need to address this, the sooner the better. Tom's no fool, he won't be put off for much longer . . .'

'Sorry.' Leah cut him off. 'Like I said, it's my school-run time. We need to be back there tonight for six p.m. sharp, to get good seats.' She whistled, and two Pomeranians trotted to her side. She clipped on their leads and walked out.

'That's right, fly away with Yin and Yang,' Joey called after her. 'It'll come back and bite you on your bum. Don't say I didn't warn you.'

Eddie wiped his mouth on a serviette. 'Still not listening to you eh, lad?'

'Nope, but she will have to soon. I know young Tom is unhappy, he wants to know his dad and who can blame him. I can understand that Leah is frightened that the lad will want to live with Dan, him being rich and all that, but I know Tom, and he really loves his mum.'

'Precisely. What do you say, Bertie Basset? Give me your paw.' Eddie snapped off one of the gingerbread man's legs and dropped it into Bertie's mouth.

Joey picked up the pink icing gun and watched his cousin stride off down the street. He was proud of what she'd achieved over the past nine years. Not only did she own seven Dog Friendly Cafés along the East Yorkshire coast, she had also opened a Pilates class upstairs, and it was very popular. Personally, he didn't know how she coped, but she seemed to thrive on the pressure. She'd got herself a great team, and they gelled. In the past, many a time Joey had found her in the early hours doing her accounting until he persuaded her to employ a friend of theirs. It made sense, and it gave Leah more time with Tom.

Joey often wished he'd thought of the idea of a dog friendly café himself because it had proved to be a brainwave, a great money earner and so good for the clientele. Leah even had 'a naughty corner', and many of her customers preferred it to the busier parts of the café. Why, ordinary folk would come in for coffee just to see and pet other people's dogs - and Joey loved that. Every one of the seven cafés had become the friendly social hub of the town they were in.

OUTSIDE THE PLAYGROUND GATES OF NORTHSIDE PRIMARY School, which were locked until the janitor appeared when school ended at 3.15 p.m., a stranger lurked, pretending to take photographs of wild birds. It was Ruby, newly arrived from London, on the trail of her best friend's grandson. In her colourful clothes she didn't exactly blend into the landscape and in fact looked rather like a bird - a tropical one - herself. She grinned; she'd always considered herself to be a super sleuth.

Leah drove into a parking space behind the school, parked then got out and began to lift the little dogs out. Immediately, another car blocked hers in. The driver - a man - jumped out and hurried away. Ruby's camera clicked as she caught Leah and the dogs in her lens.

Leah sighed. 'Damn. I always get blocked in.'

Ruby called, 'Ram it! That's what I'd do. What a cheek.'

'I can't possibly do that.' Leah laughed in disbelief.

'Sure you can.'

'That would be like me grabbing your very lovely camera, throwing it on the ground then stamping on it.'

Ruby held the camera protectively to her breast. 'Hey, it was just a suggestion.'

Leah smiled. 'Sorry. What are you taking photos of?'

Ruby looked to the skies, wishing she didn't have to lie. 'Tits,' she said, and tried not to laugh. It was the first thing she could think of. 'The Greater and Lesser Tits,' she added vaguely. 'Just tits in general.' It really was quite hard not to laugh, but Sophie would skin her alive if she screwed this up. More soberly, she went on, 'They are such pretty birds, don't you think?'

Leah shrugged. 'I've not heard of them. Neither the Greater nor the Lesser.'

Ruby gestured flamboyantly around her. 'They're everywhere if you really look.'

Just then, a big-breasted woman walked past, making Ruby want to laugh again, then a man with a huge nose struggled out of a car.

'And then there's the rare, almost extinct Knob-nosed Albatross,' Ruby couldn't resist saying, then she shrugged. 'Anything wild really.'

'The kids are wild,' Leah said.

'Pfft. They don't frighten me.'

The bell pealed out, and there was a noise of thundering feet. The kids screamed as they ran towards the gates, looking for whoever was collecting them, nearly knocking the caretaker over. Ruby fell backwards into the bushes as a dozen kids rushed past her, then another dozen.

Tom immediately went to help. He held out his hand and smiled at her.

Ruby took his hand and seemed intoxicated with him. She

smiled back, saying, 'Thanks, kid.' It was a shock. The lad was the spitting image of his dad.

'This is Tom, my son,' said Leah proudly.

'Hi, Tom. Charmed to make your acquaintance. It's not often a young man takes my breath away, but you've done just that.' Ruby flicked a leaf off her camera. 'Can I take a photo of your cute dogs?'

Tom nodded as Ruby took several photos of the Poms with Tom.

'If you write your email address down, I will let you have copies,' she told Leah.

'Thank you; I have a card here.' Leah handed over her business card.

Tom watched Ruby turn back to photograph more birds.

'Enjoy school today?' asked Leah.

The boy nodded. 'We've been rehearsing. We did my roots again. I told the teacher about you and Grandad Thomas, but I wish I had my daddy's roots too.' Tom looked sad. Then in a small voice he asked: 'Mummy, have you found my daddy yet?'

Ruby spun around.

Leah seemed dumbfounded. 'I . . . I think he works on an oil rig.'

Tom frowned. 'Don't you know? You promised you'd check, but I can check if you like?'

Leah saw and heard Tom's disappointment, and the sadness in his voice hurt her deeply; if only things had worked out, but the woman at Ryan's HQ had been adamant: Dan was out of the country and didn't want to know.

Ruby interrupted, 'Hey, what's that, Tom? Wow.' She was genuinely excited as she took photos of a majestic bird soaring on the thermals.

Tom explained, 'That's a Red Kite. They get their quarry

from roadkill, and sheep carrion mostly, but we have to be careful with our little Pomeranians as I reckon they could easily kill one. They do catch the occasional rabbit.' He pulled a yo-yo from his pocket and started to play with it, up and down.

Ruby watched him. 'Are you an ornithologist, Tom?' She gave a rich laugh. 'Well, I thought it was a pterodactyl.'

Tom thought this was hilarious. 'No, silly, it's a bird of prey.'

As Leah dreamily watched the yo-yo going up and down, a memory of a hotel terrace flashed through her mind and she couldn't help but smile, but the memory was tinged with regret and had to be banished from her mind as it hurt too much. She had often asked herself why it still hurt and each time she came back to the same impossible conclusion. How could you fall in love after only a few hours?

It was time to go, Ruby thought, before her cover was blown. She held her hand out. 'I'm Ruby, by the way. I'm sure we'll meet again, Mrs . . .'

'Oh no, it's Miss - Miss Leah Jensen.'

Ruby nodded. 'Did his dad leave?'

Leah shrugged. 'He was never really around. Nice meeting you, Ruby. Come on, Tom.' No, I can't and won't get into a conversation about Dan with a complete stranger, she thought.

Ruby studied a photo of Tom on her camera. Then she pulled an older picture of another boy from her pocket. Just as she had spotted from the start, there was a very close resemblance. This charming young lad just had to be Dan's son and Sophie's grandson.

miles out of Whitby before she drew into a lay-by to enjoy the sea view. Picking up her mobile phone, she sent one of the photos of Tom to Sophie. Almost immediately, her phone began to ring.

'Hello, so what did you find out?' asked Sophie, sounding eager.

'More or less what you suspected. I've taken several shots of both Tom and his mum Leah. Begrudgingly, I am forced to concede he has a look of Dan,' replied Ruby, knowing full well that would annoy Sophie.

'Begrudgingly? Of course, he looks like Dan! Why, he's the mirror image of him at the same age. So, what else did you learn?' Sophie enquired with just a faint note of desperation.

'Leah isn't married, so you may be onto something there, but don't start getting excited yet, you'll only be disappointed if he turns out to be no relation. However, she did say that Tom's dad hasn't been around, but Tom wants to know his dad - that much is obvious. He's been studying something do with lineage at school, and it sounds like he does miss having a father figure in his life. Having said that, we've no proof that Leah didn't search for Dan. If I'd been in her position, I'd have found Dan come hell and high water, so he could cough up for the boy's upkeep. Kids aren't cheap these days, you know.' Ruby idly watched a surfer taking in some of the big rollers and wished she'd been brave enough to learn to surf when she was younger and slimmer.

'So, what's our next move?' her employer asked.

'I come back, and we weigh up our options, that's what we do. You're not diving into this head first, Sophie; we must let Leah think this is her idea. Now I'm sorry but I must dash as I need to find a loo before I drive back. Why I couldn't be chauffeur-driven, I've no idea,' complained Ruby.

'Because Sisco is Dan's chauffeur, that's why. I'll see you

when you get back late this evening. Drive carefully with the rest of those photos, they're precious,' said Sophie.

'Oh, and I thought you cared.'

'Don't push it!'

Ruby laughed into the phone. Thirty-odd years of being best friends meant they almost knew each other inside out, but first, she needed to find a loo.

LEAH AND TOM WITH YIN AND YANG FOLLOWING THEM entered the café. The dogs went straight to Joey for a treat.

'OK, take these to your bed,' Joey said, affectionately stroking both dogs before they trotted off to their cosy bed in the back. 'I love these boys; they're so obedient.'

'Thanks to me going to puppy school with them,' Leah reminded him.

'And me babysitting,' Joey protested. 'Fancy a cuppa?'

Leah nodded, watching Tom go into the side room.

'Have you decided whether or not to look for Dan again?' Joey placed a cup of tea on the table.

Leah shrugged. 'I'm still mulling it over. Of course, I want Tom to know his dad, but Daniel Ryan comes from a very powerful family with a great deal of wealth behind them. I don't want Tom taken away from me. That kind of power can move mountains.'

'Daniel Ryan is not a devil, he's a man, and his son deserves to know him,' said Joey, trying to get her to see reason.

'Don't you think I know that? I'm just scared. I tried so hard when I had Tom, but I got nowhere - it was like there was a very high wall between us. Look, I will do the right thing, just give me time to get my head around it.' Leah drank her weak black tea in silence.

'Can't you tell Tom?'

'What - that I was his father's hooker?' Leah shuddered. 'No way.'

'You could explain we were doing it for Grandad Thomas,' said Joey.

Tom, who was sitting with his back to the wall listening to the conversation, heaved a sigh. His plan was starting to work; he would get to see his daddy soon. The next step was ready. He went to sit in the dog bed and pet his beloved Pomeranians and take in the new piece of information he'd just been given.

'I want my mummy to understand that I need to meet him. That's all I'm asking. You are lucky. We see your mummy and your daddy in the park. If I can meet mine, I will be happy,' said Tom as he cuddled his dogs.

Joey walked through at that moment, saying, 'It's time to get a move on for the family tree thingy. You need a change of clothes. Are you worried about it?'

'Not really. I know all about our family – well, most of our family. Enough to get me by.' Tom grinned. 'Sorry boys, but you have to stay at home for this one. Better keep safely away from the fireworks.'

'What do you mean? There won't be any fireworks,' Joey said.

'True – it's just that there'll be a lot of family secrets let out of the bag tonight, judging from some of the things I've heard in the rehearsals. We've all been doing lots of research.'

'I bet you have,' Joey said thoughtfully.

6

HOME TURF

Dan Ryan stepped down from the Learjet onto the tarmac at Heathrow airport like a Greek god stepping onto the peak of Mount Olympus, every bit the billionaire in his dark Armani silk suit, white shirt, plum-coloured tie and gold cufflinks. His elegant leather shoes shone like mirrors, but that was down to his mother always fussing about well-polished shoes.

His efficient PA, brunette Chelsea Saffer, was climbing down the aircraft steps behind him. She was smartly dressed in a fitted jacket, a matching short skirt that showed off her legs, and high strappy heels that Dan thought might get caught in a hole at any moment.

Then his heart leaped as his pride and joy, his Newfoundland dog Hero, came racing to meet him. Sisco, Dan's chauffeur who helped to look after the big dog when his master was away, gave a helpless exclamation as the lead was torn out of his hand by the excited animal who was overjoyed to see Dan. Hero shook his head and drool flew, hitting Chelsea's pristine suit.

Chelsea screamed dramatically.

Dan had instinctively ducked and the drool missed him by

millimetres, but he was used to his hound, so he merely grinned and said fondly, 'That's my boy. Missed me, did you, old feller?' as he stroked Hero's head.

'I hate drool! Ugh. That thing stinks.' Chelsea glowered at the huge dog.

Scotty, who was watching, suddenly grabbed the trailing lead and said, 'I think he needs to relieve himself. I recognise the signs.' Then, 'Oh, shit,' as Hero pulled the little man across the private airstrip at a rate of knots.

'Not necessarily, Scotty,' Dan chuckled, 'but if he does, we have poo bags, right?'

Hero pulled Scotty to his chosen spot, where he cocked a leg against a wire fence and did a lengthy steaming wee that he'd obviously been holding in.

Chelsea shuddered. 'Disgusting. Why here? Why now? And why does *he* have to come with us? Can't you kennel him? This is preposterous, dragging a mutt around with us.'

'I have business here, remember. The one that pays your exorbitant salary - and just so you know, I will never kennel Hero. He's my boy, the nearest thing I have to a son.' Dan walked over to take Hero's lead, leaving Chelsea in no doubt where she stood in the queue.

Chelsea looked at the dog with hatred and ground her stiletto into the tarmac.

Scotty walked up to her and muttered, 'You had better get used to being in the UK fulltime. Your boss is planning on living in England again, instead of coming and going from New York and Paris.'

'Huh, not if *I* have anything to do with it!'

'That's the thing; I don't think you do.' Having delivered that putdown, Scotty walked quickly away before a stiletto could do him some damage.

The chauffeur-driven four-wheel drive pulled up a few minutes later and Dan opened the tailgate for Hero to jump in.

Scotty looked furtively around. 'I've checked for snipers; we're safe to proceed. All is OK on the western front. I wasn't in the SAS for nothing.'

'Good man, Scotty,' said Dan with a smile, humouring his bodyguard as he climbed into the front seat. Scotty and Chelsea got into the rear.

Sisco pressed the button to wind up the security window, before saying to Dan, 'He wasn't in the SAS. Think they'd take that little feller? You do know that he's a fruit cake – a Dundee one as he's Scottish.' Sisco snorted at his own joke.

'He knows I worry about security. OK, OK, I agree he's a fruitcake, but he's a good friend of my mother's and like you he is part of the family,' Dan said peaceably.

Without more ado, they set off in the direction of Dan's temporary home, the Hambourne Manor and Country Estate in St Albans, just north of London. The owner was a wealthy horse-breeder who had moved to Newmarket and now rented the place out. Dan had signed a two-year lease, enough time for him to find a permanent home, apart from the flat he owned in the Barbican near the Ryan HQ in the City of London. He'd bought a penthouse apartment in New York and one in Paris too – great places to stay when he was in the head office there or off doing one of his frequent bursts of travelling - but his heart had always remained in good old Blighty. He knew Hero would love the indoor swimming pool, and as he'd had all his horses transported here from their livery stables, the Hambourne estate would soon feel like home.

Dan looked around as the big car purred onto the M25. Loosening his tie, he relaxed into his seat and closed his eyes. The vehicle jolted and Dan's eyes shot open again. He looked in the passenger side mirror and saw Hero's head lolling. Who would ever have thought that a big black bear-like creature would become his best friend and confidant?

Closing his eyes once more he settled back in his seat for the hour-long journey to what he was now calling his great adventure. At least that was what his mother had called it when she persuaded him to move back to the UK lock, stock and no smoking barrels.

LEAH AND JOEY ESCORTED TOM BACKSTAGE AT THE SCHOOL. Leah ran her hand through the boy's hair, but he shrugged her off.

'You can leave now, Mummy. I know exactly what I'm gonna say.' Tom gave a high-five with Harry. 'I can't wait, can you?'

Harry grinned and nodded as he walked back to his own mum and dad.

Leah felt she needed to advise Tom - but she could hardly tell him about his dad now in a school full of people. My goodness, she realised she was more nervous than her eight-year-old son, she couldn't even think straight. 'Look, darling,' was all she said in the end, 'just concentrate on Grandad's veteran days and you'll be fine.'

'I must say something about you too, Mummy,' Tom beamed.

'Be kind, be truthful of whoever you talk about. That is all we can ask.' Leah blew Tom a kiss.

Seeing this, Tom's friends made funny faces and laughed; he joined in too.

Leah and Joey moved to their seats, but Leah was still nervous and very fidgety.

'Aren't you excited? His first public appearance and he doesn't look a bit bothered.' Joey offered Leah a Bon-Bon.

'No, thanks. Oh Lord, I'm scared he'll play a wrong note.' Leah wrung her hands together.

'Oh no, his piano lessons are going great. Miss Hudson is a marvellous teacher. He's always raving about her.' Joey popped another sweetie into his mouth. 'I've not met her yet, but he really enjoys going to her house for his lessons. Oh, lookie here, they're starting.'

The stage curtains drew back and the children acted out some of the yesteryear themes while Tom played a simple tune on the piano.

Then Harry and Troy marched onto the stage in different uniforms. Three little girls baked in the background on pretend cardboard cookers.

'That's a bit sexist, isn't it?' Joey whispered.

'No, it's in years gone by,' Leah answered.

'My grandad is a doctor, and he saves people's lives,' piped up Harry.

'My grandad is a butcher and he feeds people,' said Troy.

Tom, whilst banging the keys of the piano, said, 'And my grandad was a soldier, and he fought our enemies.'

The play carried on to the modern day. Tom changed key and played a different, simple tune.

Harry stepped forward. 'My daddy is also a doctor, but my grandad says he gets paid too much money because he's always on the golf course.'

Everyone laughed.

Gaining in confidence, Troy too moved to the front of the stage. 'And my daddy is an artist,' he told the audience. 'He paints cows instead of eating them, and he demonstrates about animals' rights.'

People laughed and a few gave a little cheer.

Looking nervous, Tom stood up and stepped away from the piano. Into the sudden silence he said: 'And my . . .' He scanned the audience for Leah and blurted out: 'And my mummy was my daddy's hooker and plaything.'

The audience gasped. All eyes turned to Leah, who was left open-mouthed.

Joey hooted with laughter. 'Some kids have great imaginations when they haven't got a father around to rein them in,' he said loudly and clearly.

Leah laughed nervously. It had been a long time since she had wished for the ground to swallow her up.

Thankfully, the audience erupted with laughter too.

Leah sighed with relief - then she saw her son's sad little face. And it broke her heart.

LEAH RAN UP THE STAIRS, MOMENTARILY STEPPING ON, THEN skipping over one creaky step. Her mind was still whirling, and she knew now she had to address the root problem. Her son wanted to meet his father. Joey was right - it was time.

Leah walked into Tom's room. He was jumping on his bed playing with Yin and Yang. Leah raised her brow in mock sternness.

'Are you really angry, Mummy?' the little lad asked.

'For telling the truth? No. As for telling the truth to a school full of parents, I should be.' Leah sat on the bed and patted the place beside her. Tom snuggled up to her.

'What is a hooker, Mummy?'

'Well . . . let's just say that it's someone who falls in love for one night only.' Leah sighed. That was the truth on her part at least.

'I'm glad you loved Daddy, but I do miss him.'

'Me too. I did love him. Now . . . teeth?'

Tom grinned, showing his teeth to his mum.

'Done them. I've just to say my prayers. Goodnight, Mummy. I love you.' Tom kissed Leah.

Leah hugged him back. 'Love you for . . .'

'. . . ever more,' Tom finished off.

'Night-night, darling.' Leah tip-toed out, then stopped for a moment behind the door, which she always left open.

Tom cuddled the dogs and pointed to the stars through the window where the curtains hadn't quite met in the middle.

'You see that star shining brightly in the sky?' he told them. 'That one is the mummy star, so my mummy's and your mummy's hearts shine from there.'

Leah was captivated, hearing this, but she felt terribly guilty for listening in.

'That's the daddy star, the one next to the mummy star.' Tom audibly gulped. His voice was so sad. 'Don't know if my daddy is shining from there, but you're lucky we see your daddy in the park. I don't see mine. I think he's lost.'

Leah almost flat-lined. What on earth was she doing to her son? Making her way slowly down the steps, she stood on the creaky one, and sure enough, it creaked.

Tom laid his head on the pillow as he heard his mum step on the squeaky step. He smiled, then closed his eyes.

JOEY LOOKED UP AS LEAH WALKED IN. 'WELL, DID YOU ASK him why he said it? I have to admit I was shocked. You could have knocked me down with a feather, and that's no mean feat.'

'No feather could ever knock you down, Joey. Anyway, he must have overheard us in the café. He asked me what a hooker was.' Leah frowned.

'And you said?'

'Someone you fall in love with for one night only.' She reached for Joey's cup of tea and refilled it from the pot.

'Huh. That's a cop-out.'

'Really? I thought it was an accurate description, for me anyway. I'm scared, Joey. We saw the results of that lawsuit a few years ago. I couldn't bear to lose Tom as that girl did, but I do reckon I have to face facts, find Dan Ryan and confront him for once and for all.' Leah placed the cup down and Joey picked it up.

'At last she sees sense! Just remember, you could be opening a can of caviar - or a bucketload of worms. But as I see it, you have no choice. Oh, to see the look on Dan Ryan's face when you walk in. I wonder what his wife is like?' Joey sipped the warm liquid with a slurp.

'I won't drop him in it. That's not my intention. I want him to acknowledge the fact that Tom is his son. I don't want his money as we have enough, but I would like some commitment from him, for Tom's sake.' Leah reached for the iPad. Dan's photo was smiling back at her. *Poldark* fans would be after him; he was definitely an Aidan Turner lookalike, she thought dreamily. If only things had been different. *If, if, if.* But the cold, hard facts were that he had never returned her calls nor had he replied to her emails. Now, however, she was going to find out why.

'You don't want a lot then. He's going to be a very busy businessman according to the iPad. And let's say he doesn't want to know. What then?' Joey interjected.

'Whose side are you on?' Leah stuck her tongue out at her cousin. 'His or ours?'

'Why, yours of course,' Joey promised, reaching for the biscuit tin, 'but you have to be ready for these things, Lee-Lee. I so don't want you to be hurt, and these businessmen types can be ruthless. I mean, just look at that face. Good-looking, I have to agree, but is he ready to become a daddy again?'

'He may not be a daddy. He may love Tom as soon as he sees him.' Leah sneaked another look at the iPad. Oh Lord, he was even better-looking than she remembered. He was more mature, more muscular and she liked the laughter lines around his eyes. She looked at his eyes and her heart skipped a beat. Was she going to come out of this intact? There was a price to pay here and Leah knew it was she herself who would be paying it. This man had broken her heart once before without even knowing it: was there a slim chance that this time, he could mend it? Only the next few weeks would tell.

7

ANOTHER TRIP TO LONDON

Having travelled down to London in a first-class carriage, Leah managed to get some of her emails up to date. Joey had driven her to York and booked her an open ticket for the non-stop journey, paying the extra for a better seat as he knew she wouldn't have squandered the cash herself. It was a welcome change, Leah decided, even if she was reluctant to admit it. Free food and drink and a gorgeously comfy seat and quiet carriage made the expense well worth it. And after all, this trip was intended to be the one that would change all their lives, so it had been a good idea of Joey's to start off in style.

The passing scenes went past in a blur of images, then she saw Alexandra Palace on one side and the Emirates football stadium on the other and knew they were close to Kings Cross. As the train glided slowly into the station, Leah felt butterflies begin to flutter in her stomach.

LEAH TOOK A CAB TO HER HOTEL IN RUSSELL SQUARE, WHICH
was a short distance away; then after checking in and leaving
her luggage in a pretty bedroom overlooking the park, she took
another cab to the Ryan Empire office block in the City. Paying
the cabbie off, she realised her hands were shaking.

'Are you going for an interview, love? I wouldn't worry, you
look stunning,' said the taxi driver in a kindly way.

'Here's hoping, and thanks for the history lesson on the way,
You were as good as a Blue Guide,' Leah said genuinely. The
cabbie waved away her tip and once she'd hopped out, he
immediately picked up a couple carrying briefcases who'd just
emerged from the building.

Leah moved towards the automatic front doors of the tall
glass building. She backed off twice, but then her phone rang
and her son's photo appeared on her iPhone.

'You should be at school, Tom,' she said gently.

'Sorry, Mummy, I was so excited I was sick at school so
they sent for Joey,' Tom apologised.

'Sweetheart, I will call you as soon as I know anything. You
remember what we said about Dan being a very busy man. So
be patient. Now you go and lie down and get Joey to spoil you
once you feel well enough. Try and be calm. Bye, sweetie, I
love you.' Leah turned back towards the prestigious doors. This
time she didn't hesitate; she'd come this far and wasn't about to
give up now. Her son's happiness was far more important.

As she walked into the building, Leah took stock of the
layout and the luxurious interior. She was looking for information about where Dan's office might be, then she saw the lift.
That was surely the place to find the CEO's information.

Leah looked very business-like as she walked past the huge,
impressive reception desk. She didn't realise she should sign in
– nor did she spot the short Security man lurking behind the
desk.

Scotty craned his neck. ''Scuse me, miss, do you have an appointment? Miss – miss, you can't go through there without a pass.'

Leah tried her best to blag it. 'Yes, I have an appointment with Mr Dan Ryan.' She handed Scotty a business card. He tried to turn it over but Leah snatched it back. 'This is my card. Dan gave me it a while ago and he said if I needed him I had just to get in touch.'

Scotty looked her up and down. 'That's definitely an old business card. I will just check. Please wait here. What's your name, madam?' Scotty moved behind the desk and disappeared.

Leah leaned over. 'Leah Jensen.' She checked the clock in the foyer. It was 9.30 a.m, the second of May. From this vantage point she could see the elevator information. *Chief Executive - Floor 5.* Feeling as if Joey was pushing her forward, she tip-toed away, then ran for all she was worth as the elevator doors opened as if on command. Leah jabbed the number 5 button several times. Then again.

Scotty looked across from the security desk. As he reached the lift, the doors began to close. Leah hit out at Scotty with her bag in a half-hearted manner, just to keep him at bay without hurting him.

'Sorry. I am family,' she said. 'I promise.'

Scotty staggered back as the handbag whacked him on the shoulder, sending him off-balance. Feeling like a twit, the little man saw the lift doors close on him.

LEAH TURNED THE BUSINESS CARD OVER AND OVER IN HER hand. She looked at the words and a small smile appeared on her lips. *You are an extraordinary, gorgeous girl and far too*

good for this game. What an entrance. Dan xx P.S. Do something amazing with your bonus.

If only she could have gone back in time, Leah thought sadly, and explain to him that she was pregnant - and not have to go through that interfering woman on the phone who had insisted he had left the country and wanted nothing more to do with her. If she had rung once, she'd rung a dozen times, and each time she had met a brick wall. Had the woman been instructed to blank her if she got in touch?

The lift door opened and Leah took a right turn, stopping at a door with a sign saying *Mrs Sophie Ryan, Deputy Chairwoman.*

'Oh, so he *is* married.' Leah's heart sank - but what could she expect? So many years had passed since their magical meeting. She couldn't expect Dan to have remained celibate, as she herself had done. Hearing the second lift arrive, she shot inside Sophie's office without knocking and immediately sought refuge in the coat closet. Women's voices could be heard, coming up the corridor. As the voices came closer and the office door opened, she dived down out of sight.

CHELSEA HANDED DAN AN ITINERARY. HE LOOKED AT THE details.

'What time do we need to be there?' he asked.

'Seven thirty, just as you said,' Chelsea commented. 'I wish we could give it a miss and go out to dinner, but your mother is patron of this charity and she insists we go.'

Dan glanced up from his papers. 'I wouldn't dream of missing it, Chelsea. I hope you've put everything in place for these old soldiers.'

'Of course I have. I've even got them fancy dress. All my own idea.'

'Well done, may I ask what the theme is?'

'No. I want to keep it as a surprise for you. I will bring your clothes around later. *He* can go back to the house and stay there.' Chelsea pointed to Hero.

The Newfoundland dog raised a massive, sleepy head then flopped down with a big sigh almost as if he knew what the unfriendly human was saying.

ALONG THE CORRIDOR, RUBY YAWNED AS SHE PLONKED HERSELF into a comfy office chair then spun herself round, just for fun. Today she was wearing tailored white trousers with a bird-of-paradise blouse. With her big personality and rich Caribbean voice, Ruby brought warmth on the coldest day.

Sophie Ryan was ever the elegant and well-groomed businesswoman. Her clothes spoke volumes about her station in life. 'Ruby, dear,' she addressed her best friend and PA, 'do we know what's happening this evening?'

Ruby laughed wryly. 'Some joker left it up to that silly tart Chelsea to organise whilst I was playing detective for you up in Whitby. I'm not too keen on Dracula, to be frank, but the people up there on the coast were very friendly. Wish they were more like that down here. Yes, it's a cute little place, and I found what you were looking for all right, didn't I?'

Inside the cupboard, Leah gasped and almost let out a cry as she recognised the voice.

Ruby spun around, viewing the office suspiciously. 'Did you hear something? I'm going to check.' Jumping off the chair, she went to the coat cupboard and peered in. All she could see was a row of coats hanging from the rack almost to the floor.

Ruby didn't fancy bending down to look in case she couldn't get up again. She shrugged and closed the door.

Leah let out the breath she had been holding. Sweat was pouring down her back.

Sophie said, 'Well, I never heard a thing. Of course, it could be a ghost.' And when Ruby uttered a quiet scream, Sophie hastened to add: 'Come on, we'd better go and find out from Dan what exactly the plan is for this evening. I don't trust a word Chelsea says and I am a Patron, after all. Mustn't let her make a mess of it.'

As Leah heard the two women leave the room, she let out a long breath and then quickly vacated the closet. She stretched, feeling a bag of nerves. On the desk she saw elaborate engraved invitations for the event she had heard them talking about: the Veterans' Dinner Dance. Guiltily, she picked one up, then put it back. She was fighting with her conscience but eventually she picked it up again and hastened out of the room before the women came back, forgetting to look to right or left and stuffing the ticket in her bag as she went.

Sophie and Ruby marched into the outer office of Dan's suite where Chelsea was stood looking out of the window. Hearing them enter, she turned and snapped, 'I'm sorry, you can't disturb him.' To Sophie's astonishment, the younger woman even went and stood in front of the door to Dan's office, effectively blocking them. One of these days, Sophie thought angrily, Chelsea would go too far.

'I'm his mother, you silly girl!' Sophie admonished her. 'Of course I can disturb him. I need to know what has been arranged for this evening. And why were you standing gawping out of the window instead of working, which is what he pays you to do! And seeing as I am owner of half of this company, I insist you get on with some work.'

Chelsea ignored her. Such remarks just rolled off her thick skin. 'I have it here, Mrs Ryan,' she said haughtily. 'Everything is as you asked. And sometimes I look out of the window when I'm thinking.' She lowered her voice and muttered snidely, 'Something you two never do.'

'I beg your pardon?' Sophie scowled at Chelsea.

'I just said I was thinking about the itinerary.'

Ruby mumbled, 'Yeah, I'll bet.'

Chelsea continued, 'Your costumes are being delivered this afternoon.'

Sophie repeated, 'Costumes? What costumes?'

Chelsea sighed and it was obvious she had had enough of the older women. 'Yes, *costumes*,' she said rudely. 'You did say you wanted a veteran theme?'

Sophie turned to Ruby. 'I did?'

Ruby nodded. 'You did, girlfriend. It ain't often I agree with *her*, but you did.'

Chelsea picked up the phone. 'I will get them delivered to your apartment if you like, Mrs Ryan?'

'Very well. I hope they are appropriate?'

Chelsea blinked, and Sophie could have sworn there was a momentary smirk on her lips. 'Very, very appropriate. I'm sure you'll love them.'

Sophie watched Chelsea through slit eyes; she had never and would never trust this girl. 'Now, I need to see my son.'

Chelsea jerked a thumb at the window. 'He's out with that disgusting mutt.'

Sophie stalked past her and checked her son's office. 'Then we shall see you both this evening. And Hero is no mutt. He's a pedigree Newfoundland, for your information.'

Ruby leaned toward Chelsea. 'The costumes better be

good,' she hissed. A long-time fan of the annual Notting Hill Carnival, she knew a good costume when she saw it.

Again, there was that suggestion of a smirk as Chelsea said sweetly, 'Oh yes. Right up your street, Ruby.'

AS SOPHIE AND RUBY WALKED OUT OF THE OFFICE, THEY passed a woman bending to fix her heel in the corridor.

Sophie barely noticed, so livid was she. 'The gall of that jumped-up little cow. I'm his mother - how dare she speak to me like that?'

Ruby laughed. 'Oh, that girl, she dares all right. She's after your son, as you well know. Even after all these years she won't let go or give up – and he's too trusting to see it. Gold-digging skinny trollop that she is, she wants his dosh.'

Ruby glanced briefly at the woman mending her heel, but then turned her attention back to her best friend.

LEAH WALKED INTO THE OUTER OFFICE, STILL REELING FROM realising that she'd just seen the same woman who had been taking photos of birds by Tom's playground at Northside School.

Chelsea looked Leah up and down with a toss of her head. 'May I help you?'

'Yes, I have an appointment with Dan Ryan.' Leah straightened her skirt.

'No, I'm sorry but you don't. I know exactly what Dan - I mean Mr Ryan - is doing today.'

'I can assure you I have legitimate business with him. Will you kindly tell him I'm here.' Leah looked directly into

Chelsea's eyes, knowing from instinct that this woman was trouble; she had the exact same annoying voice as the PA who had blocked her from speaking to Dan. Well, this time she would no longer be at her mercy. She would *insist* on seeing him, come hell or high water. However, Leah had reckoned without the little security man. Small he might be, but dogged with it.

Having tracked her on the camera, Scotty dashed in; he tried to grab Leah's arm but she wrestled herself free and darted through the adjoining door into Dan's office and slammed the door.

Chelsea opened it and screamed, 'Get this woman out of Dan's office. Now, Scotty!'

Leah was beginning to enjoy herself, regardless of the consequences. She jumped onto the desk, making the papers fly.

'I just want to see Dan,' she told Scotty. 'I have business with him, and it can't wait.'

'So why run? I'm not getting any younger,' Scotty said crossly, out of breath after all the exertion.

'I don't know who she is but *get her out*!' Chelsea spat out at the security man.

'Oh, don't get your knickers in a twist, love,' Leah said to Chelsea. 'I no longer take any notice of you. And as for you, little man, you'll have to catch me.' She burst out laughing.

Scotty grabbed for Leah's leg. He missed, but even he couldn't resist a smile. This was a great game and was brightening up a miserable day at the office. Personally, he couldn't see any harm in this Yorkshire lass. Nor could he stand Chelsea – no one could if truth be told.

Chelsea was fuming. 'Do something, you useless squirt,' she hissed. 'I want her out of here before Dan gets back.'

'Hey, don't be rude to him. Manners are free!' Leah

chuckled gaily and then jumped down and barged past Scotty before running into the corridor.

SOPHIE AND RUBY WERE ON THEIR WAY BACK TO DAN'S OFFICE when Leah bumped into them, pelting hell for leather along the corridor.

Ruby was shocked. 'You!'

Leah laughed in mock hysteria, saying, 'Hang on, that's *my* line. You!'

Scotty caught Leah this time and took a good hold of her wrist; without hurting her, he led her away and into the lift before the other two women could react and think what to do. Elated, he puffed, 'Gotcha this time.'

SCOTTY ESCORTED LEAH OUTSIDE INTO THE BUSY STREET AND released her wrists. 'Look, young lady, if you know what's good for you, you'll not come back. I'm too old for this malarkey. What's it all about, anyway, all this drama?'

'As I said, I want to see Dan about family business.' Leah tried to tidy her hair.

'He's got his mother, and he's got us, his staff. We're his family. He's married-'

'He is? Oh, that's sad.'

'Let me finish. He's married to his business. Now please, be on your way, dear.' Scotty shooed her away.

'I only want to talk.' But Leah knew this was the end of the road. She'd messed up, big time.

Scotty winced as he watched her straighten her spine and walk proudly away. He called after her, 'Make an appointment if you must speak to him,' but wasn't sure if she had heard.

SOPHIE TURNED TO RUBY. 'WAS THAT LEAH?'

'Yes.' Ruby grinned. 'Got plenty of spirit, hasn't she? She took me by surprise; I didn't expect her to come to London so soon.'

'Quickly, we must find her,' Sophie said, turning to walk down the corridor towards the lift.

'Oh, she'll be back,' Ruby said, following. 'It's no use chasing her - she'll be gone by now.'

'I am going to see if I can find her. If you are my friend, then you will escort me.' Sophie jabbed at the button for the lift and soon they were alighting in the foyer.

'Can you see her?' Ruby asked Sophie.

'No, I can't.' Sophie walked towards the huge plate-glass windows and peered out. 'I can't see her outside either.' She looked at Ruby. 'She had better get back in touch or we will be going to Whitby. My God, how could we have let her slip through our fingers, once we had her with us?' Tears stood in the older woman's eyes.

'Sophie, stop panicking, honey, she will get in touch. You know your Ruby - I can feel it in these old bones.' But Ruby too was concerned. If only Scotty hadn't interfered - but no doubt that was what he was paid for. Perhaps the whole bird-watching escapade had been a serious mistake, and she and Sophie should have gone to Whitby on a straightforward mission together. Ruby sensed that Leah was the kind of person to prefer straight dealing. Oh dear. Slowly, she went back to the office, singing under her breath the words to Bob Marley's 'No Woman No Cry'. That just about summed it up.

8

FANCY DRESS

Leah sat on the bed in her hotel room, staring out at the people walking their dogs in the park across the road. A tiny dappled dachshund sniffed around the flower beds while his owner strolled along looking at his phone. A huge Golden Retriever ambled by, accompanied by his walking companion, a smart Beagle. Four poodles of varying sizes and colours danced around them. Elsewhere, a whippet stood unmoving at the foot of a majestic tree, observing a pair of squirrels running up and down the branches. Despite its owner calling, 'Percy, come on!' the dog took no notice. All around, happy folk were patting their pets, unclipping their leads and joyfully seeing their best friends gather in a big pack to play. For a moment, all of Leah's cares disappeared. Dogs certainly knew how to live in the moment, she thought, and every single one of them, and their owners, would be welcome in one of her dog friendly cafés up north.

Tearing herself away from the window, she looked at the kettle and biscuits on her hotel room tray. Lord, she missed that strong coffee Joey made for her when he knew she was in a flap. She took the ticket to the dance out of her bag and stared at it. Struggling with her guilt for taking the ticket in the first place and then her sense of failure that she'd not even seen Dan, and the fact that she knew Tom would be so sad, her emotions were so raw that tears streamed down her face. Through them, she read the words on the invitation. *The Glaston Hall Hotel Veterans Fancy Dress Dinner Dance. Location: The Strand. Theme: The Land Army. Appropriate Fancy Dress a must!*

'I can't cope with that,' she wailed, then blew her nose.

Just then, her phone rang and Tom's face flashed on the screen. Leah quickly composed herself then answered.

'Hiya, sweetie. Well, I've got an appointment later this week to see your daddy,' she lied convincingly.

'Wow. I'm so excited, Mummy! Did you see him?'

'No, but I told you he'd be busy. We mustn't expect too much from this first meeting. Now, promise me you'll go to bed when Joey and Grandad say it's time, and I will call you tomorrow evening. Be a good boy for me, won't you. I love you, Tom.' Leah wanted to run back to Whitby, but she knew she couldn't.

Switching the mobile off, she picked up the hotel phone.

'Hi, this is Leah in Room 229. I'm wondering if you could find me a number for a fancy-dress shop. I know it's short notice but I need a costume from the World War Two period and I need it for tonight.' Leah listened. 'Did you say Angels, and it's in Shaftesbury Avenue? Thank you, that sounds perfect.'

Apparently, she could either take the 38 bus or walk there within ten minutes or so. Jotting down the details before she forgot, she then consulted the A-Z of London that she'd bought all those years ago for her trip with Joey to Madam Butterfly's. Even thinking about it now made her have butterflies of her own! But at least the big shop seemed to be within walking distance; apparently it was dead famous and she should find exactly what she needed.

Heading out of the door, Leah ran down the hotel steps and out on to Southampton Row feeling a lot more optimistic.

PESSIMISM WOULD HAVE BEEN MORE APPROPRIATE, IT SEEMED, for Leah had been forced to take what Angels had left. A lot of their costumes for that period had already been hired by a film company. Now as she joined the queue to get inside the Glaston Hall Hotel, Leah felt an utter fool in the 1940s police uniform and helmet, but the worst thing was the ridiculous handlebar moustache that went with it.

In front of her in the queue were several old folks in military uniform, medals attached, some tottering whilst clinging to their Zimmer-frames or sturdy walking sticks; other veterans were in wheelchairs, accompanied by their carers. Everyone had to show their ticket to the doorman.

Leah flashed her ticket and the doorman grinned at her get-up. He allowed her in no problem and she sighed with relief. She gazed up at the glitterball over the dance floor and wondered, as she had so often, whether she had been a magpie in a previous life because she loved shiny objects and was a collector of such things. This dazzling light would look so great in her bedroom. She knew it might be tacky in some people's eyes, but that was just too bad.

The elderly guests were thoroughly enjoying themselves as the band played wartime tunes, talking to each other and reliving the past. Of course, some were too young to have been active in the last war themselves, but all the male guests had done their National Service and been involved in conflicts around the globe. Their fellowship was good to see and made her heart sing. How her grandad would revel in this atmosphere. He admired these brave veterans so much.

Just then, Scotty walked past Leah, giving her a momentary shock. He ignored her, however, and now Leah was glad she was wearing such an unflattering costume. Sophie and Ruby were, she saw, dressed as old washerwomen, with 1940s-style turbans on their heads so their hair wouldn't get caught in the mangle. Leah giggled. Some mean so-and-so had stitched them up good and proper.

Sophie was obviously annoyed. Leah overheard: 'Just wait until I get hold of Chelsea.'

'Oh no you don't. I get first go. She's mine - seriously.'

Then Leah saw Dan and her heart skipped several beats. He was dressed, she presumed, as a gentry landowner or gentleman farmer employing the Land Girls, some of whom were dancing with other guests. He was leaning over to listen to Chelsea, who was dressed in a form-fitting 1940s vintage fishtail dress with a plunging neckline that showed off her assets. Lady Muck, Leah thought disgustedly.

She sat herself down at a table with several veterans, and greeted them warmly. She didn't dare eat or drink in case her 'tash unglued and fell off. Scotty walked past, once more ignoring her, but from under her disguise she could watch Dan without anyone knowing, or so she thought.

The gentleman to her left smiled at her, then asked, 'So, what's a good-looking policeman like you doing here?'

'Me? I need to speak with someone.'

He laughed. 'What, you want them to come down to the station with you? Must be important to come to this gaff with us old farts.'

Leah laughed with him. 'My grandfather is an old fart. I mean he was in the army.'

'My name is Phil, by the way, Officer, and I was an RAF

chap – in the air. But that was a long time ago and since you are a police officer I had better tell you the truth: that right now, I'd rather be in bed reading a good book than dancing to Glenn Miller. Long gone is the day I did anything more exciting under the sheets.'

Leah grinned. 'Ditto, as it goes - but a good book is very tempting. I'm Leah, by the way.'

Scotty walked Leah's way again, and this time he stopped and stared at her. 'Excuse me, can I see your ticket?'

Leah stuttered, 'I . . . I . . .'

Phil came to the rescue. 'We gave them to the doorman, old fellow,' he said smoothly. 'My carer and I.'

Scotty looked at him with a wry smile. 'Yes, of course, sir, my mistake. We're searching for a gate-crasher.' Yet still he hovered from a distance.

At that precise moment, Hero bumbled across to Leah, pushing his nose into her hands.

Leah said softly, 'Hello, and who do you belong to?'

'Is it exciting being a gate-crasher?' Phil asked.

'Terrifying. But I had to do it. You see, my son's father is in this room and we need to talk,' Leah explained, petting Hero who had plonked himself beside her and rested his gigantic head on her knees.

'I will help you - as long as you keep me away from those washerwomen,' Phil said.

Leah watched as Ruby and Sophie walked across the dance floor. They were obviously fuming, as Sophie was rolling up her sleeves and Ruby was holding her back. Unfortunately, in those get-ups they did look a bit like the Ugly Sisters in *Cinderella*. Leah couldn't help but smile at this. 'It's a deal.'

Frank leaned in closer. 'Who is the father of your son?'

Leah looked across at Dan. 'The man in the posh evening

suit, next to his PA. She's got on a blonde wig and is dressed as the glamorous lady of the manor.'

Phil looked over at the throng. The band were now playing a Vera Lynn number, with a lookalike singer belting out the words onstage while the glitterball shone patterns everywhere.

'Oh, her? She's dressed as Doris Day, but you're too young to know that.'

Leah looked across at Chelsea. 'Am I?'

'Yes. So, does he know you're coming to see him or will it be a shock?'

'No, he doesn't know and yes, it will be a huge shock, but I won't spoil his evening. That would be so unkind.'

'That's my girl. I know you're not here to upset the apple cart tonight. That's why I am helping you.' Phil spared a look at Dan and Chelsea.

'Getting to talk to him is the first hurdle,' Leah told him. 'Dan has a piranha by his side and I fear it's the same piranha that I spoke to almost nine years ago, and on many occasions afterwards. She wouldn't let me anywhere near him.' Leah watched Chelsea enviously as she laughed up into Dan's face.

'You do know she's after him, but she doesn't like his dog. I saw her push him away earlier.' Nothing escaped Phil's notice.

Leah stroked Hero as she whispered little nonsensical things to him. 'But he's beautiful.'

Phil added, 'You've no need to worry, Constable Leah. Your Dan isn't interested in her. I can tell.'

'He isn't?' Leah said, turning her attention to Dan. 'That doesn't solve my problem though, does it?'

'Leave that to me.' Phil manoeuvred his electric wheelchair across the dance floor, which was clearing now that 'We'll Meet Again' was over and the band were playing a medley of other popular wartime numbers. Leah watched as the old gentleman spoke to Dan, then pointed over to her. Dan glanced across at Leah.

For a split-second Leah felt as if her disguise had been peeled away. Their eyes locked for what seemed like an age. Then Leah broke the spell. She looked away, and when she glanced back, Dan was talking to Phil again.

Her new friend drove his wheelchair back across the floor, a devilish grin on his face.

'Give me it straight, Phil. What did you say?' Leah couldn't wait to find out. Dan's expression had given nothing away.

'I told him my carer wanted to dance and didn't have a part-ner, so he's going to save you a dance a bit later.' Phil grinned. 'Not bad for an old Biggles, am I?'

'Heck, what do I do now? Oh, thank you, Phil.' She hugged him.

'I'm hoping he'll recognise you.'

'Oh Lord, I'm hoping he won't.'

'Oh, that's just pre-combat nerves. Chocks away!'

As the band struck up with 'Pennsylvania 6-5000' people started humming and singing the one-line refrain and those who were mobile got onto the dance floor. It was then Dan asked Ruby to dance. The washerwoman's smile lit up her face. It was obvious there was a very special connection between them.

Phil and Leah watched with interest. Ruby's dancing style was quirky, and they couldn't help but chuckle. Dan was laughing too as if he was really enjoying himself. Leah still felt conflicted about Ruby - quite miffed, if truth be known, that the woman had been blatantly spying on her and Tom. They couldn't know about Tom being Dan's child, could they? Surely not. The more she thought about it, the more of a muddle she got in.

When they'd finished the dance, Dan took Ruby back to her seat, then offered his arm to his mother and walked her onto the dance floor just as two singers joined the musicians and the band struck up with 'Chatanooga Choo-Choo' to a roar of approval from the guests. As Dan and Sophie bopped around the floor with all the other couples, sometimes joining in with the words, tears pricked at Leah's eyes. She could see the love between mother and son - and she prayed she would always have that with Tom. This was why she knew she'd better get it right tonight, if only for her son's sake.

Once a puffed-out Sophie was back with Ruby and the women had ordered another drink, Dan walked across to Leah's table. After nodding politely at Phil, he turned to Leah and said, 'Excuse me, Constable, may I have the next dance? Although two men dancing together, the squire and the village bobby, will set the tongues wagging I've no doubt.'

The elderly gentlemen at the table laughed heartily and Phil's eyes twinkled with mischief.

With no further ado, Dan swept Leah into his arms for 'The GI Jive'. Doing her best to follow the beat while dancing in his arms, she felt dizzy, as if she was on a merry-go-round. It would be fatal to look up into his eyes.

'You know, you remind me of someone, Officer,' Dan said into her hair, 'but for the life of me I can't think who. But whoever she is, she is beautiful.'

'Well, that's a bit of a cheesy line,' Leah laughed. 'Besides, you don't know what I look like. I could be a spotty teenager behind this moustache.'

'Huh, I'm mortally wounded.' Dan looked down into Leah's eyes. 'But seriously, you do remind me of someone I once knew.'

'A good memory?'

'Memorable.'

'Then why did you forget her name?' admonished Leah as her heart was pumping fast in time with the music.

As the band finished the song to a rousing chorus of cheers, they didn't let up for a second but immediately launched into 'Little Brown Jug'. The joint was really jumping!

Dan wouldn't let go of Leah – he simply jigged away with her, and flustered, she tripped over his feet. Dan caught her just in time, but by then Leah's helmet had fallen over her face, and her moustache was half-hanging off.

Dan laughed heartily. 'Take them both off, Constable.'

As Leah reached to peel off her moustache, her helmet fell on the ground, nearly causing another jitterbugging couple to trip, and her hair tumbled around her shoulders.

Dan looked into her wide eyes and exclaimed, 'You!'

'Oh, I'm so sorry,' Leah babbled, 'I don't want to spoil your night but I do need to talk to you. Please, Dan. It's important.'

Just then Scotty ran up, shouting, 'Hey, you!'

Leah took off at a run - but why, she had no idea. Scotty was hot on her heels, running after her as fast as his short legs could carry him.

Dan looked stunned. As Leah scurried past Phil, she blew him a kiss, but her path took her near the bar; she saw the deep scowl on Chelsea's face, but that was too bad: she had to get out of there - now. This had been a massive mistake, Leah fretted as she pelted at top speed out into the Strand, then hid in a doorway, trying to control her emotions and hide from the curious sideways glances of passers-by. Gate-crashing a private dinner dance, then seeing Dan with his mother and Ruby, as well as stroking and whispering sweet nothings into his beloved dog's ear. What had she been thinking of!

RUBY AND SOPHIE HAD BOTH OBSERVED DAN DANCING WITH the policeman; they'd been chuckling about it until Leah's disguise fell away, and then it all happened so quickly: Scotty making chase after the fleeing young woman.

Ruby looked around for Sisco in the foyer. 'Hey, Sisco, we need a lift sharpish.'

'Of course, where are we headed? And isn't it a little early to leave?' he asked as he put down his *Racing Post*.

'We are chasing that blonde policeman, who is a woman.' Ruby was deadly serious for once.

'No kidding - he's a woman, is he? I didn't notice. Take my arm, Sophie. We need to get a spurt on. Let's hope she hasn't gone too far.'

'We need to divert Scotty too,' said Sophie, who was getting breathless by then.

Scotty was nowhere to be seen and soon they were hastening up the Strand, looking into every shop doorway and scanning the pavements on either side. It wasn't long before they found Leah; she was standing weeping on the corner of the street where *The Lion King* was playing.

'Leah, why are you hiding? Come on, come back with us to the party,' Ruby said gently. 'You're very welcome, you know, dear. There's no need to run away from us.'

Leah was shaking her head, crying, 'What am I going to tell Tom? How can I go back to Whitby and disappoint him?'

Sophie took her hand. 'Please, Leah, I need to know if Tom is my grandson.'

Leah turned and looked her in the eyes, with tears running down her face. 'Yes, he is, but did you see Dan's face? Your son wasn't happy, and he's never going to believe me now.'

9

THE CRANE

A s the three women stood in the doorway, oblivious to the crowds and the heavy traffic, Sisco drew up at the kerb, let down the window and said: 'Hurry up, ladies, before a real policeman gets me for obstructing the traffic.'

'Of course. Please get in the car, Leah, and let me explain.' Sophie sounded so sincere that Leah caved in. She was shaking all over as she climbed into the car.

'This was all my idea,' Sophie went on as they drew away from the kerb. 'I'm truly sorry about Ruby's deception, but she was simply taking my orders. She didn't mean you any harm, I promise. None of us would ever want to hurt you.'

She turned to Leah. 'You know what? I think we need a plan. I'll get you in to see Dan, but first of all, we must let him cool down. I know my son. We can talk tomorrow. Where are you staying and what is your mobile number?'

Leah should have been pleased - but she couldn't let Ruby's part in it go. She gave Sophie her details, then whipped round to Ruby, practically snarling, 'You were taking photos of the birds. And I believed you.' Her eyes blazed.

'What can I say?' The big woman shrugged. 'I'm convincing, aren't I? The truth is, I do have a genuine love of feathers.' Her expression was so naughty that in other circumstances Leah would have seen the funny side. But at the moment she was far too upset.

'How did you know?' she asked Sophie.

'Dan mentioned you, and I was curious. You see, I could tell something had happened that was out of the ordinary. And as a fan of Agatha Christie, I turned detective and eventually found you.'

'Agatha Christie solved murders,' Leah muttered grumpily.

'Now, dear, don't get upset. I think we both want the same thing,' said Sophie, trying to defuse the atmosphere.

'I still don't understand,' Leah said. 'How do you know about Tom, if Dan doesn't? And why would Dan mention me?' She looked from Sophie to Ruby.

Sophie sighed. 'To be fair, we knew about you nearly nine years ago.'

'But *how*?' Leah was shocked.

Ruby threw her arms in the air and almost clipped Sisco's ear and knocked his chauffeur's cap skew-whiff. 'Picture this if you will. Scotty, Dan's mini-minder - you met him back there – well . . .' she cleared her throat '. . . he told us Dan wanted a high-class hooker.'

Sophie jumped in with: 'Scotty was out of his depth. I had to help out. I chose you, Leah, with the help of my old friend Madam Butterfly.'

Leah whispered, 'You know Madam Butterfly?' She blushed. 'I'm no longer that person.'

Ruby gave a mocking laugh. 'Oh yeah? Once a bitch always a...'

Leah kept her eyes on Sophie. 'I want you to know that your son left me a generous pot of money – unasked for, I may add. This sum enabled me to pay for my grandad's operation which we couldn't get on the National Health. He was in so much pain that I had to do something! So I came down to London from Whitby and well, you know the rest. It was a one-off. I could never regret it. Grandad had his operation and it was successful, so it was all worth it. With the remainder of the money, I set myself up in business.'

'Ooh. You must have been *sensational* in the sack, girl,' Ruby grinned as Sophie threw her a warning look.

'Getting to see Dan won't be easy, as for one thing he has a hectic schedule,' Sophie said thoughtfully. 'But we want to help.'

Ruby interrupted again as the car approached the turning off Southampton Row into Russell Square. 'Don't forget little Miss Money-Grabber who is always at his side.'

Leah leaned forward and said to Sisco, 'I'm staying at the President Hotel over the road. Could I get out here, please? Thank you.' She was feeling very shaken still and slightly sick. All she wanted now was to be back in her room.

'You mean Chelsea,' she replied to Ruby. 'Yes, I've met her.'

'And you weren't turned to stone?' Ruby whistled. 'I am impressed.' Her tone became serious. 'Listen, Leah, going back to Dan, you've got to understand that he's had several short-term relationships since your night together, and two of those women tried to catch him in the child-trap thing. It was all very unpleasant. So it's only natural that he finds it hard to trust women now. And surely Tom could be fathered by-'

'I slept with Dan,' Leah interrupted. 'No one else.'

Ruby mimicked her: '"I slept with Dan. No one else". What – didn't you have boyfriends up in Whitby?'

Leah glared at her. 'Not really, and not for a long time until I met Dan. And after that . . . I was so busy and I had

Tom. Do you have children? No? Then perhaps you won't know first-hand how a child can fill your time and your heart. I have my family in Whitby and they give me all the love I need.'

There was a short silence, then Sophie asked Sisco to release the electronic door lock so that Leah could climb out.

'Meet us tomorrow morning in the reception area at Ryan's, and we'll find a way.' Sophie touched Leah's hand. 'Don't worry. Is ten o'clock all right?'

Leah nodded.

'Sisco, please walk Leah back to her hotel,' Sophie instructed the chauffeur. 'And just so you know, you are sworn to secrecy.'

Sisco nodded then added under his breath, 'They don't realise I'm only human and can forget on the odd occasion.'

LEAH GOT OUT OF THE TAXI IN THE CITY THE FOLLOWING morning and looked around. The streets were thronged with business people staring at their phones as they hurried along. Should she go straight in? She held a cake box in her hand. It was her trademark, always to take a cake when she visited someone. Unfortunately, the cakes were not home-baked this time, but she'd seen some gorgeous ones in a café in the Brunswick shopping centre near her hotel. Then she thought, *What am I doing? Does Dan look like he eats cake?* Dilemma, dilemma, what on earth was the matter with her? She was usually so decisive. Just as Leah was dithering, her mobile gave a beep: a text message.

Hey, Leah, we are around the side of the building.

Leah strode around the corner and stopped dead in her tracks – for there was Ruby, standing next to a huge crane.

'I've had a great idea,' Ruby said proudly. 'And it involves you going up on the crane platform.'

'Oh no, if you think I'm risking life and limb on that, you can think again.' Leah stared at the crane. True, she'd done some daredevil stunts in her time, but she was older and wiser now.

'If you want to see Dan, it's the best way,' Sophie advised, giving a thumbs-up to the crane operator. 'His office is on the fifth floor and it will give him such a surprise to see you outside his window. We'll make sure you are perfectly safe. Leah, if you can do wing-walking, this will be a breeze.' Sophie beamed and Leah could tell that she had done her homework.

Leah thought of Tom, waiting at home, and caved in. 'Oh, all right, I'll give it a go,' she said, then asked Ruby, 'Can you please hold these cakes until I get this harness on?' She was so pleased she'd put smart jeans on and a crisp linen top. Perfect for the job in hand.

'You didn't have to bring me cakes,' Ruby simpered.

'They're not for you,' Leah snapped, looking at the crane with trepidation.

'You're so easy to wind up, girlfriend.'

Ruby checked Leah's safety harness, and then she handed the young woman several sheets of card. Leah glanced through them quickly, then asked for a pen to add some words of her own. She then took the box of cakes from Ruby.

'Are you sure this will work?' she asked Sophie. 'More to the point, will Miss Money-Grabber be there?'

Ruby shook her head. 'Chelsea's out on an errand, and yes, it will work. Trust us. We've got your back.'

Leah stepped onto the crane. The driver checked her harness himself, gave a nod then closed the safety gates around her. He then got back in the cab and the platform began lifting. Leah peered down and clung to the safety bar with a shaking hand.

The crane rose higher in the sky.

WHEN HERO BARKED LOUDLY AND RAN TO THE WINDOW, DAN looked up from his computer screen. 'What is it, boy? What's going on?'

Hero cocked his head to one side and began whining. Dan followed his eyeline. 'Good Lord!' He did a double-take at the crane platform that had appeared outside. The last time he'd seen it, two men in hard hats had been travelling up in it. Now he saw Leah - looking incredibly sexy in hip-hugging jeans. It was hard to believe his eyes: Dan blinked several times.

Leah showed him a note. *I only want to talk.*

Dan darted over to his whiteboard and turned it around. He scribbled quickly: *I'm busy!* Although why he'd put that, he didn't know.

Balancing precariously, Leah unhooked her safety harness. She opened the cake box, tilted it and showed him the creamy contents. Then she screamed as she lost her balance and dropped one cake. In slow motion, Leah watched the cake as it fell to the pavement, missing Ruby by millimetres.

Grinning all over her face, Leah wrote: *Oops. Only one left. What a shame. Now we'll have to share.*

Dan was frantic. This was one gutsy lady, but he was so worried about her safety. *Hook the damn thing back on,* he wrote. *Now!*

Leah scribbled and held out another sign. *Nope. I just want to talk.*

Dan scrawled urgently: *OK, OK, come down safely, then we will talk!*

LEAH STEPPED OFF THE CRANE WITH A GREAT SENSE OF RELIEF, then immediately panicked because she would soon be talking to Dan.

Ruby pointed to the splattered cream cake. 'What a waste. But back to the subject at hand, I have to say I told you so. My plan worked.' She preened herself.

'Only because I unhooked my safety harness,' said Leah, stepping out of the said harness with the aid of the crane driver. 'But thanks, Ruby, it was a great idea and I appreciate it.'

'Well, we women have to stick together,' Ruby said as she saw Scotty marching towards them. He must have been told by Dan to come out and fetch Leah.

The little man grabbed Leah's arm none too gently, but she easily shrugged him off.

Scotty screwed his eyes up at her. 'You wanna watch out, you do. Gawd knows what my boss wants with you, trumped-up little agency temp. And why were you on the crane? Is an interview so important to you?'

Without replying, Leah followed him into the building and across to the row of lifts, watched by the glamorous receptionists at the long front desk.

In silence they ascended to the fifth floor.

Scotty opened a door and practically pushed her inside. 'Someone will be in to see to you soon.'

He left the room. Leah made a face at him, then screamed as a voice came from behind her.

Dan's deep voice was laced with fury. 'Is this some kind of joke? Well, I don't think it's funny.' In truth, he wasn't sure how to deal with this situation.

Leah jumped back - and dropped the remaining cake. 'Damn. Look what you made me do.' Lordy, even with a frown on his face he was better-looking than she remembered. Distinguished, that was the word.

'Save your explanations and excuses for now. Scotty!' he bawled, and the little man reappeared. 'Get someone to clear up this mess, then bring the car round to the front, will you? As for you, madam, we will talk as we travel. I will drop you off at your hotel. My mother tells me you are staying near Euston station.'

Leah was a little deflated as they set off a few minutes later. She didn't want to tell Dan about their son in the car, but at least this way, he was a captive audience.

THEY WERE IN THE COMPANY MERCEDES, WITH SISCO DRIVING and Scotty sitting beside him. The car was moving past St Paul's Cathedral towards Fleet Street when Dan finally spoke.

'So, what kind of a stunt was that back there with the crane?' he demanded. He was furious although he didn't know why. Maybe because she really could have fallen. 'A, I don't think you were insured to be on that platform, and B, what is so urgent that you couldn't wait for an appointment like any normal person?'

'I already phoned for an appointment; however, your PA told the little man to get rid of me.' Leah was wringing her hands; this wasn't going well.

Scotty scowled and Dan pressed the button to bring down the privacy screen. Scotty was not to be beaten; he placed a suction-pad receiver on the glass so that he could hear all of what was being said.

Sisco tutted. 'One day, mate, you'll get the sack.'

Scotty sat back, smug that he could hear every breath. 'I'm in with the top brass,' he replied. 'Sophie wouldn't allow him to sack me. Besides, Dan relies on me.'

As they argued, Dan was addressing Leah. 'So, you just

want to talk. Then go ahead, talk, before I'm tempted to inflict corporal punishment for the crane stunt!'

Leah licked her lips; she was a tad nervous. 'Ha, corporal punishment. I never took you for a woman beater.'

'I'm not, and I said I was tempted. Different thing entirely.'

'I don't suppose you remember me. Or the night . . .'

Dan touched the pulse-point on her throat very gently. 'Of course I remember you, Leah Jensen,' he said gruffly. 'You were my girl for hire and made my night very pleasurable. Your disguise flummoxed me yesterday.'

Leah lifted a finger to her neck and put it on the exact spot where Dan had placed his: her pulse was racing. 'You were my first and my last client,' she managed to say. 'That morning you gave me a bonus.'

'A bonus? Ah yes, I remember it well.' Dan moved nearer. Inhaling her scent. 'You earned it, if my memory serves me right.'

'It doesn't matter what I did to . . .'

The car cornered wildly as Scotty deliberately grabbed the steering wheel. Sisco fought for control.

'What are you doing, you crazy little squirt!' Sisco pushed Scotty off.

Leah fell against Dan in the back of the limousine. They were so close, Leah could feel his warm breath against her hair.

Scotty had a quick glance back. He grinned.

Leah composed herself then pushed away.

Dan was amused. 'So, you came back for more, did you?'

'No!' Leah gave him a filthy look. 'I told you – I need to talk. It matters, what you left me with.'

'Eleven thousand pounds if I remember rightly. OK, OK, I'll let you get to the point. Just spit it out.'

Leah looked at her hands. 'Well, it's a delicate subject.'

'I'm waiting.'

'It's hard to . . .'

'I am still waiting.'

Leah looked out of the window, and that was when the car passed a branch of Gap. Like manna from heaven. Seizing the initiative, she shouted: 'Stop the car. STOP!'

10

THE MANNEQUINS AND THE MADMAN

Sisco braked and the big car screeched to a halt outside the shop, but not before the driver of a bus had tooted rudely at him.

Leah undid her seatbelt and waited while Dan did the same, then she took him by the hand and tugged him onto the pavement. 'Come on.' She pointed at the window display. 'There - in the window. What do you see?'

Dan stared at the two little mannequins of boys dressed in shorts and summer shirts posing with a beach ball. 'I don't understand,' he said, genuinely baffled. 'What are you getting at?'

Scotty watched on from the car and made a move to get out, but the door was locked. Sisco grinned. All Scotty could do was look on at his boss and Leah and wonder what they were talking about.

When Leah made no reply but just waited, Dan said sulkily, 'OK, I see two little kids playing with a ball.'

Leah sighed. 'Are they boys or girls?' she asked patiently.

'They are boys – what's that got to do with anything?'

Leah was frustrated. 'Now do you see? Yes, they are boys!

And that was your bonus. Your life-changing bonus was a boy. Our beautiful son, Tom.'

Dan stared at the window display; his face drained of colour as he put an involuntary hand onto the glass. After a moment or two, he turned back and ushered Leah into the car.

Scotty saw Dan's face and scrabbled with the receiver, only to drop it down the side of the seat.

In deathly silence Leah watched the streets go by. She dared not move, she dared not say one word. When the car stopped near the President, she made to get out but Dan put a hand on her arm to stay her.

'It's taken this long to tell me?' he asked quietly.

'I'm sorry, but I did try to get in touch. I tried on several occasions but was turned away each time. I thought you didn't want to know so in the end I gave up.'

Dan looked at her as if she'd crawled out from under a stone. All he said was, 'I need to see my lawyer.'

Leah gasped. 'Your lawyer? Dan, there was no one after you. You were my first and my last client. It was just once. Let me explain.'

'No, no explanation. You expect me to believe that I was your last lover? Never! In all these years? Please, don't take me for a fool, Leah.' Dan indicated that the conversation was over and signalled to Scotty.

Sisco released the door locks and Scotty jumped out, ready to open the door for Leah. He was half-sorry to see her go.

Standing on the pavement with tears running down her cheeks, Leah watched the car accelerate away. She had failed.

DAN LOOKED UP AT THE BIG HOUSE ON HARLEY STREET. THE discreet sign outside read *The Elixir Therapy Centre*. 'What name did you book me in under?' He was feeling upset and miserable and ready to snap anyone's head off.

Sisco winced. 'Scotty booked you in. He didn't tell me the name he put you under. Just say you're the two o'clock appointment, I guess.'

Dan nodded. Looking around to ensure that no one had seen him, he made his way inside the building, checked in with the practice receptionist, and was directed along a corridor to a door on his left.

When Dan walked in to the therapist's office, his immediate reaction was - *woah*! Greg Biggs was aged around forty, and his longish hair stood out as if he'd been plugged into an electric socket. He was just like the proverbial nutty professor.

Greg's penetrating eyes took in Dan's appearance in one easy glance. He offered Dan his hand and they shook in greeting.

Greg then spread his arms in a flamboyant gesture. 'ALL RIGHT! Put your feet up, Mr Bean. Oh, firstly, have you been to the little boys' room, had a tinkle, shut off your phone, your emails, messages - to keep all those pesky little people away?'

Dan lay down on the couch and put his feet on the cover provided. *Mr Bean - what was that all about? Some kind of a joke?*

'Yes,' he replied.

'Goody gum-drops. Right, tell me in your own words what's troubling you, Mr Bean.'

Dan suddenly understood. He raised his eyebrows and thought, *Thanks for booking me in as Mr Bean, Scotty. I owe you one.* 'I want to discuss a hooker. Please call me . . .'

Greg interrupted, 'Jelly Bean, I know. A hooker, you say?'

Dan added awkwardly, 'Yes. She came from Madam Butterfly in Soho. Or so my man said.'

Greg's eyes widened. 'Ah, your man? You like to swing it about. A bit of both sexes?'

'No! He is my security guard, my man. She's a hooker. Professional, lady of the night kind of thing.'

'Oh, that kind. Do you have her number or that of Madam Butterfly?'

Dan sighed. 'No. But I am confused about her. I think I have feelings I shouldn't have.'

'What kind?'

'Well, sexual.'

Greg smiled. 'Normal feelings then?'

'No.'

'Feelings about her boobies or her botty? Kinky feelings?'

'Feelings about her bungee jumping.' Dan shuffled about on the couch as if he was uncomfortable.

Greg moaned, 'A bungee-jumping hooker. I really do need her number.'

Dan's brow was creased. 'Well, it is because of my status. It's awkward.'

'What status is that, Jelly Bean?'

'I'm a . . . a banker.'

Greg shouted quickly, 'ALL RIGHT, now we're getting to the nitty-gritty. So the bungee-jumping hooker has contaminated you and you don't want your colleagues to know?'

Dan protested, 'No. Absolutely not. She is a clean person and she tells me I was her only client. She smells . . .'

'UGH. Get rid . . .'

'She smells wonderful. But I can't have a relationship with her.'

Greg blew out a breath and mouthed silently, 'Can I?' He composed himself. 'You believe you were her first?'

'Yes. *Yes.* She was my one and only date with a hooker. And she tells me I was her first and her last too.'

'Her last? How long ago was this, and do you believe her?'

'It was a few years ago. I suppose it's possible, but . . . Oh, I don't know. And yet my gut tells me I should believe her. Is she truly a hooker?'

Greg bit his lip as he pondered. 'Hmm . . .' Then he decided: 'My advice is just forget her.'

Dan whispered, 'I can't. She says she is the mother of my son.'

'Does she, indeed. Interesting.' Greg thought for a while, before concluding, 'Well, status or no status, Jelly, you're stuffed. Like a turkey with tinsel around its bum kinda stuffed. I take it you want to see your son?'

'Of course. I must see him if he's mine. I just don't know if he is mine. I'm at a loss, to be honest. Confused. That's why I'm here.'

'I understand your confusion - who wouldn't feel confused in these circumstances. And if, as you and she both say, you truly *were* her only client, she could hardly be a hooker. My wife is a hooker a million times over, the way she takes money from me. And the portions I get in return aren't massive, far from it. Once a week if I'm lucky. So I could do with a hooker. However, to clarify the matter, Mr Bean, I will get out my big dic.'

Dan leaped off the couch immediately and so did not see Greg reaching for a huge book.

'I'm sorry, I have to dash. I have a very important rendezvous,' Dan stammered and made for the door.

Greg was taken aback. 'Wait up, Jelly, not so fast. You need to check this out.'

Dan held his hands up in front of him, almost closing his eyes in case he saw something he shouldn't. 'Sorry, got to go.'

Greg was at a loss. 'But we haven't finished, Jelly. My big dic can solve everything.'

Dan exited the room, thinking, *I'll bet. But I don't want a big dick, thanks very much, Professor Branestawm. I'm straight.*

Greg meanwhile gazed down at his big dictionary, his finger on the word *hooker*.

DAN RAN OUT OF THE BUILDING AS IF THE DEVIL HIMSELF WAS chasing him and jumped into the car without waiting for Sisco to open the door. The chauffeur looked surprised.

'That bad, was it?' he asked as he switched on the engine.

'Worse! He's more of a fruit cake than Scotty. Get me out of here quick, Sisco.' Dan's mind was in a whirl. A hooker, a big dick. What on earth was happening to him? Barely hours ago, she'd danced with him as an old-fashioned policeman and he'd thought she was some sad, lonely carer in his arms, and then she had become a kind of Cinderella running like the wind to get away. Then today she had casually stood outside his office on a crane with bloody cream cakes, nearly causing him to have a heart attack when she undid the safety harness. Finally, she'd given him the shock of his life when she'd told him that he was a father – that he had a son! There was no doubt about it: this woman was rocking his safe world.

'Back to the office?'

'No, to a bar. I need a stiff drink. That geek was getting his big dick out. He said he was sex-starved.'

'No kidding.' Sisco couldn't wait to tell Scotty about this.

'By the sounds of it, he thinks his big dick can solve everything.'

'So do most men, but it's a bit extreme coming from someone in his kind of profession.'

Dan's phone rang and he let it go to voicemail. Then he listened to the message with the loudspeaker on.

'Hi, it's Greg Biggs here.' Dan had given the number to the receptionist when he paid. 'I just thought Jelly Bean would like to know that I was talking about my *big dictionary* when I referred to my "big dic". I think he got the wrong end of the stick - so to speak, hahahaha. It's a running joke with my other clients. Big Dictionary. *ALL RIGHT.*'

The line went dead.

Sisco looked in the mirror and saw Dan with his face in his hands. 'Jelly Bean? Big Dictionary?'

Their eyes met in the mirror; they both burst out laughing hysterically.

Dan had employed Sisco for just over ten years and the chauffeur had become a great friend. The best, in fact. Friends like him you only came across once in a lifetime if you were lucky, and Dan knew that. Sisco had also saved his life and that was one of the reasons he was acting as Dan's chauffeur and driving him around now. Sisco was ex-military, but he'd fallen on bad times and found himself sleeping rough.

Dan remembered the winter evening well. He'd seen Sisco sitting in a doorway across the street when he was on the way into an expensive department store near the office. Once he'd bought his mother her favourite perfume and Ruby hers, he had then made his way into the coffee shop next door and bought a sandwich and some chocolate, and a coffee to go.

When he emerged, Dan had walked across the road and handed the homeless guy the snack. The fellow took it with polite thanks - and that was when Dan noticed the regimental badge.

'Is that your badge?' he asked.

'Yeah, why? It's not stolen, if that's what you think,' Sisco had replied, just a tad on the defensive. 'I earned the right to wear it.'

'I'm sorry. Enjoy your sandwich.'

'Thank you.'

Whenever Dan came out on the street, he would look for the soldier and buy him a sandwich, some fruit and a hot drink. And each day they spoke more until one day Sisco told Dan that he just wanted a chance to work, that he wasn't a drinker like some of the people on the streets. The rest was history, so they say.

LEAH HAD TAKEN A SHOWER AND THEN PACKED UP HER policeman uniform and walked round to Angels with it. She was back and was sorting out her belongings, ready to go home, when there was a knock on the door. She opened it and was surprised to see Sophie and Ruby standing there. Without a word she let them in, closing the door behind her.

Sophie sat on the edge of the bed. 'I take it yesterday didn't go well?'

Leah shook her head. 'No. It was disastrous. I suppose I need proof to convince Dan. You see, I know categorically that Tom *is* Dan's son, but he seems to think that I'm some kind of gold-digging fraud.'

Ruby put in, 'Well, you could be trying to extort money. You wouldn't be the first.'

'I am not! My son wants to know his daddy. That's it. Period.'

Ruby tutted. 'I'll bet.'

Leah stared at Ruby. 'Why don't you give it a rest, woman? I need to ring my son.'

'He'll be fine.'

'How would you know? My cousin Joey is looking after Tom, and he will have his hands full when Tom gets to know that I've failed. He is going to be absolutely devastated. He's at that age when he's questioning everything – and all the other children at his school know who their fathers are and can speak about them. All my little boy wants is to see his daddy.'

Sophie got up from the bed. 'I will ring your cousin, Leah, and I will assure him that everything is fine. Just calm down. We will think of something else to make my son want to listen to you. He's just being stubborn.'

Leah wrote the number down for Sophie, apologising for being a little overwrought.

Ruby's voice softened. 'Yes, you will need proof, Leah. Little Miss Chelsea will insist.'

Sophie grimaced. 'Yes, my dear. Dan will want DNA tests done.'

'I know, but he told me he wants to see his lawyer.' Leah was so hurt.

Sophie looked thoughtful. 'You just need Dan's DNA?'

'Yes. And funnily enough I do have it, since his hair is still in my snake ring from nine years ago.'

'He isn't going to believe that,' shrugged Ruby.

'Well, I do,' said Sophie, 'but I agree that he probably won't.'

'No, I guess not.' Leah clasped her brow. Another headache was on its way.

'And Tom's too, of course – we'll need young Tom's DNA.' Sophie raised her hands in frustration. 'My son can be such an arse- an idiot!'

Ruby finished the sentence off. 'An arsehole. Don't pretend to be all prissy. We know that's what you meant.'

Sophie consulted her watch. 'We need to leave. You too, Leah. I'll phone Joey later, if that's OK. Right now, we need to move.' She scowled at Ruby. 'Come on, so-called friend. I have a son to work on and I believe I may need your help.'

'Son of a new grandmother,' put in Leah.

'I liked you the first time I saw you!' exclaimed Sophie.

Ruby addressed them both. 'You, Leah, have given Sophie a grandson and you need her help to get Dan on board with this. You, Sophie, want to see your grandson and become part of his life. So stop playing "let's get to know you, doggy doggy" and stop sniffing each other's-'

'We get the picture, Ruby.' Sophie picked up Leah's coat and bag and handed them to her. 'Let's get back over to the office. Sharpish.'

SCOTTY CAME TO ATTENTION AS HE SAW LEAH WALK IN, WITH Sophie and Ruby following her through the revolving door. He rushed over.

'Is this woman bothering you?' he asked Sophie.

'No, Scotty, we're good,' she reassured him. 'Leah, how about I call your cousin Joey, whilst you talk to Dan.'

Leah touched Scotty's shoulder. 'See, little man? I told you I was family.'

'Presumptuous or what!' huffed Ruby.

Sophie and Leah walked away towards the lift. 'I know he's my darling son,' Sophie was saying, 'but he's gone too far this time.'

Scotty turned to Ruby. 'That crazy woman had Mr Dan ranting on about God knows what. Mannequins playing ball was one thing I heard. I've not seen him like that since the flying hooker business.'

Ruby shrugged. 'It will do him good to get his blood pressure up. He's usually far too laid back - doesn't take life nearly seriously enough.' She nodded to herself. 'That Leah has style. Clever girl.'

They all reached the bank of lifts at the same time, and the flashing light showed that one was on its way.

'Beam us up, Scotty,' grinned Ruby, and was gratified to see Leah burst out laughing.

11

DNA AND DENTISTS

As the lift juddered, Ruby yelled out, 'We're breaking up, Captain!'

'Hold her steady, Scotty, or they'll burn up and disappear,' Leah instructed, joining in with the role play.

'I will, Cap'n, that I will,' Scotty replied.

'I'm surrounded by Trekkies,' complained Sophie.

'Stop that, woman. You know you love Captain Picard - and they say that Sir Patrick Stewart is from Yorkshire, just like Leah.' Ruby winked.

'Well, I suppose I wouldn't say no,' admitted Sophie.

LEAH WAS WAITING IN SOPHIE'S OFFICE. DAN'S MOTHER HAD just called Joey and delivered Leah's message.

Ruby was busy looking up Dan's diary on the computer. 'I'll just check his appointments.'

But Sophie was adamant. 'Whatever he's got planned, he'll have to cancel.'

Leah shook her head. 'He was so angry. He won't see me.'

Sophie put an arm around her shoulder. 'I'm sure he will be fine. I'll go ahead and deal with any obstacles.'

'In that case, what are we waiting for?' Ruby asked. 'Let's go and see him. Right now.'

Leah hesitated, but Ruby grabbed her arm. 'There's no time like the present.' She marched Leah into the corridor. 'Let's just hide here behind this wall, until we get Sophie's cue.'

'And that is?'

'When she'd got Miss Smarty Pants out of there. Hold on, here she comes.'

Chelsea left the office with hips swinging. She pouted as she saw herself reflected in the mirror on the wall, and then got in the lift.

Ruby turned to Leah. 'That's got rid of her. OK, girl, go and give him both barrels.' She smirked. 'He gave you both of his.'

Leah was too nervous to laugh. She set off and walked through the outer office with Ruby following, then knocked and walked in, closing the door in Ruby's face.

Dan was looking out towards the crane and didn't turn immediately, assuming it was Chelsea come back for something. Hero, however, greeted Leah enthusiastically and she stroked him, wishing his owner was this amenable.

Dan swung around. 'You again! What is it this time?'

Leah looked sad. 'I need a sample of your DNA - please.'

Ruby barged in at that point, saying, 'I said both barrels.'

Dan stood up. 'What are you talking about? Ruby, please leave. This is my problem.'

Ruby shook her head. 'The gall. Had you not blasted your barrels years ago there would be no problem! No barrels - no problem.'

Dan looked as if he couldn't believe this was actually happening. 'What exactly do you know?'

Ruby actually looked embarrassed. 'Only what Scotty told me,' she lied.

At that moment, Chelsea stormed in. Some instinct had made her head back to Dan's office. 'What's *she* doing here?' she shouted, staring at Leah.

Sophie now joined them. 'What on earth is going on? I can hear you down the corridor, Chelsea.'

'It's nothing, Sophie. Nothing I can't deal with.' She advanced towards Leah.

Leah moved nearer to the desk. She sat on the edge and dangled her legs.

Dan watched her, a flicker of amusement on his face.

Leah wasn't prepared to let Tom down – and she wasn't scared of the other young woman. No one was going to stand in her way.

'We need to discuss this,' she said steadily. 'I'm willing for Tom to have his DNA test if you don't believe me.'

Sophie looked at Dan in shock, pretending not to know. 'What's she talking about, darling?'

Chelsea immediately went for the jugular. 'Another false paternity claim,' she snapped. 'Dan, don't you dare agree to a DNA test until we've spoken to our lawyers.'

Ruby nudged Sophie and hissed, '*Our* lawyers? She has ideas above her station, that one.'

Sophie turned to Chelsea. 'I think we need to leave them alone to talk. Don't you, Chelsea?'

'No!'

But Ruby frog-marched Chelsea out, with Sophie closing the door behind them all to give Leah and Dan some privacy.

Dan put his hands up, indicating his negative feelings. 'Sorry, Leah, but my PA is correct. I have had many women . . .'

Leah gasped. 'And they think I'm the slut!'

Dan smiled. 'I deserve that. What I meant to say was that I've been the victim of several unfounded paternity claims before this, but I didn't sleep with any of those women.'

'You did with me! But you know what, Dan, screw your DNA sample. Your dog has more sense than you.'

Leah walked out as the red mist descended and threatened to consume her. Arrogant bastard. Exactly who did he think he was?

Chelsea passed Leah in the corridor, saying spitefully, 'You do realise that the last woman to claim is now bankrupt because we counter-claimed. And her son is with foster parents. We are that powerful, lady, so get lost while you still can.'

Back in Sophie's office, Leah was trying not to break down and cry, whilst Sophie was pacing the floor.

'Chelsea is just trying to frighten you,' Sophie said, trying to comfort the younger woman.

Ruby opened the door and hurried in, saying, 'Quickly, ladies, I have a plan.'

'I won't do it, whatever it is,' Leah said brokenly. 'I will not lose my son. I've been afraid of this his whole life long.'

Sophie looked surprised. 'You're going to let Chelsea win?'

Leah was confused. 'No! But I can't lose my son. I won't. The risk is too great.'

Sophie frowned. 'Maybe Tom should decide that.'

The next day, Dan was back in Harley Street to try out a new dentist that had been recommended to him by his mother. He shuddered as he passed *The Elixir Therapy Centre* and headed for the dental surgery next door. The waiting room was very luxurious and while he waited, he looked without seeing at a copy of *Country Life*. When the receptionist told him to go straight in, he entered the surgery and took a seat in the chair. He could see the TV screen hanging from the ceiling.

Lewis Brown, dentist to the stars, was fifty-plus and very eccentric. He slapped a plastic bib on Dan, making his patient feel about three years old, and then put a pair of dark glasses on him, to block out the glare of the overhead examination light. He then pressed a switch and the chair rose in the air.

'Any problems, Mr Ryan? Open wide and I'll just take a little look.' Lewis checked his mouth.

Dan grunted. 'Women problems. That's all.'

'See a gynaecologist. Hahaha.' Lewis was amused by his own joke.

'No. I mean I've got a problem *with* a woman.'

Lewis peered over his own, horn-rimmed glasses. 'Ah. We all have those problems from time to time.' He tapped a back tooth with a probe, saying, 'Aha. I think we'll X-ray this area. Now then, I'm a little bit longer in the tooth than you - excuse the pun - so if you need advice, chomp away.'

Dan opened his mouth, but before he could speak, Lewis stuck a piece of card between his jaws and a cotton-wool sausage roll along his upper gum. 'Yes, I know it's uncomfortable, but keep still . . . Don't move now!' He went out of the room and did the X-ray then came back and removed the painful bit of card and the roll. Phew, Dan felt he could breathe again.

After he'd examined the X-ray and pronounced himself satisfied, Lewis carried on, 'I mean, my first wife - what a corker, but all she was after was . . .'

'Your money?' mumbled Dan.

Lewis shook his head. 'My sister.'

Dan nearly choked.

Lewis then checked his molars, pausing to say, 'The second wife, all she wanted was . . .'

'Your money?' dribbled Dan.

'Nope. Guess again.'

'Your dog?'

'She'd never get my dog. No, she wanted a partnership in my business. So if I were you I'd steer clear of the lot of 'em. Now what were you saying?' He squirted some liquid into Dan's mouth.

' . . .'

'I gave up after four marriages, now I'm celibate. It's just me and my Bedlington terrier Gnasher.'

Dan laughed and did choke this time. Bedlingtons were such peaceful woolly dogs, about as far from Dennis the Menace's dog Gnasher from the *Beano* comic as you could get.

'Married to your business, then?' he managed as the chair shot down again unexpectedly. 'Oops!' Strange that there was no dental nurse to help him off with the bib or dark glasses, or offer him a glass of 'pink drink' to rinse with, he thought, considering the extortionate fees he'd no doubt get charged by Mr Brown.

'Ha! Funny. Well, all that seems to be healthy enough. Now pop along and see the hygienist in the next room, and make an appointment for three months from now with the receptionist when you leave. Good luck. Cheerio!' Then the dentist left the room and Dan heard him calling, 'Next one in, Sandra!'

TWO WOMEN WAITED IN THE HYGIENIST'S ROOM. THEY WERE dressed in disposable overalls and large white masks which almost covered their faces, distorting them, reminding Dan of the Hall of Mirrors he'd been taken into at the fairground when he was a child. One woman was checking the dental utensils while the other pulled on rubber gloves.

'Take a seat, please.'

Dan did climb into the seat, but he felt uneasy: something was amiss.

The other woman grabbed the chair remote and as soon as Dan was seated the chair flipped back and he almost fell out. He gripped the sides. What was happening today? These chairs should come equipped with seat-belts, he thought nervously. Ruby, who was stood behind him, stifled a snigger – which made him open his eyes wide. What was going on?

'Sorry, Mr Ryan, she's new.' Leah had assumed a Scottish accent.

Dan was a little disconcerted. 'No disrespect, but I find it strange that you won't show your faces. Is this a new practice? I don't recall this when I've been to a hygienist before.'

'Aye, 'tis for safety reasons,' Leah cooed. How Mr Brown could have let them loose like this still amazed her. Surely it wasn't ethical, but Lewis, who knew Sophie well, wasn't your usual dentist, and she doubted that Dan would ever come back here after this. 'Open wide.'

Dan closed his eyes momentarily.

Leah reassured him much like she did when she took Tom to the dentist. 'There is no reason to be afraid, Mr Ryan, I willnae hurt you.' Gently, she used a cleaning tool the way she'd been shown. 'Could I have suction, please?'

Ruby used suction, but couldn't resist muttering, 'Be afraid, be very afraid.'

Dan was alarmed. 'Who are you? Do I know you?'

Leah put a calming hand on his shoulder. 'She's new, remember. Ignore her.'

Dan stared closely at Leah's face but she turned away.

'I'm sure I know you. Your voice sounds familiar. Your perfume is . . .'

Ruby panicked. She put the gas mask over Dan's face. 'This won't take long, sir. Just relax, take a deep breath. In out, in out, shake it all about.' She pressed the mask harder.

Dan struggled.

Ruby was imitating a Borg from *Star Trek*. 'Resistance is futile. Give me the swab or you will be assimilated.'

Leah spun around. 'Ruby!'

Dan was even more alarmed. 'I knew it.'

He tried to rise but Ruby pushed him back, snarling, 'You know it makes sense.'

'I know it does not!'

Ruby fired the rinse gun, making Dan wet through to his skin. She fired again. 'If you hadn't sired the child, you wouldn't be in this predicament!'

Leah protested. 'Hey, I'm not a brood mare.'

While Ruby was distracted, Dan snatched the rinse gun. He pulled Ruby's mask down then fired the gun, aiming it at Leah.

'I didn't expect you to pull a stunt like this,' he said. 'Stay back.'

'Desperate women take desperate measures,' said Ruby.

Leah ripped off her mask. 'I am not desperate!'

Dan pointed the water nozzle at both women. 'Don't come near me, either of you, or I will shoot.'

Leah took a step forward. 'Give me a swab for your son's sake. Please!'

Dan shook his nozzle. 'Not until I've seen my lawyer.'

Ruby laughed mockingly. 'What's your lawyer going to do? Assure you you're not the kid's father, when you could be? Get real, Dan.'

Dan was affronted. 'I've told you - until I've seen my lawyer and she gives me the green light, my DNA sample is off-limits. You understand?' He struggled out of the chair, threw the rinse nozzle into the water fountain and backed towards the door.

'Dan, please be reasonable, for Tom's sake,' Leah begged. 'He just wants to know you.'

'Tom being your son?'

'Tom being *our* son.'

'So you say. Well, I'm leaving now, and don't you dare follow me. Oh, and just for the record, this was a very stupid idea.' Dan scowled. 'I've a good mind to report that clown Lewis to the Dental Council for letting you two loose here. I suppose he's one of my mother's cronies, is he?'

Ruby shrugged. 'Yes. And I thought it was genius had you not been so clever.'

At that moment, Sophie herself walked in - with Tom. Dan did a double-take and had to clutch hold of the dentist's chair. The boy definitely resembled him. Could the lad really be his child?

Tom looked sad. 'Why are you so cross? I only want you to be my daddy because you are. Mummy says so.'

Dan was confused. 'There are no guarantees that I am your flesh and blood,' he said gently. Seeing the child's pain and incomprehension, he got down on one knee, whilst keeping an eye on Leah. 'The thing is, Tom, we have to get lawyers involved when someone is as rich as I am.'

Tom was flabbergasted. 'We don't want your money, we have lots of our own. My mummy doesn't tell lies.'

Dan glanced across at Leah. 'I'm sure you believe she doesn't.'

Tom punched the air with frustration. Dan frowned; both he and his mother were renowned for throwing their hands in the air when they were frustrated.

Tom's bottom lip trembled and Dan caved in. He smiled at the boy. 'OK, OK, let's do it.'

Tom grinned. 'Everything will be fine, you'll see. Thank you.' He unexpectedly slipped his small hand into Dan's big one, and looked up at him like a fawning puppy.

Dan tried to catch Leah's eye, but she was feeling very upset and just looked away. When she was alone, she would tear up the business card that Dan had given her all those years ago. He'd obviously not meant what he'd written.

CHELSEA PACED UP AND DOWN HER OFFICE, SQUEEZING HER stress ball as Dan watched on. She was very agitated. Looking down at the wet object, she screamed as she suddenly realised it was Hero's slobbery ball she'd been holding. 'Ugh!' She slung it across the room, narrowly missing some photos in frames. Hero plodded over to rescue it.

Rubbing sanitiser all over her hands, Dan's PA ground out, 'I cannot *believe* you gave your DNA.'

'I did it for Tom. Poor little lad. None of this is his fault. There's no harm done - on the contrary. It will prove my innocence and help Tom understand, and that will be that.' Dan passed her the signed letters, then Chelsea saw him brush his thumb over his other palm, looking down at it fondly.

'What's wrong with your hand?' she snapped.

'It was rather touching - he held my hand,' Dan said with a smile. 'He's just a little boy who needs a father.'

'Well, *she's* after your money and you're just too damn besotted with the kid to see it!' Chelsea marched out, kicking the slimy ball in anger and nearly treading on one of Hero's enormous furry feet.

The big dog dashed over and fetched it back to Dan.

Stroking his best friend, Dan confided, 'Anyone would think she owned Ryan's. Come on, boy, let's go for walkies.' And he laughed out loud as Hero nearly knocked him over in a rush to fetch his lead.

THE TELEPHONE RANG JUST AS CHELSEA MARCHED BACK TO HER desk in the outer office. 'Dan Ryan's office . . . Very well - just one moment.' She rang through on Dan's phone. 'It's the Lab,' she said.

Dan answered. 'OK, put them through. Hello? . . . I see. It's very important it gets done today. I will come over now and wait for the results.'

Dan put the phone down as Chelsea walked in, asking, 'Is there a problem?'

Dan nodded. 'My DNA has been contaminated. I need to give it again.'

'Why would you bother? I mean, this is downright crazy,' Chelsea grunted, then stalked out in disgust.

12

A CAT'S BOTTOM

L eah, Joey and Tom entered the DNA Laboratories. By coincidence, they were situated in Southampton Row, near Leah's hotel and the park where she had watched the dogs and their owners enjoying some exercise.

She was so glad to have Joey with her at this important moment in their lives. It had been hard for him to leave Whitby, as their office was in Grandad's house, and from there Joey liaised with the other cafés Leah owned and dealt with any problems arising whilst keeping an eye on Tom senior. It was a demanding and responsible job, and he and Leah loved working together. But just for now, the Dog Friendly Cafés would have to look after themselves. Fortunately, the cousins were scrupulous in only employing dog-loving - and human-loving - staff.

Dan was seated in the foyer and Sophie was at the desk waiting. Scotty had come too. After having a word with Sophie, he walked over and took hold of Tom's hand.

'Sophie has asked me to take you for an ice cream,' he said gently. He turned to Leah. 'Would that be OK? There's a Pizza Hut just down the road which has amazing ice creams. We can wait there until you call us, and don't worry. I'm good with kids.'

Leah nodded. She took his mobile number just in case and watched the pair of them walk out. Her son was chatting happily to Scotty.

Joey looked at Dan, then nudged Leah. 'Wow, he's even better in the flesh.' He called over, 'Hiya, Dan, I'm Leah's cousin, Joey.'

Dan nodded, then stuck his head in a magazine.

Sophie looked across. 'Ah, Leah, I thought you and Joey should be here when they announce that I'm a grandmother.'

Just then, a red-headed assistant came to the reception desk. In her hands she held the required tests in sealed packs. 'Daniel Ryan?'

Dan stood up and approached the desk. 'That's me.'

'I believe you are aware that there's been a problem and so I need to ask you to provide us with another sample. If you could follow me into this side room.' She spoke in a matter-of-fact voice.

Dan was taken aback. 'Oh, very well.' He'd hoped to have some privacy. 'I can do it right here, and I will wait for the results.'

'I could wait with you,' offered Joey.

Leah had had enough. 'OK, everyone, let's go for a coffee. Give the man some space. Eh?'

Dan actually smiled and said, 'Thank you.'

RUBY HOOPED HER ARM IN SOPHIE'S. 'SOPHIE, OLD FRIEND . . .' She stopped mid-sentence as she saw a blonde-haired woman going into the laboratory.

Sophie stopped. 'What? What's wrong?'

Ruby squeezed her arm. 'Oh, nothing. You guys go on and I'll join you in the pizza place. Mine's a cappuccino, by the way. I just need the ladies' room and I won't tinkle in a café.'

'Why ever not?' asked Joey. 'There'll be clean bogs in the Pizza Hut.'

'Joey, they are toilets not bogs,' corrected Leah. Trust him to show her up.

'I just wanted to shock Ruby,' Joey said.

'I don't shock easily,' laughed Ruby.

'No, she doesn't. You used to tinkle anywhere and everywhere if my memory serves me right,' Sophie giggled.

'Well, I'm older now and more careful about whose seat I occupy - and it won't be a pizza place toilet, that's for sure. I will be back before you know it.' Ruby left them on the pavement and walked swiftly back to the Lab.

RUBY QUIETLY ENTERED THE BUILDING, THEN HUNG BACK AS she saw Chelsea talking to the receptionist. The young woman was wearing a blonde wig. Minx! You're up to something, thought Ruby. Remaining concealed, she waited. Dan reappeared in the reception area soon afterwards. Chelsea, meanwhile, had vanished.

Dan handed his sample over to the assistant.

'Thank you. I will phone you as soon as the test comes back.' The assistant smiled almost apologetically.

Dan shook his head. 'No, I'll wait here for the result, but first I need some air.' He walked right past Ruby as she pretended to be looking at some posters. No doubt he had a lot on his mind.

Ruby breathed a sigh of relief and sneaked into the reception area and listened. Chelsea had magically reappeared and had her back to her. She was talking to the assistant and Ruby heard everything.

Chelsea was holding out an envelope. 'This should be enough to mix up this sample.'

'Look, I can't do this again. It's not only very wrong, it's more than my . . .' The assistant was cut short.

Chelsea handed her another envelope. 'Here – that's double. And if you don't keep your part of the deal, I will ensure you lose your job!' She made to storm out, but Ruby stood in her way.

'I wouldn't do that if I were you.'

The laboratory assistant spun around. Her face went scarlet. She held the envelopes out, blustering, 'I'm sorry. I didn't want to do it. She made me!'

Ruby waved them away. 'Keep the money. Now I am going to watch you do this test and see that you hand it over to Mr Ryan. In person. OK? Then you will keep your job and this woman here will lose hers if I have anything to do with it.'

LEAH HAD DECIDED NOT TO GO WITH THE OTHERS TO PIZZA Hut. She was stressed out by the situation and also Joey was chattering so much it was driving her mad. She'd have a lie-down, she decided. Tom was happy and the others had promised to meet her back at the hotel in an hour's time, hoping that by then, they'd have the result.

Exactly on time, Dan walked through the hotel lobby followed by his entourage, and they headed en masse towards a group of sofas and chairs.

When Leah came down to meet them, still white-faced but feeling a lot better, Dan was apologetic. 'Sorry it took so long.

It made sense to bring Tom back to your hotel. We need to go somewhere private to discuss the results. I have them here.'

Tom looked up at his mum. 'Can I come?'

Leah nodded. 'Of course. This is important to you.'

Dan reluctantly agreed. 'Very well. Just the three of us then.'

Joey poked Dan. 'Did you have a sneak preview?'

Dan said quietly, 'I feel a hundred per cent sure the result will be negative.'

Chelsea, who had joined the party, moved possessively between Dan and Leah. 'You need one of us with you, Dan.'

Dan looked across at Sophie. 'Yes, I suppose you're right. Mother, would you join us?'

Chelsea was left open-mouthed. Ruby guffawed in satisfaction.

'You're so dead,' Chelsea hissed. 'You and that bitch of a mother of his.'

Scotty reprimanded her. 'You shouldn't speak about Sophie like that.'

'Why not? She screws up everything!' Chelsea went off in a huff.

'Why on earth do you tolerate that woman?' asked Ruby.

Scotty shrugged his shoulders. 'I don't know. I suppose I feel sorry for her.'

'Sorry for that devious little untrustworthy cheat? You must be barking. Even Hero knows she's bad meat. Just be careful, Scotty. After all this time you're losing your touch. I tell you, she's *baaad*.' Ruby walked away, leaving the security guard standing by himself scratching his head.

THE ENVELOPE WAS LAID ON THE TABLE IN ROOM 229. DAN, Tom and Leah just stared at it. A knock came on the door.

Joey poked his head in. 'Do you need some back-up, Leah?'

Leah nodded. Joey came in, closing the door behind him, and moved to Leah's side.

The door opened again. Dan sighed.

Ruby kept the door slightly ajar. 'We need to be your witnesses. We'll wait in the doorway.'

Dan passed the letter to Leah. 'Would you like to open it?'

She nodded. 'Yes, thank you.' With shaking fingers, she tore the envelope open.

Tom urged Leah, 'Quickly, Mummy.'

Leah was nervous but she didn't know why: she knew Dan was Tom's dad.

Dan interpreted Leah's reluctance. 'Tom's not my son, is he?'

Leah was angry. 'You men are impossible. Women don't conceive by themselves, now do they? It takes two!' She glanced at the letter then handed it to Dan. 'Of course he's your son.'

While Tom yelled, 'Yes, I am your son!' and danced about, ecstatic, Leah hissed at Dan, 'Think back; we used *your* condoms that *your* company made. They must have been faulty.'

Dan felt like he'd been punched. It was a long time ago, but she was right - they had used his condoms.

Uninvited, unwanted, Chelsea had tagged along and now stood in the doorway behind Ruby. Hearing the news, she wailed, 'Impossible. That's impossible,' but no one heard.

Tom went to Sophie and hugged her round the waist. 'Which means I am your grandson,' he told her.

Sophie hugged him back. 'You certainly are, my darling. "My grandson", that sounds so good.'

Tom looked at Dan's stunned face. 'It must be a shock, Dan. Mummy, can we get a strong coffee for Dan.'

Leah smiled. 'Joey sometimes makes one when he's worried about something.'

Dan took a seat. He put his head in his hands.

Ruby passed Chelsea who was still open-mouthed. 'How the hell did this happen?' the girl said.

Ruby laughed. 'Seriously, I saw you try and sabotage this a second time. So don't try anything else or I will see you finished for good.'

Joey asked Ruby, 'Can you tell me why Chelsea has the face of a cat's bottom?' He puckered his lips tightly.

'Oh, she always looks like that.' As far as Ruby was concerned, the girl had got her just deserts and now Dan was safe from her wiles. 'You know, Joey, I just can't wait to see what happens next,' she added. 'Can you?'

Tom looked at the test certificate. He frowned. 'Grandma, what does it mean exactly? I mean, how did I become Dan's son?'

Leah sighed, and answered for Sophie. 'I told you, Tom, we can discuss this when you're sixteen. We agreed.'

Tom nodded. 'I suppose so.'

'You're a little young to know all the ins and outs right now,' Joey said kindly, thinking that 'ins and outs' were exactly what the Hokey Cokey was all about.

Sophie put her arm around Tom's shoulder.

'I'm sorry I'm such a shock,' the little boy said to Dan. 'I'm sure you'll get used to me when I come for a sleepover.'

Dan groaned.

Leah looked at Tom's reaction. 'You go with Sophie and get

the coffee. You remember what I told you about what shock can do to a person?'

Tom nodded gravely and took hold of Sophie's hand.

As they walked out, Ruby walked in. 'Come on, Dan, surely you realised there was a possibility that Tom was yours?'

'Truth is I didn't,' he said dully.

'You do know your precious Chelsea was trying to doctor the test results, don't you?' she nagged him.

'No, I had no idea. *Come on, man-up, mate,*' he whispered to himself. Then he stood up and held his hand out to Leah for the test results sheet.

'They've not changed. You are still his father,' Leah said as she handed it over.

Dan walked over to the window. He looked down at the certificate and the words blurred in front of his eyes. Blinking, he looked again - and this time he knew beyond doubt that he was Tom's father. At that moment it became clear to him that his life had changed – for ever.

13

DAN'S ESTATE

As the limousine travelled up the long driveway to Hambourne Manor, Tom pointed to the horses grazing on both sides of the road. Leah was in awe as she saw a white mare galloping along the fence side. Unbeknownst to her, Dan was watching her reaction.

'Welcome to my home, Leah and Tom. We can see the horses later. Let's get you all settled in first,' he said.

Leah could have sworn she saw his shoulders relax. She was right. Dan couldn't wait to rip off his tie.

'Is it good to be home?' she asked.

'It sure is, but Hambourne isn't mine: it's on a two-year lease until I find my own country place to buy. My mother always said that home is where the heart is, but I reckon home is where my animals are - and when I have to go back to London, I always make sure I take Hero with me.'

The car stopped; Dan unbuckled his seatbelt and stepped out then held the door open for Leah and their child.

'Your horses are beautiful.' Leah was enchanted by the fields full of healthy-looking horses grazing.

Dan pointed to one. 'It's my passion to breed rare and

endangered species to save them from extinction. That grey mare is a Lippizaner.'

'I didn't know they were endangered.' Leah was startled.

'Well, they're on the endangered list. Thank heavens I have the financial means to breed them.'

Sophie, who was walking with Hero, now approached them. She had so much poise, Leah thought, like a true lady of the manor. She and Ruby kept their own suites at Hambourne; even Chelsea had a suite there, since when Dan wanted to spend a day or two away from the office, she sometimes had to stay over. Today, she had stubbornly refused to go back to the London HQ of Ryan's and was following them around, green with jealousy.

Sophie kissed her son. 'Darling, I'd like a family photo of my grandson and his parents with the house as the backdrop. And Hero too, of course.'

Dan shrugged. 'One family photo. Just the one.'

As if that was going to happen. Sophie took plenty of photos and managed to get in the frame for the final one with Ruby and the others.

Chelsea took that photo before walking inside the grand house in total disgust. In the distance, the lake at Hambourne shimmered in the sunshine.

DAN WADED WITH TOM ON A FLOAT BOARD IN THE SHALLOW end of the indoor swimming pool. Hero rescued him by pulling the board in, time and time again, much to Tom's delight. He laughed and squealed.

Dan looked up at Leah who was sat on the side of the pool with Joey, their feet dangling in the water. 'Come on in, the both of you.'

'I can't, I have no swimwear,' Leah replied.

'It's never stopped you before,' Joey said cheekily. 'Thankfully Scotty lent me some swim shorts.' He jumped in, making a big splash and deliberately soaking her as they'd done since being children.

'Hey!' she shouted, wishing she could jump in and duck him.

Dan waded to the side of the pool. 'Did he mean you go skinny dipping?'

Tom giggled. 'She goes in the sea in her undies!' he called.

Dan held out his hand. 'I won't tell if you don't.'

Leah bashfully turned her back, stripped off and slid into the heated pool. She was really pleased she'd had a quick shower and changed into her best turquoise matching bra and cute knickers. The water was refreshing and she struck out to the end of the pool. Hero followed her, towing Tom behind him.

'Mummy, look I'm right behind you,' Tom yelled.

Joey swam up. 'This is better than the sea in Whitby. It's warmer for a start.'

Dan swam towards them and Leah struck off to do the crawl to the other end. He threw a ball for Hero and Tom giggled. They all ended up at the shallow end with Joey keeping up the rear.

'I think Tom approves, Dan. Not only of the swimming pool but especially his new pastime being towed around by your lovely dog,' said Joey honestly.

Dan swam underwater, then surfaced and lifted the little boy out of the water. Tom was so happy, the happiest she'd ever seen him. Leah caught her breath and tears stood in her eyes for a moment. It was a beautiful sight to see her boy so happy. Then Dan pretended to be Jaws. Tom was hysterical. Leah laughed at their antics.

Then Dan chased Leah - and it got a whole lot more exciting.

Tom screamed, 'Mummy, quick. Swim, swim fast.' He jumped up and down in the shallow end.

Dan grabbed Leah by the arm as she swam away and she turned in his arms. As they looked into each other's eyes the world seemed to stand still.

Sophie and Ruby watched on from the side of the pool.

'He seems bewitched by her,' said Sophie, with a certain amount of satisfaction.

'Oh stop it. Aren't you satisfied you've got your grandson? If it's going to progress, let it be organically, Sophie. No interference or matchmaking as it will only end in tears. I don't want to see you hurt, old woman, and I certainly don't want to see Leah hurt. She looks like she's getting in too deep as it is.' As Dan and Leah continued to splash and frolic in the pool, she saw Chelsea watching them from a poolside lounger, a look of scheming fury on her face.

LEAH JUMPED OUT OF THE POOL AND JOEY JOINED HER.

'How could I ever think that Tom was better off without his dad?' Leah said as she picked up a towel from the pile beside the pool and patted her wet hair.

Joey smiled at her. 'You never really had a dad for long, so you've had no experience. Grandad was your father, wasn't he?' Then he hugged her and held her for a moment.

Tom was shouting. 'More, more!'

Dan pleaded for mercy. 'No more. I'm exhausted. We will be shrivelled up like prunes if we don't get out, now.'

Dan and Tom climbed out of the pool hand in hand, and Dan wrapped his son in a big soft towel. With very bad timing,

Chelsea got off the recliner and hurried over to monopolise Dan – just as Hero walked up the ramp out of the pool, then shook himself hard – all over Chelsea.

'Right on cue. Nailed it,' Joey said.

Chelsea cursed. Her make-up was running and her smart suit was wet through. 'I hate that dog!'

Dan frowned. 'That's my boy you're talking about.'

'Me? I'm your son,' Tom piped up.

Sophie laughed. 'Not you, Tom. Hero had the title before you. Can you break it to him gently?'

Tom put his arms around the big dog. 'Hero, I will share the title, it's only fair.' The Newfie licked him with a huge pink tongue, which made him giggle happily. Tom was perfectly at home with dogs, even if Hero was many times bigger than Yin and Yang, the Pomeranians.

Ruby sighed. 'How magnanimous. You know, Sophie, your Alex loved Dan, and Dan will love Tom.'

'Huh. Alex was desperate for his child to inherit.'

'Must have been, to pick you over me. But seriously, Alex was yours, just not for long, sadly, and he was so grateful to you and he *was* in love with you.'

'Oh stop it, Ruby, you'll have me believing all this crap.' Sophie gave a wobbly smile. She still missed her late husband even if there was sometimes a twinkle in her eye when she saw a handsome man.

CHELSEA MADE ANOTHER ATTEMPT TO BE THE CENTRE OF attention. Once everyone was dry and sitting around the pool, she took a piece of paper out of her briefcase and took it over to Dan.

'I've made a list of the weekends you will be available to

see your son,' she said self-importantly. 'I'm sure his mother will be too busy to come with him.'

Tom stared at Dan. 'I thought you liked my mummy?' he said, and bursting into tears, he ran away from the pool.

Leah confronted Chelsea. 'How could you do that to a little boy?' And she quickly chased after Tom. However, her son had disappeared.

FIVE MINUTES LATER, LEAH WAS FRANTIC. EVERYONE HAD BEEN looking, checking places on the big estate, but the boy had vanished. 'Dan,' she implored. 'What are we going to do? Where can he have got to?'

Scotty jogged up; he was breathless. 'It's all right, Leah, I have found him. He just wants the two of you to go and talk to him. Stubborn little boy.'

'Oh, he can be.' Leah sagged with relief. 'Thank God. And as for you, Scotty, I'll never be able to thank you enough.'

'Where is he?' Dan asked. He too had been searching every-where he could think of.

Scotty pointed. 'The far barn.'

Dan gasped. 'My God! There's dangerous machinery down there.' He started running.

Leah quickly followed.

Dan scanned the barn as he opened the door. Leah pulled the door wide open and the setting sun filtered in.

'Tom! Tom, pet, it's us,' called Leah.

There was a noise from overhead, up above the hay bales.

Tom answered, 'Watch this, Mummy. *Woohoo! Woohoo!*' He swung upside-down on a bungee rope, missing Leah but he slugged Dan, then he bounced back up.

Dan was bruised, but immensely relieved that they had found him OK. 'Careful, son.'

Leah grabbed Tom on the way back down. 'We've been so worried whilst you were having fun. Why did you run away?'

Tom looked worried again. 'I thought you liked each other.'

Leah frowned, finding it hard to think of the right words. 'We do sort of like each other.'

Dan hugged Leah. 'Of course we do.'

Tom was unconvinced. 'Other mummies and daddies kiss.' He sounded sad.

Dan kissed Leah, catching her off-guard.

Leah turned to her son. 'Tom, we hardly know each other.'

Tom ignored his mum's protestations. 'Other mummies and daddies live together.'

It was Dan this time who protested, 'Surely you can't expect that?'

Leah unhooked Tom from the bungee harness.

The boy suddenly asked his mum, 'Do you have your phones with you?'

Dan answered, 'No. Why?'

Tom looked sheepish. 'Because they disturb grown-ups and you two have to talk and not argue.' Then he legged it, shouting, 'I want normal parents.'

The barn door slid shut and Dan heard a clicking sound.

'He's locked us in, dammit. Is this your idea of a joke?' He rounded on Leah.

'Hang on a minute. I've done nothing wrong.'

'Huh. It's obviously Joey who locked the door, Tom's not strong enough.' Dan tried to force it open but it was immovable.

'He wants us to talk, so let's talk,' Leah said, getting a glimpse of the muscles on his arms. This was stupid: how could the sight of his biceps give her butterflies? What was happening to her?

'I won't take orders from a child, Leah,' commented Dan, pushing at the big barn door again.

'He's our child. He has a say.'

'I know he has a say, but not on how we run our lives. He is a minor, not the grown-up here.' Dan looked around at Leah. 'Or do you think he should run the whole show?'

'No, but what I am saying is he's a little boy who desperately wants us to get on, so that he can see more of you. Try and understand it from his point of view. He wants to know we are friends, that's all,' Leah explained.

'I think he's already put my pyjamas next to your pillow,' Dan replied without turning to her this time.

'You wear pyjamas?'

'No. It was a metaphor.' And at her silence: 'Would it matter if I did?'

'Er . . . no,' Leah said, her nerves going into overdrive imagining him without pyjamas.

'Good.' Why on earth it bothered him that she might not approve if he didn't wear pyjamas was insane, but everything about this woman rocked his safe world and made him question his sanity.

He knew it was futile, and sure enough, when Dan tried to open the door again, it refused to budge.

'Now would be a good time to say thanks for the bonus. You enabled me to set up in business and pay for Grandad's operation. I will be forever grateful for that.' Leah's voice was getting fainter and fainter.

'Surely you earned a lot on the game?' Dan surmised.

Leah felt as if she'd been punched in her gut. 'You were my first and my last client,' she said hotly. 'I told you that at the time. It was an act of desperation for Grandad's sake. I was a hooker for one night only.'

'Sounds like the title of a Bond film. Do I believe that?'

'It's true.'

'I'll reserve judgement, if you don't mind.'

'Big of you, Dan.'

'Actually,' he coughed, 'you were my first lady of the night - and my last.'

'You expect me to believe that?' Leah could hardly suppress her laughter.

'Touché.'

Leah climbed the haystack. Dan was still concentrating on the door.

'I'm getting bored now,' she sang out.

Dan turned, but he couldn't see her. 'Leah. Where the hell are you?'

Dan heard a yelp, then a *boiiing*, and saw a figure hurtle towards him. Leah bounced out of reach just in time as the bungee lifted her back up again. Dan tried but failed to grab her. He was concerned – she was so reckless!

'You could hurt yourself, Leah.'

'I embrace risk, remember? You should try it some time.'

Laughing hysterically, Leah bounced three more times before Dan finally caught her. They fell into the hay and stared at each other, and Leah stopped laughing.

Dan murmured, 'There's something incredibly sexy about a woman on a bungee rope.'

'Mmmm . . . and something incredibly sexy about the man who unhooks her.'

Dan unhooked her. 'I really was your first and your last?'

'I swear on our son's life.'

Dan kissed her neck. 'Don't suppose the bonus paid for anything else?'

'Like what?'

'Like a proper kiss.'

They kissed with a frenzy.

'I think we should stop,' said Leah weakly.

'I agree - but there's just one thing wrong with that theory,' whispered Dan as he rained kisses on her ears, her neck and back to her lips.

'What's wrong with that?'

'I can't stop.'

'Oh. Good.'

This time when they kissed, it was deep and hungry and uncontrollable as they ripped at each other's clothes. And this time when they made love, it was as though they'd been waiting for each other all these years.

14

THE APHRODITE

As the lovers dozed, the doors of the barn suddenly opened wide. Ruby stood looking around. She flicked the light switch on and the barn was illuminated. Leah blinked rapidly. She and Dan were covered in a horse rug, but she was naked beneath Dan's shirt. Her still-damp underwear-cum-swimwear lay strewn about her.

Ruby looked quizzically at the pair. 'Why are you in the dark, or shouldn't I ask?'

Joey, who'd come in after her, took one look at Leah's face and quipped, 'Read the signs, dear, read the signs. They look very loved-up to me.'

Dan stood up, bare-chested. 'Oh – and you made sure of that by locking us in, didn't you,' he said.

Joey put his hands on his hips. 'Ooh, hark at her, getting all shirty. Please tell me what I'm being accused of, 'cos I ain't guilty.'

Ruby spoke up for Joey, to whom she had taken a real shine. 'He's been with me and your mother all this time.'

Dan brushed straw off his jogging bottoms. 'It's not what you think.'

Joey smiled. 'Yeah, right. So your name isn't Humpty Dumpty and you didn't fall off the wall and onto my cousin. Well, I don't buy it, Humpty.'

Leah opened her mouth at last, but decided not to deny it. 'Where's Tom?' she asked. 'I need to speak to him and find out who locked us in. Dan was trying for ages to unlock the door from this side but in the end we had to give up. I'm sure Tom isn't strong enough to lock it.'

'Well, don't look at me, nor Sophie, nor Ruby,' Joey said.

Ruby protested. 'It's just like Joey said. We three have been together. Sophie has bathed and fed Tom and put him to bed - and she won't be happy if you wake him.'

As they left the barn, with Leah wearing her damp knickers, Dan's shirt and Ruby's jacket, Dan went to switch the light off, but before he did so, he glanced at the bungee and the haystack. He wasn't going to forget what had happened here in a hurry; whatever kind of magic hold this woman had over him, he sure did act on impulse whenever Leah Jensen was around.

THE NEXT DAY, A KNOCK CAME ON DAN'S OFFICE DOOR ON THE estate. He opened it and ushered Sisco in.

'Sisco, I need the impossible. It must never get out that Leah was a . . .' Dan paced around the room.

Sisco said solemnly, 'I never came across any reference to it when I Googled and did the usual checks on her.'

Dan sighed. 'Let's hope we can keep it that way.'

'I hear you were blaming Joey for locking you in the barn.' Sisco cleared his throat. 'If that's all for tonight, I have an errand to run for Ruby. Wish me luck! She wants to come with me and when she starts singing her gospel tunes, I get hoarse 'cos I have to join in with her.'

Dan grinned at the thought of the two of them singing along in the car. 'Yeah, sure. We are eating here so I will get Cook to save you and Ruby some food.'

'Thanks, that'll be great.' Sisco went to the door just as it began to open and Sophie walked in.

'Hi, Sisco.'

Sisco nodded and left, closing the door behind him.

Sophie hugged her son, saying, 'This has been one of the best and worst days of my life.'

'Worst?'

'Yes. When Tom went missing, I was imagining all sorts of things.' Sophie sat down opposite him. 'I feel all topsy-turvy.'

'Well, how do you think I feel? Three days ago, I wasn't a dad. I didn't have a complication like this in my life.'

'Surely Tom isn't a complication?'

'I wasn't meaning Tom.'

'Oh, I see - you mean Leah. She's so pretty, I'm surprised I don't remember you dating her, but my memory is not so good these days.' Hiding her face, Sophie turned to pick up a mint from a dish on Dan's desk. 'Did you go out for long?'

Dan raised his brow. 'Come on, Mother, I thought it was you who picked her for me.'

'Oh.' Sophie deflated. 'So you know.'

'Yes, I know. I was rather surprised I have to admit.'

'Well, darling, I wasn't going to let you have any old trollop, was I? Madam Butterfly only supplies the very best girls. I don't suppose you know that I went to school with Shelley Collins – that's her real name - did you? Believe it or not, we were both at boarding school together and while the rest of us went off and did boring things, Shelley set herself up in Soho. To my mind she's no different from that woman who does *Millionaire Matchmakers*.'

'I'm just so pleased you were part of it but I'm ashamed that you somehow heard about my very first meltdown. It was all the pressure at work.' Dan smiled at his mum. 'I'm glad you had my back. And you chose well.' He let out a long breath, feeling more confused than ever.

BEFORE GOING DOWN FOR DINNER, LEAH HAD SHOWERED AND shampooed and made herself up before putting on her best dress. She was a woman on a mission. She unhooked the baby/dog gate at the entrance to Dan's home office and walked through to stand on the lush white carpet. As usual, Dan was staring out of the window; it was where he did a lot of his thinking. Hero followed Leah through and trotted over to his master.

Leah sighed. 'White carpet, baby gate? Bit stupid, isn't it?'

Dan replied whilst still looking out of the window, 'It's to stop Hero making a mess apparently, according to my PA.'

Leah couldn't help herself. 'You own a beautiful, black, hairy Newfoundland dog. Why on earth have a white carpet?'

Dan turned to look at her and caught his breath. Red and sexy took on a whole new meaning to him as he stared at the figure-hugging dress. 'I didn't choose the carpet.'

Their eyes met properly for the first time since the barn episode. 'I can guess who did.' Leah noticed a beautiful gold and turquoise decorated egg in a glass cabinet. The gems glittered. 'That's beautiful,' she said. 'I remember it from before. You'd just bought it on the same day when we met for the first time.'

Dan strode across to the cabinet. He unlocked it, then passed the egg to Leah. 'Your dress is beautiful too.'

'Thank you. This is made by Fabergé, if I remember rightly. Exquisite colours too.'

'Fabergé eggs usually have wonderful colours.'

'Oh my gosh, here - take it from me before I drop it.'

Dan chuckled. 'I bought it in a moment of madness. I too liked the colours and you had the same reaction last time.'

'You remember?' Leah said almost shyly. 'Two moments of madness in one day?'

'Possibly. Now, would you like something to drink – an aperitif?' Dan placed the Fabergé back, but forgot to lock the cabinet.

'Just some water, please. I think we need to talk, Dan.'

Dan took a bottle of Perrier out of the fridge and poured out her drink. He was so close, his fingers fleetingly touched Leah's hand and they both glanced at each other. Both felt the touch; it was like an electrical charge.

'Not here, later,' Leah managed to say.

Joey and Sophie walked in, followed by Chelsea, as Leah took her first sip.

Sophie looked enquiringly at her son. 'What, later? You should do what, later?'

Leah stepped away from Dan.

'Nothing, Mother.' He kissed his mother, then Joey put his cheek out - but Dan ignored him.

'Shucks, a girl can hope, can't she?' Joey joked.

Chelsea glowered at Leah. 'What's that *thing* doing in here?'

'If you mean Hero, I let him through,' said Dan, winking at Leah.

Chelsea frowned. 'He's not allowed on my carpet.' She turned her back on the others, trying to shut them out. 'I've arranged for a conference call at 10 a.m. tomorrow as you asked.'

'Ah. No, that's been changed. Marcus is going to take it at the main office,' Dan informed her. 'I have another appointment.' He put an arm around Sophie. 'I've just been showing Leah the Fabergé I bought on the day we first met. She loves the colours.'

Sophie admired it through the glass. 'The diamonds are almost flawless. Just like something else that day, I believe.'

Joey looked at it. 'Like me, obviously,' he preened.

Chelsea narrowed her eyes. She moved between Leah and Dan. 'I know of no other appointment.'

Dan shrugged. 'I don't have to run everything by you.'

Chelsea was gob-smacked again.

'I suggest we go into dinner. I for one am starving,' said Dan as he took his mother's arm.

THAT EVENING, WOKEN BY THE COMINGS AND GOINGS OF GUESTS retiring to their rooms after dinner, Tom climbed out of bed in his pyjamas, picked up a parcel and went to knock on Dan's bedroom door.

'Come in,' Dan said, and gave the little boy a welcoming smile. He wasn't sure how to handle this dad thing, but he reckoned he was going to have to go with his gut.

'Are you cross with me, for making you and my mummy talk? I mean, you just needed to break the ice. That's what my great-grandad says. *Break t'ice.*'

Dan couldn't suppress his laughter. 'Does he talk with a broad Yorkshire accent all the time?'

'He does.'

'I don't suppose you're going to tell me who locked the door, are you?' Dan asked his son.

Tom shook his head. 'Great-grandad Thomas, I call him just Grandad even though he is really, really, really old, well, he says we should never tell lies, so the best thing is to say nowt at all. So my answer is - nowt.'

Tom held out the parcel for Dan. Surprised, he opened the box, took out what was inside and after a moment or two asked, 'Is it a robot?'

Tom nodded. 'Yep. If you talk to him, I will see you and hear you when I get home from school. Grandad Thomas ordered it for me on the internet, specially, to give to you.'

Dan switched the robot on. 'Then I shall put him on my desk and talk to him. I'm not too bad with technology.'

Tom was impressed. 'That's cool. Many old people don't understand it.'

Dan stared at Tom. 'You think I'm old?'

Tom was baffled. 'Well, yes.' He looked eager and at the same time apprehensive as he asked, 'Did you and Mummy make friends?'

'I'm going to take her out tomorrow. We need to talk. I was hoping to talk to her tonight, but we had such good fun playing cards with my mother we didn't have time. Will you be OK staying here with Joey and Sophie?'

'May I go swimming again?' Tom looked excited. 'And play with Hero?'

Dan smiled. 'You certainly can, but don't get lost again, whatever you do. Seriously, you think I'm old?'

'I think anyone older than twenty is old,' the boy said solemnly. 'Ancient even.'

Dan glanced at his watch. 'Come on, Tom, let's get you back to bed before your mum has my guts for garters.' The little boy giggled happily as his dad took him back to bed.

LEAH WAS STROKING A GREY MARE AT THE FENCE SIDE AND saying non-sensical things to her as the horse nuzzled her velvety nose into her hands. Leah kissed her, murmuring, 'Your owner has a soft side, I'm beginning to find out.'

Tom came running up with Hero trotting behind him.

'Mummy, quickly, Daddy needs to talk to you. He said that Harry and Troy are coming from Whitby to stay here, and you're going out with Daddy.' Tom skipped excitedly, dying to see his friends from school.

Leah looked surprised, but reluctantly stopped fondling the mare. She glanced up to see Dan near the house, talking to Chelsea.

'Did he say where I was going with him?' she asked, still watching them.

'No, he just said he was taking you out to talk. I expect it's about arranging to see me on a regular basis,' Tom replied as he reached up to stroke the mare.

'Sweetheart, I thought we agreed not to rush your father into anything. Let him go at his own pace, remember,' Leah cautioned gently as she took Tom's hand and walked towards Dan and Chelsea.

Without saying so much as a 'good morning', Chelsea rudely addressed Leah. 'Sisco and Ruby will be here soon with two other brats. Although why, I've no idea.' And she moved away back to the house.

Leah enquired, 'Did she mean Troy and Harry?'

'Yes, my mother thought it would be nice if we brought them down for the weekend, so Tom has got some pals to play with,' Dan explained. He gave a grin. 'And that's not all: Yin and Yang are coming too. No boy should be without his canine mates.'

Leah laughed. 'Yes, I can't imagine how your mother got him here without them. He loves those boys so much - just like his dad loves Hero, I reckon.'

'I want to take you away for a short stay,' Dan said, a note of tenderness in his voice. 'No distractions. We need to talk about Tom and our situation.'

CHELSEA COLLARED SCOTTY. 'SO WHERE IS HE TAKING HER?'

Scotty shrugged. 'I just go with him, he doesn't consult me.'

'Yes, but that's the thing, he normally consults *me*! Remember - make sure there's no funny business. She's after his money, you do know that?'

'Funny business?' the little man scoffed. 'When he never laughs? What are you on about!'

Chelsea frowned. 'Money-grabbing, I tell you. It's written all over her silly face.'

'If you say so, although I've seen no sign of that. However, I'll keep my eyes and ears open.' He went off into the house to collect his bags.

DAN HELPED LEAH INTO THE HELICOPTER, CLIPPED HER IN THEN sat beside her. The pilot jumped inside and greeted them, before doing some checking of the controls.

'The flight won't take too long,' Dan reassured her, 'and Simon is a very experienced pilot. We'll be meeting up with our next mode of transport soon.'

'I'm intrigued, but I like surprises so I don't want you to tell me where in the world we are going, yet.' Leah paused. 'I thought this visit was to talk about Tom?'

'Ah, after we've had some R and R. We just need to relax and enjoy the flight and have a day or so to talk, without anyone else putting their oar in. My mother is wonderful, but when she gets the bit between her teeth, she generally gets what she wants – which is to see more of Tom. Mind you, how can I blame her? She is over the moon at being a grandmother, and she and Tom already love each other.'

'Your PA has a lot to say for herself, even about things that don't concern her,' Leah couldn't help commenting. She'd had just about enough of the other woman's rudeness.

'You have to forgive Chelsea. The way she acts is partly my fault. I suppose I've let her position run over into my private life at times. I have never encouraged her, you must understand that.'

'Dan, it's not really any of my business, I was just observing, that's all,' Leah said simply, but the voice in her head was screaming, *Of course I want there to be nothing between you both, only professional stuff, but Chelsea seems obsessed by you and believes you are hers!*

'At least this way we will get to talk.' Dan put his finger to his lips as he saw Scotty approach. 'He's like an old washerwoman gossip too.'

Leah laughed, feeling quite giddy that she was going to fly in a helicopter with Dan. She wondered how much it had cost to hire this machine – then realised that of course he must own it!

Scotty climbed in and Simon closed the door behind him, then helped to buckle the little man in safely.

Leah waved to Tom and Sophie. 'They get on so well - to think they've only just met.'

'They do, don't they. It's as if they've known each other a lifetime, but I guess she's waited a lifetime for a grandchild.' Dan pointed to his horses cantering as the helicopter took off. Studying Leah's profile as she watched the horses, he asked curiously, 'I take it you love horses?'

'Yes, ever since I was a nipper. Grandad Thomas did three

things: he taught me to swim and to ride, and he took me out in the country for walks. He has a friend who owns a riding school, but I think my love for horses came from Thomas himself. I have just recently had to retire my mare, but I ride the school horses when I get the chance.'

As the engine started up and the helicopter began to ascend, Leah looked across at Scotty. 'Are you feeling all right?' she mouthed.

The little man did his best to grin, whilst he held onto his stomach. 'Not my favourite mode of transport,' he managed, shaking his head then groaning.

It was Leah's first ever experience of travelling by heli-copter but she took to it with no problem.

Scotty observed the couple as the helicopter flew through grey clouds to blue skies. His boss and Leah seemed to be getting on very well, he thought, before gritting his teeth and closing his eyes: he didn't dare look out of the window. The helicopter landed at Jersey airport where a chauffeur-driven Mercedes was waiting. After shaking hands with Simon the pilot, Leah, Dan and Scotty - now feeling much relieved to be back on terra firma - got into the big car.

'So, we're in Jersey, are we?' Leah asked. 'Very nice, it's been on my bucket list for a while.'

'Your *bucket list*?' Dan enquired with a grin. 'That sounds so dated.'

Leah got comfortable. 'Yes, my son tells me I'm old-fash-ioned. Sorry, I meant *our* son.' She pointed to Scotty in the front seat and added less cheerfully, 'I can tell he still doesn't trust me, despite the test results.'

'No, he doesn't – but remember, he's paid not to trust anyone. As for a bucket list, Tom thinks I'm ancient too. I was mortified to be classed as old.'

Leah chuckled merrily and Dan sat back and drank in her smile as if it was nectar.

It didn't seem long before they arrived at St Helier harbour, and the Mercedes parked not far from where a large yacht was berthed.

'Here we are, at the *Aphrodite*,' Dan announced.

When the chauffeur opened her door, Leah got out and began to make for a smaller yacht. Dan steered her towards the *Aphrodite* and was gratified by her look of awe.

Scotty ushered them quickly up the gangplank, but he was too late. A flashlight went off and Leah spun around as a press reporter pushed through the small gathering of journalists to ask: 'New ladyfriend, Mr Ryan?'

Dan ignored him.

'I'm his charlady . . . I make a great cuppa,' Leah called over her shoulder.

Dan whisked Leah quickly out of sight. 'Say nothing to them, Leah, they hound us like wolves sometimes.'

As they entered the main bar, she stopped. 'Gosh. I bet this is expensive to hire. I'd like to pay something towards it.'

Scotty's mouth dropped open. He gawped at Leah as if she had two heads.

Dan chuckled. 'You want to pay, do you? For what, exactly?'

Leah shrugged. 'For the charter, of course.'

Scotty whispered, 'Is she having a laugh?'

Dan didn't enlighten her. 'I've put you in the Master Stateroom,' was all he said. 'I will show you through.'

'There's no need, Dan, a single bunk will be fine.'

He took her elbow, informing her, 'We don't do bunks on the *Aphrodite*.' And he escorted her out.

It had been a long journey, and Scotty made straight for the

bar. He deserved a drink after that helicopter ride. 'My usual -
Navy Seal, please.'

The little man then tried to mount a bar stool, but it was
impossible. The barman poured equal measures of Jagermeister,
tequila and rum into the shaker, then passed Scotty his folding
stepladder. With great relief, the little fellow used it to clamber
up then hoist himself onto the stool. Thank God no one was
watching! He then folded the steps and handed them back over
the counter to the bartender before taking a refreshing swig of
his favourite drink. There wasn't much a Navy Seal couldn't
cure, he thought contentedly, from heartache to bellyache.

15

A SCREAMING ORGASM

The *Aphrodite* gained speed as she left the confines of the harbour and entered into clear blue waters, sailing around the headland to hug the coastline. The paparazzi were left far behind on the quayside.

'I thought we'd anchor in a secluded bay. It will stop the press from having a field day,' Dan said as he escorted Leah to the Master Stateroom. 'And here we are.' He held the door open for her as she stepped into the room.

'Thank you. Oh wow!' Leah stopped in her tracks. Everything about the room screamed quality. 'This is beautiful and my favourite colours.' She hastened towards the panoramic window, trailing her fingers on the wall as she went. She touched the curtains, the cushions. 'The colours are like sand and turquoise sea. I absolutely love it here. Thank you, Dan.' Secretly, she was awed by her surroundings and thought the rental must have cost him a packet.

Dan smiled. 'I'll let you get unpacked. Join me in the bar when you're ready - and please stop worrying about the money. I can read your thoughts, you know.'

Leah nodded. 'All right, I promise.' She added, 'You might have to drag me away from this room though. The only other luxurious room I've been in was nine years ago.'

'Really? Don't you go on holiday?'

'Yes, but we usually only stay in a cottage. Nothing on this scale, but they're all very nice,' Leah explained.

'Is that all you can afford?'

'No, not any more, but we do enjoy renting a cottage in the countryside because it's so different from where we live in a seaside town - although there is nothing quite like riding on the beach.'

Just then Dan's phone rang. 'Excuse me,' he said, adding, 'so I will meet you in the bar when you're ready.'

Leah watched him leave the room. She could hear him talking on the phone as he walked away. Closing the door behind him, she felt the cushions on the window seats and couldn't resist their softness. She gazed out to sea and wondered exactly what she and Dan would be talking about later. Picking up one of the scatter cushions, she cuddled it as she sat, entranced by the breath-taking view.

Scotty was propping up the bar when Leah walked in about fifteen minutes later.

'May I?' she asked, as she took the stool next to him. 'Gosh, these stools are high, aren't they?'

'Yeah, they sure are. Stay and chat. Have a Sex in the Sand cocktail,' Scotty said and winked.

'You mean Sex on the Beach.'

'Ha. I'm wrong again. I pride myself on being wrong most of the time.'

Leah sipped her delicious orangey and peachy cocktail whilst wondering what Tom was up to. She took a sly glance at Scotty. 'Do you have to fly with Dan, even if it makes you so sick?'

Scotty slugged his cocktail back. 'Oh, I'm feeling a whole lot better now. I'm off-duty - but I can still fight off a masked marauder.'

'I'm sure you can. Fancy another - or should you sleep it off?' Leah asked after a while when there was still no sign of Dan.

'Why not. I'll have another Navy Seal - and how about a Kinky Organism for you?'

'Screaming Orgasm,' corrected Leah in a whisper.

'Same thing, isn't it?' Scotty looked at Leah who was trying her best to suppress her mirth.

They both burst out laughing then downed the cocktails, ignoring the bartender's raised eyebrows. Scotty ordered more, then Leah fell off the bar stool, at which they both laughed helplessly again.

'Another?' Scotty enquired.

'I shouldn't really.' She looked at the door.

'Oh, if he's on a phone call he could be hours,' the little man said, slurring his words slightly.

'In that case, yes, thanks. I will have a Gamble.' Leah thought the gin in it would sit nicely with the first two cocktails. She was already feeling pretty light-headed though.

'And I will have a Brain Eraser.'

'A Brain Eraser?' Leah starting laughing and couldn't stop. 'What's one of those, Scotty?' she managed.

'It's a cocktail,' Scotty said with dignity. Then: 'Tell me, Leah, do you like a gamble?' He burped and said, 'Pardon.'

'Depends. Will we get into trouble?'

'Maybe.'

'In that case, bring it on.' Leah drank up. 'What are we waiting for?'

Scotty almost fell off his stool too, but Leah caught him just in time. While the barman stared, the two of them giggled: 'Whoops-a-daisy!'

THE YACHT WAS WELL ON ITS WAY TO ANCHOR IN THE BAY AS Dan walked around in the Stateroom with his iPhone to his ear. He was distracted when he thought he saw a figure drop by his window and then there was a loud splash. No, it couldn't be what he thought. He glanced out but saw nothing.

A little while later Dan was once more immersed in his iPad when he heard screams and shouts, then an engine started up.

'What the hell?' Dan saw his speedboat race past with Scotty at the helm. A second later, a water-skier literally flew by, doing acrobatics.

'Scotty? Leah? Oh my God.' Dan dashed out onto the deck. He heard the speedboat engine come from the starboard side this time. It whizzed past him.

Leah waved frantically, but she was laughing.

'Leah, what are you doing? Of course, she can't hear me out there,' Dan said out loud.

Leah did a stylish little jump then waved at Dan again. She was showing off her prowess on the water-skis.

'Oh God. You'll hurt yourself.' Dan ran to the bow as they passed the yacht again. He clenched his fist at Scotty. 'Bring Leah back at once!' he bawled. But again, he knew that his voice wouldn't be heard over the sound of the engine.

Scotty was having the time of his life as Leah twisted and

turned on the skis. She motioned for Dan to come out on the water to join her. Then she jumped high, missing the bow and Dan by millimetres.

'Get me a vessel, I need to stop these drunken lunatics!' Dan shouted to a member of the crew as he ran to the stern.

Leah leaped again, and at that point, Scotty turned the speedboat and raced towards the *Aphrodite*.

'Come on, Dan, be a daredevil, embrace risk!' Leah hollered, but he couldn't hear her. She then spotted a jet ski come from behind the yacht.

Scotty also saw the jet ski as it moved in front of them. He quickly turned the speedboat – and that was when Leah lost her balance for a moment. On regaining it, she realised that the jet ski was pulling Dan on a 'banana boat' – an inflatable small craft. Panicking, she screamed: 'Duck, Dan, duck!'

Dan saw Leah hurtling towards him on the water skis. He ducked as Leah jumped over the banana boat and lost his own balance in turn, falling into the sea.

Leah looked back, then laughed at Dan's predicament. Gulping and looking furious, he was clinging to the banana boat for dear life.

BACK ON THE *APHRODITE*, WHICH HAD DROPPED ANCHOR NOW, order had been restored. Dan had taken a shower and when he walked into the bar, he was wearing clean slacks and a open-necked short-sleeved shirt.

Leah looked up from drinking her water. She giggled. 'Sorry I knocked you off your banana.'

'It's not funny. Either one of us could have lost life or limb. I will have a beer,' Dan said to the bartender. He went and sat on the periphery of the bar and motioned that Leah should sit with him.

Leah got down from her stool and slightly unsteadily made her way across to him, the after-effects of the cocktails still in evidence. 'Dan, relax, it was harmless fun.'

'Huh. I'm afraid I can't agree. But look - we're mooring soon. There is a very good taverna on the sea-front. We'll have dinner there if that's OK - unless you'd like to eat here?'

'The taverna sounds lovely, thank you.'

'Scotty will accompany us but he won't be sharing our table.' Dan tutted. 'Seriously, you should be more careful when drinking and water-skiing. I shall be having a word with him.'

'Don't tell him off, it was my idea. I was the one who got him drunk and suggested we have some fun. I was bored when you didn't come back. It was all my idea, Dan, honestly.'

Scotty was hanging back in the doorway; overhearing her defence of him, he stepped into the bar, saying, 'Is there any strong coffee going?'

'Take a bucketful, Scotty.' Dan looked across at Leah. 'Then have a sleep. Please be ready for seven p.m. Sharp.'

Leah whispered, 'Thank you, Dan. I owe you one.'

'I suggest you take a rest too. You look tired out. I'm just going to make a few more calls.' Dan stood up. 'I will give you a knock around seven o'clock too.' He bent down to kiss her cheek and she watched him walk away.

Scotty held onto his head. 'Thanks for not dropping me in it. We both know I was the one who plied you with drink and then challenged you to a dare.'

'Oh, don't worry about it. I had a great time. Right - I'm going for a lie-down. If I were you, I'd do the same.' Leah moved to the bar. 'Could I please have another water to go.'

DAN AND LEAH WERE EATING AT THE TAVERNA. HE WATCHED with amusement as she devoured the fresh cod, with buttered new potatoes and samphire. She had a healthy appetite, he was pleased to see.

'Do you like shellfish too?' he asked as she cleared her plate.

'Of course, I come from a seaside town. Fresh fish is in abundance. Plus I just love eating good food and this is good.'

'It doesn't show.'

'Oh, I keep fit with Pilates and horse riding when I'm not running my coffee shops and doing the school run. Tom likes to ride so we try to get out at least once a week but it's difficult in winter. We have to ride in the floodlit school then, and getting a free hour in the arena there is hard. Mmm, that was delicious.' Leah put her knife and fork down and caught her breath when she saw that Dan was watching her intently. 'I have to admit I'm surprised that you have horses. I got that one wrong.'

'I will show you around properly when we get home,' Dan said before taking a sip of wine.

'Thank you, that would be lovely. Tell me, where do you actually come from?'

Dan pondered, scratching his chin. 'I was brought up in several cities. London, New York . . .'

'Paris?' Leah asked.

Dan laughed, 'Not quite Paris, but Zurich. However, my father was born on the Greek island of Alonnisos. He was a bit of a hero.'

'Wow. Tom will love that his grandfather was a Greek hero.'

'And you? Where do you actually live?'

Leah laughed. 'We've never really had a chance to properly talk to each other, have we? I come from Whitby in Yorkshire.

Did you know that Dracula came ashore on our beach disguised as a huge black dog? Not unlike Hero, but of course Dracula was vicious. Hero is not.'

'Dracula vicious? Never. But what I do know is that I shall have to visit this Whitby. It must be a great place.' Dan gazed into her eyes.

The music struck up.

'Would you like to dance?' Dan put his wine glass down.

Leah took his hand as they walked to the dance floor. 'At least I can be myself this time.'

'Ah yes, your policeman stunt.'

'I was so scared coming down to London to search for you. You seemed to vanish from the face of the earth once we parted,' Leah murmured as she swayed gently in his arms.

'You tried to find me when you found out about Tom?'

'I did try, but my grandad was having his operation, thanks to you, and I was thrown into my café business at the same time when the owner had to sell up - again thanks to you. I tried several times to find you, but I was always told you were away or not interested: you'd disappeared.'

'You dealt with your grandfather, a new business *and* our son's birth?' Dan stopped momentarily.

'I just had to get on with it. It's what we Yorkshire lasses do.'

'Well, I'm amazed.'

Leah laughed as they danced some more. 'You make it sound like women have never had children before. Hello, we women do it every single day. All over the world.'

'Hm, but what did you do about childcare?'

'Oh, that was sorted out between me, Joey, Grandad Tom and the staff, and a few dear friends. You don't have to worry, Dan. Our son has had a lot of loving and a very good upbringing.' Leah fastened her eyes on Dan's chin, not daring to look up at him as they were so close.

SCOTTY OBSERVED THE COUPLE WITH INTEREST, DESPITE HIS hangover. He just wished he knew what they were talking about, as he was on orders to report back. However, they looked happy.

Dan and Leah swayed with a perfect rhythm, almost as if they'd been together for a lifetime. Then while the band had a break, the music changed to Beyoncé, singing 'Crazy in Love'. Leah broke free of Dan and did a little jump. As she danced, she suggestively shimmied near Dan. Amused by her little show, he then tried to join in, but they just ended up laughing. It looked quite magical to other people in the taverna. The two dancers were like a couple in love, enjoying a night out.

Scotty continued to watch on, amazed that his boss was actually relaxing, laughing even. Miracles would never cease!

DAN AND LEAH WALKED BACK TO THE SPEEDBOAT AND LEAH climbed in with the help of Dan, who said to the crew member, 'Take us back to the yacht, please, then return to pick up Scotty.'

'You can't leave him, Dan.' Leah scanned the jetty for her little pal but couldn't see him.

'They'll come back for him, I promise. Just relax.' Dan leaned back and spread his arms across the back of the leather seats.

Leah closed her eyes; she could feel him next to her, but not quite touching. She knew she'd be lucky if she came out of this with her heart intact. Leah wanted to keep her feet firmly grounded, but being so close in this boat made it almost impossible.

Over on the shore, Scotty saw the speedboat disappear and shook his fist at Dan.

Dan touched the nape of Leah's neck. 'Look, I think he's realised we've left him behind.'

Leah laughed rather shakily, thinking she might be going to die of bliss, and then the featherlight touch was gone. But they had both felt the electricity crackle between them.

BACK ON THE *APHRODITE*, DAN WALKED LEAH INTO THE BAR and asked her to take a seat whilst they had a nightcap. He brought her a glass of mineral water and placed it on the table beside her. 'Are you sure this is all you want?'

'Yes, thank you. I'm not normally a big drinker. You must understand this afternoon was a boredom thing.' Leah took her glass from him.

'Ouch. I do realise it was down to me that you got smashed out of your skull with my security man and then went water-skiing to try and break a leg. I know it was my fault and unforgivable of me. I brought you here to talk and then I took a business call. I don't blame you at all.'

'Maybe I should have come looking for you.'

'Or maybe I should have cut the phone call short. It was rude of me not to.' Dan took a sip of his brandy; he was about to say something when Scotty bowled in. 'You got here then?'

'No thanks to you, boss,' Scotty complained. 'Did I miss anything?'

'No, not a thing, Scotty, so whoever you're reporting back to, just forget it.' Dan finished off his brandy and held his hand out to Leah. 'I shall walk you to your room. I suggest you get an early night as we'll be exploring the island in the morning.'

Leah took hold of Dan's hand, saying, 'Goodnight, Scotty, I had fun today, thank you.'

Scotty nodded. 'So did I, young lady, so did I.' And it was true. The little man watched them leave then walked out in the opposite direction. He had a phone call to make.

16

REAL ALE

L eah put on cream slacks, a turquoise top and sneakers and was thankful that Joey had had the foresight to bring her some extra clothes when he came down from Whitby.

'I wonder if I will need a mac?' she mused aloud.

'First signs of madness so I hear, talking to oneself.' It was Dan, standing in the doorway.

'Sorry, but you must know how unpredictable the British weather is.' Leah grabbed her raincoat and walked across the room. 'I slept amazingly well. These beds are really comfortable. Did you sleep?'

'No, I could hear someone snoring.'

'Me?'

'I hope it wasn't you. No, it was Scotty. I should have banned him to the hotel on the headland.' Dan pushed a strand of Leah's hair behind her ear; how could he tell her that he had lain restless and horny while thinking about what had happened nine years ago and the day in the barn when history had repeated itself. He was longing to take her in his arms again, but instead he said, 'Right, let's get going.'

As she walked past him, her delicate scent floated by with her. It was like an exquisite flower.

OUT ON DECK, DAN AND LEAH WERE HELPED INTO THE speedboat. Leah turned. 'Is Scotty coming with us?'

'I'm afraid he's still suffering from a hangover, so we'll have to go it alone.' Dan added, 'He only does this on the rare occasion, and after all, we all need to let our hair down once in a while.'

Leah self-consciously patted her loose chignon. 'I'm afraid I too take the blame.'

'He doesn't need too much encouragement, Leah, so don't beat yourself up.' Dan took a seat.

'Am I allowed to know where we are going or is it a surprise?'

'Just a secluded beach where we can talk, without Scotty listening in. He's a great security man and takes everything seriously, but he can be a bit of an old woman. You know, fussing about every little detail and eavesdropping when he shouldn't.' Dan smiled at Leah.

There was no doubt he was good-looking, she thought, with his wavy haircut; he was cleanshaven and had the most amazing long eyelashes that outlined his lovely green-blue eyes.

What was she doing? Assessing him from under her lashes as if he was a suitor. Her mind sprang back to their time in the barn. How on earth did they end up making love on the hay? It was almost as if they had gone back nine years, to when they had first met. To when she had been escorted onto the Byzantine Hotel roof and to the point when she had checked she had her condoms with her . . . but then something strange had happened: someone had pushed her off the roof and the multicoloured foil packets had flown through the air like heavy confetti. Thankfully, Dan had informed her that he had a supply of them, since he owned his own condom company. The more she thought about it, the more this had confused her over the years. Had it been a faulty batch?

'You're very quiet. Is it something I've said?' Dan asked.

Leah blushed because of her thoughts. 'No. I'm just thinking about Tom and the last few days. I'm sorry this has been such a bombshell for you. No warning, no phone call to try and break the news gently.'

'I imagine the dental hygienist routine was Ruby's idea,' he said and drew his brows together in mock sternness.

Leah giggled. 'You know Ruby better than me.'

'I do - and it was right up her street. And the crane stunt?'

'Ruby.'

'I thought so. Ah, we are here at Portelet Tower, or Janvrin's Tomb.' Dan looked at her sneakers. 'You might want to take your shoes off and paddle in the shallows.'

'And here was me thinking . . .'

'What – that I might carry you?'

'No. I just thought the boat might get nearer, that's all.'

'Well, I'm carrying the picnic basket and I'm taking my shoes off and turning up my trouser legs.'

'In that case, I will paddle too,' said Leah with a smile.

'Good girl. It's nice that you're not prissy, like some women I know.' Dan rolled up his trouser legs. 'Are you ready for an adventure?'

'I must admit, I didn't take you for a paddling kind of guy.'

'Live and learn, young lady, live and learn.' Dan put his foot in the water and shuddered. 'It's chilly.'

Leah boldly stepped into the water. 'Not for a northern girl. Live and learn, young man, live and learn. Come on!'

DAN PLACED THE PICNIC BASKET ON THE BEACH ALONG WITH his shoes. Leah was already on the beach and scouting around.

'What are you looking for?' Dan ensured that the picnic basket was away from the water's edge before he joined her.

'I'm looking for young crabs that have been trapped in the shallow rock pools. I try and move them to a deeper pool where there is cover,' Leah said.

'That's very thoughtful.' Dan watched her gently place a small crab out of harm's way.

'Grandad Thomas always taught us to help the sea creatures and all the wildlife around where we live. When I was young, we raised a fox cub. He used to run down the hedgerow when he heard me. We still try to carry on the tradition with Tom and his friends, and last year we successfully saved five hedgehogs from a terrible fate.' Leah was lost in her story, then she glanced up to find Dan watching her intently. 'What?'

'I was just thinking what a well-rounded young man our son will grow up to be.'

'You think so?'

'Yes, I do. Look, here's another sea creature who needs rescuing.'

'Should I take it?'

Dan lifted the crab onto his hand. 'Ouch, he's biting me.'

Leah laughed. 'Here, let me. You need to pick them up carefully, like this.' She took the crab gently by his shell so that he couldn't dig his pincers into her too.

'You make it look so easy.'

'It is, Dan, and one of the main reasons I do it is that the shallow pools can get warm at this time of year and can in extreme cases kill these little guys and girls.' Leah found one more and rescued it.

'Shall we go up to the tower? We'll have to be careful as these rocks are quite slippery.' Dan stood up and went to retrieve the picnic basket.

They made their way up to the tomb and Leah read the plaque outside. 'Gosh, that is so sad,' she said. 'Poor Philippe, captain of the *Esther*, catching the plague in 1721 and not being allowed to go home again, nor to see his wife and his family, and being buried here on this islet. I don't think we appreciate how good we've got it today.' She sighed, then asked: 'So, what things did you want to talk about?'

'Well, I often wondered what happened when I left you that morning at the Byzantine Hotel.'

'You did?' Leah was astounded. *Now, now, calm down*, she told herself.

'Well, I slept some more,' she said aloud. 'You left early, if I remember right.'

'Very early.'

'I took a leisurely bath. Then I met Joey outside the hotel. Oh, but first when I went to the desk, the concierge there gave me your gift. It was a wonderful gesture,' Leah remembered. 'I'd never had such a lovely phone before.'

'I'm so glad you liked it. But what I'd like to know more is how you got to be there in the first place. I mean, I have heard some of it, but I'd like to hear the full story.' Dan held his hand out. 'First we should have some lunch. Let's find a nice place to sit. I think there is a blanket in the basket.'

'You thought of everything,' beamed Leah.

'Not me. My staff got this ready, so let's enjoy it.' Dan seemed reluctant to let go of her hand, but he had to release her as he opened the basket.

Leah took the blanket and laid it in a grassy dip which was warmed by the sun. 'This place seems idyllic even though it is a tomb. I hope Philippe doesn't mind.'

Dan laid out the food, which had been wrapped superbly, onto the plates.

Not knowing what to expect, Leah had feared the butties might be delicate finger sandwiches so she was pleasantly surprised to see chunky cheese and pickle sandwiches.

'I'm surprised at these butties,' she blurted out.

Dan grinned at her. 'I get enough of those delicate finger foods. I need a proper sandwich.'

'So do women.'

'Then why do we put up with the other sort? Here, have a humongous cheese sandwich.' Dan handed her a doorstep-sized butty.

'This is what I call a proper sandwich, thank you. Have they packed any water?' Leah asked.

Dan frowned. 'I forgot to ask for water, but we do have a bottle of the finest wine.'

'Well, just a small one then and a packet of crisps, please. I love eating crisps inside a butty.'

'And so do I – how's that for a coincidence.' Dan watched Leah pull her sandwich apart and pile on the crisps. He followed suit. Then he bit into his sandwich. 'Mm, this is nice.'

'And the first time you've had crisps on your butty,' Leah observed.

Dan grinned. 'Caught out bang to rights. But I have to say, Leah, it tastes very good.'

'I'm pleased you approve. I personally think it's the only way to finish off a cheese butty - and several other butties, come to think of it.' Leah accepted a glass of wine.

AFTER A LEISURELY LUNCH AND A COUPLE OF GLASSES OF WINE, Leah realised their conversation had been just small talk. Dan was laid back, his hands behind his head.

'I feel so tired,' he admitted.

'Close your eyes and I will tell you the full story of how I came down to London all those years ago,' suggested Leah.

'I might just do that.'

She settled herself and thought how best to start. At the beginning, she decided.

'Well, a few weeks before I met you, I found out that my grandad needed a complex new knee operation that was not covered on the NHS list. He was in a lot of pain and Joey and I were desperate to help him. It meant we would have to raise money for his operation. We booked it with the pioneering surgeon then had a deadline in which to find the fee. I tried various little jobs and then the pair of us did several money-raising jaunts, which included a wing-walking stunt, a para-chute jump and water-skiing, to name but a few. The deadline was looming close and Joey suggested there was a way we could earn more money more quickly. He seems to know about these things as he's lived away from Whitby and done all sorts.'

Leah took a deep breath before saying in a small voice: 'I was loath to do anything like that. In fact, I was ready to run a mile. But love for my grandad saw me through. It was the only way we were going to help him.' She looked down at her hands. 'Thankfully, I got you - and the rest, as they say, is history.'

When there was no response, Leah looked across at Dan. His eyes were closed, his breathing deep and even.

'Oh, you heard none of that. You are so tired and the wine must have just tipped the scales. I think I will just rest my head here next to you for a while; the temptation is just so great,' Leah said softly.

Lying down, she sighed contentedly. 'If only life was this relaxed all of the time.' As her eyes closed, she too drifted off.

LEAH SHIVERED, THEN NUZZLED IN CLOSER TO THE WARM BODY beside her until the breeze got up a little stronger and her shivers got much worse. Opening her eyes, she propped herself up on her elbow to watch Dan, who was still asleep. She could watch him all day like this. Goodness, his eyelashes were long - just like Tom's. As she scanned every single millimetre of his face and committed it to memory, she felt a spit of rain.

'Darn it, the British weather.' Standing up, she pulled on her mackintosh, but as she put her arm in the sleeve she looked down at the beach, then exclaimed, 'Oh no! Dan, Dan, wake up! We have a big problem.'

17

STRANDED

Leah was starting to feel giddy with worry. She checked for her phone, then remembered that she had left it on charge in her stateroom on the *Aphrodite*.

'Dan,' she said more loudly.

His eyes opened slowly. 'Gosh,' he said woozily, 'I must have fallen off to sleep for a few minutes.'

'I think we both went to sleep but it's more like a few hours. We're stranded by the tide. I'm just hoping you brought your phone with you?' But Leah knew the answer before he shook his head.

Dan sat up. 'No – for once I thought I'd leave it behind because I didn't want any interruptions. What do you mean, we're stranded?' He looked around and then stood up and checked again. 'Oh Lord, we are completely cut off. Let's just go down to the water's edge and see how deep it is.'

'I think we should stay high up so we can call for help. If we see anyone on the mainland we can wave or maybe start a fire.' Leah grabbed his arm. 'Don't think of swimming. Look down there, that looks like a riptide.'

'How can you tell?'

'Because I've seen them before, that's how.'

'But the weather's closing in.'

'And we'd be better staying on land. At least if we see anyone we can wave and shout.' Leah moved a little away. 'Look there, now you can see the riptide.'

'I can see a lizard, but no riptide.' Dan pointed to the building just a few yards away. 'I wonder if there's anyone there?'

'There was no one when I last looked. Will anyone miss us from the yacht, do you think?'

Dan scoffed. 'Would *you* search for your boss if he had gone missing with a woman friend and obviously wanted some privacy? So, in answer to your question, no, I don't think so. My crew would be too worried about annoying me.'

'What about Scotty?'

'Possibly, but only possibly.'

Leah picked up the blanket to stop it getting wet because now the drizzle was starting in earnest. 'Let's just go nearer to the tower. We might be able to get shelter.'

'I suppose we should, at least until the rain stops. You do realise we could be here a while.' Dan felt such a fool for letting this happen.

'I guess so, but if my company is so bad, we can both stand at either end of the tower.' Leah yawned. 'I don't know why I'm so tired as I slept really well last night. And then when you fell asleep without listening to my explanation as to why I was in London all those years ago, I must have dropped off myself.'

'I'm sorry, I didn't mean to fall asleep on you and I will be honest - I don't remember any of what you said.' Dan felt doubly ashamed that he'd been so remiss.

'Oh look, it's no biggie. I can tell you again sometime, but right now I think we need to either get out of the rain or shout really loudly for help, because if not, we've got a long wait."

Dan started laughing.

'What's so funny?'

'Just that I can run a multi-million-pound business – well, several, actually - and yet I get us stranded on the only beach I chose out of many this island has to offer. I read about it in the middle of the night when I couldn't sleep and found that it's one of the most beautiful beaches in the world. We're certainly getting a good look at it.' Dan spotted someone across the water on the mainland. 'Hey, help, we are stranded. Hey!'

The man waved back, but soon went out of sight.

Leah was disappointed. 'I think he's gone, Dan. Let's just go into the tower before we get wet through.'

'Yes, I suppose that makes sense.'

Leah took the lead. She marched up to the entrance only to leap back as a kit of pigeons flew out into the air.

Dan caught her in his arms as the blanket fell to the ground. 'Wow, I wasn't expecting a flock of birds to fly out,' he said.

'No, neither was I.' Leah had a firm hold of Dan's arm; she could feel the muscles under his jacket and admitted to herself that his biceps felt good and strong.

Dan put his arms around her waist, he was looking over her shoulder. 'Actually, we wouldn't like to stand in all that bird poo, would we?' His eyes were crinkling up around the edges.

In that moment Leah felt total happiness. Being with this man felt so comfortable and right, as well as exciting. 'I think this lunch on one of the most beautiful beaches in the world has turned out to be a bit of a disaster,' she said lightly.

Dan looked to the heavens. 'I think the rain is slowing down, so we may salvage this date yet.'

'It's a date, is it?' Leah felt like she was tempting fate. 'A lunch-date?'

'What kind of date did you think?'

'Oh nothing, I just wondered.'

Dan was just about to kiss Leah when they heard an engine. They both looked down and saw Scotty waving.

'Mr Dan, Mr Dan, we've come to rescue you,' shouted Scotty.

Dan dropped a quick kiss on Leah's lips. 'It looks like your hero has arrived to rescue us just when things were getting interesting.'

'Yes, it does.' *And just when I didn't want rescuing,* thought Leah.

'The rocks will be extra slippery after the rain, so let's take care. Come on, Leah.' Dan tugged her hand.

'We need our picnic basket, they're too expensive to leave,' Leah said, pointing to the basket in her sights.

'This is something I could easily get to like about you. You always do the right thing,' Dan said softly.

'Not always,' Leah mumbled, wishing she had persisted in getting in touch with him before Tom was born, rather than let herself be put off. Why on earth had she listened to that catty woman, especially now she had met Chelsea and got the measure of her. 'Will you tell me something?' she asked.

'Yes, anything.' Dan looked at her tenderly.

'How long has Chelsea worked for you?'

'Strange question.' Dan took a deep breath. 'Ten years, I think; seems like a lifetime sometimes when she whines on like she does.'

And one more question. That night when I bungee-jumped into your arms, did it have anything to do with her? Oh, how Leah ached to ask that question. Because the more she thought about that night, the more she thought he'd been running away from something or someone. Was it Chelsea? Did they have a bond, did she have a hold on him? Or was it like the old veteran had said: 'She's after him, but he's not interested.'

'Take my hand, Leah, it gets a bit steep down here,'

said Dan.

Leah put her hand in his, they looked at each other and Dan saw such a sadness in her face.

'Don't worry, we'll get you into the speedboat safely,' he promised.

'I know.'

'Then why the sad face?'

Quick, think, think. 'I was just thinking about Philippe and his family,' Leah lied, on the verge of tears. 'It was so tragic that he spent his last days quarantined on his boat without his family being able to go to him. That must have been so hard, and then he was buried here, still alone.' Leah cleared her throat and hoped she'd pulled it off as she didn't want Dan to know what she was really feeling.

Dan squeezed her hand. 'You're a sentimental woman. Right, here we are, thank heavens.'

A younger crew member helped Scotty assist Leah into the boat. She didn't feel like saying she could manage when there were gentlemen about to help her. Dan got in too.

'Thank you, Scotty. It's such a relief to see you as we thought we would be there until the tide went out again,' Leah told him politely and she and the little man high-fived. Maybe it was a good thing that Scotty had arrived when he did, Leah thought privately; if not, she and Dan would have probably got into a bigger mess than just being stranded. Things were moving much too fast and she was worried about losing control. And yet she couldn't help but think about what might have happened . . .

AS THEY WENT BACK TO THE YACHT, THEY WERE BOTH VERY quiet. Dan's thigh was touching Leah's as they were squashed together because Scotty was sitting in the bows with them.

'Chelsea has been calling you, boss. Apparently, she needs to speak to you quite urgently,' said Scotty with a wink at Leah.

'Did she say what it was about?' Dan asked.

'She muttered on about some stock prices, but I wasn't listening. I was hungover, as well you know.'

'So you were, Scotty. I remember your snoring keeping me awake. Remind me to banish you to a cabin as far away from mine as possible.' Dan smiled at Leah. 'You slept well, didn't you?'

'Yes, I did. I wasn't disturbed,' Leah replied. *More's the pity.* There it was again, that naughty inner voice.

'Did you get anything sorted about young Tom?' Scotty asked her.

Leah was quick on the uptake. 'Well, as you know we've got a few school holidays coming up so Dan is going to work around them, and then after the summer holidays we will fix up something more permanent, won't we, Dan?'

'Absolutely.' Dan's eyes were laughing at her again. 'Leah has everything organised.'

'I thought Chelsea was going to look at your diary, Mr Dan?' Scotty rubbed his hands together. 'I am personally going to enjoy seeing what happens when the shit hits the flamin' fan.'

'She was,' Dan replied, 'but I'm letting Leah take care of that as she is Tom's mother.'

See how you feel about that, *Chelsea Saffer,* Leah thought to herself. She shuffled about a bit, trying to get comfortable, and Dan stretched his right arm over the back of her shoulders.

'So, we are going back tomorrow and Sisco will be driving Joey and the kids home to Whitby, so I thought we could fly you straight home, Leah - if that's OK with you?'

'Yes, that's fine. I will have to collect the rest of my things from your place another time. Although I can talk to Joey about that when I ring Tom.'

'Well, actually, it's my mother's birthday next week and we are having a birthday bash. I was hoping you could be there - you, Tom and Joey, that is - and your grandfather if he wants to come.' Dan couldn't gauge Leah's thoughts.

'Grandad isn't a social animal, but I can ask him. As for us three, I will do my best to free up the time.' Leah went quiet. 'What can I buy her, Dan?'

'Don't you think you've given her enough? She has Tom. I reckon she'll be happy enough with him.' As they came alongside the *Aphrodite*, Dan said: 'We're here now, so when we're back on board I will give you some time to talk to Tom and Joey. We can have dinner here if you like?'

'If you're not too busy. It sounds like you need to speak to Chelsea again.' Leah took his hand and was helped up onto the *Aphrodite*.

'Again?' Dan queried.

'Wasn't it Chelsea you were speaking to yesterday while I was in the bar with Scotty?' She had felt so jealous, and that was when her reckless spirit took hold.

Dan looked surprised. 'No, it was Stephan.'

'Oh. I just assumed because you were so long . . . I'm sorry,' Leah said simply.

'No need. I would have assumed the same. Stephan is my cousin's son. I was helping him with a business crisis, that's why the call took so long. Right - shall we meet in the bar at seven?' Dan seemed eager to get away from her, Leah noted.

She just nodded and watched him walk away from her. Then she thanked Scotty again and went to telephone Tom.

AT SEVEN O'CLOCK SCOTTY FOUND LEAH LEANING ON THE RAIL looking out to sea. She was wearing navy-blue slacks and a cream linen blouse with high-heeled patent shoes.

'Mr Dan won't be too long, he's on the phone with his PA,' Scotty informed her.

'Thank you.' Leah kept on staring out to sea.

'Are you all right, lassie?'

There was a long pause. 'Yes, but I just wonder why he really invited me here, 'cos it sure isn't to talk about Tom. Because as you can see, he's not here. You know the man is so overworked he fell asleep at the tower?'

'Is that why you got stranded?'

'I must admit, I'm not used to drinking wine on a lunchtime so I fell asleep too,' Leah confessed.

'So you slept together?'

'No! Well, yes - but not in that way. I mean, I just closed my eyes and when I woke up, we were lost at sea, so to speak.' Leah turned to look at Scotty, who was laughing.

'You're so easy to wind up,' he chuckled. 'But seriously, I've been telling him for weeks to take a break. I know he's tired out. I see a lot more than Dan and the others think. I know they reckon I'm stupid and I don't take things in, but I know more than they give me credit for.' Scotty moved to one side to let Leah go past him. Kindly, he added: 'I'm hoping he will be better company for you tonight. You don't deserve to be kept waiting like this. If I were him, I'd think I was very lucky indeed.'

Leah dropped a kiss on the little man's cheek. 'I'm sorry if I was rude to you before, and I hope I didn't hurt you with my bag when I slugged you.' She then walked away.

Scotty sighed happily and touched his cheek where she'd kissed him. He had a lot of time for this young lady. She could make his boss seriously happy.

18

THE LIGHTNING TREE

Leah walked into the bar to see that a table had been set near to the window looking out to sea. For some reason she felt that Dan had estranged himself from her; he had gone quiet on her ever since Scotty had mentioned Chelsea's call. Did he have some kind of emotional tie with the woman? Is that why the latter was so spiky? But then there was also animosity between Chelsea, Sophie and Ruby - so what was going on? *What kind of hold did she have over him?*

As Leah pondered these thoughts, Dan walked into the room and strode across to the dining table where she was waiting.

'I never knew gannets could be found around Jersey,' Leah said as she watched them dive expertly after a shoal of fish.

'I believe they're the Alderney Gannets. They are precision personified and I could watch them for a lifetime.' Dan put a hand on her shoulder as they watched for a few peaceful minutes.

Dive after dive, the birds flew like spears into the water. Then, as suddenly as they had started, they flew off.

'It looks like the shoal have swum deeper,' Leah said.

'Yes. My captain says it's usually the dolphins and the whales that send the smaller fish towards the surface.' Dan held a chair out for Leah.

Leah sat opposite Dan as he took his seat. He sighed and said, 'What am I going to do with you, Leah Jensen? In just a few short days you've turned my world upside down.'

The waiter came over to their table and gave Dan and Leah a menu each. Leah licked her lips.

'Gosh, this puts my café food to shame. I think I will have the lobster pasta to start and maybe the Beef Wellington for my main, please,' she said to the waiter.

'Make that two.' And then Dan pointed to the wine list and winked at the waiter. When they were alone again, he said, 'So, you told me about your riding holiday - what date is it? If I can get the time off, I will bring Galahad up for a couple of days.'

'Ooh, Tom will love that. I will give you the exact days when I consult my diary.' Leah saw the waiter bring two glasses of wine on a tray. 'Oh, I can't drink more wine, Dan. Look what happened to us at lunchtime.'

'I think they were exceptional circumstances, don't you? Besides, we go back to drinking water, coffee and tea tomorrow. And the wine I have chosen is fit for a queen to go with our starter.'

'What kind of wine is it?' Leah asked.

'It's the Windsor Great Park sparkling wine. It goes superbly with the lobster.'

'When you put it like that, how can one resist.'

'That's my girl. Now, how was Tom?'

'Well, I think he would have liked to speak to you, but I wasn't sure if you were busy still talking to your PA. So, I said you might phone him in the morning.'

Dan was apologetic. 'I'm sorry, this dad role is so new to me I hardly know what to do right.'

'It will come over time. However, I will warn you, when you get those three boys together, they can be quite demanding, so be prepared for that. On the whole they're good lads.' Leah pointed to the hump-back whale as it surfaced. 'Wow! Look at that! Oh Dan – a real whale!'

The awe-inspiring creature was only a few feet away.

'The captain was right – that *is* why the gannets were having a feeding frenzy. The whales had obviously brought the fish to the surface. Lucky for the gannets.'

Leah accepted her starter from the waiter. 'Thank you.' She immediately gazed back at the whale as it flapped its tail in a dive. The sight made her gasp. 'Don't you just feel privileged when you see nature so close up?' she said emotionally.

'I do.' It was true – Dan did feel choked up.

'Tom would have loved this, he's a great nature-lover.' Leah raised her glass. 'Cheers! This has made my time here extra special.'

'What, me or the whale?'

Leah replied naughtily, 'Why, the whale of course.'

'Oh, I'm crest-fallen.'

'A week ago, you would never have given me a thought, so how you can be crest-fallen is an impossibility. What I shall say is, you're a close second.'

Dan clinked his crystal glass with hers. 'I shall take that as a compliment.'

They tucked into the pasta with a lobster bisque sauce and they chatted between mouthfuls.

Dan enquired, 'So, what do you think of the wine?'

'Definitely fit for a queen. It's from the Queen's vineyard, did you say?'

'You knew the Queen had a vineyard in Windsor Great Park?'

'Not until you told me earlier.'

'At least I know you're listening.'

'Why wouldn't I? And yes, it's delicious.'

'Oops, look over at the skyline, I think there's a storm brewing.' Dan pointed to the horizon.

Leah shivered. 'I'm a bit scared of storms.'

'It may blow over if we're lucky,' he reassured her.

EVEN THOUGH LEAH TRIED TO ENJOY HER BEEF WELLINGTON and the bottle of Malbec, a rich red wine from South America that Dan had ordered to go with it, she sensed that the storm was indeed coming closer. At one point she physically jumped when she saw lightning flash across the sky.

'Are you OK?' Dan touched her hand, rubbing his thumb over her fingers. 'You're shaking.'

Leah gave him a scared little giggle. 'Oh, I'm sure I will get over it. If you count the number of seconds between the lightning and the thunder . . .'

'That's the number of miles it is away from us, or so we're told,' Dan finished for her.

'I thought it was a Yorkshire saying or an old wives' tale.'

'Are you calling me an old wife, Leah Jensen? Shame on you.' Dan grinned.

'Sorry, I think everything great comes from Yorkshire. I'm a bit biased, I suppose,' Leah said, trying to eat humble pie.

'From where I'm sitting, yes, I agree - everything great does come from Yorkshire.' Dan looked satisfied as Leah blushed. He raised his glass. 'I think we ought to drink a toast to our beautiful son.'

Leah raised her own glass. If she wasn't so worried about the storm, she could feel quite heady at his words. She still didn't know quite why he had brought her here. They'd not had long conversations about Tom, nor had Dan made a move on her, but more importantly they hadn't discussed what had happened in the far barn. Was that because it had meant more to her than it did to him?

EVENTUALLY THE LIGHTNING STOPPED AND THE RUMBLES OF thunder receded towards France.

Leah saw Scotty walking down the side of the yacht. 'He looks so lonely,' she mused, taking a sip of her red wine. 'What's his story, Dan?'

'The truth is, I don't really know. He's a friend of my mother's and he's just stuck around, much like Ruby, although Ruby has gone off and had a few flings over the years.'

'And your mum, has she not met anyone else?'

'No, there's been nothing serious. I know my father was a hell of a lot older than her, but I think she loved him. In some ways I wish she could meet someone, but I think she's happy enough being single, especially since you and Tom came into her life. What about your-'

At that very moment, Scotty himself walked into the bar. 'Sorry to bother you, Mr Dan,' he said, nodding at Leah, 'but the captain's going to take us into harbour, just in case this storm comes back. It's just a precautionary measure.' Seeing Leah's expression, he winked to cheer her up.

'Does he think it's going to come back?' she asked nervously.

'No, no I don't think so, but it would be remiss of him not to take us into the protection of the harbour,' Scotty explained. 'He's following the weather reports closely and was prepared for rain. It can get pretty rough out here and I for one want to keep my dinner down the hatch, so to speak. I mean, it'll be bad enough tomorrow when we get on that blooming chopper again. Hate the damn things!'

'So why do you go in them?' asked Leah.

'Because it is my job. I have to look after milord here, don't I?' Scotty raised his eyebrows.

Dan indicated Scotty should leave. 'Thank the captain for me.'

'I think that's my cue to go,' Scotty winked again at Leah.

'Do you always have to wink at beautiful women, Scotty?' Dan asked.

'No, the flamin' whale spit in my eye from his blowpipe. Of course I'm winking, sailor boy, what did you think?' Scotty dodged out of the way and went off to the bridge to talk to the captain.

Leah was laughing so hard, that even Dan began to join in.

'I wonder what else he has called you?' she giggled.

'Oh, he's called me all sorts. Scotty has a right old temper on him when he gets really pushed. Thankfully he's laid back most of the time.'

'Toe rag,' shouted Scotty from the doorway, then he scampered away, laughing.

This set Leah off again. 'I think he's funny, don't you?'

'Well, he's certainly made you laugh. You're quite a pair.'

'It's sad that you're so busy, you never have time to tread water so to speak,' Leah said. 'But going back to Scotty, I think the reason he's stuck around is because he loves to be needed and as I see it, he needs you. You're like a family to him. He's probably more like a father figure to you.'

'Possibly. I'd never thought about it like that.'

Under the window, on the outer deck, Scotty listened in. He wiped a tear from his eye.

Leah was relieved when they arrived safely into the harbour and the *Aphrodite* was securely berthed.

'Would you like to take a walk before bedtime?' asked Dan.

'I'd rather try and get to sleep, if you don't mind, because if the storm comes back, I know I will be petrified.' Leah reached up and kissed Dan on the cheek. 'Goodnight, Dan, and thank you for everything. It's been a wonderful few days.'

Dan watched her retreat, noticing how she stopped and looked anxiously out to sea.

'Is Leah all right?' Scotty asked, coming to join him. 'She looked really pasty when I passed her just now. I said hello but she just ran off to her cabin.'

Dan shook his head. 'She seems very apprehensive about the weather, which is worsening every minute. The storm is on its way back from the French coast, more forceful than before. I did try to talk to her about it but she wasn't really with me; her mind was on something else that she wouldn't open up about. It's not my place to push it.'

Scotty scratched his head. 'But you're always telling folk about pushing the envelope. Maybe you should have done it. What does it mean anyway? Seriously though, if you ask me, she needs a friend right now.'

'Sometimes people just need their own space, but if it pleases you, I will go and see if she's OK when the storm kicks off.'

'What about right now, boss?' Scotty tutted to himself.

'No, Scotty, no. She said she was going to have an early night.' And at the expression on Scotty's face: 'I think sex is the last thing she wants and I'm not discussing this!'

'I'm not talking about sex, you fool. I'm talking about getting her to a hotel on dry land so she feels safe. She'll never get any sleep on this thing. It's starting to feel like the chuffin'' waltzer at a fairground.' The little man looked exasperated. 'Ask for separate rooms if you're bothered, or if you get a suite, you stay on the sofa! Good grief - *I'll* go and check on her.' Scotty thumped his fist on the table.

'No, I'll go.'

'No, you won't. I'm going.'

'*I'm* going, I said.' Dan was about to stride away.

Scotty rushed to the door. 'We go together.'

SCOTTY GOT TO THE DOOR BEFORE DAN AS HIS LITTLE LEGS were going fifteen to the dozen. Dan wasn't far behind and crashed into him. For a moment, the two men scuffled.

'I'll knock, you wazzock,' Scotty muttered through gritted teeth.

'*I'm* knocking,' insisted Dan. 'Look - you go and phone a hotel.'

The cabin door suddenly flew open. 'I will knock the both of you through to next week, if you don't stop acting like kids. Have you spat your dummies out?' Leah demanded. 'Now what do you want? Some people are trying to sleep.'

Both Dan and Scotty looked dumbfounded.

How she didn't explode with laughter was a miracle, but her eyes gave her away.

'Are you laughing at us?' asked Dan disbelievingly.

'She's pushing the flamin' envelope, that's what she's doing,' Scotty said annoyingly.

The cruiser swayed, Leah fell forward and both men reached for her. They all lost their balance and ended up on the floor.

Dan was first up on his feet. He gave Leah his arm to grab, saying, 'Come on. We're going to a hotel. All of us.'

But Scotty couldn't get to his feet; he was rolling around on the floor as the cruiser rose and plunged as the wind worsened.

Both Leah and Dan helped him up.

'I say we rendezvous back here in five minutes. In the meantime, I will go and ring the hotel and order the limo,' said Dan. 'Just pack essentials, till morning.'

Leah nodded and watched Dan hold onto the walls to stay upright.

'Urgh, I need the bathroom.' Scotty ran as fast as he could. 'Back soon.'

Leah saw the waves tripping over each other in huge breakers in the harbour, but it wasn't this that terrified her although she had a healthy respect for the sea. It was the storm, the lightning and the massive rolling thunderclaps. They terrified her and with good reason. She saw what had happened to her favourite oak in the meadows that Cyril owned. Now it was known locally as the Lightning Tree. Scorched and misshapen. Ugly, yet beautiful. A reminder that the weather was to be respected too.

Hurriedly, Leah packed a few things and went into the corridor to wait for Dan and Scotty. The latter came back first, looking a little better.

'I think I'd better take them stugregones - them travel pills,' Scotty said. 'I ain't got sea legs, you see, Leah, no more than I've got air legs.'

'Oh, you mean Stugerons – those travel-sickness pills?'

'Yeah, that's what I said. Stugregones,' Scotty snapped irritably.

'I have one here,' Leah said. 'Just get yourself a glass of water.'

Scotty did so and swallowed the pill, hoping he could keep it down. 'Ta, Leah. Now before Mr Dan comes back, can you tell me what the hell "pushing the envelope" means.'

'Well, don't quote me on this, but I think what it means is trying to go beyond what has been done before in that area of expertise.'

'Oh. Right, you mean like me: I take my job seriously, so if I foiled an assassination plot, I'd be pushing the envelope. Of course, right – I've got it now. Thank you.' Scotty breathed a sigh. 'Let's go and see where that twerp has got to.'

As the words left the little man's lips, Dan rounded the corner. 'Well, that's not exactly pushing the envelope, is it, calling your boss a twerp. Right, you two, let's get going.'

It was then they heard the violent clash of thunder in the distance. Leah scooted forward. 'I need to get on land and out of this storm,' she said firmly. Inside she was quaking, and the theme tune 'The Lightning Tree' from the 1970s TV series *Follyfoot* sounded in her head. She'd first heard it while watching her grandad's prized video, and to her it was even more chilling than the theme to the movie *Titanic*. Every time there was a storm Leah would think about her own version of the song - but her reason for being so scared wasn't just the fate of the tree in Cyril's meadow. It was much closer to home than that.

19

A DANGEROUS GAME

The limousine pulled up by the hotel doors and Scotty helped Leah out. She flinched as forked white lightning flashed across the sky.

'This way, quickly,' urged Dan as he held open the door to the foyer.

Leah dashed inside as if the devil himself was after her. She was shaking like a leaf. Dan soon had the room key-cards in his hand, telling the reception staff that they would find their own way. He handed one to Scotty and waited until the little man had moved out of earshot before saying, 'They only had one single room so I gave it to Scotty. We have a small suite. I can sleep on the sofa there or if you prefer, I can go back to the yacht.'

'It's fine, Dan. I just want to get in the room, close the curtains and hide myself until the storm passes.' Leah looked at him. 'I have my reasons to hate this weather.'

Dan led her to the suite and once inside, he went straight to the mini-bar, saying, 'I'll get you a brandy.'

'Why?'

'Because you're trembling, that's why.'

Leah sat on the sofa. 'Very well, thank you. Then I'll turn in, if that's all right with you?'

'Of course it is.' Dan poured two brandies. He handed Leah a glass and cradled his own in his hands. 'Is it anything you want to share?'

Leah pondered, but not for long. More than twenty-five years had passed and she still couldn't talk about it. She shook her head. 'I'm sorry. I just can't go back to it. Not now.'

Dan watched as tears filled her eyes. 'Just remember I'm here should you need a shoulder to cry on.'

'I may take you up on it, one day,' said Leah as she slugged the rest of the brandy down. 'Do you need a duvet?'

Dan nodded. 'There's usually an extra blanket in the wardrobe. I'll make do with that.'

They walked through into the bedroom. The elegant room had a huge four-poster bed, an expensive heavy cotton duvet too, but Leah barely noticed; she just wanted to get her head onto the pillow and fall asleep, away from the storm, away from the memories of that tragic night.

WHEN DAN SAW THAT LEAH WAS STILL SHUDDERING uncontrollably, he could hold back no longer and took her in his arms.

'I can't leave you alone in this state. Where has my funny girl gone? The one who only ten minutes ago was telling me and Scotty off like two naughty kids. Hm?' Dan pushed her chin up so he could see into her eyes. 'Where's my feisty York-shire woman who does amazing things like climb onto cranes and almost slugs Ruby with a cream cake, all with no safety harness on. Where is she, Leah?'

Leah swallowed hard to try and stop the sick feeling

engulfing her. 'She's just scared of the storm,' she said in a tiny voice. 'It will pass. I will close the curtains.'

'Let me do it, then I will leave you in peace.' Dan reluctantly gave up his hold on her. He crossed the room, looked out of the window and noticed that the storm seemed to be dissipating before he closed the heavy curtains. Then he went to the wardrobe and got himself a blanket and pillow. 'If you need me, I'm just through in the next room.'

The moment Dan left the room, Leah quickly undressed and put on her pyjama shorts and T-shirt top. It wasn't until she slipped between the sheets that she appreciated the quality of the fresh-smelling bedlinen. She closed her eyes and hid under the covers, eventually falling asleep.

DAN LAY DOWN ON THE COUCH, THROWING THE BLANKET OVER himself. He frowned: it was a real fear - a phobia even? - that Leah had about storms. He hadn't wanted to push her into talking about it. He knew people would only ever talk if they wanted to. He smiled to himself. Scotty had been the rudest he'd ever been to him tonight, but Dan knew the little guy had really hit it off with Leah and had wanted to amuse her. Chuckling to himself, he closed his eyes.

He must have slept for several hours because he woke with a start and had to blink several times before he could focus. Leah was standing in her pjs, looking at him with puppy-dog eyes. She was quivering and then he knew why; the storm was back with a vengeance. Dan threw off his blanket and stood up.

As the thunder crashed, Leah flew into his arms, crying, 'Oh no, no no no!'

'Hey, Leah, don't be afraid. I'm here for you.' Dan gently lifted her into his arms, took her through into the bedroom and laid her on the bed. He lay down with her, just holding onto her and soothing her.

Leah let go and sobbed from her heart, wrenching sobs that shocked Dan to the core. He held her through hours or minutes that could not be counted, until the storm had virtually passed.

'What's this all about?' he asked. It was time to talk.

'I don't want to die. Not now,' Leah sobbed. 'Not like them. Not like them.'

'Like who, Leah?' he murmured.

'I was eight, the same age as Tom. The tree was struck by lightning and then it fell on our car.'

'Oh Lord.'

She sobbed into his shirt. 'I must have lost consciousness. When I came round, I couldn't see them. It was dark and I was trapped in the back seat. I should have died with them.' She wept again, as if her whole being would break under the weight of her grief. 'It seemed ages before I heard the sirens, saw the flashing lights. I should have died like my parents. Sometimes I wish I had!'

'No, don't say that. You are here for a reason.' Dan brushed her hair tenderly and wiped her tears. 'I never realised they had died. But of course, it makes sense. Your grandfather brought you up, didn't he? And that's why it was so important that you got the money so quickly.'

Leah nodded, exhausted from emotion. 'Maybe I'm overreacting, I don't know. I've just been frightened of storms ever since.'

'Understandably so.'

Just then, there was a knock on the suite door, and when Leah called, 'Come in,' wondering who it could possibly be, Scotty flounced in.

'Has he touched you?' he demanded. 'Mr Dan, I hope

you're not taking advantage of a poor, vulnerable young woman. I told him he'd to take the couch,' Scotty said sternly.

Leah wiped her tears with a tissue that Dan handed her. 'No, Scotty, Dan has been the perfect gentleman.'

'Oh, good. I just wanted to know if you were all right when the storm started again. I was afraid for you,' the little fellow said. 'Very well, I will be off then. Sorry to disturb you both.'

Dan was riled. 'Wait a minute - what exactly did you think I was going to do?'

'Take advantage. You good-looking types generally do sweet-talk the ladies.'

Leah crept further under the bedcovers, saying, 'I am in the room, you know. Come on, boys, it's nearly morning and we will all be flying back.'

'Ah, well, that's the other thing. Joey rang to say, because of the storm up north, Tom's school has been flooded and it will take a couple of days to sort it out. Harry's mum rang and then Troy's dad, so the boys don't need to get back to Whitby so urgently after all. So we can go back to Hambourne to be with them, I reckon, and Sisco can take you all home at his leisure.'

Dan raised his brow. 'Good thinking,' he said. 'I knew there was another reason I employed you.'

'Thank you, and I knew there was a reason I stayed with you.' Scotty walked out laughing, with his parting shot being, 'See you at breakfast.' Dan followed close behind and double-locked the door.

'Has the storm gone?' Leah asked.

Dan drew back the curtains. 'It has, and it's not as oppressive as it was last night.'

'Thank you,' said Leah, feeling quite awkward.

'For what? Have you tried to talk about the accident before?' Dan queried.

'No, I don't like remembering.' Leah wrapped her arms around herself.

'Have you thought about a therapist or being hypnotised?'

'I told you – I try not to think about it.' Leah shuddered.

'I can look into finding a good therapist for you, if you like?' Dan offered.

Leah's brow was furrowed. 'I suppose I'm not going to get the better of this unless I face up to it.'

'I'll see what I can find out.'

'I'd prefer it if Chelsea didn't know about this,' Leah mumbled.

'You have my word,' replied Dan. 'Do you want to use the shower first?'

'I think I've put you out enough. I'll take the bath after you've showered, if that's OK.' Then Leah grinned. 'Wasn't it sweet of Scotty to defend my honour like that?'

Dan couldn't resist. 'Yes, he was certainly pushing the envelope of insolence, wasn't he?'

'I've always had to defend myself before, so I really appreciated him having my back.' Leah climbed out of the bed to reach her bag. She bent over to take out her comb and started to run it slowly through her hair. When she straightened up, Dan was watching her.

'You certainly know how to raise a man's blood pressure, in that get-up,' he remarked slightly hoarsely.

'And here's me thinking you hadn't noticed,' Leah flirted wickedly.

'What?'

'Maybe we could share the shower?' Leah was playing with fire and she suddenly loved it.

'Minx. I should have known you were up to something.' Dan covered the short distance between them.

'It was all I could think of to get you to notice me.' Leah

moved so she was standing right up against him and what she found didn't disappoint.

'Notice you? It's taken me all of my strength to keep my hands off you. You saucy little baggage.' Dan swept her into his arms. 'I think a cold shower is called for.'

Leah wriggled in his arms as his tightened.

'If I remember rightly, you Yorkshire women can cope with cold water.' Dan kicked the bathroom door open and reached to turn on the shower. Then he stepped out of his clothes and Leah's eyes widened at his arousal. Dan grabbed her around the waist, slipped her pjs off and lifted her under the warm cascading water and pressed her against the shower wall. Kissing her passionately, he sank himself into her as she wrapped her legs around him.

Leah yelped, not with hurt but with excitement, and as they moved together, they both forgot about the consequences.

As Leah dried her hair, Dan fastened on a clean shirt, leaving it open-necked.

'I'll go down before you,' he said. 'We don't want Scotty to suspect what we've been doing, or he may have my guts – or should I say my nuts?'

'You're not frightened of the little man, are you?' Leah said, feeling a little deflated that he wanted to keep their relationship quiet.

'No, but I'm pretty sure he's reporting back to someone. That's why I think we're better off keeping it to ourselves. By the way, are all Yorkshire women so hot?' Dan teased.

'I don't know. Maybe you should try a few more on for size, that way you'll know,' Leah said smartly. Then: 'Well, off you go - I'm starving.'

PRETENDING THAT NOTHING HAD HAPPENED WAS GOING TO BE
very hard, thought Leah as she saw her flushed cheeks in the
mirror.

'What on earth made you do that, you silly girl!' she
scolded herself. 'Neither of you need this complication.'

There was a knock on the door. Leah opened it. It was
Scotty.

'I'm on my way, I just fell asleep in the bath,' Leah lied.

'Funny, His Lordship said you were taking a shower,'
replied Scotty with a frown.

'Oh, I changed my mind. I needed a soak in the Dead Sea
salts. It was lovely,' stuttered Leah, hoping she'd got away
with it.

The little man gallantly walked Leah down to the restaurant.
'I just hope he wasn't coming on to you,' he grumbled protectively. 'Not that he slings it about or anything, but he definitely
is attracted by women who do dangerous things.'

Dangerous things? Oh dear Lord, they hadn't used a
condom. And it wasn't for the first time. That episode in the
barn . . . *I think* I've *just done a very dangerous thing,* Leah
thought and froze. OMG. She stopped in her tracks just before
the restaurant door.

'What is it? You look like you've seen a ghost.' Scotty held
the door open.

'Erm, I have forgotten something, but it will be OK,' she
said, trying not to panic.

Dan was sitting there drinking an orange juice. He stood up
and pulled a chair out for her before handing her the menu.

'I think I would like Eggs Benedict, if they're on the menu,'
said Leah, not really wanting anything to eat.

'I hope so because I'm having the same,' said Dan.

'Can you order for me, please? I just need a couple of moments.' Leah got up and walked out before Dan or Scotty could say anything.

AS LEAH WENT TO SIT AT THE TABLE AGAIN, SHE NOTICED DAN was back in his work mode. He was on his phone, but looked up as she re-joined them - and he winked. A wink that set her heart all of a flutter.

'Like I said, I haven't got the papers with me at the moment, but I will call you this afternoon as soon as I get back. Speak to you then,' said Dan with a huge sigh after he'd disconnected the call.

'Is there anything I can do?' asked Scotty as he tucked into a Full English Breakfast.

'You just stick to your security work. But thanks for the offer.' Dan looked at Leah. 'I was hoping to come with you, but I will have to visit Whitby another day.'

'Oh, that's fine,' said Leah nonchalantly. She was thankful when the distraction of their breakfast arrived, although she'd lost her appetite for no apparent reason. This was the second time he'd said he wanted to visit Whitby. That was definitely a result!

20

BACK TO REALITY

L eah relaxed and stared out of the helicopter at the billowing low clouds. She turned to find Dan watching her.

'You should be living a better life,' he said gently.

'My life is fine, Dan, I thoroughly enjoy it.'

'We could look for a new house together.' He gazed straight into her beautiful eyes.

Leah gasped. 'A new house together? You're coming to live in Whitby with me?'

It was Dan's turn to gasp.

Hurt was quickly hidden from Leah's face. 'I thought not. Where has this come from, Dan?'

Scotty listened and observed.

'I'm going to buy you a house,' he said.

But Leah was shaking her head. 'I already have a home, thank you. A lovely home. I don't need or want another.'

Dan looked shocked. 'My son-'

Leah interrupted, 'Our son has a good home-life. He goes to a great school, has lovely friends. Why would you want to disrupt that?'

'I thought that was why you came looking for me,' Dan said. 'So I could support my child at long last.'

Leah felt anger rush through her veins. 'I don't want a house, Dan,' she hissed. 'This is not about money. This is about Tom and you getting to know each other.' She couldn't bear to look at him any more and turned back to the clouds.

Scotty gave Dan a frown but his boss ignored him; he was nursing a bruised ego at her rejection of his offer.

THE LIMO WAITED AT THE GATES TO THE HAMBOURNE MANOR Estate, and while the automatic recognition system set the gates opening, photographers clicked their flashing cameras at the car. Dan put his hand up at his side window so Leah did the same at her side.

'Why are you such a celebrity?' asked Leah.

'It comes with the territory, I'm sorry to say. It's all due to Ryan's being such big business, and in my being a bachelor. There are times it becomes very tedious. I used to have a banter with the guys, but then another type of reporter came along - the kind who writes any old thing as long as it sells. They can manufacture any story they fancy,' Dan said sombrely.

LEAH AND THE KIDS WALKED INTO THE HUGE KITCHEN JUST AS Dan and Sophie were drinking coffee.

Using his mother's phone, Tom took a photo of Dan, then one of Sophie.

'My mother assures me the boys will like chicken nuggets, made of course with the best chicken breast.' Dan looked across at Leah, but she was busy with her head in the fridge.

'Are there fries with that, Dan?' asked Troy shyly.

Dan nodded. 'Yes, Troy, of course we can arrange that.'

Leah seemed really distracted as she poured the boys a glass of milk each and then poured one for herself.

Dan watched her leave the kitchen, and then he quickly turned to Tom.

Sophie beat him to it. 'What's your home like, Tom?'

Tom sat down at the table followed by Harry and Troy. 'It's great. A kind man helped my mummy, and she now owns lots of cafés and a Pilates studio. She says she's done it all for me. But I don't do Pilates.'

Harry giggled, and Dan and Sophie joined in.

'My mummy said she's lucky, because she kissed her prince first but since then she's kissed two frogs,' Tom explained.

Harry and Troy pulled funny faces.

'Ugh. Kissing a frog,' Harry sniggered.

'Boys, I know that feeling,' said Sophie with a wicked laugh.

'Tom, you must stop telling your mum's secrets. Two frogs? One prince?' Dan asked.

Tom nodded. 'Single daddies at my school like my mummy because she's beautiful. Joey says someone will snap her up and marry her soon. I just hope I like him.'

Dan wanted to change the subject but he couldn't without one last question. 'Snap her up? Is there anyone interested?'

Tom shrugged and looked rather sad. 'I think there are lots and lots. They always seem to hang around the school gate and then I've seen them come into the café.' The boy looked at Sophie and confided, 'I wish my mummy could be happy. She gets very sad sometimes and goes riding to blow her cobwebs away, but I've never actually seen the cobwebs because she rides very early in the mornings, before I'm awake. Grandad

Thomas says women who don't blow away the cobwebs can get very stressed.'

'Men get stressed too.' Sophie looked meaningfully at her son, wishing he would do something while he still could, and not let Leah slip through his hands.

'And you three boys have all this stress to come,' said Joey from the doorway.

Dan turned back to his son. 'Horses are great creatures.'

'Yes,' Tom replied. 'I ride Cloud. I will own her soon.'

Dan raised his eyebrows. 'Soon? Why soon, Tom?' He was suspicious; had Leah been counting on getting money from him? Then he hated himself for thinking ill of her. Sure enough, he found he had been wrong-footed, as usual.

The little boy said solemnly, 'I must earn her first. At the moment, Mum and I own two legs and a head. Cyril says I will have paid her off in six weeks.'

Dan was impressed with the way Leah was raising their son. 'Commendable.'

Tom didn't really know what that meant, but his father seemed pleased.

Leah walked into the kitchen and, avoiding Dan's gaze, she picked up her glass of milk.

Tom looked from his mum to Dan then announced, 'Today has been my perfect day because I now have the best mummy and daddy in the whole world who are finally together again.' The lad slipped his hand in Sophie's and smiled up at her.

Dan and Leah stared at each other in shock. It was Leah who gulped and broke the silence. 'Come on, kids, perfect day or not, it's bedtime.'

Tom climbed into one of the three beds whilst Harry and Troy squabbled over which bed they wanted.

'We had to squeeze another bed in,' Sophie explained.

'Oh, they'll be fine, but thank you so much. The boys stay over with us and the room is smaller than this one,' Leah said politely, musing that this room could have accommodated at least two more beds.

'Us?' Dan queried, on the alert once more.

'We live with Grandad Thomas,' said Tom with a sleepy yawn. 'And Joey, of course.'

'It's time we let you boys get some rest. All that fresh air has worn you out, hasn't it, Troy?'

Dan seemed awkward as he stood with his hands clasped firm behind his back. He didn't know what to do at a child's bedtime.

Leah bent down to kiss Tom on the cheek, whilst Harry and Troy giggled.

'Mum, I'm getting too old for sloppy kisses,' he complained.

'We agreed that I get one bedtime kiss until you are ten years old and then we discuss it further,' Leah said firmly, trying not to laugh.

Sophie jabbed Dan's shoulder. 'Go on,' she urged.

Dan moved to the bed. Tom immediately reached up and offered his cheek. Dan kissed his son with a great deal of satisfaction. Then the raw emotion of the moment hit him right behind his eyes and in his heart. So much so that it almost felled him. He stepped away from Tom - but not before both Leah and Sophie had seen the expression on his face.

IT WAS EARLY MORNING WHEN LEAH LEFT THE MANOR HOUSE and took a stroll down towards the stables. She breathed in the refreshing country air of St Albans before hearing music and curiously following the sound. She opened the door to the viewing gallery and was surprised to see Dan riding his dressage horse to music.

Seeing him in such control over the beautiful stallion gave her goose bumps. It was obvious that this was Dan's passion. Horse and rider were so much into the zone that he didn't realise he was being observed. Tears fell down Leah's face; it was almost as if she was seeing Dan for the first time. She hastily ducked as he glanced up.

Dan slowed the pace and let his horse walk at a relaxed gait, head down with loose reins. He dismounted outside the viewing booth, briefly looked in but saw no one. Shrugging, he loosened the girth.

Peeping through the window, Leah watched Dan as he tenderly caressed his horse's face. Sensing a presence, Dan glanced across again and this time he saw her. 'Hello, Leah, it's good to see you.'

Leah smiled awkwardly. 'Hello.'

Dan stroked the stallion's glossy coat, saying, 'I love riding to music. It's very therapeutic. Did you see?'

Leah nodded. 'A little. It was beautiful.'

Dan pointed to his horse. 'Would you like to try?'

Leah shook her head, not wanting to show herself up. 'He'll be tired, but I'll help you cool him off. Give him a rub down.'

Dan laughed. 'Oh, I imagine he'd get into a sweat with you rubbing him down. As I do.'

'You do?'

'I think you know I do.'

Leah looked down in embarrassment and kicked at the floorboards.

'Come around into the school, through that door,' Dan said as he fastened his horse's girth again.

Leah walked up and opened the door then went into the huge indoor school.

Dan held his hand out to her. 'At least ride him back to his stable. Come on, I'll give you a leg up.' He whistled to his horse who had walked away. Galahad came ambling back to Dan, who gave Leah a hitch up into the saddle.

'He's lovely,' Leah breathed. 'It's early for you to be riding, isn't it?'

'It is, but I love this time of day. We'll give Galahad a rub down and then we can have breakfast together before everyone even wakes up.'

'I'd like that.'

'So would I.' Dan grinned as Leah's feet only just reached the stirrups.

'I will do without.' Leah folded each stirrup over the opposite side of the saddle. 'I learned to ride on donkeys most of the time with no bridle or saddle on because they were in the field. I suppose you had expert tuition.'

'Yes, I suppose I did - but I look at it this way. If you can ride, what does it matter whether you learned in a field on a donkey or in a school on a pony?' Dan snorted. 'In fact, I imagine the donkeys would be much livelier to ride on than the riding school's over-worked ponies.'

As they strolled back to the house, Dan stretched and said, 'It's the best time of the day, is this. No unwanted interruptions, a decent healthy breakfast with someone you admire.'

Leah stopped. 'Me?'

Dan stopped too. He looked down at her, tucked her hair behind her ear. 'Would that be so bad?'

Leah felt her colour rise. 'You certainly know how to charm someone, Mr Ryan-Savidis.'

AFTER A RELAXING BREAKFAST EVERYTHING SEEMED ROSY IN Leah's world. Even the tea tasted extra-special as they talked, mostly about riding and horses.

'There are several beautiful beach rides I know and not just near me. Bamburgh and Seahouses in Northumberland are favourite rides,' Leah told Dan.

'Sounds wonderful. I'm sure Galahad would like a canter on the beach.'

Leah got up. 'I have enjoyed our early morning rendezvous, thank you, but now I must check on the boys. Tom is normally ravenous by now.'

'We'll catch up later,' Dan promised as Leah reluctantly walked away from the table.

LEAH WAS IN HER BEDROOM PUTTING ON HER WATCH WHEN HER son rushed in. Tom was holding a morning newspaper and tears were streaming down his face. Leah ran forward. 'What's wrong?'

The little boy showed Leah the headlines. *Billionaire has bastard child with hooker.*

Dan knocked and walked in. 'Tom, you ran out. Why?'

Leah thrust the paper at him. 'Here! It makes great reading for a young boy.'

Dan scanned the headline. 'Oh no. I was afraid of this leaking out.'

Leah looked astounded. 'You think this is coincidence?'

Dan frowned. 'Don't you?'

Leah shook her head. 'No, I do not.'

Tom grabbed Leah's arm. 'Everyone at school will know.'

Leah touched her son's head and brushed his hair with her fingers. 'Tom, darling, you already told them.'

Dan looked shocked. 'He did?'

Tom defended himself. 'They didn't believe me! I'm a bar, bar, bar steward!' And he suddenly pelted from the room.

Leah dashed after him, wondering not who but why that bitch Chelsea would hurt Dan's little boy - surely that wouldn't endear her to Dan?

Angrily screwing the paper up in his hand, Dan hurried after Leah and the weeping child.

TOM MADE FOR THE BIG DINING ROOM, AND WHEN LEAH AND Dan caught up with him, they found him being cuddled by his grandmother. Harry and Troy sat nearby looking downcast and Ruby was keeping an eye on them.

'Who got him into this state, Dan?' Sophie demanded. 'Except I know already, don't I? But this time, let me tell you, she's gone too far.'

Dan was taken aback. 'Who are you talking about? How come you both know whose bright idea this was?'

It was Ruby who answered. 'Chelsea, of course,' she snarled. 'Who else?'

'I was hoping to protect Tom, to keep him out of the tabloids. Why would Chelsea do such a thing?'

'Are you for real, Dan? Why can't you see what everyone else here can?' Ruby tutted and went to sit beside Tom's friends to cheer them up with more toast and chocolate spread.

21

IF THE CAP FITS

A short time later, Chelsea strolled into the dining room. 'Morning, all,' she said carelessly.

Joey shook the morning paper at the young woman. She took it off him and scanned the headlines.

Joey prompted, 'What have you got to say to that?'

Chelsea shrugged. 'If the cap fits . . .'

Leah almost jumped down her throat. 'It *doesn't* fit. Not at all. Dan, I must talk to the press and put them right. Immediately!' And she set off down the hallway. Dan, who had remained surprisingly quiet whilst Chelsea had been so rude, went after her. Joey too followed in his wake, after giving Chelsea a scowl that could have scorched her. He hated to see his beloved cousin, who was more like a sister to him, being so upset.

Troy whispered, 'Uh oh. I've not seen your mummy like that before, Tom.'

Dan shouted down the corridor, 'Leah, wait up!'

LEAH STRODE ANGRILY TOWARDS THE STABLES. A YOUNG groom watched as Dan ran into the yard.

'How dare she? Who does she think she is? "*If the cap fits*", indeed!' Leah scoffed.

'Leah, wait up. I will drive you to the gates - where the press are waiting. If we're going to do this, we need to do it together.' Dan reached Leah and put a steadying hand on her arm.

Joey wasn't far behind. 'Can I come too?' he asked. He was still seething.

Dan nodded. 'Of course.'

Leah was still ranting, tears shimmering in her eyes. 'How did they find out we were all here?'

'That photo was taken when we arrived,' Joey said. 'There were no press hanging around at the time, so the photo must have been taken by one of us. Sophie was in the photo so she couldn't have taken it. That leaves only your PA and Scotty, as Sisco is in the clear - so it's between Chelsea and Scotty. And if you look at the angle, it is taken from a taller person's perspective. So my money is on Chelsea.'

Leah agreed. 'I know it was her,' she said savagely.

Dan tried to calm the situation. 'Sisco is trying to find out where the photo came from. Let's go and get the press sorted first.' He opened the passenger door for Leah before he got into the driver's seat of his Range Rover.

Leah turned in her seat to talk to Joey, who'd jumped in the back seat.

'Who else could it be?' she asked.

'Well, I suppose she's going to blame me,' he said. 'I was actually standing next to her, and she did take a photo on her iPhone. I saw that much. My own phone was in my man bag.'

'You actually saw her take a photo?' Dan asked.

'Oh yes, I heard the distinctive click. In fact, she took at least three,' Joey confirmed.

'And you didn't see anyone else suspicious?' Dan asked.

'No, but to be honest I was watching Tom loving the attention,' Joey said.

Dan couldn't help but smile, although he said, 'The poor little chap was so upset just now.'

'Well, it's cruel to do that to a little boy. If she'd done it to me, fine, but when she does it to my son, it becomes personal,' said Leah through gritted teeth.

'You seem sure it was Chelsea - and don't get me wrong, if we can prove it, there will be big trouble.' Dan brought the vehicle to a stop. He pointed to the river, twisting and turning in the valley below. The view was breath-taking.

Joey sighed. 'Of all this I could be mistress.'

Leah couldn't help but laugh. 'In your dreams, matey.'

Joey grinned. 'If only you were gay, Dan.'

'This is not a Jane Austen novel, Joey,' his cousin teased him. 'You are not Eliza Bennet and Dan is *not* Mr Darcy.'

The joke lightened the tension as Dan drove on towards the gates: sure enough, the reporters were there today and perked up when they saw the car approaching. The photographers lined up their shots as Dan walked with Leah to confront them, and he was surprised how well she coped with them.

'Hi guys, I'm Leah, and I'd just like to put the record straight, seeing as the newspaper headlines have just upset our young son. The truth of the matter is, I had a fling with Dan, and it was a long time ago. I'm appalled that you've labelled me so offensively. I've never been a hooker.' To her surprise, she burst out laughing. 'I run a chain of dog friendly cafés up north – it's not quite the same thing, is it? Put yourselves in my shoes and see how you'd feel about your child reading that filth. I'd like a retraction, if you please.'

The celebrity journalist Pete Hardy sneered, 'That's your story – but it's not what the concierge at the Byzantine Hotel said.'

Leah kept her cool. 'Oh yes? Well, he was wrong.'

Hardy came back at her: 'He said you bungee-jumped onto Mr Ryan's terrace from the hotel roof.'

Leah laughed in his face. 'Oh that. It was just a dare. What can I say?' She turned to Dan. 'I like risky encounters.'

Dan laughed too. 'As do I. And preferably private, without the whole world and his wife knowing about it.' His tone hardened. 'And without journalists like you using such tales to discredit Miss Jensen here, and hurting our young son.'

'So it was not for money?' clarified one reporter.

'No,' said Dan quietly, no trace of a smile now. 'What we shared had nothing to do with money.'

'OK, we'll back off,' Pete Hardy confirmed. *Boring!* he said to himself.

'And you will rescind all comments by tomorrow,' Dan added with steel in his voice.

'What is happening now?' one reporter asked. 'Will you and Miss Jensen be getting married?'

'Don't push it. And for your information, this is our business. *Period.*'

The reporters began to disperse as Dan and Leah walked back to the vehicle. Joey, however, was pouting.

'What's the matter?' asked Dan, noticing.

'Well, they never asked me for my opinion.'

Leah glanced at Dan and whispered, 'Thank heaven.'

'I'm sure they will ask you next time,' Dan said kindly.

'Oh, well, that's all right then. I can practise what I might say.' Joey got into the vehicle with a smug look on his face.

Leah and Dan shared an amused look.

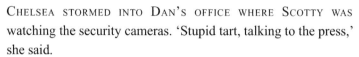

CHELSEA STORMED INTO DAN'S OFFICE WHERE SCOTTY WAS watching the security cameras. 'Stupid tart, talking to the press,' she said.

'Can you blame her?' Scotty said. 'I don't. You're about as subtle as a brick. You'll have to think of something else to upset the applecart.'

Chelsea scowled. 'I don't know what to do next. Haven't you got any ideas?'

'It's your grudge, not mine. I think you should leave them alone.' Scotty switched off the recorder and walked out, leaving Chelsea to ponder on her next plan.

BACK AT THE MANOR, DAN WAS KEEN TO LIFT THE MOOD.

'Who wants to go and see the horses?' he asked, and was gratified when three small hands were raised. 'And you, Leah, what about you?'

'Oh, Mummy will come. Won't you, Mummy?' Tom looked at her with pleading eyes.

'We can all go,' said Joey. 'Come on, kids, I'll race you. Hero? Let's catch 'em, boy.'

Leah said to Dan, 'Looks like we're all going to see the horses.'

'Good. I can't wait for you to see some of them. You'll be surprised, I hope.' Dan held out his hand. 'Let me show you my pride and joy. She is the sweetest pony I've ever come across.'

'Pony?'

'Yes. And I'm sure you will love her as much as I do. She's black and hairy and comes not far away from you, I believe.' Dan tugged her hand.

'I'm intrigued. Lead on.'

DAN LED LEAH DOWN TO ONE OF THE AMERICAN BARNS AND opened the sliding door. They moved slowly and calmly down the central walkway. The loose boxes were all spick and span, Leah noted. Then they heard whinnying as the black Dales pony popped her head over the door. It was obvious she had a great affection for Dan, as he had for her.

'Gosh, I'm surprised Chelsea allows you to keep this looker. Oh God, Dan, she's beautiful.' Leah stroked the jet-black mare with her long mane. 'Where did you find her?'

'Dreamer comes from the very best Dales stock. I have several, but this little lady is very special to me. She's from Royal stock, you know.' He opened the stable door and then stood back for Leah to go in before him.

The mare was whinnying softly.

'She has such a kind eye.'

'She does,' confirmed Dan. 'One of the first things I look for in a horse.'

'But she also has a nice nature,' said Leah as she stroked the velvet coat.

'You want to tack her up and let the kids ride her in the school,' Dan urged. 'She's a good girl with kids.'

In fact, Dan was amazed and almost reduced to tears as he watched Tom ride Dreamer around the indoor school. The boys had all taken turns.

'He's a great little rider.' Dan turned to Leah.

'He should be, he was taught bareback like we were,' chimed in Joey.

'So that's the secret of a great seat?' Dan smiled. 'I will have to try it.'

'I thought you would have noticed before now - we all have great seats,' said Joey, patting his bottom.

'Don't worry - I had.'

'I think Dreamer needs a rest, Dan, and a rub down,' Leah said, always mindful of an animal's comfort. 'Tom, bring her over here, love. We need to rub her down and give her a break.'

Hearing her phone ring, she stepped away from the circle to answer it, saying, 'Hi, Annie, is there a problem?'

Dan watched her and Joey watched him.

'Do you think there's a problem?' asked Dan.

'Nothing she can't deal with. My cousin leads a busy life so this is a great break for her, but Annie will sort out whatever's wrong with Leah's guidance. If needs must I will go back today and take over,' said Joey magnanimously, thinking he'd been away for far too long already.

'Then I shall fly you up.'

'Ooh-er. You fly?'

'Don't look so surprised. It's easy - why don't you take lessons?'

'Oh no, no, no, the only flying I will be doing is when I'm a fairy at Christmas in the local pantomime. I'm an expert at that and I don't mind admitting it.'

Leah joined the group again.

'Everything OK?' Dan asked.

'Nothing that can't be solved. I just had to reshuffle some of the staff.' She looked at Joey. 'It's all sorted for the moment.'

'For the moment?' he asked. 'You sure?'

'Yes, we're going home tomorrow, remember? The kids need to get back, and so do we. Which begs the question, how are we all going to travel? We won't all fit into one car.'

'Sisco will use the people-carrier,' Dan informed her, thinking how empty Hambourne would feel without them all. 'He'll get you back home safe and sound. I have to fly to Paris tomorrow so I'll need Scotty to drive me to the airport. Problem sorted. Come on, kids, let's take this mare back and give her a little treat.' Dan took hold of the reins and they all walked Dreamer back to the stables.

After giving the Dales mare a rub down and a scoop of pony nuts, the little group strolled contentedly back up to the house with faithful Hero following.

'Oh my goodness, where are *our* dogs?' Tom looked around worriedly.

'They're with Ruby,' Joey told him. 'She has found a new vocation as dog-sitter, Tom, so don't worry. She told me she planned to pester Cook to make liver cake.'

'Yuk - liver cake!' Troy exclaimed.

'Hero loves it,' said Dan.

'Sounds gross.' Harry held onto Hero. 'Look, he's going faster, he knows what you're saying. If he had the right kind of ears, he would have pricked them up. I just bet he would.'

'Well, I can bet Cook has something special for you boys too,' Dan teased.

Ever hungry, Joey's own ears pricked up. 'Quickly, I'll race you to the kitchen,' he challenged the lads as he set off like a proverbial bat out of hell.

The boys screamed and set off after Joey, who was a great favourite with them all, but Harry was soon winning because Hero pulled him swiftly to the house.

Dan laughed heartily as he watched them all. He turned to Leah, only to see that she had a sad look on her face. 'Is something wrong?'

'I was just thinking that Tom and his friends have had such a great time here, and I wanted to say a huge thank you. Tom is on holiday from school soon until September and we are going away for a week. If you wanted to visit, you could.'

'That sounds good. Anywhere I know?'

'Well, let's just say Galahad might like it if he wants to gallop on a beautiful beach. I'm taking Powder up for Tom, but Joey and I will be hiring horses at the local riding school. I'll send you the details.' Leah was glad she couldn't see his face, but when he opened the door for her, she had to meet his eyes.

'I may not be able to manage a whole week, but I will come and spend a couple of days with you all,' Dan confirmed.

Leah hadn't realised that she had been holding her breath. 'Please don't bring Chelsea,' she said before she could stop herself.

Dan shook his head. 'Absolutely not.'

'And when do you want us to arrive for Sophie's birthday?' enquired Leah.

'That's up to you. Your calendar is very busy, I know, but I'm sure my mother would love you and Tom to be here. I will catch up with you on that. Right now, I need to see if Sisco has found the culprit responsible for the photo.'

They went inside the house and changed their boots for shoes.

'I've had fun this morning, thank you,' said Leah. It was so hard to let him go.

'So have I.' And Dan excused himself as he saw Sisco.

Leah watched him go. She truly had enjoyed herself, which made the next few minutes only more bitter by contrast.

She was making her way towards the kitchen when Chelsea came out of a side room and immediately launched into: 'Did the reporters believe you?' Her face was screwed up into a hateful sneer. 'You must be good at lying, that's all I can say.'

'No more than you. I notice you are an out-and-out liar,' Leah said politely.

'Yes, but he doesn't think I'm a liar. He still has doubts about you and your brat,' Chelsea said with so much venom.

'Oh, give it a rest,' returned Leah, tired of her low jibes.

'Bring on the weekend, and we'll soon see who has the ace card,' Chelsea threw over her shoulder as she marched away. 'Let the battle commence, bitch!'

22

OH, WHAT A DRESS!

L eah was busy making shortbread in the kitchen at the back of the café. It was an hour till opening time. She knew she spoiled some of her customers by baking especially for them, but due to the popularity of her café she had to buy in some things. Thankfully a school friend had started her very own cottage bakery business after speaking to Leah, and Leah in turn had put several potential clients her way, including some of her cafés. It worked for both women, and worked well.

Joey flew into the kitchen. 'Phew, hide me in here.'

'Why?'

'Larry the show whippet's after me for a biscuit. His ears went up when he heard my voice. In fact, just give me a doggy biscuit and I will brave the assault.' Joey held his hand out.

Leah passed him three biscuits. 'That should keep him quiet. Now get out of the kitchen!'

'Just one more thing - what dress are you wearing on Saturday night? We don't want to clash, do we?' Joey knew he was pushing it. 'Tell you what. You think about it and I'll just go and give Larry his treats or all hell will break loose.'

As Joey walked out, Leah put a floury hand through her hair. What *was* she going to wear? It's not as if her social life was exactly buzzing: her wardrobe wasn't full of cocktail dresses. Dan had seen her red dress so she couldn't wear that. A whisper of a smile hit her lips at the thought; he'd loved the red dress.

Joey popped his head around the door again. 'Do you want time off to go to York to look for a dress? I can take care of things here.'

Don't look a gift horse in the mouth, Leah decided and untied her apron. 'I've set the timer, so keep an ear out.'

'You might want to brush the flour out of your hair before you set off,' Joey advised her.

'Thank you.' It was so thoughtful of him. 'I will bring you something nice back,' she promised.

'I'll hold you to that. Remember, I look pretty in pink.'

Leah parked up near Clifford's Tower and walked into town. She scoured the usual designer shops, or at least those she knew about. There was nothing that she liked, nothing that seemed to make a statement.

That was when she saw it in the shop window. It was long, with a V-shaped neckline and matching V-shaped back, and it was in her favourite colour, turquoise. The material was taffeta, so it was dressy too.

She looked up at the shop name and was shocked to see it was a charity shop. A quick glance around ensured there was no one who knew her. She laughed to herself. Who was she kidding? She often went into the charity shops in Whitby. Walking inside, she asked the assistant what size the dress was.

She held her breath and then let it out with relief as the young woman said it was a size twelve.

'I know it's a fag, but could I try it on, please?' asked Leah.

'Yes, I'll take it off the mannequin. Just a mo.' The assistant carefully removed the dress and handed it to Leah. 'I love the material, but I've never heard of the maker,' she commented.

Leah looked at the label and gasped. 'I'll try it on and see if it fits. Can I come out to show you?'

'Of course. To be honest if I'd been a size twelve instead of a sixteen, I would have bought it myself,' the girl said cheerfully.

Leah carried the long dress into a cramped changing room and changed into it. Coming out, seeing that the shop was still empty, she posed for the assistant.

'Oh, that colour does suit you!' the girl exclaimed. 'I take it you're buying it?'

'I've been traipsing around York for two hours and now I've found the perfect dress. Yes, thank you, I do want it. I'll just take it off.' Leah returned to the poky cubicle.

'MUMMY, HAVE YOU BOUGHT ME A BIRTHDAY PRESENT FOR MY grandma?' Tom asked that evening after school.

'I certainly have. I've bought a present from you and one from me,' confirmed Leah with a smile.

'I have some money in my money box. I don't expect you to buy it, Mummy,' said Tom generously.

'You're a good boy, Tom. Look, I bought you a birthday card too for Grandma Sophie,' added Leah.

'I can't wait to see all the dogs,' Tom told her.

'What dogs?'

'Newfoundland dogs. They are doing a display in Dan's lake,' he told her. 'I'm going to be rescued.'

'Oh, you are, are you? And when was this arranged?' Leah wanted to know.

'We arranged it with Ruby and Joey,' said Tom with a yawn.

'We?'

'Yes, Grandma's going in the lake with me. She promised and she said Hero will make a splash, as will my Daddy,' Tom said with a grin. 'I dote know anything else.'

Leah laughed. 'You dote know? I think you mean don't.'

'Grandad says dote,' protested Tom.

'Grandad's prerogative,' said Thomas from behind them.

The boy spun round. 'I live with you, so it's bound to rub off, isn't it?'

'I suppose, but I dare say you need to try harder and so will I,' Grandad Thomas said rather eloquently.

Leah joined in the laughter, then caught Joey spying into her dress bag.

'Wow, that looks nice. Must have cost a fortune - I didn't know Jason Wright had a shop in York.' He caught Leah's eye. 'Is it a proper dance that Sophie's having then?'

'She said she was having a band and a dance floor and Grandad's thinking about coming, aren't you, Grandad?' Tom looked up at his beloved grandparent.

'Well, I need to make sure this fella's good enough to be your dad, don't I?' Thomas winked at the lad.

'I see you've taken the ticket label off this Jason Wright number. Expect you didn't want us to see it – but I reckon it cost you well over a grand,' Joey said knowledgeably.

'Get your hands out of that bag! I'm not showing it off until Saturday night. Not for anyone. As for the price, let's just say it was a steal.' Leah winked at Joey.

'Whatever, you'll still look better than that bitch Ch-' Joey darted out of reach as Grandad Thomas went to swipe him with a tea towel, shouting, 'Language!' Tom screamed with excitement.

CHELSEA MARCHED INTO THE OFFICE AT HAMBOURNE MANOR and threw her phone down on the desk.

'What's eating you?' Scotty asked. He'd been perfectly happy, sitting reading the paper and working out which horses to back, and now his peace had been disturbed. Like everyone else, he was getting tired of the PA's filthy temper.

'What do you think? She's not even here and he's arranging time away. He's never had as much time off as this in years. When I suggest he needs a break, he books a week away with his mother!' Chelsea dragged a Post-it note out of her drawer. 'I can never get him alone - and I need him alone.'

'If I were you, I'd give up,' the little man said sagely. 'You've been trying for years and I hate to say it but he just doesn't seem interested in you, Chelsea love.' Scotty ducked as the Post-it notepad flew across the desk at him.

'Get out if you've nothing useful to say. I've got to find a way of ruining this party and making it look like her fault.' Chelsea put her hands on her hips and demanded: 'Are you in?'

Scotty was already shaking his head. 'I strongly advise you to forget this whole idea. Don't spoil Sophie's birthday, please.'

Chelsea glowered. 'Who cares about her and her birthday. Bring on the fireworks.' And she made to leave the room.

Scotty blocked her exit route. 'Think about what you're doing,' he urged. 'This is too big. He has a son now and Leah will always be a part of his life because she's Tom's mum.'

'Get out of my way, shrimp, or I'll hurt you,' threatened Chelsea, raising a fist.

'Promise me you'll think about the consequences. You do this, and you'll lose the job of a lifetime.' Then Scotty stood to one side and let her stomp past him.

Watching her make off down the corridor, he hoped she would reconsider whatever monstrous plot she had in mind. In his opinion, the woman was more than a bit unhinged.

SISCO PICKED DAN UP AT HEATHROW.

'Where's Scotty?' asked Dan, jumping into the front seat and buckling up.

Sisco shrugged. 'I think he's gone on an errand for Sophie.'

'Are we all set for tomorrow? I want everything to run smoothly for my mother's birthday.'

'Yes, everything seems to be on track from what I can see. The marquee is in place, as is the dance floor, the stage for the band and the singer, and the bar. Of course, they will be using the smaller marquee down by the lake for the water displays. Oh, and the water tested clear for algae.' Sisco set off out of the confines of the airport.

'And the star attraction we mentioned: was that possible to arrange at such short notice?' Dan asked, pulling at his tie and undoing the first couple of buttons on his shirt.

'Oh yes, they will literally be blown away,' replied Sisco.

'And only we know about it?' Dan smiled across at him.

'SAS honour.'

'That'll do for me. I just love surprises and my mother will love it too. They all think I've been to Paris on business but in reality, I've been practising so I hope it goes without a hitch. When are you picking up Leah and her family?'

'Very, very early tomorrow. I like it that she can get the three youngsters, the cousin and her grandfather ready so early in the morning. We should be down here around ten-thirty a.m. The way she was reeling off the orders on the telephone the other day, she must have a logistics program in her brain.' Sisco turned the car on to the motorway and put his foot down.

'And the one thing we can't predict?' asked Dan with a sigh. 'Chelsea?'

'I was thinking more of the weather,' Dan said wryly. 'We know that Chelsea is a law unto herself.'

Sisco snorted. 'I think the weather will be perfect. Not so sure about her.'

'So, there are no storms predicted?' Dan suddenly looked serious.

'No, just a slight breeze and clement weather. I think I'll take the back roads if you don't mind,' Sisco said, slowing down. 'The motorway looks like it's building up into a tailback or maybe there's been an accident. I'll just whip off here,' and he took the next exit off the M25.

LEAH CAREFULLY REMOVED THE DRESS OUT OF THE BAG AND showed it to her friend. 'Ellie, just come and see if you can do anything with this.'

'You say you didn't notice it straight away?' her friend said as she looked at the small tear in the garment. 'This is why it was in the charity shop, but you know what? It'll be a cinch. Try it on and let's see what magic we can work in an hour. Keira will come down when she's finished preparing the addition.'

When Leah tried the dress on, Ellie whistled. 'Wow. That's all I can say - wow.' She picked up her pins.

'Shall I stand on the stool?' asked Leah. 'I feel like a teenager going to a school prom.'

'You look like one,' said Ellie, with a genuine smile. 'It used to be you helping me find a fella, now I can help you.'

'Oh, I'm not finding a fella. No, I'm definitely not looking,' Leah remarked thoughtfully.

'Well, they'll be like bees to a honeypot with you in this. And we've known each other far too long for me to take you at your word. There must be something about this guy or you wouldn't have gone with him in the first place,' said Ellie, putting the pins in place.

'It was a long time ago, and I'm doing this for Tom.'

'Poppycock! Leah Jensen, you have a soft spot for this man,' her friend said sternly. 'Now come down off the stool, step out of the dress very carefully and then you can fetch me and my sister a coffee from your lovely café downstairs.' Ellie took hold of the dress as if it was the wedding gown of a royal princess.

'And a cake?'

'Need you ask, darling? Do you really need to ask . . .'

LEAH TOOK THE COFFEES AND A COUPLE OF MELTING MOMENTS back with her just in time to see Keira joining Ellie at the sewing machine.

'Just give me two minutes and then you can try it on,' Ellie said, licking her lips as she saw Leah place the cake plate down on the side.

'And in the meantime, have a look at this. Your boobs shouldn't protrude too much with this little glitter brooch pinching the dress in.' Keira handed Leah the little gem-filled brooch and chain.

'Oh Lord, it's wonderful. Thank you, Keira, I just love the colours - turquoise and the most wonderful shades of lilac and pink.'

'Who will be the Belle of the Ball?' the sisters said together.

23

GREAT ESCAPES!

'Have the boys packed their wetsuits?' asked Joey excitedly. 'Ooh, I'm feeling as giddy as my giddy aunt.'

'Which one? Your aunts always seem so very strait-laced to me.' Thomas gave a great yawn then said, 'I'm off to my bed, lads and lassies. Goodnight, you two. Don't go staying up late as we have an extra-early start.'

Leah kissed her grandad on his cheek as did Joey. Then the old chap went out of the room and up the stairs.

'So, have you got your wetsuit? I've got mine, and I look a right stunner in it.' Joey grinned wickedly.

'Please tell me it's not a mankini,' half-joked Leah, placing the dogs' food into a backpack.

'It's a pink and blue wetsuit and I have a life-jacket too,' her cousin said, posing on the spot as if he was modelling it there and then.

'And I thought it was only the kids getting rescued. Now do I need my wetsuit? I'm not going in, am I?'

'According to Tom you are, but don't worry. I've got your wetsuit in my case so you can't wriggle out of the fun today -

and I mean, who would want to? I've seen the way Dan looks at you.' Joey gestured at the dogs' rucksack. 'I hope Sisco is bringing a minibus.'

IN FACT, SISCO WAS ON THE DOORSTEP AT 5.30 A.M. AND HE *was* driving a minibus.

'Morning all,' he said as Tom let him into the kitchen at Abbey Bridge Road.

'We'll make you a cup of tea and toast just as you asked,' said Tom, eager to please, while Harry held a chair out for him.

'Thank you, son.' Sisco smiled at Harry and ruffled Troy's hair.

'I'll put the cases in the boot and sort all that out,' Joey offered. 'We've had our breakfast, and Leah and Grandad will be down very soon. I'm as chuffed as the kids, I can tell you. Do we know what the surprise is?' Joey was doing his best to find out.

Sisco tapped his nose and grinned. 'I'm not privy to that.' He took a swig of his tea and quickly buttered his toast and spread a heap of Leah's homemade strawberry jam on top.

'No? Well, a girl can only try. Come on, kids, get your rucksacks.' Joey twirled around and nearly tripped over the dogs. 'Oi, watch it, you two. I can't have my good looks spoiled, not when I'm going to be the star of the show.' He pirouetted then left the room on the tip of his toes like a ballerina.

Sisco chuckled, ate some more of his toast and took a big drink of tea.

'Oh, thank the Lord you had the sense to come in a minibus,' said Leah as she came into the kitchen carrying a leather suit- carrier. 'This is Grandad's and mine, and Joey's things are through in the hallway, I'll just-'

'It's fine - I know how to handle a lady's dress,' interrupted Sisco. 'I've had good training with Sophie and Ruby.'

'There may be *two* ladies' dresses,' Joey teased as he came back inside.

'There better not be,' Thomas interjected.

'Only kidding, Grandad, only kidding,' Joey replied with a sneaky little grin at Sisco.

DAN WAS BUSY TALKING TO HIS LOCAL NEWFOUNDLAND CLUB team when Chelsea sauntered across in her high heels, which dug into the lawn.

'Seriously, your mother wants this?' she sneered.

Dan took her arm and, excusing himself, moved a distance away. 'Yes, my mother does want this – and if you're not interested, then please leave.'

Chelsea smirked. 'She's just sucking up to your ego, and the same goes for the dog meat on legs. Well, if you haven't forgotten, there's a business to run.'

Dan was white-faced and fuming. 'That's enough. I suggest you go back to the house, take the company credit card and go shopping. I'll give you a limit of £500. Because as you say, this is really not your style. Now go before I change my mind.'

'But-'

'I'm changing my mind.'

'OK, I'm going,' Chelsea snarled as she tottered away on the heels that were sinking into the grass. Thinking he could get rid of her with a measly £500. How dare he! Then she muttered, 'I will get you to hear me out, Dan Ryan, and when I do, you won't be so goddamn cocky.'

She was still grumbling away to herself when she passed Scotty and made towards him. Fearing she was on some sort of rage trip, the little man moved deftly away before she could grab him, causing Chelsea to stumble and fall over, snapping her heel in the process. 'Stupid idiot! Clumsy fool!' she screamed at him, standing and wiping mud off her clothes and hands.

Scotty shouted back to her, 'I would have helped you up if you hadn't tried to swipe me. I may be a short-arse but I'm fast!'

Chelsea got up and the other heel sank in. 'Ugh . . .' Snatching up her broken shoes, she marched furiously back up to the big house, her stockinged feet covered in mud.

Scotty went over to Dan, who had resumed talking to the women and men who were standing around with their Newfoundland dogs. On seeing Scotty, he stepped away and asked, 'Are they here yet?'

Scotty shook his head. 'No, but what's with Chelsea kicking off?'

'I don't know, nor do I care, but there's no way she's spoiling my mother's special day. I've sent her shopping - she does that best.' Dan couldn't help but grin. 'What happened? Did she try to slug you?'

'She certainly did. You need danger money in this job! But seriously, Mr Dan, she's hacked off with something and I think it's called not getting her own way.'

'Coo-ee, coo-ee! What time does the event start, your mother sent me to ask,' enquired Ruby, looking around at all the Newfoundlands walking alongside their owners. 'Wow, more Heroes and Heroines – great. By the way, Danny Boy, you might want to leg it up to the house. Tom and his family have just arrived and your mother has a new admirer - Leah's grandfather. She's asked him if he's got his dancing shoes with him . . . and he has!'

'She likes to dance,' Scotty said fondly.

'Come on, we'd better get back there before she asks him to marry her.' Dan took Ruby's arm.

'Would that be so bad? She loves older men or you wouldn't have been born.' Ruby stepped up a gear to keep up with Dan. 'What's the rush? Can't wait to see your . . . your son?' She still couldn't quite get her head around these recent developments.

When Tom saw Dan, his face lit up and he pelted over to him, crying, 'Daddy, hello!'

'Hello, my boy.' Dan looked around. 'Where's your mum?'

Tom grinned impishly. 'Did you miss her?'

Dan laughed. 'Now that would be telling, wouldn't it?'

'She's taken Grandad to show him his room with my grand-ma.' The boy and his friends were staring and pointing at all the dogs. 'Where's Hero, Daddy?'

'Oh, he's in the house for now. We'll get him out when he's ready to rescue you kids,' Dan replied, then he looked up as one of the bedroom windows opened.

'Oh, look at those big black behinds! Aren't they just gorgeous,' called Joey, peering out.

'Is he talking about mine? I never knew I had a BIG black behind,' said Ruby, scrutinising her posterior.

'Uh-oh,' warned Tom. 'I think he was meaning the dogs', Ruby. Joey is really on top form today - he's had us all singing on the way down. Even Sisco was singing too.'

'Sisco, singing? Are we talking about the same man here?' Dan found that hard to believe.

All three boys nodded. 'We sang the Yorkshire Anthem,' they said proudly together. 'And the Horse Song.'

'Yorkshire Anthem?' repeated Dan, trying not to seem igno-rant. He'd never heard of a Yorkshire Anthem. 'Horse Song?' He must ask Leah about it, but he was saved from embarrass-ment as just then, his mother and their guests emerged from the Manor.

Sophie was holding Thomas's arm, with Leah and Joey hot on their heels.

Thomas held out his hand to shake Dan's. 'I'm Thomas Jensen, pleased to meet you.'

'Grandad, where's your Yorkshire accent gone?' asked Joey, astounded to hear the posh voice.

'You're not the only one who can speak nicely. Besides, we are in company, so you just mind your manners,' Thomas warned him.

'Pleased to meet you too, Thomas. I hope you will enjoy my mother's birthday,' Dan stated, as if it was a foregone conclusion. 'Mother, I will leave you and Ruby to entertain Thomas whilst I go and get things sorted. Leah, Joey and you boys, you're with me.'

'And what about me?' asked Scotty as he moved into the circle of people.

'Could you make sure lunch is being organised for around one-thirty? There will be a lot of hungry mouths to feed,' Dan replied. 'Right, come on, kids.' He winked at Leah.

'That wink was for me,' Joey said in a stage whisper to Leah.

'In your dreams,' Leah laughed. As she saw Dan and the kids jog down towards the lake, she turned to Scotty and said, 'Scotty, when you've finished sorting lunch, would you be a love and take my boys for a wee? They're in a cage in the bedroom. I just want to let them settle for an hour before I bring them out.'

'I will, Miss Leah,' said Scotty bashfully.

'Scotty.' Leah went up to him. 'It's Leah, remember? Think of our cocktails on the yacht and the fun we had. So - just Leah, eh?'

Scotty nodded. 'All right - Leah.' They smiled at each other, then he said, 'Oops, I'd better dash, I've got two jobs now.' And he hurried off into the house.

'The way you phrased that, it sounded like you wanted him to take the kids to the loo,' Joey criticised as they walked down towards the lake.

'You always take things so literally. Bloody hell, Joey, lighten up.'

'Huh, Grandad tells me to behave and you tell me to lighten up. A girl doesn't know *what* to do,' Joey said offendedly.

'A girl *does* know what to do. Just be yourself, Joey,' Dan told him as he walked up and kissed Leah on the cheek.

'Ooh,' said Troy. 'Kiss alert. Kiss alert.'

Tom and Harry laughed.

Dan was appreciating how Leah was blushing, then his smile died as he saw Chelsea walking down by the lake. She was flirting with one of the guys whom Dan had hired to run the day's event and she was wearing very short shorts, a sparkly top and designer shoes.

'Is there something wrong, Dan?' asked Leah as she saw his expression; she turned to see who was in his field of vision.

'Nope. Now let's go and watch some of the warm-ups with the puppies. Even they are amazing with this breed. You'll love them, Leah.' Dan got a hold of her hand and squeezed it.

'You can hold my hand if you like, Dan,' Joey said with a flutter of his eyelashes.

'Don't push it, Joey,' countered Leah.

'Never mind, I'll hold Tom's hand,' Joey said sadly.

'No, you won't,' said Tom as he scampered off followed by Harry and Troy.

'Who am I, Billy no-mates?' shouted Joey, chasing after them.

THE PUPPIES ENTERTAINED THE CROWD BY RESCUING GREEN canvas gun-dog dummies; even puppies as young as five months old enjoyed retrieving - and their crimped puppy coats were so cute. There was also a demonstration of obedience in a roped-off ring, and in another, full-grown dogs were pulling carts, their tails wagging in obvious pleasure. Barks were coming from tethered dogs wanting to get into the water to show the youngsters how a rescue was done.

'Ladies and gentlemen, lunch is being served in the two larger marquees,' a very attractive male voice informed them down the Tannoy system.

Joey came running up like a turkey in a flap. 'Gaydar, Gaydar, where is that voice coming from, Dan? That's one of my lot and no mistake.'

Dan pointed to the little pink tent.

'I might have guessed it.' Joey thanked Dan. 'I must go and meet my soulmate.'

'Joey,' warned Leah, stopping him for a moment. 'Don't wear your heart on your sleeve. Besides, he might be in a relationship.'

'My heart is permanently on my sleeve – why, you can see it thumping. There, look.' He pointed to his sleeve and moved his pecks. 'I must be off. Enjoy yourself in the water this afternoon.'

'But you're supposed to be going in,' Leah said.

'Like billy-o I will. Ta-ra.' And Joey danced off towards the pink tent.

Dan laughed. 'He's so funny it's refreshing.'

'Yeah, well, you told him to be himself, so be warned.' Leah chuckled. 'But yes, he can be very funny.'

'Let's go and have some lunch with my mother and your grandad, not forgetting the lovely Ruby.' Dan took her arm. 'Where are the kids?'

Leah pointed to the trampoline. 'You go and find your mother. I'll collect the boys and meet you in the marquee.'

'See you soon,' said Dan, bending slightly to kiss her cheek. He was feeling so happy, it could have been his birthday, not Sophie's.

LEAH WAS HEADING BEHIND A LARGE TENT WHEN SUDDENLY SHE was swung around. Chelsea dug her fingernails into Leah's arm, and there was a wild look in her eyes. As Leah gasped with shock and pain, she heard the other woman hiss, *'Bitch!'*

24

THE TROUBLE WITH MICROPHONES

'Are you crazy? What the hell is wrong now?' Leah said, forcing Chelsea's hand away and rubbing her arm, which showed red indentations where the woman's nails had punctured the skin.

'I've marked your card, dirt bag. Dan is *mine*! He may not know it yet but he is, so you can take yourself and your bastard kid back up to the cesspit you came from,' Chelsea growled, disappearing before Leah could reply.

Leah went to the trampoline and said, rather shakily, 'Come on, kids, it's lunchtime.'

'Aw, Mum,' moaned Tom.

'OK, two more minutes. Move up, I'm coming on board.' Leah removed her shoes and hoisted herself up on to the trampoline; she needed to let off a bit of steam, and a laugh with her son was just the way to do it.

More than two minutes later Dan strolled up to see the kids and Leah having a whale of a time joining hands and jumping around in a circle.

'Leah, Leah, I need a wee,' Troy said suddenly.

'Well, don't do it on Dan's trampoline. OK guys, that's

enough. Let's go and get lunch.' Leah looked across. 'Hi, Dan, how long have you been there?'

'Just arrived,' fibbed Dan.

'Right, you boys go to the loo first-off. There's one over there.' Leah pointed.

The three friends jumped down and ran off to clean up before lunch.

Dan helped Leah off the trampoline. 'Did you enjoy yourself?'

'So you *were* watching?' Leah ran a hand through her hair.

Dan looked at the angry red marks on her arm, but he didn't say anything.

'Come on, the kids are coming out of the toilets. We need to get a move on, or my mother will think we've got lost.' Dan walked with Leah as the kids joined them.

'Did you wash your hands, guys?' asked Leah, feeling somewhat giddy and berating herself for it. Why on earth did her knees want to buckle underneath her, when the conversation had been about loos, for goodness sake. Her heart sank as she saw Chelsea looking her way and scowling.

'Dan, can I ask you something?' she said as the boys ran on in front of them.

'Anything.' Dan leaned in to her.

'Well, I just wondered-'

'Coo-ee! Dan, honey, we're over here. Quickly, I need to ask you something and it's secret,' called Ruby in a hushed voice.

'Sorry, Leah, I'll get back to you on that question. The boys are in there. I'll just be one moment.' Dan pointed to a marquee as he went off to talk to Ruby.

THE LUNCH STARTED SMOOTHLY WITH NO MORE SIGHTINGS OF Chelsea. Joey arrived, accompanied by another young man.

'Just bring another chair up, Joey, and introduce your new friend,' said Sophie, who was completely monopolising Thomas.

Dan was sat at the other side of his mother, with Tom next to him.

'Well, everyone, this is Ben; he does several shows a year in this area of Hertfordshire. He also commentates for the local riding clubs, Dan, so if you wanted to hold a horse show, he's your man.' Joey smiled across at Dan. 'We've also nick-named the pink tent "Priscilla" after our favourite comedy film.'

'It's only right it has a name,' nodded Thomas. 'Do tents have feelings?'

Everyone laughed, then Tom simply said, 'I'm not sure, but the people and the dogs in them do all have feelings and my mummy says you should always consider people's feelings.'

Dan looked fondly at Leah and smiled. When she smiled back at him, he saw the glitter of tears in her eyes; she quickly blinked them away, but Thomas had noticed too.

ONCE EVERYONE HAD FINISHED EATING AND HAD CHANGED INTO their wetsuits and life-jackets, Dan collected Hero to do some of the easier rescues. The first one was to pull in the three little boys and their appropriate adult, who was Leah. When the boys screamed, 'Hero! Hero!' the big Newfie walked into the water at a steady stroll then swam strongly to all four of them. Tom grabbed hold of his water harness as instructed and Hero happily towed the three kids and Leah safely to the shore.

Joey was waiting for them on the shoreline, wearing his

pink and grey wetsuit and with Yin and Yang sitting obediently by his side.

'Where do you want the boys, Dan?' Joey asked, shivering and looking longingly back at Priscilla the pink tent.

'With you, in the dinghy. Hop in and we'll get the kids in too.' Dan urged the kids to climb aboard. 'Come on, boys, let's give Hero one more rescue to do, then we'll rest him.'

'Grandma, watch me!' shouted Tom.

'It comes so naturally from his lips,' Thomas remarked to Sophie on the shore. 'You'd almost think he'd been calling you it all his life.'

'You're right, he's taken to saying it like a duck to water,' said Sophie, peeping at Thomas out of the corner of her eye. 'But then we have to remember there was always half a chance I hadn't croaked it by the time he, I mean Leah, found his dad.'

'Yes,' said Thomas thoughtfully. Then he beamed as the kids giggled when the oarsman started rowing them into the middle of the lake.

Joey leaned over the side and put his hand in the water. 'By heck, it's freezing,' he shuddered, then spotted the men treading water out by the floating buoys. 'What are they doing over there?' he asked the oarsman.

'Just a safety aspect,' the man replied.

'You mean we could be like the *Titanic*?' Joey stifled a yell and stage-whispered to himself, 'Calm down, Joey dear, don't get your knickers in a twist.'

When the oarsman had spun the boat about, the man said, 'Right, boys, pretend we're in trouble and shout for Hero.'

The kids and Joey screamed for help at the top of their voices whilst a photographer took photos and videos. Hero diligently swam out to the rowing boat and took the rope young Tom was holding out for him.

Leah was on shore watching an older dog pull in another

boat. She saw the dog sink a little then submerge, and she realised the rope was around his neck. Swiftly, she jumped into the water to rescue the old dog.

Dan ran up and helped the animal out. 'That was quick thinking,' he told Leah, shaken.

'Not really. Just instinct, that's all.'

He held out an arm for her to get up the bank. 'What did you want to ask me earlier?'

Leah opened her mouth to speak but something made her look across the grass to where Chelsea stood, her face a mask of hatred. 'It was nothing, Dan,' she said. 'In fact, I've already forgotten. As my grandma used to say, "It must ha' been sommat and nowt".'

Dan grinned. 'So you can talk this lingo too?'

'I can. And I'll teach you some day,' she said. 'Let's go and see if the old dog is feeling better, eh?'

The animal was wrapped in a towel and was being dried and comforted by his female owner. As the couple moved on, Dan linked arms with Leah in an open display of closeness. 'You do know you are a bewitching, beguiling woman, Leah Jensen.'

Leah smiled. 'Am I?'

'I hope you enjoy the surprise that I have prepared for my mother, you and our clever, adorable son.'

'Oh, I think the boys have had an absolute whale of a time already. Am I allowed to know more?' Leah knew the answer before Dan even shook his head and they both laughed.

The older dog was dry now and obviously feeling much better; seeing Leah, he trotted over to her as if he knew she'd saved him.

'Thank you so much for saving his life. Lomond is my world. I love him so much and I hadn't seen that he was in difficulties. I'm Jackie, by the way,' the woman said, with her curly dark hair framing her pleasant, round face.

'You're welcome. It was just lucky I happened to be watching.' Leah didn't want Lomond's mum to feel bad. She grinned to ease the tension. 'He seems none the worse for it.'

'Oh, he loves going under the water, but the fact that the rope had got tangled around his neck was a big shock.' Jackie petted her beloved old dog. 'Every year I say I'll retire him - and then when the time comes, he always whines to go in.'

Dan stroked the Newfoundland dog and looked into Lomond's trusting brown eyes. 'How about working him in a pair and letting a younger dog take the strain?'

'Good idea, Dan, thank you again,' responded Jackie as they saw Lomond walk to the shade near their caravan and lie down with a contented sigh.

Joey and Ben were just chatting about animals when Ben made an announcement.

'They're just having a fifteen-minute break, then we're going to do the *pièce de résistance*,' he told Joey, then he got up. 'But first I need the little boys' room. Can you look after the loudspeaker while I'm gone? Just say something if you like.'

'What's the special secret bit of the show then? I mean, these dogs are pretty impressive already.'

'No one knows as it's a surprise for Mr Ryan's mother, but I think your cousin Leah and Tom are involved. Just knock that switch down when you want to speak, and flick it back up when you've finished. You can announce the spectacular surprise if you like when I get back. In the meantime, remind everyone where the coffees and teas are, et cetera.' Ben winked and left the tent.

Joey looked at the microphone. Daringly, he moved the switch down and announced, 'Ladies and gentlemen, children and dogs, refreshments can be taken in the two large marquees, thank you.'

He went to flick the switch back up, but something caught his eye out on the lake and he mumbled to himself, 'Ooh, I bet there's a lot of Chilly Willies out in the lake today, so beware of shrinkage, you blokes, and don't despair if you think it's disappeared. It hasn't, it's just hibernation of the nth degree.' He then noticed the switch. 'Oh fuck.'

Joey looked outside apprehensively and saw several people tittering whilst others were outright laughing.

Ben literally flew into the tent. 'Joey, what are you doing?'

'Sorry, I got distracted. I saw a bird flying down to the lake and forgot that I hadn't flicked the switch off. Honestly.' He saw Grandad Thomas marching towards the pink tent with Sophie. 'Help! Let me get under this desk, Ben. My grandad is on the warpath. Don't let him catch me.' And he scooted under the desk.

'Ben lad, where's that grandson of mine?' Thomas asked sternly.

'He's gone to fetch me a coffee. I'm parched.' Ben smiled weakly, hoping Thomas would believe him.

'Come on, my dear, let's go and search for the scoundrel,' said Thomas to Sophie.

'He was just being himself. Just like Dan said,' Sophie said, trying to defend him.

'Oh, get on with you, Sophie love. I know you've got a soft spot for the lad. It's true - he's a lovable rogue,' commented Thomas whilst nudging Sophie and pointing under the desk.

Sophie tried not to laugh.

As they left Ben's pink palace, Thomas called behind him, 'You can get out from under the table now, Joey, and mind your words when there are kiddies around.'

'Yes, Grandad,' came the muted response and as Joey

squeezed from under the desk, he said fearfully, 'Has he really gone?'

Ben laughed. 'Oh yes, he's gone. Now let me show you how to work this microphone properly.'

Before long, Dan came into Priscilla to announce, 'Joey, it's your turn to get wet.'

'Do I have to? I don't really like the cold,' moaned Joey.

Ben raised an eyebrow. 'I never took you for a Miss Scaredy- Pants.'

'Well, maybe I could go in the lake,' Joey sighed and reluctantly walked out with Dan as Ben told everyone over the Tannoy that a surprise dramatic double rescue was about to take place.

'So - what do I need to do?' asked Joey. He was fearing the worst.

25

BEAUTY AND THE BITCH

At 3 p.m. Dan asked Leah and Tom to swim to a certain spot in the water and Joey to make for another place across the lake.

'Remember to splash about. Shout "Dog! Dog!" and not "Help!" as people have heard that and called the emergency services before now,' Dan explained.

'But if I shout "Dog!" or "Bitch!" won't Chelsea come and rescue me?' Joey knew it was rude but he couldn't resist making the comment.

Dan ignored him even though Leah stifled a laugh. Dan showed her and Tom where they should swim out to. He pointed to the other side of the lake. 'There will be stewards near to you for safety reasons. They are Navy personnel and underwater divers, so please don't worry.'

'Ooh, that's nice. Sailor boys,' returned Joey, looking at the stewards in a new light.

'You'll be fine, Joey. We all will,' said Leah reassuringly.

Dan quickly jumped in the Range Rover and disappeared beyond the lake. He drove around a clump of trees and out of sight to a waiting helicopter.

Several men were standing near the helicopter and two Newfoundland dogs stood with them, wearing their own life-jackets.

'Are we ready, guys?' Dan asked, as he helped them get the two dogs into the flying machine.

Leah and Tom trod water whilst waiting for the finale.

'Hear that, Tom?' Leah pointed. 'It's coming from beyond those trees. Over there, darling.'

'What is it, Mummy?'

'Look, you can see it now,' said Leah, quietly amazed.

The helicopter beat its way around the lake and hovered near Leah and Tom, sending the surface water spraying.

'Ooh, look at Dan's chopper,' shrieked Joey camply.

The first Newfoundland dog jumped bravely out of the helicopter and Dan followed. As quickly as the dog submerged into the lake it re-emerged and swam strongly towards Leah and Tom, who were waving, calling 'Dog! Dog!' and splashing. Dan quickly swam after the dog, then the helicopter flew on towards Joey, who was caught up in the excitement and had forgotten all about the cold.

The second dog dived into the water followed by a handler. The applause and cheers were deafening, as was the sound of the helicopter as it flew back beyond the trees.

Leah was full of joy as the Newfoundland dog, and Dan,

rescued her and Tom. Once again, she saw Dan as a man, not a businessman but just a human being in touch with animals and nature and connecting with his son.

'Grab the strap on Bruno's life-jacket, Tom, and let him pull you into the shore,' Dan said loudly because of the clatter of the receding helicopter. 'Leah, grab me around my waist and I will hold on to Tom.'

JOEY SQUEALED, 'COME TO MAMA, BABY, COME TO MAMA.' And when he noted how handsome the man was, who was accompanying the dog, he added in a whisper, 'And bring your Daddy, baby, bring your Daddy.'

'Just take hold of his life-jacket and he'll pull you in,' instructed Joey's human rescuer, but there was no doubt who the heroes of the day were.

'Is it true you are in the Navy?' asked Joey, feeling rather breathless.

'Yes, the Special Forces,' said the man.

'Ooh, I'm *sooo* impressed. I've seen you people on TV. I think you're ever so brave.' Joey grabbed the dog's strap on his life-jacket. 'Good dog, now please take me back to dry land before I really do shrivel up and disappear.'

LEAH GRABBED DAN AROUND THE WAIST FROM BEHIND AND IT felt so good.

Dan looked over his shoulder at her. 'How you doing?' he asked.

'I'm fine. Just wanted to say thank you for this. I know it's done for your mother's birthday, but you're making Tom really happy too,' she said into his ear.

'I'm doing this for you too,' Dan whispered back.

There was no time to say any more as they'd reached the bank.

Bruno had completed his rescue in style. As Dan helped Leah out of the water, the huge dog shook himself all over them. Sophie was laughing and Thomas was keeping Yin and Yang amused just a little way up the bank.

Kye the Newfoundland bitch meanwhile was trying to pull a very resistant Joey back onto terra firma.

Chelsea stood at a distance staring at them all like the wicked godmother at a christening. If looks could have killed, Leah knew she'd be in trouble. She turned away to see Joey being helped out of the water, by his male rescuer this time. He was almost swooning; he couldn't have been more obvious if he'd tried. When Leah turned back, she saw that Chelsea had disappeared and Dan was heading up the field with Tom to meet Sophie and Thomas.

'What's the matter, cousin?' asked Joey on seeing a worried look on Leah's face.

'It's *her* - she keeps singling me out. She makes sure no one hears her but me, and she is being downright awful,' Leah said bitterly. 'I think she's up to something.'

'Then you must tell Dan. He needs to know the kind of woman he employs,' confirmed Joey. For once, he was being deadly serious. He loved his cousin and didn't want any harm to come to her. She didn't deserve anything but happiness.

Leah was shaking her head. 'I can't. Don't you see, he has to find out for himself about her. He'll just think I'm being spiteful. I will not be the one who causes trouble. In fact, I feel sorry for her in a way.'

'Oh stop it, Leah!'

'Stop what?'

'You're too soft for your own good. Let the woman be seen for who she really is. Surely he must know the truth about her by now.' Leah nodded and walked away just as Ruby approached. Joey accepted a towel from her.

'Who must know what?' Ruby asked as they both watched Leah follow Dan.

'Dan must know what Chelsea is like,' Joey said. 'Surely?'

'You can forget that,' Ruby shrugged. 'We've been trying for years to get him out of her grasp. I mean, there's no denying she's a great organiser, but she makes everyone else do her work while she swans around, *and* she gets up Sophie's nose. They clash like the titans. Me, I think she's a-'

'A minging little maggot,' Joey interrupted. 'I mean, her name doesn't really suit her, does it? All the Chelseas I've known have been F.A.B.'

'I couldn't have put it better myself. "Minging little maggot" - I like it. And you've made me think, Joey: I must look into the name thing. There's something in the back of my mind about when she first arrived. I'm sure I saw her application form - or was it her birth certificate? - and her initial wasn't C. I think her name on the form was something beginning with M,' mused Ruby.

'Yes - Maggot!' grinned Joey, and the pair smacked palms in a triumphant high-five.

LEAH HAD JUST LAID THE BOYS' CLOTHES OUT AS THEY WERE being allowed an hour or two at the main party before going to bed.

Dan had disappeared, saying he was helping the Newfoundland team settle the dogs and that he'd meet Leah at the party around 7.30 p.m. That didn't give her much time to get ready, but Leah knew she must take a quick shower. Only, when she got under the hot spray, she wanted to linger for a while, and that was when she had time to think. Dan had said he was doing the water rescue for her too. What did he mean by that exactly? Was he trying to rescue her from something or someone? Did he know Chelsea was behaving in a threatening way to her - or was he truly just blinkered where his PA was concerned?

Stepping out of the shower, Leah pulled on her dressing gown then quickly dried her hair and pinned it up into a loose chignon. She applied her make-up before slipping on her under-wear, including stockings and suspenders, because they made her feel sexy. Carefully lifting her dress out of the suit cover, she put it on over her head then looked in the mirror. The dress was truly stunning; it flared at the waist and reached the floor and just showed enough cleavage to be tempting, thanks to the pretty brooch Keira had made for her. After applying another coat of lipstick, she left the room.

Several people turned to look at Leah as she walked down the stairs, but she didn't notice; she was busy scanning the hallway for Dan. Chelsea was there, of course, observing her with a look full of malice on her face.

'Oh Lee-Lee.' Joey hugged her. 'You look beautiful.'

Dan was talking to a guest. Sensing her presence, he turned around, smiled at Leah and her heart skipped a beat.

'Let me introduce you to Oliver,' he called, coming to meet her at the bottom of the stairs. 'He was the pilot flying the heli-copter today. Oliver, this is Leah, Tom's mum.'

Oliver smiled pleasantly, holding out his hand to be shaken. 'Pleased to meet you, Leah. I've heard a lot about you.'

'You have?' She was shocked. What on earth could Dan have said? 'Nice to meet you, Oliver. I wish I knew something about you as well.'

'Oh, your son and his friends were very enlightening about

you. I can fill you in about me and Danny Boy here whilst he seeks out his mother,' Oliver said with a grin at Dan. 'By the way, beautiful dress, Leah.'

'Thank you kindly,' Leah said as Dan went to get drinks.

A small, attractive brunette joined them and said affectionately, 'He's very good with compliments is my husband when I'm on the warpath. He thinks I will let him off the hook because he's being gallant. How do you do, Leah. My name is Beth.'

'Oh, and why are you on the warpath, Beth?' asked Leah politely.

'Because he left me to feed and settle the dogs so that he could come and have a beer.' Beth accepted a glass of champagne from Dan. 'Thank you, my second-favourite man.'

'I brought you a glass of champagne, Leah. By the way, you look like a beautiful goddess,' Dan said, handing her the glass. 'And so do you, Beth.'

'Thank you,' both women said simultaneously and Leah blushed a little as her eyes caught Dan's and held his gaze.

As they chatted for a few minutes, no one noticed Chelsea reach under the nearby table where glasses of champagne and white and red wine stood. Pretending to look for something on the carpet, she nimbly tied Leah's dress with a thin cotton thread to the white linen table-cloth.

As she scooted out from under the table, she bumped into Scotty.

'Whatever are you doing on the floor?' asked Scotty suspiciously.

'Shush, you imbecile. I lost my earring, that's all.' Chelsea tossed her head and walked away.

'I don't trust you,' muttered the little man, whose security training kept him alert. He knelt down and could see the thin thread attaching Leah's dress to the tablecloth. Carefully, he snipped the cotton with his Swiss Army penknife, which he carried with him everywhere. 'The little minx,' he murmured to himself.

'What on earth are you doing down there?' asked Dan as he looked quizzically at his security guard.

'I dropped my glasses,' lied Scotty as he quickly retrieved them from his pocket and held them up to show Dan.

Leah looked around. 'Here, I'll give you a hand up.'

Scotty took hold of Leah's outstretched hand and heaved himself to his feet. 'Thank you.'

'Shall we take a seat?' suggested Oliver.

As Leah moved away from the tables with the wine on them, Scotty saw Chelsea tense eagerly . . . but when the wine stayed put on the table, her face went red with frustration. Scotty walked up to her and said, 'What the hell are you playing at?'

'What do you mean?' Chelsea could barely speak she was so angry.

'You know exactly what I mean. I'm warning you now: you're playing a dangerous game here,' said Scotty.

'Thanks to your interference, little man, I'll have to think up another genius idea,' Chelsea spat out.

'Just you be careful, woman. This is starting to look desperate,' Scotty muttered as he walked away. He knew he would have to keep an eye on things; he didn't want Sophie's birthday celebration to be ruined.

Chelsea glanced across to where Leah was sat with the snivelling little brats who were asking if they could run around the outside terrace. Well, maybe that kid Tom could trip - that would wipe the smile off darling Mummy's face!

26

STAINS - AND SINS

Chelsea picked up a couple of glasses of wine and walked out onto the terrace. 'Hi, Tom, where is your mummy?' she asked sweetly.

Tom frowned. 'She was in there, but I can't see her. Why?'

'She wanted a glass of red wine so I have one here for her.' Chelsea held it out.

'I can take it to her, if you like,' said Tom magnanimously.

'Oh look, she's over there in the drawing room. Thanks, Tom. Don't spill it!' she added, smirking and following him back inside.

Tom walked into the room with Harry and Troy behind him, but just as they reached Leah, Chelsea stuck out her foot and tripped Troy, who fell like a skittle into Harry, who crashed into Tom. The glass of wine was sprayed onto Leah, all over her beautiful dress.

Despite her shock, Leah looked up just in time to see Chelsea high-tailing it back onto the terrace.

All three boys' faces crumpled up.

Joey ran to Leah's side. 'I saw the whole thing,' he burst out. 'She deliberately tripped Troy up. What a witch!'

'Oh Mummy, your beautiful dress.' Tom was nearly crying.

'It was an accident,' Leah said cheerfully. 'I will go and change and we can send it to the cleaners. Don't worry, boys.'

Dan walked up. 'What on earth has happened?'

'We didn't mean to,' said Tom.

'You didn't do it!' Joey exclaimed.

'Like I said, it was an accident,' Leah said quietly. 'Joey, come and help. If we get my dress into water straight away, we might save it.' She put a comforting hand on Tom's shoulder, then walked away.

WITH HER COUSIN'S HELP, LEAH GOT OUT OF THE DRESS AND gave it to him to hold. 'I'll just clean up and get changed, and I'll see you back down there.'

'Yeah, I'll get the stain in water right now; fingers crossed, it'll come out.' Joey left without a backward glance.

Leah put on her little red dress and looked in the mirror. Tears welled up in her eyes; she dashed them away. If the dress was ruined then so be it, but it was the way that bitch was going to let the boys take the blame that hurt. As Leah opened the bedroom door, she bumped into Dan.

'Oh.' Leah stood back. 'Sorry, Dan.'

'It's fine. I was on my way up to see you. Just exactly what happened back there?'

'Someone tripped Troy and he bumped into Harry and Tom, and as Tom had been told to bring me a glass of red wine, it went all over me.' She shrugged. 'That was the intention, I believe.'

'There was a mention it was Chelsea,' he said. Then: 'Are these tears in your eyes?'

Leah nodded. 'I've never had such an expensive dress in my life. It was so special. I loved it.'

'So did I. Did you actually see Chelsea trip Troy?'

'I can't say who it was. I wasn't looking.'

'No one seems to have seen who it was. I will ask Joey.' Dan dropped a quick kiss on Leah's lips. 'He will tell me. Right - let's go back to the party. My mother will be cutting the cake soon.'

'Yes, let's.' Leah was hungry – she also wanted to see if the cake was as good as the ones she had made.

AFTER A SHORT SPEECH BY DAN AND RUBY, THE CAKE WAS CUT and the streamers, sparklers and singing of 'Happy Birthday' were followed by a big round of applause.

'Gosh, I feel like a new bride at her wedding!' exclaimed Sophie. 'It's the next best thing, cutting a very special birthday cake.'

'What about you?' Joey asked Ruby as he tucked into his huge slice – well deserved, he thought, after being rescued from the lake. 'Don't you get cake?'

Ruby looked fondly at Dan and Sophie and said with a twinkle in her eye, 'Of course. I get the works - I'm family. My slice will be humongous. Now, did you see Chelsea too?'

'Yes, nasty piece of work that she is. I mean, it was clever, I grant you.' Joey folded his arms and prepared to gossip. 'It's obvious she wants Dan,' he said, pursing his lips.

'I know, we've been thwarting her for years,' Ruby confided. 'There was a period though when she seemed to have a hold on Dan. When she first came to work for him, there was a stage when she had him wrapped around her little finger.'

'The novelty must have worn off, obviously.'

'Yes - and with a bang. Just before he had his er . . . little encounter with Leah, he and Chelsea had a big argument - and that was when he went crazy and got himself a girl. Well, Leah.' Ruby looked at Joey. 'I know I shouldn't judge, but Leah doesn't seem like *that kind of girl.'*

Joey chose his words carefully, 'It was a spur-of-the-moment thing. We needed cash for something very, very important to us.'

'Oh, might I ask what?'

'I'm not supposed to say, but seeing as you twist my arm, it was for Grandad Thomas. He was in a great deal of pain and could barely walk due to a problem with his knee; he needed an operation but it wasn't available on the NHS. We'd gone through the usual things of trying to raise money – like a water-skiing display, dog walking, cleaning windows – why, I cleaned so many windows my hands were chapped for months. Then there was the wing-walking I did,' Joey fibbed.

'Wing-walking?'

'Oh yes. It was exhilarating, absolutely exhilarating,' Joey fibbed even more, loving having a captive audience.

'Wasn't it cold?' Ruby frowned.

'Oh freezing. When you're twenty thousand feet up, it always is,' he said airily.

'Joey.' Leah, who was sitting nearby, could take no more of this.

'Yes?'

'Who did the wing-walking?'

He looked a tiny bit shame-faced. 'Oh, I remember now - it was you, Leah. I just wish I'd had the guts to do it. Hah hah, Ruby, I had you there for a minute. It was the twenty thousand feet that did it. Found out. Huh!' Joey laughed simultaneously with Ruby.

As the music struck up again, he said to Ruby, 'Do you want to dance with me?'

Ruby looked Joey up and down. 'Yes, I will dance, thank you - but I have to say it's such a shame you bat for the other side.'

Joey grinned and held out a hand. 'Come and jive and we'll see who's best.'

AFTER HUNTING AROUND, SCOTTY LOCATED CHELSEA PEEKING out by the curtain. 'So, this is where you're hiding. That little show was despicable, even for you.'

'Go away, little man, I'm spying. They've not been dancing together, so that's good. But I think Dan knows it was me who wrecked her stupid dress and he's on the warpath looking for me.'

'It will all end in tears,' warned Scotty as he moved away.

'Yes, but they won't be mine,' Chelsea vowed. She peered around the curtain, again trying to see where Dan was, but he and Leah had disappeared.

DAN BENT DOWN TO GIVE TOM A CUDDLE AND A PECK ON THE cheek.

'It's a pity we couldn't stay at the party longer,' yawned Tom.

'I think all three of you are tired. Besides, your mum says it is bedtime and we grown-ups need to do more dancing, although with chocolate cake inside, it's going to be quite hard,' Dan grinned. 'I owe your mum a dance if she'll have one with me. What do you think, boys? Will she?'

Troy answered, 'Leah is a great dancer.'

'I seem to remember she is, in all disguises.' Dan looked at Leah and she actually blushed.

Leah quickly kissed Tom. 'Did you enjoy dancing with your Grandma Sophie and Ruby?'

Tom nodded. 'And Joey too. They won the best jive prize together, Joey and Ruby.'

'I think the judge couldn't decide between them,' Leah laughed.

Dan loved the way mother and son were so connected. 'Well, boys, it's time we said goodnight. I thought we could get up early and go riding in the school here tomorrow. I will give you all a lesson in dressage.'

'Yes, please!' all three boys chimed at once. Brought up in the lovely coastal area around Whitby, they could all ride.

'Right oh, lads. We're off now.'

There was a chorus of 'goodnights' and Leah left the room followed by Dan.

Dan put a staying hand on her shoulder. She turned into his arms and they kissed, then they heard giggling as three pairs of eyes watched from around the door.

'Back to bed. At once!' Leah commanded mock-sternly. She pulled out of Dan's arms and they went back down the stairs in silence.

'So, will you dance with me?' he asked.

'I can hardly say no, can I?'

'Well, you could, but I'd be mortally wounded,' he confessed.

Leah felt her heart flutter. 'Huh, mortally wounded. That's a laugh.'

'OK, I'll be sad,' he said softly as they reached the bottom of the stairs. His breath touched the nape of her neck. Then his lips followed. 'You know, a man could become addicted to you,' he almost groaned.

Leah bit her lip. 'Dan, this is moving too fast. Slow down, buddy.'

'OK, OK, I'll try,' he replied. As they walked back into the room that had the mobile dance floor, Dan took Leah into his arms.

'You'll let me know about your dress, won't you? I really thought it was great - or is it you who is great?' he said flirtatiously.

'Flattery will get you nowhere, Mr Ryan,' Leah replied. They danced in silence for a while until Ruby's large presence intervened.

'Hey, Dan, surely it's my turn to dance with you by now. Leah's not hogging you the whole night long, I won't allow it,' she joked.

'It seems like the other women in your life are demanding your attention,' Leah said, a little sadly. She had wanted the time in his arms to last forever.

Dan apparently felt the same, as the look in his eyes when the music stopped was full of regret. He dropped a kiss onto her forehead. 'Maybe we can catch up later?'

'For a dance, yes, I think we can.' Oh, why had her words come out like that, Leah agonised. She wanted to take them back, just as she wanted to rush him off to the bedroom, but she didn't want to be the one doing all the running. She went off to seek the comforting presence of her grandfather, but Thomas was otherwise occupied - seemingly captivated by Sophie's charms. *Talk about keeping it in the family,* Leah thought wryly. *We're both smitten with the Ryans – mother and son!*

27

BEAUTY IN BLUE JEANS

Darting back upstairs to her room, Leah changed into her jeans and sensible shoes then went outside, taking the path towards the stables where the lights were still on.

Sliding the door open, Leah saw a young groom look up.

'Is it OK if I come in?' she asked.

'Yep, of course. I'm just giving Galahad and Ebony a carrot or two before bedtime. I always like to make sure all the horses are accepting treats, as it usually means I can sleep well.' He added in a friendly tone, 'Do you want to help? By the way, my name is Quinn.'

'Hi Quinn, I'm Leah,' Leah replied as she closed the door quietly behind her, not wishing to spook the animals.

'I know who you are. Here then, here's the bucket of carrots. You know, I thought you might still be dancing with the boss,' Quinn added shyly.

'Maybe I should be dancing, but not everyone wants me to dance with Dan, it seems. I just need some space for a while, Quinn, just to process what's going on here because I sure as hell don't understand it.' Leah breathed a sigh as she took the bucket of carrots from Quinn.

The young man reassured her: 'If it helps, I don't think it's personal. Anyone who's ever shown the slightest interest in Mr Ryan has been got rid of swiftly and efficiently.'

'You've seen it first-hand?' Leah asked, then immediately went on, 'No, I don't want to know. And I won't get you into trouble for tittle-tattling with me.' Leah gave a big chestnut a carrot and watched him crunch it noisily to bits.

'Galahad has three carrots, not just one,' the groom informed Leah. 'I think he can count, so he'll know he's owed two more.' Quinn chuckled. 'And madam here gets so excited she smacks her lips. Just like that.' He did a demonstration.

Leah laughed at the black Friesian called Ebony, who then copied him with her own soft lips. 'She's beautiful,' Leah said dreamily. 'I've always dreamed of owning a Friesian.'

'Stick around and maybe you will,' the young man dared to say.

'Ah yes, but with your own admission I may be got rid of.' Leah went back to the bucket and collected two more carrots. 'Sorry, but I have to give this lovely lady three too.'

'I'm surprised that *she* hasn't got rid of these horses and us,' the young groom said in a low voice, 'and poor Hero is always getting in the line of fire. She hates dogs too. In fact, the only thing I've heard she does like is shopping - but I shouldn't harp on about she who I will not name.' Quinn gave a lengthy sigh, which made both horses look up at him.

Pulling himself together, he remembered his manners, saying, 'Can I make you an instant coffee in a jam jar, Leah, whilst you finish feeding these spoilt creatures their carrot treats?'

'Yes, please, it's a long time since I had a jam jar full of coffee.' Feeling much more cheerful, Leah was stroking the mare when Joey suddenly opened the stable door and walked in, with Ben following.

'Lee-Lee, you're missing the big show-down. Dan has collared Chelsea and there's a humdinger of a row going on outside.' Joey pointed to the house.

'Good. I want to miss it,' Leah said as she finished feeding the horses.

Quinn came back carrying a jam jar wrapped in a piece of rag. 'Here we go, your coffee, madam. Watch out though, the glass makes it very hot.'

'Ooh darlin', do you have a couple more?' Joey asked.

Quinn indicated the little kitchen at the end, saying, 'Through there,' then to Leah: 'Want to go into the next block? They'll be waiting for their carrots too.'

'And the ones in the paddocks?'

'Already been done.'

'Then let's do the next lot.' Leah picked up the bucket which she'd put down, but then the door flew open again.

'Here she is, the stupid cow who's blaming me for the wine her precious son tipped over her dress,' Chelsea screeched. 'Look at her, consorting with the stable boy. I can guess what they've been up to!'

Leah went white, as did Quinn.

Dan was right behind her. In a strong voice, he said: 'I will not have shouting in my stables, nor will I have you accusing Leah of something she hasn't done. As for your other insinuation, Chelsea, I will try to pretend I didn't hear it.' He looked absolutely furious.

Joey stuck his head out of the kitchen. 'I saw you push Troy, Chelsea, and I'm not the only one. Ruby saw you too.'

'Huh. That fat cow lies through her teeth too. I hate her!' And then Chelsea did what she always did when losing an argument – she made a dramatic exit, with the horses looking on.

'You're to go back to London and I'll see you when you've calmed down,' Dan called after her, his voice unsteady from anger.

Then Dan looked at Leah with the bucket of carrots in her hand and for a split-second he was lost for words. 'So, Quinn, how many more need to have their bedtime snack?'

'Just the giants,' Quinn told him.

'I was helping,' Leah explained, then: 'Dan, I'm so sorry your mum's birthday party has been disrupted because of me.'

'Not because of you, Lee-Lee,' Joey loyally defended his cousin. 'It was her. It's always her.'

'Well, let's not dwell on that, eh. Let's just feed these horses.' Leah held out the bucket to Joey. 'It's heavy, you can carry it, you lazy lump.'

Dan grinned, and the tension eased out of him. 'Come on,' he said, 'we can all go.'

It was Dan who took the bucket from Leah, his fingers touching hers lightly, then their hands met and held each other. 'Is this what taking it slowly is?' he asked gently, as the others left the stables.

Unable to speak, Leah simply nodded.

'Well, I still want my dance,' Dan added. 'Even in your jeans.'

Leah nodded again. What on earth was wrong with her? She felt tongue-tied and giddy.

The adjacent American barn had loose boxes down either side; 'the giants' as Quinn had called them, waited patiently for their carrots. Several whinnied a hello.

Leah and Joey fed the Suffolk Punch mares, the Shires and the Clydesdales. The Ardennes and the Percherons were next in line.

'I'm just stunned,' Leah said simply. 'Are all these on the danger list?'

'Some are in very grave danger.' Dan stroked Clara the Clydesdale mare. 'Clara here was in very bad shape when she came to Hambourne, but next year we will mate her. There are only sixty of these beauties left in the UK.'

Leah gasped. 'Only sixty?'

'Yes, and I have five of them, including one stallion,' Dan told her.

'He doesn't get many oats then, does he?' Joey said.

Dan grinned. 'Don't you worry - he gets enough. Some people want Clydesdale crosses.'

After they had finished feeding all the horses, Dan said, 'Let's go back, shall we?' He was looking at Leah.

Leah nodded. 'It was nice meeting you, Quinn.'

'Nice meeting you too. I'm off to me bed now. Goodnight, all.' And Quinn tactfully disappeared.

'Goodnight,' Dan called after him.

Joey and Ben followed the other two back to the house, where the music had become slow and seductive, as befitted the late hour.

'I believe this dance is mine,' said Dan, taking Leah into his arms.

Joey and Ben watched on as the couple moved slowly around the dance floor. 'What do you think?' Joey asked. 'Are his intentions honourable?'

'Well, mine aren't,' Ben mumbled.

Joey tossed his head. 'I beg your pardon, but if you're gay you shouldn't be fancying my cousin.'

'I don't fancy your cousin, numskull. I fancy *you*,' Ben tutted. 'I thought you knew. I thought I'd made it obvious. All day I've made it obvious.'

'So, what are we waiting for? My room or yours?'

'That's easy. I don't have a room, so it'll have to be yours.' Ben winked. 'I've always wanted to stay in this house.'

As they danced, Dan held her close so she breathed in his cologne. Leah inhaled blissfully, wishing she could stay like this all night.

'If only I could get inside your head,' Dan whispered.

'Really?'

'Yes, really.'

'I can tell you what you'd find. It goes something like this: "Tea or coffee? Sugar and milk? Gingerbread man or woman? Red Velvet sponge or treacle flapjack?" It's hardly mind-blowing, Dan.' Leah looked up; he was smiling.

'It's kept you in a job for a few years,' Dan said, respect in his voice. 'And it's kept our son in school without being on the breadline.'

'It certainly has. I saw a niche market and went for it.'

As the music stopped, Dan said, 'I will walk you to your room and be very courteous when I say goodnight, because we are taking things slowly and getting to know each other. Come on, you look tired.'

'I am very tired,' admitted Leah, yawning. 'It's been a long day.'

As they turned to go, Ruby came up to them. 'Is it your bedtime already, people?'

'It's mine, for sure. I'm really looking forward to a sleep-in,' Leah told her.

'And I'm getting up early to give the kids a dressage lesson.' Dan looked at Ruby as she put her head on one side. 'Yes? Is there something you want to say, Ruby?'

'No, no, not a thing.' Ruby really wanted to know if they were sharing a bed. They had shared a barn not so long ago, she thought, but for once she kept her thoughts to herself and all she said was: 'Goodnight then. Sleep well.'

As Ruby watched them walk away hand-in-hand, her curiosity kicked in and she simply couldn't resist the impulse to follow them; she watched as they kissed, then saw Dan turn away and walk towards his own room. Alone.

LEAH STOOD WITH HER BACK AGAINST THE DOOR. DAN HAD kissed her slowly and thoroughly and she was totally turned on. Oh, how she wished she'd never suggested taking it slowly, because right now she could be in his arms, making love, making magic. Dear God, it was going to be impossible to get to sleep tonight. But she was wrong.

After having a second shower that night, to wash away the evening with its triumphs and disasters, Leah climbed between the sheets, her muscles aching. She tossed and turned for a while, but even thoughts of Dan kissing her couldn't keep her awake.

AS RUBY WENT BACK TO JOIN THE REMAINING FEW PARTY-goers who were still awake and enjoying themselves, she saw Sophie getting up from her seat.

'Has Dan gone to bed?' Sophie asked.

'Yes - and alone too. Did you hear the fracas earlier?'

Sophie shook her head. 'No? Tell me more.'

'I reckon it was about the wine spilled on Leah's dress. Dan was really arguing with Chelsea.' Ruby shrugged. 'If it'd been up to me, I would have sacked her for what she did. I saw her deliberately push Troy and he fell against Harry who then fell onto Tom. It was like a line of dominos. That's how the wine ended up on poor Leah's best party frock.'

'Yes, I saw that bit. The cheeky cow, trying to frame my grandson.' Sophie huffed in disgust. 'So, he's had a ding-dong with Chelsea - about time too. When is he ever going to see the light where that young woman is concerned!'

'According to Scotty, she left in a huff.'

'Good. She shouldn't be allowed to get away with things like that. Well, Ruby, I must be getting old because I'm tired. This Birthday Girl needs her beauty sleep.'

'Is Thomas still here?' Ruby looked around for him.

'No, he went up not so long ago. I have to say, he's a good dancer,' Sophie mused.

'That's true. I'm only sorry I didn't get a chance to dance with him. He seems a very charming man with an equally charming grandson. They're a nice little family, and I even include Joey in that statement.'

'Oh? But you were the one who says - and I quote, "Once a bitch, always a bitch",' Sophie reminded her.

'Well, a person can change her mind. I'm actually getting rather fond of Leah. Come on, it's time we went to bed and please don't bang on my door in the morning. I shall still be fast asleep.' Ruby grinned, knowing full well she would be up before Sophie.

LEAH WOKE UP VERY LATE FOR HER, AS IT WAS GONE EIGHT o'clock. She felt tired and a little out of sorts. Luxuriating in the comfortable bed, she knew she would soon have to get up, jump into the shower, see where the boys were, check on Grandad Thomas and find out what Joey got up to last night . . .

Climbing out of bed, she crossed to the window and saw Joey and Ben walking down to the barns. The easy and intimate way they touched hands told her that Joey was losing his heart again, and she was glad. He had been lonely too long. With no further delay she washed and dressed and almost ran down to the stables.

'Wow, Mum, you look like a cow girl!' exclaimed Tom when he saw Leah's turquoise checked shirt, corduroy jeans and smart leather boots.

'Thank you, Tom. Have you enjoyed your dressage lesson with Dan?' Leah asked as she caught Dan watching her.

All three boys nodded their heads.

'They have all managed a half-pass,' said Dan.

At that moment Sisco came running in, panting, 'Boss, we have a problem.'

'What is it?'

'There's been a fire on the fifth floor at the Ryan's head office. The alarms and sprinklers worked fine, but there's a certain amount of damage,' Sisco informed him, looking distressed.

And that was the moment when everyone knew that the party was finally well and truly over.

28

THE KISS

Back at the Amazing Dog Friendly Café, Leah was serving a regular called Freddie with his pot of tea and cheese on toast when Joey came out of the café toilet looking very smart in his new jeans and white shirt that showed off his tan.

'What do you think, Lee-Lee?' he asked nervously.

'Lovely. You look really handsome. Joey, when you meet Ben, why not take him around the town and show him the sights before you bring him back here for his lunch,' Leah suggested.

'Oh, great idea. I could tell him about Dracula - take him to my old haunts, so to speak,' Joey enthused. 'Thank you, Lee-Lee.'

'You're welcome, now get a move on or you'll miss the bus. I have some lavender scones and bacon butties to make.' Leah shooed him out, then grinned to herself as she watched him walk proudly down the street.

JOEY ARRIVED AT THE STATION TO FIND THAT BEN'S TRAIN WAS running a little late. It gave him time to call in the Whistle Stop Tea Rooms for some chewing gum. He wanted his breath fresh just in case he got a welcoming kiss. Ah, but did he want all Whitby to see a kiss between him and Ben, he wondered. Oh well, he had a few minutes to decide.

When he saw the train pulling in, he muttered, 'Oh my giddy aunt I'm all of a flutter,' and his stomach lurched. 'Coo-ee, Ben, I'm here!'

Ben came up and hugged him, saying with a grin, 'Hiya, Joey. Wow - that was a long journey. I had to change at Northallerton and then at Middlesbrough. I'll come in the car next time.'

Hah, he's thinking of coming again already. 'Here, let me take your case. We can leave it with the lady in the Tourist Information.' Joey moved towards Ben who instantly grabbed him and kissed him. He was so shocked he swallowed his chewing gum.

'Are you OK?' Ben asked.

'Nice to see you,' Joey choked. 'Yes, I'll be fine.'

As he followed Joey towards the Tourist Information, Ben looked around.

'What a quaint town. I love it already,' he said.

'Oh, you should come when it's Goth Week. It's fabulous,' Joey said.

'If that's an invitation, then I'd love to come,' replied Ben.

After leaving Ben's luggage with the lovely lady, Joey told her: 'We'll be back for five-thirty when you close. I'm just going to take my friend on the Dracula tour. I will start at the Whalebone Arch.' He took Ben outside. 'I hope you can make it up this hill.'

Ben looked at the hill. 'I've been sitting on my bum in a

train for hours on end, so a walk even up that beast of a hill will be fine.'

'We'll go the scenic route, so if you see any shops you want to go in, we have plenty of time,' Joey said, and was taken aback when Ben grabbed his hand. He let go, saying sadly, 'I'm not sure Whitby is quite ready for this,'

'Whitby might not be, but I am,' Ben told him, grabbing his hand a second time.

'Ooh, well, in that case, I'm game,' said Joey meekly.

As they strolled hand in hand up one of the side streets, they looked in the window of a jewellery shop.

'Those are beautiful,' said Joey, pointing to a pair of cuff links made from the world-famous Whitby jet. 'I think I will let Leah know about those. They would look great on Dan, don't you agree?'

'Yes, he wears the kind of suits and shirts that would make the most of them, I guess.' Ben was curious. 'I can't help asking: how on earth did your cousin and Dan ever get together?'

'Oh well, they met on an . . . er . . . on a date. She literally fell for him on their first date.' He cleared his throat.

'She took a fall?' Ben frowned.

'Yes, from quite a height too. Luckily he caught her.' Joey looked all day-dreamy. 'She fell into his arms.'

'You'd have thought they'd have used a condom in this day and age,' Ben pondered.

'Well, it was over eight years ago, in the dark ages,' Joey laughed. 'Anyway, who cares? Tom is lovely and I can't imagine our family without him. In fact, it was Tom who recently got them back together. They'd split up for some strange reason.' Joey hoped he'd pulled that one off. He didn't want Ben to know anything about Madam Butterfly. Good cause or not, some people would never understand that they were doing it for love.

'He seems smitten, but then she's such a lovely person, Leah,' added Ben, a little out of puff as they'd started to climb the steep hill again. 'So, where are your parents?'

'In the back of Burke,' Joey replied.

'Where's that?'

'In the Australian Outback apparently. I live with Leah and Grandad because it's nice to have the company. So we're staying with them. Is that OK, Ben?' Joey asked.

'Yeah, sure. Wherever I lay my hat is home, as long as it's next to yours this weekend,' Ben grinned. 'Was that too cheesy?'

'Ooh no. I love it,' Joey gave Ben a squeeze as they walked on.

As they got to the top to the Whalebone Arch, Joey sat on the seat, saying, 'That hill gets harder to climb, but the view is so worth it. Look, don't the Abbey ruins look all mysterious? You should see them in the moonlight or even just at night because the ruins are all lit up. They also say that sometimes, you can see the white lady in the window openings. Of course, I've seen her.'

'You have?'

'Yes, usually when I'm tanked up and my eyes look in two different directions. I've never seen the haunted hearse though, which has a scary headless coachman and is pulled by four black Friesians. The horses and hearse jump over the cliff apparently,' Joey said in his best Dracula voice.

'I'm so pleased you asked me here. It's so beautiful, looking down across the harbour to the red tiled rooftops and the church above them,' Ben said, taking in a deep breath of the sea air.

'If you fancy another climb, there are a hundred and ninety-nine steps up to St Mary's - that's the church where the hearse is.' Joey said slyly, 'Shall I tell you about Dracula and how it is said he came to shore as a huge black dog?'

'Like a Newfoundland?'

'Maybe with bigger teeth. Hero is such a softie,' laughed Joey and he gasped as he realised Ben was going to kiss him again. Wow, this was going to be a great weekend.

But all too soon the weekend flew by, full of magic moments. Joey was falling in love. He only hoped Ben felt the same. Best of all, Grandad had accepted him into the bosom of the family and had treated him like one of his own.

AS THE TWO YOUNG MEN WAITED AT THE STATION ON THE Monday morning, Joey said, 'Shucks, we never did finish the Dracula tour, but it was worth it to call in and have a reading with that gypsy.'

'Do you believe in that kind of thing?' asked Ben, still rather dubious. 'I mean, she told you we would be with each other forever.' He rubbed the silver and jet ring that Joey had bought him.

'I know - and here you are leaving me . . .' Joey tailed off.

'But I will come again, if you ask me?' Ben replied softly.

'Then come when you next have time off. Ring me and let me know, and I will get time off again.'

'That's a promise. Now come here and give me a hug and a kiss,' Ben said, hoping the moment would stand still for an hour or so.

After their goodbyes Joey waved Ben off as the train pulled out of the station. Ben blew him a kiss. Satisfied, Joey ran all the way back to the café, his heart light.

29

THE HOLIDAY

Northumberland

Time passed, and apart from the odd phone call from Dan to Tom, Leah had not heard from Dan since that morning in the stables. Before they parted, Dan had held her hands, kissed her and said, 'I will see you in Northumberland.'

Now, as Leah stared out at the gannets feeding in a frenzy below them in the sea, Joey grabbed another ham sandwich from the picnic they had made to eat outside their rented holiday cottage and said, 'A penny for your thoughts.'

'Oh, I think you know my thoughts,' she replied, taking a gulp of water and almost choking as it went down. 'This is supposed to be our holiday, so why am I so miserable?'

'Is it because it's day two and Dan hasn't turned up yet?' Joey pushed the sandwiches at her. 'You're barely eating. What gives, cousin?'

'I know I'm worrying about nothing. He told Tom he would come, and he wouldn't let our son down.' Leah took a cheese sandwich and put it on her paper plate.

'You sure about that?' Joey had no illusions about men.

'I am. Anyway, when Tom comes back from the bathroom, I'm taking the dogs for a walk on the beach. I need some space. Is that OK with you?' She felt guilty, knowing it was a bit selfish.

'Course it's OK. You walk the boys and I'll take His Lordship over to the hotel for a hot chocolate after a whizz up and down the High Street.'

'Thank you. A walk on the beach always helps me to feel better.' Leah said goodbye to her son and Joey, and set off along the rocks. Yin began whining and Yang was jumping about, all excited. Curious to know what the fuss was about, Leah joined her dogs by a small rock pool.

'Oh baby, what are you doing here?' Leah asked the little Eider duckling who was swimming up and down in the rock pool and couldn't get out. The duckling was quacking and trying to escape but the rocks were too high. Leah gently picked him up out of the water and he quickly snuggled up to her warmth.

'Come on, boys, let's put him back with the creche.' Leah knew the Eider ducks had a creche near the water's edge and obviously this little one had been left behind as the tide had retreated.

Picking her way carefully over the beach, aware that the tide was turning and was about to start coming in, she stepped onto the rocks and placed the Eider duckling down next to another.

'There, the babysitter won't even know you've been missing,' she said cheerfully, then jumped back as a wave threatened to wet her feet. 'Come on, boys, let's get going.' She sprinted laughing up the beach with Yin and Yang running after her, yapping their heads off.

She stopped to take one last look at Bamburgh Castle,

standing majestically on the edge of the beach like a bodyguard protecting its shores.

'Come on, I suppose we'd better go back.' Leah loved this place so much, it was like a second home.

As Joey and Tom walked towards the High Street they chatted merrily, having been up to the stables to check on Powder. The pony had been happily eating the hay that Leah had fed her earlier that morning. Tom had given her an apple and promised her they would ride out in the afternoon. Powder too loved cantering down the beach and Tom enjoyed the thrill of riding her.

As they reached the small roundabout, Joey looked down the road from Alnwick and saw a posh horse box being driven towards them. The Ryan emblem was plastered on the lorry; what's more, there was a massive black Newfoundland sitting in the cab.

Joey grabbed Tom's hand. 'Quickly now, let's get back to the cottage.'

'What's the rush?'

'We just need to see your mummy. Come on.' Joey was walking extremely fast.

'Mummy's over there,' Tom pointed.

Joey bawled at Leah with his arms flailing, 'In the words of Mrs Bennet, "He is here. He is here".'

'Who is here?' Tom was baffled, and Leah was gazing around too.

Reaching her, Joey gestured at the horse box just negotiating the roundabout. Her heart lurched, and the only words she could utter were simply, 'You are right. He *is* here.'

'Too damn right he is. Go and brush your hair and teeth

then we'll walk back to the stables. I did wonder why the yard girls were getting the stables cleaned out.'

As they walked back to the holiday cottage, it had only just registered with Tom who 'was here'.

'Daddy said he would come. Why did you doubt him, Mummy?' the boy asked as he danced with Yin and Yang on the causeway.

'It wasn't that I doubted him,' Leah said, and shot a look across at Joey who mouthed 'liar'. 'It was that I've not heard from Dan for a while. He'd spoken to you, but not me.'

Tom frowned. 'But I told you he was coming. Didn't I?'

Leah watched her son's bottom lip tremble. 'You know what? I think you did. I must have forgotten.'

Joey smiled. He loved his cousin for being so forgiving and thoughtful.

Tom nodded, happy again. 'Does Daddy know where to come to find us?'

'He has all our numbers, he can ring,' Joey said as they walked up to the cottage.

Tom immediately got his phone out and checked it.

Leah unlocked the door with shaking hands.

DAN WAS TALKING TO THE OWNER OF SLALEY HALL STABLES, whilst Quinn was settling the horses in and Hero was stretching his legs.

Dan walked back up to Quinn, saying, 'We need to check into the hotel at the bottom of this street. It's overlooking the harbour. Then you can finish for the day. I will sort the horses out this evening. After all, I'll have three people to help me.'

'Thanks, boss, I am a bit tired,' Quinn said as he tied the last hay-net up. 'There we are. I've sorted the water, everything else is in the horse box - and you have a spare key for that, don't you?'

'Yes. You need to get some sleep - you've driven most of the way here.' Dan saw how shattered Quinn looked. It had been a very long journey, up from St Albans.

They walked out of the stable yard with their bags in their hands and headed down towards the harbour. Dan had clipped on Hero's lead for the walk down the High Street.

A SHARP RAP CAME ON THE COTTAGE DOOR.

Tom shouted, 'He is here! He is here!'

Leah scowled at Joey. 'My son is going to know every line from *Pride and Prejudice* before his next birthday because of you.'

'I know, it's fabulous, isn't it? He'll be an expert on Jane Austen. Wow.' Joey ran to the door and opened it. 'There are two good-looking guys here – shall I let them come in?'

Dan unclipped Hero and the huge dog ambled in. Yin gave a token bark, but Yang closed his eyes and went back to sleep.

'The Poms look tired,' remarked Dan as he hugged Tom and kissed Leah.

'They've just been on the beach,' she replied bashfully. She wanted to look at how well his shirt clung to his muscles, but she did not dare.

'That's a pity, I was hoping to take Hero there.' Dan was waiting for Leah to look into his eyes.

'Me and Tom can take him. You and Leah have a coffee and one of Leah's home-made ginger biscuits. Maybe she'll have one then too. She's hardly been eating anything,' announced Joey.

Leah glared at her cousin.

'I'd love a cup of coffee and a biscuit, if it's no trouble.' Dan grinned at their bickering.

'No trouble at all. Go and sit in the lounge, there's a lovely view over the harbour.' Leah walked into the kitchen and switched on the kettle. She heard the front door go and screamed when Dan put his arms around her waist and snuggled into her.

'I've missed you,' he murmured.

'Really?'

'Yes, really. It's been difficult. Part of the fifth floor was damaged, but thank God the building itself was untouched, as were the offices above and below. The sprinklers came on the moment the fire started, but as you can imagine, it was a mess. I've hardly slept . . .' Dan tailed off as Leah turned in his arms.

'You look exhausted,' she said, noting the grey shadows under his eyes.

'I am - so much so that I need a bed right now.' Dan's legs felt shaky with fatigue. 'I don't even think I've got the energy to eat a biscuit or go back to the hotel.'

Leah pointed up the stairs. 'Use my bed, it's the room at the back.'

'You are my angel, but you must wake me up to feed the horses.' Dan kissed Leah's forehead. 'Promise?'

'It depends - you look all in. Which horses am I feeding and what am I feeding?' Leah wanted to know. 'Just in case.'

Dan took a key out of his pocket. 'This is the horse-box key. I've already bagged up their feeds with their names on. They have haylage on a night. Thank you.'

'Go up to bed now,' Leah instructed as she switched the kettle off.

Dan walked to the stairs and climbed them. Leah could tell by the slowness of his steps just how tired he was. He'd soon be out for the count and would be sleeping like a baby.

WHEN JOEY ARRIVED BACK WITH HERO, TOM IMMEDIATELY looked around for Dan.

'Where's my daddy?' the boy asked.

'He's tired out, darling, he's in bed,' Leah said.

'You wasted no time,' Joey whispered.

Leah sighed. 'He's tired out, Joey. I'm amazed he's here at all. No wonder he's so jiggered.'

'Poor guy. Of course, he's tired.' Joey ruffled Tom's hair and switched on the kettle. 'Come on, let's all have a cuppa.'

After a refreshing drink and a few biscuits, the quartet set off for another walk; Hero was full of energy, relishing the sea air and barking at the gulls. On their return, Leah was surprised to see Dan sitting drinking coffee in the kitchen.

'You should have stayed in bed, you were all in,' she admonished him.

'I will be fine after some caffeine. I've had a good hour's nap. Besides, I need to feed the horses, and you've promised to help, Leah.' Dan smiled tiredly and Leah's heart melted.

'I have to feed Powder too,' Tom announced. 'And I will have to tell her I'm sorry. I promised her a ride on the beach this afternoon.'

'We can all go together,' said Joey, opening the biscuit tin and handing round some of Leah's gingerbread horses to make them laugh.

AT A HOTEL A HALF-MILE UP THE ROAD, CHELSEA LOOKED down her nose at the room she'd just walked into, even though for any normal person it was perfectly suitable.

'Naff place – ugh,' Chelsea shuddered, addressing the photo

of Dan that she'd brought with her. 'I really don't know what you see in the woman, the child and the annoying cousin. She may have you under her spell - but not for much longer.' Opening the bottle of champagne she'd brought with her, she poured a glass and raised it to her lips then walked across to the window. 'Perfect. From here I will be able to see when you go past on those ugly brutes of horses. They should be extinct by now, surely.'

She gulped down the champagne in one, refilled the glass and began to unpack.

TOM STOOD PROUDLY IN FRONT OF POWDER'S STABLE. 'DON'T you think she's the nicest pony you've ever seen?'

Dan peeked over the stable door. He looked at the pretty grey pony with the dark eyeliner-effect around her beautiful brown eyes. She was 14 hands high or so, he guessed. 'She's a beauty, son. I couldn't have chosen better myself.'

Leah and Tom were both thrilled with his words. 'I see you've brought three horses with you, Dan. Why three?' asked Leah.

'There's one for you and Joey, and Galahad for me. What's the point in having all these horses and not bringing them to such a beautiful place?' Dan walked up to Galahad's stable to change his water. He picked up two buckets, then went back for two more for his Friesian mare, who was smacking her lips at him. 'Hey, Ebony, stop trying to kiss me,' Dan teased her, before dropping a kiss on her soft nose.

'I'd smack my lips if you'd kiss me,' announced Joey, puckering his lips.

Tom giggled. He was very used to Joey's antics. 'Is that her name - Ebony?'

'It is, because as you can see, she is black. The Lippizaner is called Ivory or Ivy, and Ebony is Ebby for short. They are both beautiful animals.' Dan stroked Ebby and tried to ignore Joey's protruding lips; it was hard not to laugh.

'And which one is Mummy riding?' the little boy asked.

'Whichever one I am not,' Joey said immediately. 'Bags I take the grey.'

'That's a great choice. Ebby was for Leah anyway,' Dan told him. 'Are you hungry? We can eat at the hotel if you like?' He looked at Leah.

'Yes, please, Mummy.' Tom sent a pleading look at his mum.

'Yes, OK: does that include all of us?' she asked.

'Of course, and we can ride out on the beach tomorrow if you fancy it?' Dan suggested.

'I promised to do that with Powder.' Tom looked all serious.

'Good - I think we have a plan. Come on then, I'm starving,' Joey said, taking hold of Tom's hand. The mood had lifted and they were on holiday!

30

ARMED AND DANGEROUS

J oey had taken Tom back to the cottage. Dan and Leah sat having a drink and watching the fishing boats return into the harbour.

'This place is something else,' Dan sighed happily. He reached across and held Leah's hand. 'How did you find it?'

'I came here on a riding holiday and fell in love with it. Grandad spent hours wheeling Tom in the stroller whilst me and Joey rode up to the castle and back on the beach. We can do that tomorrow, if you'd like to?' Leah asked, trying to get her mind off the fact that Dan was rubbing his thumb over her palm, which was doing strange things to her insides.

'I'm not sure how slowly I can take this,' Dan said out of the blue.

Leah had been thinking the same thing earlier today. 'Then why wait?' she murmured. 'I've got to know you a little better and we can take this one day at a time.'

'Meaning?'

'Meaning where is your room?'

Dan grabbed her hand. 'Let's go.'

LEAH LOOKED ACROSS AT DAN AS THE SUNLIGHT PEEKED through the curtain. She wanted to be at the cottage for when Tom got up and yet she didn't want to leave the man beside her.

Dan reached across to brush the hair from her beautiful face. 'What's the frown for?' he asked.

'I'm torn. I need to be at the cottage, but I don't want to leave you. I'm in a dilemma,' Leah said.

Dan rolled across her. 'Stay a few more minutes with me, then we'll both go back to the cottage.'

Leah could feel his arousal, and it excited her. She put her arms around his neck and they got to know each other all over again.

JOEY WAS BRUSHING IVY. 'THEY'RE ALL READY FOR OUR RIDE on the beach today.'

Dan was saddling up Galahad. 'Just watch your bottom when you saddle Ivy up,' he advised, 'as she likes to take a nip.'

Tom started giggling as he put Powder's bridle on. Leah had just finished tacking Ebby up. 'It's a nice day to ride,' she said. 'Not too windy, not too warm.'

'Yes, I'm going to enjoy it,' said Dan as he went to help Tom. 'OK, Tom, what have you forgotten to do?'

The boy shook his head.

Dan bent over and picked up Powder's front legs one by one, then stretched them out. 'We do this . . .'

'To make sure the girth isn't pinching,' said Tom.

'Good boy, that's exactly right. She needs to be comfortable during the ride,' commented Dan.

'And have you done Galahad?' asked Leah as she looked over the stable door.

'Of course he has, Mummy,' Tom said, defending his father instantly.

CHELSEA WAITED BY THE WINDOW IN HER HOTEL ROOM. SHE knew Dan would be chomping at the bit - literally - to ride his precious Galahad on the beach, and she would make sure she was right behind the riding party. Reaching for her coffee, she saw the four of them doing a sitting trot down the road past the hotel. Grabbing her car keys and the tote bag instead, she hastened out of the hotel and into the car park.

Jumping into the hire car, Chelsea drove towards the castle, passing the riding party as she went. Even Chelsea had to admit that Bamburgh Castle was a sight to remember. It was a colossal structure and the most impressive building she'd ever seen.

She swung down the road towards the sea, knowing that this was the way they'd come to get onto the beach. She'd done her homework. Parking the car up, she searched around. This was the perfect spot. Chelsea laid herself down on a rug in a dune overlooking the beach - and waited.

About twenty minutes later she heard the horses' hooves coming down the lane. As the three horses and one pony with their riders trotted past her, she waited – then let the airhorn rip out twice.

She heard a scream, then the thunder of a horse galloping across the beach. Ebony had panicked and was dashing head-long, with Leah clinging on for dear life.

'Leah!' Chelsea heard Dan shout - then there was a second

thunder of hooves. She ducked as she saw Joey struggling with his mount. Tom's pony was just jogging at his side.

'That one would need a rocket up its backside,' noted Chelsea as she got up and went back to the car, brushing sand off her hands.

JOEY GLANCED ACROSS AT THE DUNES ONCE HE'D GOT IVY under control, then did a double-take. Surely it couldn't be . . . He noticed Tom looking in the same direction.

'I thought I saw Chelsea.' Tom looked worried. 'Shouldn't we go after Mummy?'

'Yes - right now, and let's hope that Dan has caught up with her,' said Joey. 'Ready to gallop?'

Tom nodded; he was a very good rider. They both set off and soon picked up speed.

Ebby was thundering down the beach. Leah was on a sixteen-hand horse that was out of control. Sand and sea were being flung up in their wake. Leah was stood up in her stirrups pulling back with her reins as much as she dared and talking as soothingly as she could under the circumstances, which in her case was nearing hysteria. However, she couldn't let the Friesian mare sense her nerves. At one point, Leah grabbed a handful of Ebony's mane just to keep herself from falling off.

Dan galloped after Leah. He shouted urgently to her, but was aware that she probably couldn't hear him. 'Leah, can you steer her into the water?' he bawled, to no effect. Then his heart sank as he saw a rocky outcrop jutting out of the sea. He urged Galahad even faster. The big horse quickly made up the ground and was side by side with the runaway Friesian. Dan pushed Galahad into Ebby's shoulder as he managed to reach her breast girth and they slowed down, but then Ebby barged into Galahad and thundered down the beach again. There would soon be no beach to gallop on. Dan was frantic.

Then something strange happened. Joey and Tom galloped up on their mounts. Ivy began to whinny – and not just the once either. She whinnied and whinnied and whinnied - as if she was worried for her best friend - and that's when Dan saw Ebby falter, enough for Leah to drive her into the surf and bring her to a halt.

The boys cantered up to the sweat-covered horse who was snorting into the waves; her flanks heaving in and out.

'Oh my God, are you all right, Leah?' Dan jumped off Galahad and ran into the surf to grab Ebby's reins. He walked the shuddering animal out of the water and then helped Leah down from the saddle.

He wrapped one arm around her and kissed her wind-strewn hair. 'What on earth happened back there?' he asked shakily and bent down to check Ebby's legs.

Tom piped up, 'It was Chelsea. I saw her with one of those things people have at football matches. It was an airhorn thingy.'

'Chelsea's in London. You must be mistaken, son,' Dan replied.

'Who's that charging down the beach?' asked Joey, shaking his head at Tom who was about to protest.

Dan looked up. 'It's Quinn.' He stroked Ebby. 'This has really scared the both of you, hasn't it?' He dropped a kiss on Leah's lips. 'I'm so sorry. I didn't know she would react like that.'

'It's not your fault, but who would do such a thing?' Leah asked. 'Surely anyone with a brain would know not to do that near horses. We could both have been killed.'

Quinn reached them, quite breathless himself. He grabbed Galahad's reins, since the big horse was amiably wandering around behind Dan. 'What's happened, boss? I saw Ebby from way down there, and could hardly believe my eyes. She's normally such a calm girl.'

'Well, someone blew a horn, right behind us in the dunes,' filled in Joey. 'And Tom thought it was Chel-'

'Chelsea doesn't know where I am and I'm sure she wouldn't do anything that cruel.' Dan loosened Ebby's girth. 'I suggest we walk this young lady back and let her cool off in the stables.'

Joey was watching Quinn; the latter looked guilty and obviously knew more than he was letting on. 'Here, Leah, jump on Ivy,' he suggested. 'I will walk back to the stables with Quinn. You, Dan and Tom carry on with your ride.'

As Joey and Quinn walked the now quiet mare on the back road to the stables Joey asked outright, 'Did Chelsea find out from you where Dan was coming?'

'Yes, it's all my fault, although to be fair, I wasn't told to keep it a secret. I mean, I know she's a mad bitch, but this is something else entirely. Who could have predicted this?' Quinn stopped and stroked Ebby. 'You could make a case for calling it attempted murder. The woman is unhinged. I don't know why she carries on like this because apart from a fling when he first hired her, Dan has never looked at her in that way again, from all accounts. Did you see her?'

Joey nodded, then added, 'Mind you, I couldn't swear on it, but Tom seemed pretty sure.'

'Yes, Tom seemed adamant it was Chelsea and I wouldn't put it past her. She's got me in trouble before. The stable lads call her "the smiling assassin",' Quinn said thoughtfully.

'I don't suppose it's any good speculating who it was. We need proof.' Joey was wondering how he could find out.

THE MOOD WAS MORE RELAXED WHEN THEY ALL REACHED THE stables at around the same time. Ebby whinnied as she saw Ivy coming out of the bridleway.

'How is she now?' Leah asked after the mare.

It was Quinn who answered. 'She's fine now. Much more herself.'

'Good, because it wasn't her fault,' Leah stated.

Soon all the horses were rubbed down and munching on hay.

'Quinn, have you seen my magic wand?' Dan asked.

Quinn walked over to the horse box. 'I'll check, boss, but I thought you had it on the ride.'

'I'll go and look in the stable,' Dan said and walked away.

Joey followed Quinn, quipping, 'You know, Leah saw his magic wand just over eight years ago and she's not been the same since!'

Quinn pulled out a riding crop with a silver end. 'It's here, boss.'

'Huh, she never told me it had a silver knob. How remiss.' Joey laughed at Quinn and the latter could barely keep a straight face when he passed the precious dressage whip to Dan.

'Thanks – I wouldn't want to lose it,' Dan explained. 'It was my father's.'

As Dan walked back to the stables, Joey was longing to launch into more innuendoes about Dan's 'dressage whip', but thought perhaps he'd made enough cheeky remarks for one day.

'You're so funny, Joey,' said Quinn as he walked away.

'No one would look for *my* wand if it went missing,' Joey tutted. And then he thought, *Well, maybe Ben would . . .*

IN THE COMING FEW DAYS THE PARTY RODE AGAIN ON THE
beach, and other than a bit of dancing about, Ebby had returned
to her normal amiable self. However, the whole sorry incident
had put a downer on the week. When it came time for Dan to
leave, Leah felt there had been a wedge put firmly between
them, and it saddened her.

His parting words lifted her spirit somewhat.

'The next time Tom is due to visit, why don't you all come
down? I know my mother would like to meet Thomas again. I
believe she was very impressed with his dancing.'

'Thank you. I will ask Grandad Thomas and let you know.'
The time for Dan to leave was imminent and Leah didn't want
him to go - it was as simple as that.

Dan gave her a peck on the cheek and helped Hero up the
ramp into the cab before storing the ramp away safely and
jumping into the cab himself. He looked down at Leah and his
heart wrenched, for she appeared so sad. He almost leaped back
out to scoop her into his arms and kiss her senseless, but in the
end he settled for a wave and a wink. It wasn't enough for
either of them.

31

QUEEN OF THE DUNG-HEAP

'What are you talking about?' Chelsea demanded.

Scotty shrugged. 'I heard Ruby and Sophie saying that someone saw you.'

'Who exactly?'

'There was a mention of Tom.' Scotty tried to placate her. 'But who's going to believe a child, I ask you.'

'Precisely! Sneaky little shit that he is,' she sneered.

'But then again, you shouldn't be doing that kind of thing.' Scotty couldn't get his head around it. 'Someone could have lost their life, and the horse could have died or broken a leg.'

'Frankly, who cares. The main thing is that Dan believes I was in London.' Chelsea shuffled a few papers around. 'I'm tired. I think I'm going home to my flat now, especially since Dan's in Rome and can't check up on me. Setting a fire here has really thrown a spanner in Mr Perfect's works.'

'It was you?' Scotty was appalled.

'No, stupid, of course it wasn't me,' the young woman said rudely. 'I've got no idea who it was. By the way, is the Fire Report back? Do we know what started it?'

'Not yet, I've not heard a thing,' Scotty said, getting a bit disgruntled.

'When is The Bitch coming to Hambourne again?' Chelsea asked.

'She's not a bitch. Leah's all right, you know. They're due to arrive on Friday, and for heaven's sake don't start anything.'

As he walked away, Scotty thought about Chelsea's reference to throwing a spanner in the works by setting a fire in the office. Was it her? As of late, he wouldn't put it past her. 'Arson and attempted murder. Whatever next?' he mumbled to himself.

'It's the first sign of madness, talking to yourself,' said Ruby from behind him. 'You're a friend of the witch, do you think it *was* her causing havoc up in Northumberland?'

'Your guess is as good as mine,' Scotty snapped and strode off before Ruby could pry any more.

Ruby shrugged and took one of the lifts down to the front entrance of the Ryan's London HQ. She had a secret mission to fulfil - and she'd better get a move on.

LEAH WAS FEELING AS NERVOUS AS A KITTEN AS SHE DREW UP in front of Hambourne Manor; she'd not seen Dan since Northumberland and wasn't sure of the reception she might get. Did he still have the same feelings for her as she had for him?

'Daddy,' called Tom as he saw his father coming up from the stables dressed in his horse-riding outfit and long leather boots. The little boy jumped out of Leah's four-wheel drive and ran towards him.

'Hi, son, it's good to see you all. Hello, Leah, Thomas and not forgetting our colourful Joey.' Dan kissed Leah's cheek, shook Thomas's hand then put a peck on Joey's cheek.

'At last. A kiss,' Joey announced, very satisfied with himself.

Everyone laughed, even Leah as it eased some of her nerves. Tom thought it was hilarious.

'Lunch should be ready very soon. I will need to get changed and you all no doubt want some time to recover from the long journey, so how about we rendezvous in the blue drawing room - if you remember how to get there. I will carry your suitcases, Leah and Thomas.' Dan grinned as Joey huffed and puffed, pretending that his and Tom's luggage was heavy.

The blue drawing room was another room with the same white carpet as in Dan's office, thought Leah. *A carpet not chosen by you, Dan.* Sad really, she said to herself as she followed Dan and Grandad Thomas. She didn't like the idea of Chelsea choosing everything here. Tom and Joey knew exactly which rooms they were in, and headed straight for them.

Dan put Thomas's case in the doorway. 'Lunch will be in around half an hour.'

'Thank you, Dan, I will be there,' Thomas replied.

As they walked towards Leah's room, Dan asked her: 'Have you missed me?'

The question took her aback. 'As much as you've missed me,' was all she was prepared to say.

'Well, in that case . . .' He dropped her bag on the floor and scooped her up into his arms. She was laughing as he carried her into her room and put her down on the bed. Then, just as he knelt next to her, there was a knock on the door.

'Mummy, I've lost Joey and I can't find the blue sitting room.' Tom sounded distressed.

Leah got up from the bed. 'The penalties of having a large house,' she sighed. 'You go and get changed and I will take our son downstairs.'

Dan nodded and watched as she walked out of the room. He

wasn't sure where he stood with her. They'd parted in Northumberland under a dark cloud, even though they'd both pretended everything was all right. What Tom had said about Chelsea was still niggling at the back of Dan's mind. It wasn't that he doubted what Tom thought he'd seen, but he was sure Chelsea didn't know where he'd been going on his short break - and if she *had* known, who the hell could have told her?

He ran a hand through his hair. No, Chelsea would never do anything so dangerous as deliberately frightening Leah's mount. He couldn't bear to think how that incident could have ended. No, surely it was impossible.

'GRANDAD, HAVE YOU SEEN MY DADDY'S SPARKLY EGG?' TOM asked as he pointed to the *Fabergé*.

'My, that is bonny.' Thomas looked through the cabinet. 'Yes, it's a blummin corker.'

Dan immediately suggested, 'Let me show it to you, Thomas. I bought it years ago, in a moment of madness.' He unlocked the cabinet, carefully took the *Fabergé* out and handed it to Thomas.

'Can I see, Daddy?' Tom looked curiously at the diamond-encrusted egg.

'Of course, my boy.' Dan smiled at his son. 'Just be careful with it, mind.'

'I promise I will,' Tom said.

Leah spotted Chelsea loitering in the drawing-room doorway, watching Tom, and wondered what her arch-enemy was up to now.

Tom took the egg from his Grandad Thomas, saying in a hushed voice, 'Wow, it's so sparkly. I love it.' Then he handed it cautiously back to Dan.

Dan replaced the egg in the cupboard, thinking how hungry the ride out in the fresh air had made him. 'If we can find Joey, we can have lunch,' he said.

'Where's Sophie?' Thomas wanted to know. He was excited at the thought of seeing her again.

Leah watched Chelsea mimicking her grandfather. On seeing that she had been observed, Chelsea smirked and walked away.

'Knowing my mother, she'll be at the table, waiting for her lunch,' Dan told him. 'She and Ruby are always at the front of the queue when food is involved, but Ruby is away until tonight.'

'Does your PA always mimic her elders?' Joey asked, unsmiling, as he entered the room.

'Shush,' Leah begged.

Dan was just about to answer when Thomas interrupted, 'Now you're here, lad, what say we go and eat.'

'Good idea.' Dan held the door and waited for Leah. 'Come on, let's go for lunch. By the way,' he added in an undertone, 'have you brought your swimwear this time?'

'I have. I wouldn't dare go in just in my underwear with Grandad being here.' Leah met Dan's eyes. 'Don't laugh like that. And you won't tell him, promise me, Dan.'

'I promise I will keep our first secret, Leah.' Dan trailed a finger over her cheek. 'Sealed with a kiss.' He dropped a quick kiss on her lips, grabbed her hand and tugged her towards the dining room.

JOEY AND LEAH HAD RACES IN THE INDOOR SWIMMING POOL, forced by Tom into swimming in all kinds of ways to slow them down.

'Mummy, you're swimming with two arms. Only swim with one!' Tom had ordered.

'Yes, sir, if I can manage without drowning myself,' Leah joked, then the smile died on her lips as something made her look up and she saw Chelsea glaring through the glass at them.

Joey stopped swimming and followed Leah's gaze. 'She hates you,' he said baldly.

'I don't know why.' Leah felt resentful. 'She's had years to hook him. It's hardly my fault if he's not taken the bait.'

Dan swam up. 'The bait? What bait? There are no fish in this pool.' He splashed Tom, who splashed him back.

Joey, quick on the uptake, said, 'Leah was wondering about the kind of bait you'd need for the fish in your lake.'

'You like to fish?' Dan asked in amazement.

'No, but Grandad does,' Leah said – and at least that was true.

LEAH WAS HELPING QUINN AND THE OTHER STABLE HANDS MOVE the muck pile back from the cobbles and had no idea that Chelsea was about to launch another attack on her. Her rival's rage was at a fearsome pitch, and the only thing on her mind was that she must get rid of Leah – by any means. Spotting her chance, she emerged from the doorway where she'd been hiding and ran at Leah like a woman possessed - and she must have been possessed to try and run on cobbles in high heels. Before she even reached her victim, her left heel caught in the cobblestones and she fell face first into the muck pile as Joey pulled Leah out of Chelsea's path.

Chelsea came up coughing and spluttering.

Joey smiled, his voice not revealing the mixture of shock and mirth he was feeling inside. 'Oh dearie me,' he said with fake concern, 'there's shit, shit, shit all over the place, and you are covered with it, lady. Pity your Jimmy-Choos let you down at such a crucial moment in your life.'

Glowering, she limped away, balling her fists at her sides and muttering, 'This isn't over yet.'

Joey then started laughing so hysterically that all the stable hands joined in too; they laughed until their sides ached as Joey mimed the accident to perfection. Leah bit her lip, for she knew she'd be the one to bear the brunt of Chelsea's wrath.

Dan came through the American barn to see Leah helping the lads.

'You don't have to do that,' he said.

'Oh, but I do. I've not had a work-out like this since last month,' Leah replied happily.

'Chelsea was down here a few minutes ago,' Joey said, his laughter finally exhausted. 'The stable yard is no place for heels but she insisted on wearing them and then fell over into the muck pile when her heel broke. She just missed dragging Leah down with her.'

'Did she hurt herself?' Dan enquired.

'Yes. Her pride was hurting her bigtime, and her Jimmy Choos were broken; other than that, she's fine. Oh – except that her clothes and face were covered in poo. That might have upset her a tad.'

'Oh no.' Dan sighed heavily. 'I'd better go and see if she's OK. Sorry, Leah, I'll be right back.'

'Or you don't have to go at all,' said Joey under his breath.

'You go, Dan. See how the poor girl is. It was quite a tumble she had,' Leah remarked, her concern quite genuine.

As Dan strode away, Joey turned to Leah.

'Honestly, Leah, you are too nice for your own good. She was going to push you into the muck pile and probably rip your eyes out at the same time. If serendipity hadn't taken over it would be you in the proverbial shit and *not* Chelsea.'

'True, but I can't help feeling sorry for her . . .'

'What? Are you for real? She's out to get you. You mark my words.' Joey stomped off to see where Tom was.

Leah looked across at Quinn, who had been helping along-side her. 'I suppose you think the same?'

'It's not really for me to say, but you need to watch your back, Leah.' And Quinn picked up the yard broom and started sweeping up again.

DAN LOOKED HIGH AND LOW FOR CHELSEA BUT EVENTUALLY had to assume that she was all right. As he walked into the blue drawing room, his mother called him over.

'Darling, do you know what time Ruby is due here? I think she will need Sisco to collect her from the station. She's been so secretive about where she went off to.' Sophie tutted. 'She's a law unto herself, is that one.'

'Thomas,' Dan asked, 'is my mum looking after you properly?'

'By gum she is. We get on like a house on fire. By 'eck we do.' Thomas smiled, he liked this here lad of Sophie's. Liked him a lot.

As Dan walked out of the room, he bumped into Chelsea. His PA had tears in her eyes.

'What happened down at the stables?' Dan asked.

'It was her – that awful Leah. She just flew at me and attacked me. I was coming down to look for you and she just went crazy. She really has got a grudge against me, and it rubs off on both the cousin and your son! They are assassinating my character.'

Chelsea looked up at him from under her Opti-tears, knowing that Dan would never suspect they were fake. They always worked on him.

IN FACT, RUBY HAD BEEN ON THE FAST TRAIN TO KINGS CROSS from Berwick-on-Tweed, enjoying the service in her first-class carriage. A ham and cheese sandwich, washed down with a double gin and tonic, should keep her going until Kings Cross, she thought. But then, of course, she had to get back up to Dan's spread in St Albans. It was a hell of a journey, but it had been in a very good cause.

As she looked out at the passing landscapes, only one thing troubled her. The man who ran the hotel near the beach had been a real disappointment. She knew data protection laws had him holding back precious information that would put Chelsea in Northumberland at the same time as Dan, but whose name had the girl gone under? She wouldn't be stupid enough to use her own. It needed more investigating.

Closing her eyes, Ruby knew the puzzle would be solved soon.

Why did the letter 'M' come to mind? Miranda? No. Milly, Molly, Mandy? No. Taking another sip of her gin and tonic, she looked out again as the countryside began to be replaced by the dreary grey terraces and churches of suburban North London. The train was slowing down; they passed Alexandra Palace and then the Emirates football stadium came into view. Ruby yawned and brushed crumbs off her lap before standing up to fetch down her coat and bag. One more short journey from St Pancras to St Albans and Sisco should be waiting to pick her up at the station there.

32

THE MISSING EGG

L eah sat in the darkness of the big drawing room wondering why Dan was taking so long to come back from the stables. She'd even thought of going to look for him. Then, when he suddenly turned up, she couldn't understand why he looked so furious.

'Joey has apparently been making fun of Chelsea. I suppose you were behind this,' he said, annoyed with Joey but taking it out on Leah.

'*Me?*' Leah was outraged. She stood up. 'What on earth gives you that idea? She ran at me and tried to push me into the muck pile - and I end up getting the blame? I hardly think that's fair, but then I forgot: you like to think the worst of me, don't you? You seem to think your Personal Assistant is Miss Goody Two Shoes. She pulls the wool over your eyes each time. Well, let me tell you this, Dan, she went for me like a madwoman. She *always* goes for me! She probably won't be satisfied until I'm dead. Remember what happened on the beach? Oh, I've had enough of this.' And Leah spun around to leave the room.

'Where do you think you're going?' Dan wasn't finished

with her yet. Why, she even had their son claiming that Chelsea had been in Northumberland - now that was well out of order.

'I'm going to get a shower because no matter what I say, you apparently believe your PA over me.' Leah spoke in a bitter tone that brooked no argument.

'I'VE BEEN LOOKING FOR YOU.' DAN HAD FINALLY FOUND LEAH sitting in the kitchen nursing a cup of tea. 'Dinner's ready and everyone is waiting for you so they can start to eat.'

'I'm not hungry, thank you.'

'You must be.' Dan softened his tone. 'Look, maybe I was a bit tough on you earlier.'

Leah caught her breath; why did she melt when he spoke like that, especially when he was being so unfair? She shouldn't be giving him the time of day.

'Come for dinner, please.' Dan held out his hand.

Leah sighed. Here she was, giving in again like she always did. But she didn't want the others thinking she was making a scene. Ignoring his outstretched hand, she went reluctantly to the dining room and forced herself to appear normal and to eat, when all she really wanted to do was to go upstairs and have a good cry. And it wasn't the first time she'd felt like that recently.

After dinner, Dan walked Leah to the top of the stairs. She had told him she needed a lie-down for an hour. In fact, she just wanted to get into the sanctuary of her room because something profoundly astonishing and unexpected had occurred to her during the meal - and she needed to process it.

'Thank you for my short break, Dan,' she said rather stilt-edly. 'Your horses are beautiful and most of the weekend was great fun.'

Dan seemed awkward too. 'I'd forgotten what fun is until you came. Maybe we could-'

Leah interrupted him. 'Not now, Dan. There's always tomorrow.' She paused, then added: 'I'm sorry you don't believe me.' She then turned and walked away without a backward glance.

Back in her room, Leah felt as if she had the weight of the world on her shoulders. She didn't even realise she was crying her heart out until the tears poured down her cheeks and fell on her hands. In that moment, it came to her that she was in love with Daniel Ryan.

Piano music filtered up from downstairs. It was 'Anything for Love' – the song made famous by Meatloaf and played now, Leah presumed, by Dan's mother Sophie. She could hear the others joining in, singing the words and laughing, and that made her feel even more desolate.

RUBY DUMPED HER OVERNIGHT BAG IN THE HALLWAY, TOOK OFF her coat and joined Tom and Thomas in the drawing room. Sisco had just brought her back from the local station and she'd sensed the strain in the atmosphere as soon as she'd walked into the house.

'What's been going on?' she asked Thomas.

But before the old chap could reply, Chelsea prowled in, demanding, 'Where is she? Hasn't she had the decency to pack up and clear off back to her slum by now – and take them with her!' She glared at the guests.

Thomas immediately stood up and said, 'Come on, lad,' and took the boy out of the room. He was fuming but the best thing was simply to go and distract his beloved grandson. It was a good thing Leah was resting upstairs.

'She won't stop trying to steal Dan from me.'

Sophie scowled. 'You are behaving disgracefully to our guests. And I didn't think my son was yours to steal. You're not daughter-in-law material, in my opinion.'

Chelsea bridled. 'Well, she's definitely not!'

At that moment, Leah entered the room, carrying an envelope.

Chelsea hissed at her, 'You've gone too far this time.'

'I've no idea what you're talking about.'

Chelsea scoffed. 'The *Fabergé* egg has been stolen. Dan is on to the police as we speak, and I'm pretty sure I know who took it. You!' Then she walked out, contented with the drama she had created.

In the confrontation, Leah had dropped the envelope. Now Sophie picked it up and put it on the table.

But this time, Leah wasn't going to let Chelsea get away with it. She caught up with her in the hallway and grabbed Chelsea's arm. Digging her fingers in painfully, she swung the other woman round. Facing up to bullies usually revealed a coward behind the bullying, and Leah had taken as much as she could stand.

'I've not taken this jewelled egg and neither has my son nor any member of my family. *So where have you put it?*' she asked with steel in her voice. For anyone who knew Leah, this was a danger signal.

Chelsea feigned surprise. 'Me? You dare accuse me, you common little tramp? I haven't touched it.'

Leah dug her fingers in harder. 'Liar! Save your lies for someone who believes them. For an intelligent man, Dan shows loyalty but no sense in trusting you.'

Chelsea spoke through gritted teeth. 'I know you are after his money.'

Leah was flabbergasted. And then she laughed out loud. 'I don't need his money - I have more than enough of my own.'

Enraged by the laughter, Chelsea took a swing at her. 'You're a slut and a thief. Take that!'

She slapped Leah's face, and as Leah went to slap her back, Dan came running down the hallway. He grabbed Leah's arm, saying, 'Stop, please!'

Chelsea cried, 'See, Dan? She's as guilty as hell.'

Leah tried to defend herself. 'You're jealous – that's what's wrong with you. You want Dan all to yourself, and my son and I have put a spanner in your works.'

Chelsea said snidely, 'At least I don't sell my body and steal, you *hooker*.'

Leah pulled away from Dan and snatched a hunk of Chelsea's hair. 'I am no thief!' she screamed. 'And no hooker!'

At that point, hearing the commotion, Joey joined them. Seeing him, Leah released Chelsea, turned and ran.

'Uh oh,' Joey said simply, noting the red mist coming down over Leah. He didn't blame her one bit. Personally, he'd have liked to take Chelsea back out to the muck heap and throw her right into the middle of it. To his mind, it was where she belonged.

Leah's thoughts were running much along the same lines. Seething with rage, she pelted down to the stables in the summer night. Grasping the rubber handles of a barrow full of horse manure, she pushed it towards the house. Sophie and Joey saw her coming. Grandad Thomas and Tom were out of earshot, happily playing Ludo upstairs.

Joey looked scared. 'Rocking-horse shit that ain't,' he commented, meeting her at the back door. 'Come on, Leah, don't do this. Don't sink to her level.'

Sophie grabbed his elbow. 'No way are you going to stop

her, meladdo. This is going to be fun. Chelsea has had this coming for a *looong* time.'

Joey gave up. He knew his cousin and she was a devil when roused.

Leah ran with the barrow into the house, the stench of the steaming manure filling the air. Grim-faced, she made for the office with the impractical white carpet, where Chelsea stood looking tearful next to Dan.

 Seeing the wild-eyed Leah bearing down on her, Chelsea screamed, 'No! Not on my beautiful carpet!'

Leah smiled. 'Think of it as a parting gift,' she said coolly.

When Dan saw Chelsea's face crumple, he appealed to Leah. 'Come on – is this really necessary? Leah, stop! I'm asking you not to do this.'

But Leah had done with trying to please Dan. Looking him in the eye, she said sweetly, 'Oh, but I want to.'

Ruby nudged Sophie. 'I like this girl.'

'Me too.' Sophie nodded.

Chelsea beseeched Dan, 'Stop her, Dan. You do know she kept Tom from you for a long time.'

Leah answered this. Addressing Dan, she said strongly: 'I did try to find you, Dan. And I'm sorry I didn't. I think Chelsea had something to do with that. Dan - you're a good-looking man, with money. Why aren't you married? In fact, why use Madam Butterfly's agency at all?'

Making a face because of the smell of the dung, Chelsea said scornfully, 'You were just a whore, a hooker for one night when he was feeling low because we had argued. It was just a tiff. He should have been mine.'

Dan remained silent.

Leah was so hurt. 'A whore, you say? Well, the whore says this white carpet is impractical, especially when you have kids in the house. As for your *Fabergé,* I could have stolen it nine years ago, so why would I do so now - tell me that. Or if you can't, *I'll* tell you why. Because I've never, ever stolen anything in my whole entire life!'

Chelsea screamed, 'You are trying to steal Dan.'

Leah's eyes screwed up. 'Why would I want to steal a man who can't even defend me? His silence speaks volumes. Good-bye, Dan!'

And she tipped up the barrow and dumped a clod of reeking manure onto the white carpet before walking out, her head held high.

Joey looked down at the carpet. He was genuinely shocked, but that didn't prevent him from quipping: 'For the second time in two days, there's shit all over the place. We have an old saying in Yorkshire: "Shitten luck is good luck" - or maybe not in this case.'

Then he left, looking for Thomas and young Tom. Sophie and Ruby followed, Sophie looking accusingly at her son as they departed, leaving him staring at the mess he'd helped to make.

MANY HOURS LATER, WHEN THE GUESTS FROM WHITBY HAD packed up and left in a very subdued mood, so different from their joyful arrival, Dan went to his home office to sit at his desk and think everything through. The stained carpet had been cleaned and the air smelled fresh. By now it was the small hours, but no way could he even consider going to bed. He was feeling wretched.

Eventually, Dan switched on Tom's gift of the bot, which he placed on the desk in front of him. He looked into the camera and said, 'Well, Tom, I promised I'd use this bot and I'm sorry you all left so suddenly this evening when we'd all been looking forward to spending time together. I want to make up for not being around until we met so recently, and . . .'

Dan kept on talking and when he'd finished, he absent-mindedly left the machine running when he finally went off to bed. He was all in; it had been a very upsetting few hours. Yawning again, he bumped into Ruby.

'Are you tired, darling?' Ruby asked. She was a night bird and rarely went to bed before about 2.30 a.m.

Dan nodded. 'Yeah, I am a bit. Goodnight, Ruby.' He bent and kissed their old friend on the cheek.

'Sleep tight.' But as she watched him walk away, she murmured, 'You deserve to toss and turn, you fool, for not sticking up for the best thing that's happened to you EVER.'

CHELSEA HAD NOT UNDRESSED YET. ALTHOUGH SOPHIE HAD asked her to leave, she had refused, saying she wouldn't be safe driving at night after a glass of wine at dinner. Now, sneaking out of her bedroom when the house had gone quiet, she tiptoed into Dan's home office and switched on the light. Careful to make no noise, she pulled out the bottom drawer of his filing cabinet and removed a small object wrapped in a scarf. A blonde wig fell out onto the floor. She picked the wig up and pushed it back in the drawer. Then she went to the desk and sat down in Dan's chair. She unwrapped the scarf, held up the *Fabergé* egg and admired it for a time before wrapping it again and putting it in her handbag. She swung around in Dan's chair and said aloud to the empty night air: 'You won't know what's hit you, Leah Jensen, when I've finished with you. Your stupid gingerbread men can't save you now.'

TWO DAYS LATER, SISCO WAS DRIVING BACK TO HAMBOURNE after collecting Dan from Heathrow. When he glanced in the rear-view mirror, he could see that his employer was lost in a daydream.

'How was Paris?' Sisco asked.

Dan looked up. 'Yeah, good.'

'I sold all your shares in that other French project, as you asked.'

Dan was looking out of the window. 'Oh good, that's great, thanks, Sisco.' It was as if he hadn't even heard him.

Sisco was freaked out by this behaviour, but even more shocked when they'd turned off the motorway and were driving through the outskirts of St Albans when Dan suddenly shouted: 'Stop the car. Stop!'

Sisco checked it was safe before bringing the big car to a halt. Dan jumped out and ran back to stare into the children's clothing store they had just passed.

Sisco got out too; he was concerned. 'What's the matter?' he asked.

Soundlessly, Dan pointed to the store window where a boy mannikin, very much like the one that Leah had made a big song and dance about in London's West End, was posed, dressed in football gear. At either side, the window dresser had artfully put footballs bouncing up and down on elasticated cords. Dan stared – and in his mind's eye, he could see a bungee rope and the beautiful, funny, sincere girl on the end of it.

What have I done? he thought as he got back into the car, into the front passenger seat this time. Despair overwhelmed him and he sank into silence once again as Sisco pulled away from the kerb.

Leah watched from the Amazing Dog Friendly café window as heavy rain fell onto the reporters gathered nearby.

Joey put his cappuccino down. 'Don't they ever give up?'

Leah peeked at Dan's photo on her phone.

'Who took that?' Joey asked, looking over her shoulder.

'Tom took it. I was going to delete it, but he will want it on his computer. Dan is his father, after all.'

Turning his attention back to the reporters, Joey started twerking at them. He'd do anything to be on film.

'Stop showing off - you'll only make it the worse for Tom. Let's give the reporters coffee and a cake each. In fact, let's invite them in before they get soaked. The poor things are only trying to do their job.' Leah put her phone down near Joey and he looked at Dan's photo, deep in thought.

'What is it?' she asked.

'He really is cute.'

'Cute maybe, but stupid for believing a liar over me.' Leah glanced out at the reporters again. 'Shall we ask them all in?'

'What? Are you crazy?' Joey was shocked.

Leah smiled. 'The good-looking one fancies you.'

Joey put a hand through his hair and checked his reflection in the mirror. In that case, you can come in and look, but honey, you can't *touch,* he thought. *Not now I've got my hubby Ben.*

Chelsea was rummaging in Dan's filing cabinet in the office at home in Hertfordshire. She was supposed to be in the City HQ, so when Dan walked in dressed in riding gear, it was hard to tell who was the most surprised.

'I wasn't expecting you here today,' Dan said. 'Not till after the weekend as I'm only just back from the Paris trip.'

'You scared me,' Chelsea accused him. She was always

good at turning the tables to blame others, he thought, but she seemed strangely flustered.

'Lost something?' he asked, wondering what she'd been up to.

'No . . . ah, here it is.' She quickly stuffed the blonde wig into her Emporio Armani tote bag.

Dan watched her. 'What's that?'

Chelsea grinned nervously, which was unusual for her, especially where Dan was concerned. 'I forgot to send it back after the dinner dance. I will do it later today as they've been pestering me.'

Dan stopped at the door. 'You can have the weekend off. Go back to your flat in London. I'm having Tom here and I don't want any upset.'

'I could sort your agenda,' Chelsea offered, loath to leave him alone when Leah might just turn up.

Dan shook his head. 'No. I'm fine looking after my son. Sisco will drop you at the station. Have a good weekend and I'll see you on Monday morning. Right - I'm off to have a shower and change.' And Dan walked out.

Sophie stuck her head round the office door, followed by Ruby. The pair of old friends had been staying at the estate to help care for the animals; and were keen to see more of Tom.

As Chelsea flounced past her, Ruby muttered under her breath, 'I wish you'd fall off those designer stilettos and break your scraggy neck. Do us all a favour.'

DAN STARED AT THE BUNGEE ROPE IN THE FAR BARN. HE climbed the hay bales and held onto the rope as if it was something precious, sighing heavily.

Sisco peered into the barn and switched on the light as the

day was turning to dusk outside. 'Just checking if you need me for anything. I've taken Chelsea to the station and seen her onto the London train.'

Without responding, Dan swung the bungee rope. He let it go and watched it bounce up and down again.

Sisco knew he was thinking about Leah. 'She's just a woman, lad,' he said gruffly.

Dan smiled. 'Yeah, I suppose.'

Sisco added, 'But what a woman, eh?'

'Yes, but we come from different worlds, and the *Fabergé* egg must be somewhere. Do you think she-' Dan exhaled as if his breath was hurting when really it was heart-ache.

Sisco shook his head. 'Nope, of course not. Don't even go there. Come on - we'd better get back and see what your mother and Ruby have made for dinner. Young Tom is coming tomorrow, and that's something to look forward to.'

Dan managed a smile. 'True. Lead on.'

33

BANG TO RIGHTS

few days later, Dan couldn't face the trip into
London and was working in his home office, reading
over papers he needed to sign when Chelsea walked
in. As usual, she was immaculately dressed and made up. With
the salary he paid her, she could afford it. She looked so beautiful, he thought - until she opened her mouth.

'Morning,' she greeted him. 'Have you seen the stock
market?'

Dan said, 'Yes, but it shouldn't concern you . . .'

Chelsea butted in. 'Oh, but it does. I'm a shareholder,
remember, and the share prices are crashing.'

Dan shrugged. At the moment, he couldn't care less.

Chelsea continued bossily, 'You need to take extra care with
your image now, Dan - it's important. A billionaire cannot be
associated with a common hooker.' She shuddered. 'You need,
well, someone like me at your side – someone who knows how
to dress and looks good in the best designer outfits.'

Dan shook his head. 'Fine feathers don't make fine birds,'
he said dully.

Chelsea sat on the edge of his desk, showing a large amount

of leg. Today she was wearing stockings and made sure that a little bit of suspender was visible beneath her Ralph Lauren skirt. No man could resist that.

But Dan ignored her.

RUBY WAS PASSING BY AND SHE HAD STOPPED TO LISTEN IN. IT was always wise to keep an eye and an ear on what Chelsea was getting up to. What she heard made her hurry down the corridor and run into Sophie's suite of rooms.

'That nasty girl is up to her old tricks,' she burst out, 'trying to convince Dan that hookers are dirty and cheap.'

Sophie nearly snarled, 'What? Our Leah is worth ten of that little tart any day. She's an honest, hard-working and all-round lovely girl, and I want her in the family, Ruby. It's time for Plan B.'

Ruby clapped. 'At last. By the way, do you remember that day at dinner a few months ago when Bitchface slipped up and wasn't answering to "Chelsea"? What was her real name – do you remember? It was in her file.'

'It began with an M, I do remember that. But I'm not sure. Why?' Sophie enquired.

'I just wondered about the hotel in Northumberland, whether she had booked under another name.' Ruby took a piece of chocolate and popped it in her mouth. 'We both know she's capable of doing that. I don't fancy asking in Human Resources at HQ as they might gossip, so let's keep trying to remember that name. It's crucial.'

PILATES STUDENTS OF ALL AGES, SHAPES AND SIZES WERE waiting on their mats in the room above the Whitby café as Leah switched on the tranquil music. One of the ladies in her early sixties cleared her throat. It was a signal that they needed to get something off their chests.

Leah looked at them all. 'You saw the article in the *Daily Mail*, didn't you?'

They all nodded, then one older lady said, 'He's a yabba dabba do! Hot, hot, hot. Will you see him again?'

Leah turned away. 'Not in that way. He doesn't want me.'

A young mum called Suzie objected strongly, saying, 'Then he's a fool. You're funny, beautiful and clever.'

Leah's eyes filled with tears; she quickly wiped them away as a knock came on the door.

Joey walked in; he was pale-faced. 'You're wanted downstairs,' he told his cousin, and the ladies all gasped. 'It's the police.'

DAN THOUGHT ABOUT WHAT CHELSEA HAD JUST SAID. 'MAYBE you're right,' he said. 'Maybe I would be better with someone like you.' But his heart wasn't in it.

Chelsea preened herself. 'Now you're talking sense. As for your son-'

The phone interrupted their conversation.

Chelsea answered, 'Hello, Daniel Ryan's office . . . Dan, it's the police.' She handed the phone to him without a flicker of emotion.

SISCO HUNCHED AWAY FROM THE DOWN-DRAUGHT OF THE helicopter rotor blades as it waited on the lawn at Hambourne Manor. Chelsea had already climbed inside.

Before joining her, Dan put a hand on his trusted chauffeur's shoulder. 'My nerves are shot to pieces. Fetch you know who.'

Sisco nodded solemnly. 'You got it.'

Dan stepped up into the helicopter and Sisco moved even further back and then went inside as the rotor blades gained speed and the helicopter became airborne.

Ruby ran into the kitchen. 'Where have they gone?' she demanded. 'Dan didn't stop to tell us anything.'

Sisco said heavily, 'It seems the police phoned Dan earlier. Apparently, they have proof that Leah did steal the *Fabergé*.'

Sophie stood at the kitchen door open-mouthed. 'Never. I don't believe it. It's a put-up job and we know who is responsible. What are we waiting for, Ruby?' And Sophie set off down the long hallway. On the way, she bumped into Scotty and let him know what was happening.

'I see,' he said. 'It's her - she's done it again. But she can't win, not this time. I won't allow it. She's gone too far.'

'Who's done what again?' Ruby asked, but Scotty had hurtled away; he was a man on a mission of his own.

IN THE POLICE STATION AT WHITBY, A MODERN LOW-RISE building on Spring Hill, Leah stood with Joey and her Pilates students. The latter had changed out of their gym-wear and followed her to the station. They none of them wanted to miss this – and anyway, they were here to support their beloved teacher and friend.

Desk Sergeant Warke tried to read the sheet in front of him, but as he'd mislaid his reading glasses, he soon gave up and peered at Leah over his glasses. 'Leah Jensen, we have brought you in for questioning about the theft of . . .'

'She didn't do it,' Joey butted in. He was shaking all over.

The door banged open, and Chelsea and Dan marched towards Leah.

Before the police could stop him, Dan confronted her, his expression unreadable. 'Did you take my *Fabergé?*' he asked.

Chelsea answered for Leah. 'Of course she did.' She turned to the sergeant. 'Shouldn't this woman be in handcuffs? I insist you put her in cuffs.' Chelsea drew herself up and said to Dan, 'She won't steal from you ever again. I'll see to that.'

The sergeant ignored her, as did Dan.

'Did you steal my *Fabergé*?' he repeated.

'You really think I could do that?' Sadly, Leah shook her head.

Dan returned truthfully, 'I don't know what to think any more.'

'Well, I think you need locking up!' Chelsea said, at which point the door burst open again, and several reporters bustled in all at once, many getting squashed in the mayhem and affording much excitement to the Pilates ladies.

'Hey, Ms Jensen, did you steal his precious egg?' demanded a ginger-haired journalist from Hull.

A second reporter with a dark, bushy beard addressed the sergeant, saying, 'Lock her up, mate. Throw away the key.'

Leah didn't miss the look of recognition that flickered between him and Chelsea.

'There will be no throwing away of any key, sir, and would you-' But Sergeant Warke was interrupted again. Several of Leah's loyal customers, who had known her for years, came in en masse.

As it happened, Sergeant Warke's wife Jenny was a regular

customer at the Amazing Dog Friendly Café; after a long walk by the sea, she would take their German Shepherd Sherlock there and have a sit-down and a natter with Leah. But he wouldn't let that influence him.

Right now, he said through gritted teeth: 'If that door bangs one more time . . .' He rang for back-up to clear the front office.

SCOTTY WAS HELPED INTO ANOTHER HELICOPTER BY SOPHIE, who thanked him profusely and promised his favourite dinner of steak and kidney pudding and apple tart with custard if he would brave the flight to Whitby. Although the little man was terrified, he didn't need any bribes to make him do the right thing. It was imperative for him to get to the police station in Whitby ASAP.

Scotty literally went a shade of green as he watched the fields zoom by. He was clutching a box to his chest as if his life depended on it.

REUNITED WITH HIS READING SPECTACLES, AND WITH EVERYONE sent away who didn't belong there, Sergeant Warke had taken all four people into an interview room and, reading from a transcript, said, 'I'm not arresting you just yet and you have the right to call for a solicitor. This is simply a preliminary interview. Now, it says here that the missing egg was found in your café, Miss Jensen.'

'The only egg I know about is my own; it resulted in the birth of our son eight years ago,' Leah said steadfastly.

'Anyone could have planted the egg in our café,' Joey protested.

'That creature took the egg,' snapped Chelsea, pointing to Leah.

'How could I? The last time I saw it, it was locked up,' Leah said.

'*You're* the one who should be locked up,' sneered Chelsea.

Dan glanced over at Leah; she looked so terribly sad and washed-out. Surely she couldn't be guilty! What on earth were they all doing here? It was his fault. But he had to know the truth.

'If it was locked up, who had access to the key? It was on your property, wasn't it, sir?' The policeman threw a questioning glance at Dan, who nodded.

SISCO GLANCED BACK INTO THE REAR-VIEW MIRROR AND nearly hit a cyclist as he saw Ruby's legs in the air and black fishnet stockings being rolled on. As he drove through Whitby, he was frankly relieved that the limo had blacked-out windows. This was a respectable town.

'Eyes averted, Sisco,' said Sophie as her legs in turn came up in the air.

Sisco drove on, but couldn't resist a quick glance.

'I saw you,' Ruby said, squeezing her generous curves into a tight skirt. 'Peepers on the road, buddy.'

'Yes, ma'am.' Then Sisco added innocently, 'But I have to check my mirror.'

Sophie laughed, before she and Ruby said simultaneously: 'Ah, we're here.'

Sisco pulled up at the kerb. He jumped out of the car quickly and opened the rear door so as not to miss this show.

Ruby scrambled out. Sophie needed help and Sisco obliged. It was hard not to burst out laughing.

'Don't say a word,' she warned him, reading his mind. 'Your job's on the line here, sunshine.'

Sisco grinned. 'The entrance is just there. Go to it, ladies, and good luck.'

Sophie and Ruby teetered inside on very high heels.

SERGEANT WARKE WENT ON, 'THE MISSING EGG WAS FOUND AT Ms Jensen's Amazing Dog Friendly Café.'

Dan gulped. 'Dog Friendly? Ingenious.'

Chelsea shrieked, 'It was her, she steals everything. Put the hooker in jail. Put the hooker in jail.'

The door banged open as she said those words, and the sergeant went to investigate, with all four people craning over his shoulders to see what was happening.

Sophie and Ruby made quite an entrance. In fact, it was an entrance that no one there could or would ever forget – even if they really, really wanted to.

Wearing flimsy mini-skirts showing their stocking tops, and see-through blouses with plunging necklines from which their boobs nearly burst out, the two overweight middle-aged women posed and flaunted themselves. Black eyeliner shaped their still-beautiful eyes, whilst glossy blood-red lipstick painted their lips. The shocked audience almost expected one of them to say, 'Looking for a good time, darling?'

Instead, Sophie said, 'Sergeant, if you're putting the hooker in jail, you put me in jail too.'

'And me,' Ruby said. And she waggled her rear at him.

Joey came out to join them and waggled his rear too. He never could resist a bit of twerking. 'And me,' he cooed.

Dan was in shock. 'Mother, what are you two doing here? Why are you dressed like that? What's going on?' The nightmare was getting worse: would he wake up in a minute? He'd certainly need therapy after seeing his mother dressed like this, but this time he'd be careful to avoid Greg and his 'big dick'.

Ruby tutted. 'Duh! I would have thought that was obvious.'

Sophie beckoned her son with a finger. 'Come here. Look at me, son.'

Ruby moved forward and toppled on her heels. Dan caught her.

Ruby bit her lip. 'Altitude sickness, that's all,' she said, tossing her head. 'I'll get used to it again soon. It's been a long time.'

The door swung open and Sisco walked in. He'd managed to find a parking space nearby.

The sergeant put his hand up. 'So, you're all sex-workers and you all want to go to jail, is that it?' His head was beginning to pound.

Sophie said, 'Yes. And we all stole the egg, so there.'

Sergeant Warke interrupted, 'No, no, no, I will be arresting Leah Jensen before this gets out of hand. First, I need an adjournment. Don't go anywhere.' He badly needed a cuppa and a paracetamol.

While the tension eased somewhat and everyone started chatting, Dan went over to Sophie. 'Talk to me and explain what is going on. And please keep your voice down.'

Sophie indicated that he should bend over to listen to her. Bracing herself, she took a deep breath and told her son the truth she had been hiding from him all his life. She whispered in his ear, 'I was working as a call girl when I met your father. It's true, darling. It was how I earned my living.'

Dan balked. 'You're kidding. Right?' But he saw the truth in his mother's eyes in her painted face, and for a moment his heart broke. 'You're not, are you?'

Sophie shook her head somewhat sadly and leaned closer to

Dan. She wanted her son to know everything. 'Only I wasn't like your Leah, who did it only once and for a worthwhile cause. For me it was a way of life. I, Sophie Ryan, am the real hooker in this room.'

Dan couldn't take it in. He felt as if he might go mad. 'Be quiet! Don't say another word - I don't want to know. Ludicrous. This is bloody ludicrous.'

Sergeant Warke came back into the room at this point. It was time to take control. 'Leah Jensen, I am arresting . . .'

She protested, 'But I didn't steal anything. What about my little boy? Dan, you can't do this?'

Chelsea laughed triumphantly. 'Enjoy your life behind bars. Thief!'

Sergeant Warke began to lead Leah away.

Leah turned again. 'Dan, say something,' she pleaded, tears in her eyes. 'What about Tom? I'm innocent - of course I am. Oh, my little boy.' She burst into sobs.

The entrance door slammed open, this time straining the hinges. It was Scotty. He held something up. 'Wait, wait!' he shouted. 'You need to see this before arresting anyone.'

The little man winked reassuringly at Leah. Then, going to the desk, he showed the sergeant footage from Tom's video bot. It clearly revealed Chelsea taking the *Fabergé* the day after Leah had left. The words she had spoken aloud at the time proved her part in the theft and her motive for setting up Leah.

While the sergeant moved to put the cuffs on Chelsea, Sophie handed the envelope she'd been carrying to Dan, who was in a state of shock. 'Open it, son,' she said quietly. 'Open it right now.'

Dan opened the envelope and a cheque fell out. Picking it up, he read out aloud, 'It's made out to me, Daniel Ryan, for the sum of fifteen thousand pounds, and it's signed by Leah.' There was a note with it. It read: *This is the £11,000 plus interest you loaned me. Thank you so much. You helped all of our family and I will never forget your generosity.*

As the sun filtered in, it illuminated the scene: the furious, snivelling Chelsea and a sombre Leah standing with Joey and the two mature so-called 'hookers'. Tom and Grandad Thomas stood for a moment in the doorway taking it in. Then the spell broke and Tom ran over to Leah and hugged her tightly, burying his face in her side.

'They said you'd been arrested, Mummy.' Tom tried hard not to cry; he didn't want to do so in front of the others. 'Have you done something naughty?'

Leah said fondly, 'No, sweetheart. Your daddy thought I had taken something that belonged to him - the *Fabergé* egg.'

Tom turned a face full of pain to Dan and said in a choked voice, 'I wanted to know you because I thought you would be a good and kind daddy, like the other boys in my class have. Now you've upset my mummy and I wish I'd never met you!'

Grandad Thomas looked around at everyone, then said in a thick Yorkshire accent full of emotion, 'By 'eck, Leah, lass - what the flippin' hummer are ya doing 'ere wi' t'rozzers?'

Ruby turned to Joey. 'Translate, please.'

'In a nutshell: "OMG, Leah, what the hell are you doing here at the police station?"'

Ruby was astounded. 'I've uncovered a whole new language.'

Leah addressed the sergeant. 'Am I free to go?'

Sergeant Warke shook her hand. 'Yes, of course you are, lass. I'm right glad it's worked out for you.'

Leah looked across at Dan and her expression spoke volumes. Joey noticed, as did Grandad Thomas.

Dan stood there in shock. He wanted to say something, to tell Leah that he'd known all along that she was innocent. But by the looks of it, he'd left it too late. His heart lurched. What a fool he'd been. If she never spoke to him again, he could hardly blame her.

Chelsea wept, 'Dan, you can't do this. Don't let them take me. She's only a hooker. A common whore.'

Dan said coldly, 'You shared my bed a long time ago, but it was never about me – I realise that now. It was and always has been about the money. My eyes are truly open now. I know who the hooker is - and it's not Leah.' He looked around. 'Where is she? Where has she gone?'

Sophie looked disgustedly at her son. 'If I were her, as far away from you as I could get. Come on, Ruby, our work here is done, and my feet are killing me.'

'So are mine.' Both women took their high heels off and made for the exit in their black-stockinged feet.

'What am I going to do?' Dan asked helplessly, feeling the worst he'd ever felt in his entire life. And he deserved it, he knew he did.

'What is the definition of a hooker anyway?' Scotty asked.

Sophie answered immediately, 'A beautiful woman who has fallen on hard times. And who needs a dictionary for that.'

Ruby and Sophie high-fived and hugged.

Dan reached for the door. It fell off the hinges.

34

L IS FOR LOVE

J oey chased after Leah and caught up with her in a side road. He grabbed her arm, halting her. 'Tell me this isn't so,' he puffed.

Leah looked at the ground. 'What?'

'You're in love with him. You always have been,' Joey stated.

'I've never fallen out of love with him,' she said quietly.

Joey nodded. 'Your Mr Bennet would definitely approve. Dan earns more than £30,000 a year - about the same as Mr Darcy had coming in. Besides,' and he quoted: '"It is a truth universally acknowledged, that a single man in possession of a good fortune, must be in want of a wife"!'

Tom and Grandad Thomas joined them, walking more slowly.

'Who is Mr Bennet and what's he got to do with it?' Tom asked.

'He's from *Pride and Prejudice* - you know, the box set they always watch.' Grandad Thomas nudged young Tom.

'Oh, *that* one,' the boy said with a look of deep disgust. It was so soppy.

A WEEK PASSED, DURING WHICH LEAH AND HER FAMILY TRIED to get back into their normal routines. Hard work always helped, Leah thought as she baked and cleaned, looked after the two men in her life and treated customers and their canine companions with a friendly welcome and delicious treats for both.

This Saturday morning, she was sitting out on the step of her café in Whitby, having a breather and enjoying the warm sea air. It was still early, and there were only two customers in the café, a pair of friends tucking into a sausage butty washed down with a pot of tea while their dogs - a Jack Russell and a Golden Retriever - watched their owners' every mouthful with close attention.

Leah waved to Tom and his friends, who were sitting on the grass overlooking the harbour. That was when her heart turned over; surely the big dog ambling towards them couldn't be Dan's Newfoundland Hero? Then she saw Scotty walking behind him, and there could be no doubt. Before she could get her head around this, Hero barked and looked skyward – and automatically, Leah looked up too.

A helicopter hovered overhead.

High above her, Dan looked nervously down at the sea. 'Are you sure this bungee rope will hold me?' he asked the safety guy.

'The rope will hold ten of you, Mr Ryan,' the safety man said confidently. 'You just need to jump.'

Dan drew in a deep breath. 'Easier said than done,' he muttered to himself. 'My respect for that woman has soared to a whole new level. Here goes – anything for love!' And then he jumped.

Gazing upwards, disbelieving, Leah saw Dan leap from the

helicopter on a bungee rope – he was aiming straight at her. She screamed, and cream cakes crushed into her as Dan scooped her into his arms and held on as the rope lifted them both into the air.

Dan grinned. 'I brought cakes,' he panted from the adrenaline rush.

Leah realised she'd been holding her breath as she managed: 'I know. I'm wearing them. Ooh.'

The helicopter moved over the bay, taking them with it.

Dan said, 'I want to talk.'

Leah looked at the water below and shivered. She clung more tightly to Dan. 'We can talk on the ground. Not in the water. Please, Dan, I can't hold on much longer.'

Dan signalled that they should be lowered, but instead of aiming for high ground, the helicopter lowered them into the cold salt water. The kids were screaming, and Hero barked crazily.

Dan and Leah were dripping wet through. Dan took a penknife out of his pocket to cut the rope.

'No, no, Dan, it's far too cold,' Leah protested.

'But I can hardly spoil Hero's day, can I?' Dan said mischievously. 'He wants to rescue us.'

'Very well,' Leah said resignedly. The fact that she was in his arms was amazing.

'You know, every time I've been ready to love you, Leah Jensen, something dragged me back and said, "No, I won't do that".'

'And now?'

'I realised I was listening to the right song, but the wrong words. I *will* do anything for love. *Your* love. Leah Jensen, will you marry me?'

'I will.'

Dan cut the rope. He kissed Leah as they fell into the water with an almighty splash. Hearing it, Hero pulled away from Scotty, galloped to the surf and dived into the water to save them both.

LEAH PASSED DAN A TOWEL AND THE LOVERS SHARED A SECRET smile that spoke volumes.

Tom raced down the hill and over to them, shouting, 'I knew my daddy would turn out to be a prince. And Hero saved you both. Hero,' he patted the big dog, who then shook himself, spraying the lad with seawater and making him laugh, 'here you are, boy. Have Grandad's gingerbread policeman. He won't mind, will you?'

'O' course not.' Grandad Thomas joined them, feeling what he could only describe as 'discombobulated' by the latest turn of events. Tom cuddled a wet Hero and watched him despatch the gingerbread man in one second. Yin and Yang came trotting up, looking for treats too.

BACK IN THE POLICE STATION, CHELSEA HANDED OVER HER worldly goods to the sergeant.

The sergeant told her, 'You may be let out on bail, but after your trial you'll most likely be locked up, which is what you deserve. Perverting the course of justice and committing a theft.'

Chelsea screamed, 'He should have been mine. *Mine!*'

'Who's that exactly?'

'Both of them! Dan and Tom. They should be mine.' She was babbling now, careless about what she said. 'I wish I'd made a better job of that horse bolting. Just think - no more Leah Jensen.' She laughed. 'The air horn worked a treat.'

A policewoman took her away to be arrested and put in a cell, while the sergeant made a note of what she'd said, to be passed on. It sounded to him a lot like attempted murder.

AT THE WEDDING, THERE WAS A SMALL GATHERING OF LOVED ones and a larger gathering of dogs. When everyone had eaten and drunk their fill, Dan stood up to say a few words. He was floating on air, and feeling much dizzier with happiness than he'd even felt on the bungee rope.

'Nine years ago,' he told everyone, 'I met a once-only hooker, the mother of our son Tom. She changed my life then and she's changing it for the better now. My mother was a hooker too, I've since found out, only she was a proper one . . .'

Ruby looked miffed. 'Me too, if you don't mind.'

Dan laughed. 'Ruby too. I mustn't forget you, must I. This is my crazy, fun-loving family who I wouldn't swap for the world.'

When everyone had cheered and toasted the happy couple, Joey received a phone call that he took outside. It was a message from a waiter at the hotel Chelsea had been staying at near Bamburgh. Dan needed to hear this.

When the right moment came, he called the groom away on some pretext. Then, showing Dan the message, he said, 'What did we tell you, Dan? Here I have the proof that it was Chelsea who scared Ebby. If her plan had worked, you wouldn't be wearing that wedding ring today. My cousin would be dead or maimed for life. This message will be passed to the police.' Although it was Dan's wedding day, the truth had to come out.

Dan had gone white in the face, and for a moment he had to hold on to the back of a chair. 'I had no idea she would stoop so low,' he said finally.

'Well, let's not allow Chelsea to spoil this day from afar,' Joey said, and the two men shook hands; a tot of brandy was in order.

TOM WAS PLAYING A MELODY ON THE PIANO. SOPHIE SAT BESIDE him, occasionally joining in with a chord or two. Dan and Leah were showing the *Fabergé* egg to Grandad Thomas for the umpteenth time. They none of them tired of holding it up and watching the colour of the jewels spark out and enchant them.

Ruby and Joey were leafing through a celebrity magazine. They marvelled at the way Leah's recipes for gingerbread people and dog treats had made front-page headlines. Her marriage to the most eligible bachelor in town was big news, obviously.

'Just one question. How did you get a photo of Chelsea at the hotel? I phoned them and they couldn't find her booked in,' queried Ruby.

'I had someone on the inside. Chelsea had booked in under the name of Martine Kidd – Mardy Kid in my opinion,' Joey said. He tapped his nose. 'You just have to know who to ask. Apparently, she'd been so rude and unpleasant, the guy took a photo of her. All we can prove, of course, is that she was in the village that day.'

'She could have killed Leah,' Ruby mused. 'I think that was the intention, don't you.' It wasn't really a question, more a statement.

Close by, Scotty read the *Financial Times* headlines out loud: '"Ryan Empire stocks soar on announcement of wedding".' That was good news, the little man thought. He might ask the barman for a Navy Seal to celebrate. Or perhaps not.

Taking no notice, Joey got closer to Ruby and said in her ear: 'Wanna know a secret?'

Ruby nodded.

Joey leaned even closer. 'I was the one who pushed Leah off the hotel roof.'

Ruby hooted with laughter. 'You gave destiny a helping hand, did you?'

Joey grinned. 'Absolutely.' He burst out laughing, then looked guilty. 'She was screaming like a banshee.'

Ruby enquired, 'Would you yourself have leaped into the darkness?'

Joey drew himself up. 'I'm not scared of heights if that's what you're getting at.' But secretly he knew he would not have been as daring as his lovely cousin. And it had been for the best of causes.

Over in another corner of the room, Dan was saying to his bride: 'I still wonder who sabotaged my condoms. Someone must have got to them as they are a hundred per cent safe, usually.'

Leah nodded, and secretly put her hand on the slight swell of her belly. 'I'd like to know that too – so I could thank them.' They kissed tenderly.

When Dan asked, everyone quickly denied any involvement, but he remained suspicious.

'You know what?' said Scotty. 'Sisco and I have been discussing this and we think we have the answer.' Together both men said: 'Chelsea.'

Scotty explained. 'She was desperate to get you, Dan, by any means. She was planning to seduce you again, become your girlfriend and get pregnant. It all makes sense, if you think about it.'

It was a sobering thought, but it did make perfect sense. Thank heavens her plan had failed, thought Dan, looking at his wedding ring which matched Leah's. Although he'd nearly ruined it all, he'd been given a second chance and now was married to the woman he loved and admired with all his heart. He was such a lucky man.

'Shall I bring Mummy's present out now?' asked Tom.

Dan nodded and put an arm around his son's shoulders.

'But I told you I didn't want a present,' Leah protested.

'I know, but I thought you deserved one or two,' Dan replied as Tom held out a large flat box and a smaller one.

Leah accepted them graciously. The large one intrigued her and as she opened it, she gasped. 'My dress!'

'Ah, not exactly. Your dress was ruined so I asked the designer to recreate it,' Dan said.

'You'd do that for me?' Leah simply replied.

'Tom, come on.' Sophie ushered him to the piano and the boy started playing 'Anything for Love'. His faltering notes made it sound simple, beautiful and profound.

Dan looked into Leah's eyes, which were full of tears. 'And I would do anything for you. Because I love you.'

Grandad Thomas was curious. 'What's in t'other box, Leah lass?'

She opened it to reveal the latest iPhone.

'Does that mean we can throw the other one away?' Tom asked.

'You still have the other one? I'm touched.' Dan gave Leah a hug.

'I dare say it still works,' she said.

'There's something else that still works an' all. Tell him, Leah,' Joey encouraged his cousin.

'Am I allowed to know what he's on about?' asked Dan.

Leah huffed and puffed. 'I . . . yes, I suppose you need to know. After all . . .'

'Get on with it, Leah.' Joey tutted and turned to address Dan. 'What she's trying to say, Danny Boy, is that she's up the duff - at least, that's what I'm guessing. She's been moody and tearful and everything she was when she was pregnant with Tom.' Joey looked at Leah's outraged face. 'Well, someone had to tell the poor guy.'

'And I was planning to tell him later – in private,' she admonished Joey from Dan's lap. Her husband, on hearing the news of a second child, had lifted her up and embraced her and now wouldn't let her go. 'But it seems you lot are always one step ahead of us - I wonder why?'

The newlyweds stared at Sophie, Ruby, Joey and Tom. Scotty looked up from reading the paper and grinned.

Dan, who was on cloud nine, managed to say: 'There are still so many unanswered questions, but I get the distinct impression you lot had something to do with bringing us back together. Mother, what do you have to say?'

Sophie winked at Tom. 'You know me, Dan.'

Tom butted in, 'I can't let you take the blame, Grandma. It was me who did it. I got in touch with Grandma Sophie and asked her to help.'

Sophie admitted, 'Yes, I was part of it.'

Ruby joined in. 'Me too.'

Joey just beamed.

Sisco added, 'And me.'

Scotty looked aghast. 'I would have helped if someone had asked me!'

As Dan and Leah looked on in total shock, holding each other's hands tightly, Tom began to play the piano again, picking out that same haunting tune, 'Anything for Love'.

Leah looked enquiringly across at Grandad Thomas; had he been part of the conspiracy too? Reading her thoughts, the old fella nodded his head and in front of them all, he declared in his strongest Yorkshire: 'Aye, I did an' all. Now then, my lass, the way I sees it, *I'd* do Owt for Love, an' that's a fact.'

Hearing this, the wedding party as one raised their glasses once more and toasted: 'Owt for Love!' - with a cheer that nearly brought the rafters down.

THE END

but not The End: follow the next episode in Two Moments of Madness

ABOUT THE AUTHOR

Gracie Bond loves a good romantic comedy, either to read or to watch on Netflix. Her favourite go-to novel is Pride and Prejudice - and more recently Something Borrowed she's happy to watch a Bridget Jones movie any time of the day. Among Gracie's interests are Newfoundland dogs, horses - and handsome Yorkshire men. Her idea of fun would be to ride a spirited horse along a Northumberland beach, followed by a pack of her favourite dogs, including their new addition to the family, Jessica the Newfoundland puppy.

Gracie lives in Yorkshire with her partner John and she has close connections with Whitby, one of the settings for this novel.

Visit her website: www.graciebondauthor.co.uk

SUBSCRIBE TO THE NEWSLETTER

The Power of positive reviews.

If you enjoyed this story and the characters within and you would like to leave a review for this book, please go to next page. As a self-published author we rely on readers who enjoy our books to leave honest, kind feedback. Thank you so much in advance. I am truly grateful to my readers.

Click on the link below.

Get your free excerpt from Dancing Queen, third in the Anything for Love trilogy today by

Gracie Bond, award-winning romance writer.

Plus, newsletter subscribers with have details of every other release in my Romantic Comedies. From time to time my list will be open to ARC Advanced Reader Copies.

Please sign-up today.

Https://graciebondauthor.co.uk